P9-CCW-355

# TURN A BLIND EYE

## ALSO BY JEFFREY ARCHER

### THE WILLIAM WARWICK NOVELS

*Nothing Ventured* • *Hidden in Plain Sight*

### THE CLIFTON CHRONICLES

*Only Time Will Tell* • *The Sins of the Father* • *Best Kept Secret* •
*Be Careful What You Wish For* • *Mightier Than the Sword* •
*Cometh the Hour* • *This Was a Man*

### NOVELS

*Not a Penny More, Not a Penny Less* • *Shall We Tell the President?* •
*Kane and Abel* • *The Prodigal Daughter* • *First Among Equals* • *A Matter of Honor* • *As the Crow Flies* • *Honor Among Thieves* • *The Fourth Estate* •
*The Eleventh Commandment* • *Sons of Fortune* • *False Impression* •
*The Gospel According to Judas* (with the assistance of Professor Francis J. Moloney) •
*A Prisoner of Birth* • *Paths of Glory* • *Heads You Win*

### SHORT STORIES

*A Quiver Full of Arrows* • *A Twist in the Tale* • *Twelve Red Herrings* •
*The Collected Short Stories* • *To Cut a Long Story Short* • *Cat O' Nine Tales* •
*And Thereby Hangs a Tale* • *Tell Tale* • *The Short, the Long and the Tall*

### PLAYS

*Beyond Reasonable Doubt* • *Exclusive* • *The Accused* • *Confession* •
*Who Killed the Mayor?*

### PRISON DIARIES

*Volume One—Belmarsh: Hell*
*Volume Two—Wayland: Purgatory*
*Volume Three—North Sea Camp: Heaven*

### SCREENPLAYS

*Mallory: Walking Off the Map* • *False Impression*

# JEFFREY ARCHER

# TURN A BLIND EYE

St. Martin's Press New York

This is a work of fiction. All of the characters, organizations, and events portrayed in this novel are either products of the author's imagination or are used fictitiously.

First published in the United States by St. Martin's Press, an imprint of St. Martin's Publishing Group



www.stmartins.com

The Library of Congress Cataloging-in-Publication Data
is available upon request.

ISBN 978-1-250-20080-8 (hardcover)
ISBN 978-1-250-20081-5 (ebook)



Originally published in Great Britain by Macmillan, an imprint of Pan Macmillan

First U.S. Edition: 2021

10 9 8 7 6 5 4 3 2 1

To Sofia

# ACKNOWLEDGMENTS

My thanks for their invaluable advice and research to:

Simon Bainbridge, Jonathan Caplan QC, Gillian Green, Alison Prince, Catherine Richards, and Johnny van Haeften. Special thanks to Detective Sergeant Michelle Roycroft (Ret.) and Chief Superintendent John Sutherland (Ret.).

During the battle of Copenhagen in 1801, the flagship commander signaled to Lord Nelson that he should stop attacking the Danish fleet and retreat.

Nelson held a telescope to his blind eye and said, "I do not see the signal." Having disobeyed the order, Nelson continued to attack and won the battle.

This incident has come to be known as turning a blind eye.

# 1

**May 19, 1987**

Detective Sergeant Warwick blinked first.

"Give me one good reason why I shouldn't resign," he said defiantly.

"I can think of four," replied Commander Hawksby, taking him by surprise.

William could come up with one, two, possibly three, but not four, so he knew the Hawk had cornered him. But he remained confident he could break free. He took his letter of resignation from an inside pocket and placed it on the table in front of him. A provocative gesture, though he didn't intend to hand it over until the commander had revealed his four reasons. What William didn't know was that his father had called the Hawk earlier that morning to warn him that his son planned to resign, which had given the commander time to prepare for the encounter.

Having listened to Sir Julian's sage words, the commander knew the reason Detective Sergeant Warwick was considering resigning. It hadn't come as a surprise, and he intended to preempt William's prepared speech.

"Miles Faulkner, Assem Rashidi, and Superintendent Lamont," said the Hawk, delivering his first service, but not his ace.

William didn't respond.

"Miles Faulkner, as you know, is still on the run, and despite an all-ports alert, seems to have disappeared off the face of the earth. I need you to dig him out of whatever foxhole he's hiding in and put him back behind bars where he belongs."

"DS Adaja is well capable of doing that job," said William, sending the ball flying back over the net.

"But the odds will be considerably shortened if the two of you work together as a team, as you did during the Trojan Horse operation."

"If Assem Rashidi is your second reason," said William, trying to regain the initiative, "I can assure you that Superintendent Lamont has gathered more than enough evidence to make sure he won't be seeing the light of day for several years, and you certainly don't need me to hold his hand."

"That might have been the case if Lamont hadn't resigned this morning," came back the commander.

William was taken by surprise a second time, and wasn't given a moment to consider the ramifications of this revelation before the Hawk threw in, "He had to sacrifice his full pension rights, so he may not be entirely cooperative when it comes to giving evidence at Rashidi's trial."

"He'll be more than compensated by the cash he found in that empty holdall in Rashidi's drugs factory," said William, not attempting to hide his sarcasm.

"Not any more he won't. Thanks to your intervention, every penny has been returned. And one thing's for sure, I certainly don't need two resignations on the same day."

"Fifteen love," conceded William.

"You're also the obvious choice to take Lamont's place as the Crown's leading prosecution witness at Rashidi's trial."

Thirty love.

William was still puzzled as to what else the Hawk had up his sleeve. He decided to remain silent until the commander had delivered his third serve.

"I saw the commissioner early this morning," Hawksby continued after a brief pause, "and he's asked me to set up a new unit that will be responsible for looking into police corruption."

"The Met already has an anti-corruption unit," said William.

"This one will be more proactive, and you would work undercover. The commissioner has given me a free hand to select my own team with the sole purpose of removing any rotten apples from the barrel, to use his exact words. He wants you to act as my point officer in charge of the day-to-day investigations, reporting directly to me."

"The commissioner wouldn't know me from Adam," came back William's baseline return.

"I told him you were the officer behind the success of the Trojan Horse operation."

Forty love.

"Frankly, it's a lousy assignment," continued the Hawk. "A lot of your time would be spent investigating colleagues who have only committed minor offenses." The commander paused again before delivering his next serve. "However, following the Lamont incident, the commissioner is no longer willing to ignore the problem, which is why I recommended you."

William couldn't return his volley, and conceded the first game.

"If you decide to take on the job," said the Hawk, "this will be your first assignment." He pushed a file marked CONFIDENTIAL across his desk.

William hesitated for a moment, well aware it was another trap, but couldn't resist opening the file. DETECTIVE SERGEANT J. R. SUMMERS was printed in bold capitals on the first page.

William's turn to serve.

"I was at Hendon with Jerry," said William. "He was one of the smartest lads in our intake. I'm not surprised he's made detective sergeant. He was tipped for early promotion."

"And with reason. The first thing we have to do is find a credible excuse for you to get back in touch with him, so you can gain his confidence and find out if any of the accusations made against him by a senior officer stack up."

Foot fault.

"But if he knows I'm a member of an anti-corruption unit, he's hardly likely to welcome me like a long-lost friend."

"As far as anyone else in this building is concerned, you're still working for the drugs squad, and preparing for Rashidi's trial."

Second serve.

"Hardly the most tempting assignment," suggested William, "spying on your friends and colleagues. I'd be nothing more than an undercover grass."

"I couldn't have put it better myself," said the Hawk. "But if it makes any difference, DS Adaja and DS Roycroft have already signed up, and I'll leave you to select two new constables to make up your team."

Love fifteen.

"You seem to forget, sir, that DS Roycroft turned a blind eye when Lamont helped himself to that bag full of money following the Trojan Horse raid."

"No, she didn't. DS Roycroft made a comprehensive report, for my eyes only. One of the reasons I promoted her back to sergeant," the Hawk responded.

Love thirty.

"Surely it should have been for everyone's eyes," said William.

"Not while it helped me convince Lamont not only to return the money, but to hand in his resignation."

Love forty.

"I'll need to discuss your offer with Beth and my parents, before I make a decision," said William, taking a drinks break.

"I'm afraid that won't be possible," said the Hawk. "If you agree to take on this highly sensitive assignment, no one outside of this office can know about it. Even your family need to believe you're still attached to the drugs squad and are preparing for Rashidi's trial. At least that has the virtue of being true, because until the trial is over, you'll be doing both jobs at once."

"Can it get any worse?" asked William.

"Oh, yes," said the Hawk. "I'm informed by the senior visits officer at Pentonville that Assem Rashidi has a meeting booked this morning with our old friend Mr. Booth Watson QC. So I'm bound to say, Detective Inspector Warwick, that what had looked like an open-and-shut case must now be considered to be hanging in the balance."

It took William a few moments to realize that the commander had served his ace. He picked up his resignation letter and slipped it back in his pocket.

⊸o⊷

"See you in a couple of days, Eddie," said Miles Faulkner as he got out of the unmarked van and began the only part of his escape that hadn't been rehearsed.

He walked cautiously down the well-trodden path toward the beach. After about a hundred yards he spotted the glowing tip of a cigarette. A lighthouse that guided the escaped fugitive safely away from the rocks.

A man dressed from head to toe in black was walking toward him. They shook hands, but neither of them spoke.

The captain guided his only passenger across the sand to a motorboat that was bobbing in the shallow water. Once they were on board, a crewman switched on the engine and steered them out to the waiting yacht.

Miles didn't relax until the captain had raised the anchor and set sail, and didn't shout hallelujah until they were well outside territorial waters. He knew that if they caught him, not only would his sentence be doubled, but he wouldn't be given a second chance to escape.

# 2

Mr. Booth Watson QC took the seat opposite his potential client, removed a thick file from his Gladstone bag and placed it on the glass table in front of him.

"I've studied your case with considerable interest, Mr. Rashidi," he began, "and would like to briefly go over the charges against you, and your possible defense."

Rashidi nodded, his eyes never leaving the lawyer seated opposite him. He still hadn't decided whether or not to engage BW, as Faulkner called him. After all, a life sentence could hang on the decision. He needed a King Charles spaniel to charm the jury, crossed with a Rottweiler who would tear the Crown's witnesses apart limb from limb. Was Booth Watson that animal?

"The Crown will set out to prove that you ran a large-scale drugs empire. They will accuse you of importing vast quantities of heroin, cocaine, and other illegal substances, from which they will claim you have made millions of pounds in profit, and that you controlled a criminal network of agents, dealers, and couriers. I will argue that you were no more than an innocent bystander caught in the crossfire of the Metropolitan Police's raid, and no one was more appalled than you when you learned what the premises were being used for."

"Can you fix the jury?" Rashidi asked.

"Not in this country," replied Booth Watson firmly.

"What about the judge? Can he be bribed? Or blackmailed?"

"No. However, I have recently discovered something about Mr. Justice Whittaker that could prove embarrassing for him, and therefore useful to us. But it will need double-checking."

"Like what?" demanded Rashidi.

"I'm not willing to reveal that unless and until I decide if I'm willing to represent you."

It had never crossed Rashidi's mind that Booth Watson couldn't be bought. He had always considered lawyers were no different from street whores: you only haggled over the price.

"Meanwhile, let's spend our limited time going over the charges in greater detail, and your possible defense."

Two hours later Rashidi had made up his mind. Booth Watson's forensic grasp of detail, and of how the law could be bent without being broken, had made it clear why Miles Faulkner thought so highly of him. But would he be willing to defend him when he didn't have a foot, let alone a leg, to stand on?

"As you know, the Crown Prosecution Service have provisionally penciled your trial in for September the fifteenth at the Old Bailey," said Booth Watson.

"Then I'll need to consult you regularly."

"I charge one hundred pounds an hour."

"I'll pay you ten thousand in advance."

"The trial could last for several days, possibly weeks. The refreshers alone will be substantial."

"Then let's make it twenty thousand," said Rashidi.

Booth Watson silently nodded his assent. "There's one other thing you ought to know," he said. "The Crown will be represented by Sir Julian Warwick QC, and his daughter, Grace, will act as his junior."

"And no doubt his son will still be hoping to give evidence."

"If he doesn't," said Booth Watson firmly, "you'll have lost before the trial begins."

"Then we'll have to grant him a stay of execution, at least until after you've taken him apart in the witness box."

"I may not even cross-examine the aptly named Choirboy. It's the not-so-saintly Ex-Superintendent Lamont I want the jury to remember, not Detective Sergeant William Warwick," Booth Watson said as the door opened and the duty officer joined them.

"Five more minutes, sir. You've already run over your limit."

Booth Watson nodded. "Do you have any more questions, Mr. Rashidi?" he asked after the door had closed.

"Have you heard from Miles recently?"

"Mr. Faulkner is no longer my client." Booth Watson hesitated a moment before adding, "Why do you ask?"

"I have a business proposition that might appeal to him."

"Perhaps you could brief me," said Booth Watson, giving away the fact that he and Faulkner were still in touch.

"The shares in my company, Marcel and Neffe, collapsed after all the negative press that followed my arrest. I need someone to purchase fifty-one percent of the stock at its current market price, as I'm not allowed to deal on the stock market while I'm in prison. I'll pay him double for the shares on the day I'm released."

"But that might not be for some time."

"I'll pay you double if you get me off."

Booth Watson nodded again, proving he was indeed a whore, albeit a very expensive one.

---

William couldn't resist making the journey back to Brixton by bus. However, this time he wasn't accompanied by forty armed police officers bent on destroying the largest drugs ring in the capital, but by a throng of housewives heading for the shops.

During the journey he peered down at some landmarks that he remembered from Operation Trojan Horse just the day before. But this bus came to a halt at every stop to let passengers off and on, and its top deck hadn't been converted into a command center from which the Hawk could oversee the biggest drugs raid in the Met's history.

Two high-rise blocks of flats came into sight. At the next stop William jogged down the steps and jumped off the bus, to find his colleague DS Jackie Roycroft sitting in the shelter waiting for him. No well-placed lookouts to prevent them entering the building this time.

As they approached Block B an old woman passed them, pushing a trolley laden down with heavy bags. William felt sorry for her, but something made him turn and take a second look before he continued walking toward the building. He and DS Roycroft stepped into the lift—no bouncer to hinder their progress—and Jackie pressed the button for the twenty-third floor.

"The premises have already been taken apart by SOCO, and they've drawn a blank. But the Hawk felt we should take a closer look just in case they missed anything. They've left at the crack of dawn," Jackie told him.

"'I have no idea when that might be,'" drawled William, "'but I'm sure it must be most disagreeable.'"

"Go on, tell me," said Jackie.

"Sir Harcourt Courtly addressing Lady Gay Spanker in *London Assurance*." Seeing the blank look on Jackie's face, William added, "It's a play by Boucicault."

"Thank you for that compelling piece of evidence," said Jackie, as they stepped out of the lift into a corridor to find a heavy door propped up against the wall.

The general handyman hadn't bothered with the numerous locks, he'd simply removed the door, leaving a cave. Aladdin's Cave?

"Well done, Jim," said William, as he entered an apartment that wouldn't have looked out of place in Mayfair. Modern, stylish furniture littered every room, a carpet so thick you sank into it, while contemporary paintings adorned every wall: among them Bridget Riley, David Hockney, and Allen Jones. Lalique glassware was scattered liberally around the apartment, reminding William of Rashidi's French upbringing. He could only wonder how such a cultured man could have ended up so evil.

Jackie began to search the drawing room, looking for any sign of drugs, while William focused on the master bedroom. It didn't take him long to accept that SOCO had done a thorough job, although he was puzzled by the lack of day-to-day objects he would have expected to find in an occupied flat: no comb, no hairbrush, no toothbrush, no soap. Just a rail of Savile Row suits and a dozen handmade shirts from Pink's on Jermyn Street, that looked as if they'd just come back from the dry cleaners. Nothing Booth Watson couldn't easily dismiss as not belonging to his client. But then he saw the initials "A.R." embroidered on an inside jacket pocket of one of the suits. Would Booth Watson be able to dismiss that quite as easily? William folded the jacket neatly and placed it in an evidence bag.

The next thing he turned his attention to was a photograph in an ornate silver picture frame engraved with *A* on the bedside table, which looked more Bond Street than Brixton. He picked it up and took a closer look at the woman in the photo.

"Gotcha," he said, placing the solid silver frame in another evidence bag.

After he'd made a note of the telephone number on the other side of the bed, he began examining the paintings on the walls. Expensive, modern, but not evidence, unless it turned out that Rashidi had purchased them from a reputable dealer who'd be willing to appear in court as a Crown witness and reveal the name of his customer. Unlikely. After all it wouldn't be in their best interest. The silver-framed photograph was still his best bet.

He paused to admire a Warhol painting of Marilyn Monroe SOCO had placed on the floor to uncover an unopened safe. He immediately went in search of the handyman, Jim, who produced a set of keys that would have impressed Fagin. He had the safe unlocked within minutes. William pulled the door open, only to find the cupboard was bare.

"Damn man. He must have seen us coming." Suddenly he remembered the bag lady who'd passed him earlier, pushing her laden trolley. He knew something about her hadn't rung true, and then he recalled what it was. Everything had been in character except the shoes. The latest Nike trainers.

"Damn," he repeated as Jackie appeared in the doorway.

"Have you found anything worthwhile?" she asked. "Because I haven't."

With a flourish William held up the plastic evidence bag containing the silver-framed photograph.

"Game, set, and match," said Jackie, giving her boss a mock salute.

"Game, I agree," said William, "possibly even set. But while Booth Watson's appearing as Rashidi's defense counsel at the Old Bailey, match is still to be decided."

⊸o⊷

No one was willing to sit at his table until they were convinced he wasn't coming back.

When Rashidi came down to the canteen for breakfast on the third morning after Faulkner had escaped, he took his place at the top of the empty table, and invited two of his mates, Tulip and Ross, to join him.

"Miles will be out of the country by now," said Rashidi as a prison officer placed a plate of bacon and eggs in front of him. He was the only prisoner whose bacon had no rind. Another officer handed him a copy of the *Financial Times*. The prison staff had quickly accepted that the old king had departed, and a new monarch now sat on the throne. The courtiers were not alarmed. The new king was the natural successor to Faulkner, and more important, would make sure their perks were still forthcoming.

Rashidi scanned the stock exchange listings and frowned. Marcel and Neffe had dropped another ten pence overnight, making his company vulnerable to a takeover bid. He could do nothing about it, despite being only a couple of miles away from the Stock Exchange.

"Not good news, boss?" asked Tulip as he forked a sausage and stuffed it into his mouth.

"Someone's trying to put me out of business," said Rashidi. "But my lawyer has it all under control."

Marlboro Man nodded. He rarely spoke, only asking the occasional question. Too many questions would make Rashidi suspicious, the Hawk had warned his undercover officer. Just listen, and you'll gather more than enough evidence to make sure they won't be releasing him any time soon.

"What's the latest on the supply problem?" asked Rashidi.

"Under control," Tulip assured him. "We're making just over a grand a week."

"What about Boyle? He still seems to be supplying all his old customers, which is eating into my profits."

"No longer a problem, boss. He's being transferred to a nick on the Isle of Wight."

"How did you manage that?"

"The transfer officer is a couple of months behind with his mortgage payments," said Tulip without further explanation.

"Then let's pay next month's in advance," said Rashidi. "Because Boyle's not the only inmate I want transferred, and it's less risky than the alternative. What about you, Ross? When will you be leaving us?"

"I'm off to Ford Open sometime next week, boss. Unless you want me to stay put?"

"No, I need you back on the street as quickly as possible. You're far more use to me on the outside."

# 3

In prison, the Jews and the Muslims are the only sects who take their religion seriously. However, it's the Christians who manage the largest attendance at any service.

Every Sunday morning the prison chapel is packed with sinners, who not only don't believe in God, but in most cases have never attended a church service before. But since attendance means a prisoner will be out of his cell for over an hour, they see the light and join one of the largest congregations in London that morning.

It takes almost the entire prison staff to accompany the seven hundred converts from their cells to the chapel in the basement, where the chaplain welcomes his flock of black sheep with the sign of the cross, and doesn't deliver his bidding prayer until the last inmate has settled.

The chapel is the largest room in the prison: semicircular, with twenty-one banked rows of wooden benches facing an altar dominated by a large wooden cross. Most prisoners know their place. The first two rows are filled with those few white sheep who have actually come to worship. During prayers, they fall on their knees and cry hallelujah whenever the chaplain mentions God. They also pay attention during the sermon. Not so the rest of the flock who make up the vast majority. They also have their own pecking order, and unlike any other place of worship that Sunday morning, the most sought-after seats are at the back.

The most powerful sit in the back row and conduct their business with those seated in front of them. Assem Rashidi sat in the middle of the back row, a position that until recently had been occupied by Miles Faulkner. Tulip sat on his left, with Ross on his right.

Slips of paper were continually being passed to the back, detailing prisoners' requirements for the coming week: drugs, alcohol, and porn magazines being the most popular items, although one prisoner only ever wanted a jar of Marmite.

"Our first hymn this morning," declared the chaplain, "is 'He who would valiant be.' You'll find it on page two hundred and eleven of your hymnbooks."

The pilgrims in the front two rows stood and sang lustily with heart and voice, while the dealers at the back, whom Christ would certainly have thrown out of the temple, continued trading.

"Three rocks of crack for cell forty-four," said Tulip, unfolding a piece of paper. "Thirty quid."

There wasn't much Rashidi couldn't supply, as long as the payments were met by the end of each week. No one gets more than a week's credit in prison. Three of the guards acted as couriers, which earned them more in a day than they received in their weekly pay packets. Two were responsible for bringing the goods into the prison, while the third, the most trusted, collected the payments from wives, girlfriends, brothers, sisters, and even mothers.

*". . . to be a pilgrim."*

The congregation sat back down, and a young West Indian prisoner stepped forward to read the first lesson.

*"And I saw the light . . ."*

Tulip handed the boss another order, for a wrap of heroin. "The bastard hasn't coughed up for the past two weeks. Shower job?"

"No," said Rashidi firmly. "Just stop supplying him, that way we'll soon find out if he's got any money on the outside."

Tulip looked disappointed.

"I think one of the couriers must be taking a cut," he said, "because our profits were down by over two hundred pounds last week. What do you want me to do about it, boss?"

"Make it clear that if it happens again an anonymous report will land on the governor's desk and both his sources of income will dry up overnight."

"Anything else, boss?" Tulip asked after he'd taken the last order.

"Yes. My evening meals last week were lukewarm by the time they arrived in my cell, so change our outside caterers."

"Will do," said Tulip as the congregation sat back down.

"The text of my sermon this week," intoned the chaplain, "is taken from the Book of Exodus, chapter thirty-four. *When Moses came down from Mount Sinai . . .*"

"What's the latest on Detective Sergeant Warwick?"

"Not much longer for this world," said Tulip. "I only wish it was me doin' the job."

"Not until the trial is over. You can then take care of Warwick. Make it a slow, painful death so his colleagues will think a second time before they cross me."

Ross felt sick.

"*Thou shalt not kill*," said the chaplain.

"Amen," said Ross quietly.

"Let us pray," continued the chaplain. The first two rows fell on their knees. "*Almighty God . . .*"

"When the time comes," said Rashidi, "send a dozen roses to his widow, and leave her in no doubt who sent them."

Ross listened carefully to every word that passed between them. He would have to get a message through to the Hawk as quickly as possible so Warwick could be warned. Like Rashidi, he also had a prison officer who could be trusted to pass on messages to the outside world, although in his case he didn't expect to be rewarded. Ross would have to make sure he was cleaning the corridor outside Senior Officer Rose's office after breakfast tomorrow morning.

"When they send you to Ford Open next week," said Rashidi, breaking into his thoughts, "get in touch with Benson, who controls the drug supply there, and warn him that if I don't get my cut, no more junkies will be transferred to Ford."

Ross nodded.

"Anything else, boss?" asked Tulip.

"Yes. Have you sorted out my other problem?" asked Rashidi, turning his attention back to Tulip.

"Sure, boss, but it won't come cheap—several of the guards will expect a backhander."

"Pay them. That's one luxury I'm not willing to sacrifice."

"Then a hooker will be brought to your cell soon after lights-out."

"Any news of Faulkner?" asked Ross, aware that all the Hawk's leads had gone cold.

"They've just offered me his cell, so I think we can assume he's out of the country by now. I've got another appointment with his lawyer tomorrow morning, so I may find out more then."

Having asked his one question, Ross continued to listen.

"Have they fixed a trial date yet?" asked Tulip.

"September fifteenth. And tomorrow I'll find out how much evidence they've come up with after raiding my apartment."

Ross knew exactly how much evidence they had, even whose photograph it was in the silver frame.

"Any hope of me taking over your cell when you move into Faulkner's?" asked Tulip.

"Consider it done," said Rashidi, who understood about rewards every bit as much as punishments. He nodded to a prison officer to let him know he would need to see him after the service.

*"The blessing of God Almighty, the Father, the Son and the Holy Ghost."*

*"Amen,"* said all three of them in unison.

⊸o⊷

"How are the twins?" asked Christina.

"I don't get much sleep nowadays," admitted Beth, who was pushing the pram as they strolled around Hyde Park together. "They always seem to work in tandem whenever they want something. I'm perpetually exhausted, and suddenly full of admiration for my parents."

"I envy you," said Christina, looking down at the twins wistfully. "How's William coping with the added responsibility?"

"He's wonderful whenever he's at home, but if I'm to continue doing my job, we're going to have to employ a full-time nanny, which will cost almost as much as I earn."

"Worth every penny," said Christina, "especially if it gives William more time to track down my husband, who seems to have sailed away for a year and a day."

"There's not a great deal he can do about Miles while he's preparing for the Rashidi trial."

"If half the things the press say about that man are true, I hope he rots in hell."

"Where no doubt he'll once again meet up with Miles," said Beth.

"Do you think their paths crossed in Pentonville?"

"William's convinced of it, especially as Booth Watson will be representing Rashidi at his trial. And that's one man who won't be allowed to attend his mother's funeral, not least because she's very much alive. Though William tells me she hasn't once visited her son in prison."

"Perhaps he'll find some other way to escape?"

"Not a chance. You can be sure he'll be accompanied by a small army on his journey from the prison to the Old Bailey after what Miles got away with."

"Miles was always going to be several moves ahead of the police. His escape would have been planned like a military operation, and you can be sure he wouldn't have left anything to chance."

Beth didn't respond. Although she looked upon Christina as a friend, she was well aware that William didn't trust her. When he'd left for work that morning, he'd suggested she just listen, as Christina might well say something she'd later regret.

"It wasn't a coincidence that the day before he escaped from his mother's funeral," continued Christina, "Miles's yacht slipped out of Monte Carlo and headed for the English coast."

"How do you know that?"

"One of his deckhands returned to Monte Carlo after they docked in New York, and later reported back to me. My bet is you won't be hearing from Miles again."

Beth recalled that Miles also had an apartment in New York. "What about the art collection?" she asked.

"Half of which in theory belongs to me. But if I had to guess, I'll never set eyes on any of those treasures again. I scour every catalog from all the leading auction houses in case one of them comes up for sale, but so far, nothing."

"What about the flat in Eaton Square?" asked Beth as they reached the Serpentine.

"The lease runs out in a couple of months, but I intend to renew it."

"How can you afford to do that if Miles has run off with everything?"

"Because my dear husband overlooked a minor detail when he burned down our country home and thought he'd left me penniless."

"I'm lost," said Beth as Christina took over pushing the pram down Rotten Row.

"My estate agent called last week to tell me the local council has granted planning permission to build a dozen houses on the site. He's already had an offer of half a million pounds for the land, and they haven't even put it on the market yet."

"Well, that should take care of your immediate problems."

"Possibly. But I won't be celebrating until Miles is locked back up, preferably in solitary, and half of the paintings are hanging in my apartment."

"Not to mention the Vermeer he stole from the Fitzmolean," said Beth. She glanced at her watch when they reached Albert Crescent.

"Make sure you tell William not to waste his time looking for Miles," said Christina as they parted. "Concentrate on the paintings. Find them, and you can be sure he won't be far away."

Beth brought the pram to a sudden halt, causing Artemisia to burst out crying. Peter joined in moments later. Was that the sentence William had been looking for, which Christina might well later regret?

"William?"

William looked up to see DS Summers pushing his way through the swing doors of the canteen.

"Jerry? What are you doing here?" he asked, knowing only too well.

"Same as you, I presume. I'm giving a talk on what it's like being a humble copper in the sticks, rather than a high-flyer at Scotland Yard."

"Hardly. I'm giving an introductory talk on drugs, to a lot of raw recruits who are just out of school and wouldn't know a drug if they saw one."

William picked up a briefcase and placed it on the table in front of him. He opened it to reveal a dozen small plastic boxes containing samples of every illegal drug from heroin to Ecstasy tablets.

"Impressive," said Summers, helping himself to a cup of tea. "But not as impressive as finally catching up with that villain Rashidi and putting him behind bars. I hope you've got enough evidence to nail him, because I'm told he's as slippery as an eel, and you can be sure he'll employ the best silk money can buy."

"You know him?" asked William.

"Only by reputation. But a couple of his lowlife scum work Romford and Barking. We've noticed that their supply chain has dried up recently, thanks to you and Superintendent Lamont."

"How do you know Lamont?"

"He was my first gaffer when I began life on the beat in Romford. He was transferred to the Yard a couple of years later, so I haven't come across him since. How is the old bastard?"

"He took early retirement, so I haven't seen him recently."

"Why would he do that?" said Summers, almost to himself. "He can't have been more than a year or so away from qualifying for a full pension." He dropped a couple of sugar lumps into his tea before asking, "So what's it like being at the sharp end?"

"I spend half my time filling in forms and arresting junkies who should be in hospital, not prison. But if you come across the new supplier for Romford, please let me know."

"You should keep an eye on the Payne family," said Summers.

"They control the drugs supply on my patch, but they're not big enough to take over Rashidi's empire. In fact, they'll be praying he gets off. Because without the shark, the minnows don't get fed."

William made a written note of something he already knew, and a mental note that Summers hadn't mentioned the Turner family.

"And congratulations," said Summers, selecting a chocolate biscuit. "I hear you're the first of our intake to be made up to detective inspector. Not that anyone will be surprised."

"Promotion has its disadvantages," said William with a sigh that he hoped wasn't too exaggerated.

"Like what?" asked Summers, rising to the bait.

"Not much overtime payment for inspectors, though we're still expected to put in the same hours."

"That's part of the deal if you want to join the officer class," said Summers. "Which is one of the many reasons I'm happy to remain in the ranks. Are you married?"

"Yes, and we have twins, so despite the promotion, we're only just about making ends meet," said William, hoping to tempt him into an indiscretion.

"That's why I'm still a bachelor," said Summers. "Better get going. I'm on in five minutes," he added, finishing his tea before grabbing the last chocolate biscuit. "If I hear on the grapevine who the new supplier is, I'll give you a bell."

The two men shook hands, before Jerry left for the classroom. William wasn't sure if the supposedly coincidental meeting had served any useful purpose. The Hawk had arranged for both of them to address the new intake at Hendon so that bumping into each other wouldn't look too obvious. But even then, he'd had to sit in the canteen drinking cold tea for over an hour before Summers had finally appeared, and he wasn't convinced he'd ever hear from him again.

The Hawk had already allocated DS Paul Adaja and PC Nicky

Bailey, a raw recent recruit, to watch Summers around the clock. Bailey was patrolling the streets of Romford as a constable, while Adaja remained undercover. Back at the yard, DS Jackie Roycroft continued to work closely with William, alongside another recruit to the team, DC Rebecca Pankhurst, who kept them all on their toes.

The Hawk wanted to know who Summers's friends were, who he met up with after work, whether there were any unexplained entries on his crime sheets. Did he have an informer? Who was his latest girlfriend? Was she a WPC?

Adaja and Bailey had been able to answer some of these questions within days, but others remained a mystery.

Summers may have been a bachelor, but when they swapped stories in the canteen PC Bailey had reported that there was no shortage of WPCs who were happy to succumb to the young detective's charms. She also told William about Summers's impressive record as a thief catcher, and the fact that his arrest record was second to none. Could they be investigating the wrong man?

William wrote his report on the Summers meeting during the tube journey back to Victoria, and would leave it on the commander's desk before he went home.

The Hawk had said just plant the seed. "Because if he thinks you might be in financial trouble, he could be back in touch sooner than you think."

*Unlikely*, thought William, *as it was Jerry Summers who'd originally come up with the nickname Choirboy when they were both at Hendon.*

⤙o⤚

"Detective Superintendent Lamont?"

"Who wants to know?"

"DS Jerry Summers, sir. You won't remember me, but—"

"Slippery Summers," said Lamont, laughing. "How could I forget? Thanks to your undercover work, we put most of the Payne gang away. So why the call?"

"I heard you'd taken early retirement, sir."

"Who told you that?"

"DI Warwick. We were both speaking to the new recruits at Hendon last week."

"Were you indeed? And what else did that little prick have to say?"

"Not a lot. In fact, he clammed up when I told him you were my first gaffer."

"You still haven't answered my question."

"I was wondering if you'd already got another job, because you never struck me as the retiring type."

"I've got a couple of irons in the fire," said Lamont, "but that doesn't mean I'm not open to offers."

"That's good to hear, sir. Because I might have something that would appeal to you. Best not discuss it over the phone. Perhaps we could meet somewhere private?"

# 4

"Would you like my seat, sir?" the young woman asked politely.

"No, thank you," said the commander, touching the brim of his trilby, and suddenly feeling his age. *Damn it,* he thought, *I'm not yet sixty,* although he had to admit his daughter was older than the considerate young woman.

Several passengers got off at the next stop, which allowed the Hawk to sit down. He opened his morning paper. POLICE CALLED TO CONTROL PICKET LINE AT WAPPING, was the headline. He began to read the article, but his mind drifted back to the meeting that was about to take place. Ross Hogan, his undercover officer, had recently been released from Ford Open Prison, so once again he went over the questions he needed answered. He felt like a child about to finally open a long-awaited Christmas present. At the next stop he stood to offer an elderly woman his seat, which she gratefully accepted. Not dead yet.

When the train pulled into Victoria, the Hawk was among the first to get off and join the lemming-like crowd scurrying toward the escalators. He showed his pass to the ticket collector at the barrier, before emerging into the bright morning sunlight.

He tried to gather his thoughts as he made his way slowly along Victoria Street in the direction of Scotland Yard. But when he was halfway down he turned right, left the crowded pavement, and entered a small quiet square dominated by a magnificent cathedral. Ignoring a few worshippers and the simply curious who were making their way toward the entrance of the Roman Catholic Church's principal place of worship in England and Wales, he walked slowly down the right-hand side of the vast red-and-cream brick building, not stopping until he reached an inconspicuous entrance that was normally only used by priests or choristers.

He opened the door and stepped inside, confident that as long as he looked as if he belonged, nobody would question his presence. As he made his way toward the vestry, a cleaner on her knees scrubbing the stone floor looked up. "Good morning, my child," he said.

"Good morning, Father," she replied as he hurried by.

On entering the vestry, he walked across to the end locker and opened it. He removed his jacket and tie, replacing them with a long black cassock, white surplice, dog collar, and bands, transforming himself from commander to canon. At least he was a Roman Catholic, and the occasional deception had been approved by the Cardinal Archbishop of Westminster, if not by our Lord.

A quick check in the long mirror on the wall before he emerged once again into the body of the cathedral. He progressed slowly toward the Lady Chapel—priests, unlike policemen, don't move quickly—and on into the nave, until he reached a familiar bronze relief of St. Benedict staring down at him. He was relieved to find the confessional box was unoccupied. He stepped inside, drew the little red curtain to show he was open for business, and prepared himself for one particular parishioner who he knew would be seeking absolution and was unlikely to keep him waiting.

Moments later he heard someone enter the box, and a familiar voice addressed him through the grille that separated them. "Father, I have sinned and seek the Lord's forgiveness."

"When did you last confess, my son?"

"It's been over six months, Father, during which time I committed a grievous sin by attending a Church of England service every Sunday morning."

The commander was pleased to find his undercover officer hadn't lost his sense of humor.

"And what did you learn from this unfortunate experience, my son?"

"That Assem Rashidi will be represented by the Devil incarnate when he appears in court next month."

"I was aware of that, my son," said the Hawk. "The Lord moves in mysterious ways. Did you find out how Mr. Booth Watson rates his chances of getting his client off the various charges?"

"He's confident he'll get him off the most serious charge, of heading up a drugs cartel, because he's convinced you don't have enough evidence to persuade a jury."

"We've got more than enough," said the Hawk, "as he'll discover when he sees the list of items we'll be presenting for the jury's consideration."

"But Rashidi assured me the flat was cleared of any incriminating evidence just before our boys turned up."

"He left behind a wardrobe full of tailored suits and a dozen handmade shirts that just happen to fit him perfectly."

"As they would thousands of perfectly innocent people, as Booth Watson will point out. He'll also suggest you have no proof that Rashidi ever owned or occupied the flat."

"Then he'll have to explain away the photograph that was found on the bedside table in the master bedroom."

"He'll say there's no evidence that the 'A' stands for Assem."

"It doesn't," said the Hawk. "But he'll still have to explain what a picture of his mother was doing on the bedside table."

A short whistle was followed by the words, "Ouch. His sweepers are going to regret leaving that behind. It could condemn Rashidi to twenty years."

"Amen to that," said the commander. "What else did you learn from the heathens while you were away, my son?"

"The prison rumor mill thinks Faulkner made it to the States. New name, new passport, and new identity. But he must still be active in the art world, because his house in Monte Carlo is on the market and there are no longer any of his pictures hanging on the walls."

"They left on the same boat as Faulkner," said the Hawk. "Although so far nothing's come up on the open market."

"Faulkner's too bright to make that mistake. He'll lie low for a bit, and if he sells anything it will be to private buyers."

"Were you able to find out his new name, or pick up any clues about where he might be?"

"No, Father. But Rashidi thought it was unlikely to be New York, as that's the first place the FBI would look. In any case, Faulkner's Fifth Avenue apartment was also put up for sale just weeks before he escaped, and surprise, surprise, minus the fixtures and fittings."

"I'm guessing the paintings are all in one place. But where?"

"I've no idea, boss."

"Then leave that to me. Your next job will be to try and find out who's running Rashidi's empire in his absence, so he can share a cell with him in the near future."

"I already know the answer to that question, but for obvious reasons I won't mention his name. I've left that particular piece of information in the usual place. However, I should warn you there's a coincidence you're not going to like."

"I'm intrigued."

"Anything else, sir?"

"Yes. After you've committed some of the more wanton sins you were denied in prison, we'll meet again and I'll tell you all about a certain Detective Sergeant Summers."

"Who he?"

"Not now. Bless you, my son, and be assured you are absolved of your sins. Go in peace."

The Hawk waited for a few moments, praying that no other sinners would seek absolution while he flicked through his notebook to check that all his questions had been answered.

Satisfied, he tucked the notebook back in his cassock pocket, slipped out of the confessional, and made his way toward an offertory box that was surrounded by candles, not many of which were alight. He glanced around before taking a small key out of a trouser pocket and deftly unlocking the box to find a few coins, mainly copper, and an empty Marlboro cigarette packet wedged in one corner.

He looked up to see the Virgin Mary staring down at him. He returned her enigmatic smile before removing the red-and-white pack and slipping it into his other pocket. He locked the offertory box and made his way slowly back to the vestry, confident no one had witnessed his sleight of hand.

A few minutes later, Commander Hawksby slipped out of the side door of the cathedral and headed for Scotland Yard. He had two things on his mind: who had taken over from Rashidi as the new drugs supremo, and what could Ross have meant by a coincidence he wasn't going to like? That would have to wait until the boffins in the basement had taken the empty cigarette packet apart and revealed its innermost secret.

⊸o⊷

"William's already left for work," said Beth, holding a baby's bottle in one hand and the phone in the other. "Can I pass on a message?"

"No, I want to tell you both the good news in person," said Christina.

"Clue?"

"You're worse than William."

"Why don't you come around for a drink this evening? It's William's turn to bath the twins, so with any luck he'll be home by seven."

"That's something I can't wait to see," said Christina. "I'll be with you soon after seven."

⊸o⊷

When the commander arrived back at Scotland Yard he went down, not up, taking the stairs to the basement, where he walked quickly toward the office at the far end of the corridor. He didn't knock before entering "spook world."

"Good morning, sir," said a white-coated lab assistant, looking up from his microscope. "It must be important for you to come in person."

"It is," said the Hawk, as he handed over the empty Marlboro cigarette packet.

"Then I'll get to work on it immediately and send the results up to your office as soon as I have them."

"I'll wait," said the commander, taking a seat.

The scientist nodded before returning to his desk. With the help of a pair of tweezers, he extracted the thin sliver of foil from inside the cigarette packet, before laying it on a bronze plate. The Hawk reflected that he would forever be in debt to Professor Abrahams for introducing him to the Electrostatic Document Analysis machine, which was now part of Scotland Yard's standard investigation kit, and had proved far more reliable than most witnesses, not least when it had come to proving that Beth's father, Arthur Rainsford, was innocent of murder.

The young scientist placed a sheet of Mylar film on top of the foil, then took a tiny roller from the shelf above him, and moved it slowly over the entire surface of the film until all the air bubbles had been removed.

He then put on a pair of dark safety goggles before switching on an infrared corona, which he held an inch above the bronze plate, scanning it backward and forward to identify any indentations on the surface. He next picked up what looked like a pepper pot and sprinkled photocopy toner across the silver paper until it was fully covered. He waited for a few moments before gently blowing the surplus toner off the plate. Finally, he peeled away the thin layer of Mylar film, and bent down to see if his experiment had produced anything worthwhile, well aware that the Hawk was now standing over him, waiting impatiently.

He stood aside to show that he'd finished, and the Hawk stared down at the tiny letters that had appeared on the surface of the silver foil. It didn't take him long to realize what the coincidence was, and the line Booth Watson would be taking when he presented the case for the defense.

"Impressive," was the Hawk's immediate reaction. But Rashidi would still have to explain the photograph in the silver frame, which Booth Watson wouldn't be able to dismiss quite so easily.

⊸o⊷

"He hasn't got back from the Yard yet," said Beth as she opened the front door to find Christina standing on the doorstep, clutching a bottle of champagne.

"Then this will have to wait until he does," she said, "which will give us a chance to bath the twins."

"But I want to hear your news!" cried Beth. "When it comes to time, William can't always be relied on. To quote him, 'crime doesn't necessarily fit in conveniently with the twins' bath time.' So, can I assume you've found a new man?"

"No, but I've found the old one," said Christina, as Beth put the bottle of champagne in the fridge. "And before you ask any more questions, the answer is no. Not until William gets back."

"Then you could be staying overnight," said Beth. They each picked up a twin and carried them upstairs to the bathroom, Artemisia and Peter basking in the extra attention they were getting and gurgling with delight. They both heard the door slam and a few moments later William marched into the bathroom to join them.

"Just in time to dry the little monsters and put them to bed," said Beth, "while Christina and I go downstairs and enjoy a glass of champagne."

"What are we celebrating?" asked William as he wrapped Peter in a towel.

"Christina won't tell us until you've put them to bed."

"Fine by me," said William, as the two women abandoned him to his task. This was always his favorite time of the day. In fact, he didn't go back downstairs until he'd read another chapter of PC Plod and the twins had fallen asleep.

He strolled into the living room to find Beth topping up Christina's glass with champagne.

"Just in time," she said, "otherwise we might have polished off the bottle before Christina gets around to telling us what we're celebrating."

"Should I assume you've got a new boyfriend?" said William, trying to look interested.

"No, you should not," said Beth, handing him a glass. "I've already asked that question, and I'm none the wiser. So, shush."

"Well then, you must have sold the land at Limpton Hall for an exorbitant amount?"

"Old news," said Beth. "Shush!"

They both stared at Christina expectantly, but she couldn't resist taking another sip of champagne before saying, "Miles is dead."

# 5

"When and where is the funeral?" demanded the commander even before William had sat down.

"Geneva, sir. Ten o'clock tomorrow morning."

"How did he die?"

"The local police report says he suffered a heart attack during the night." William opened his notebook. "A maid discovered the body early the following morning. A line of cocaine and a credit card were found on his bedside table."

"A pity. I'd hoped for a slower death," said the Hawk. "But why Geneva?"

"I expect he had a numbered Swiss bank account with no name attached."

"And a banker who didn't ask too many embarrassing questions about his last known address," said the Hawk. He paused for a moment. "Right, I want you to fly to Geneva and make sure we aren't being led down another blind alley. I won't believe Faulkner's dead until you've seen the body being lowered into the ground and the priest has given the final blessing. And don't leave before the grave-diggers have completed their job."

"I think he's going to be cremated, sir."

"Then be sure to bring back his ashes so we can display them in the Black Museum along with all the other notorious criminals who've made it to the Met's chamber of horrors."

"Should I take anyone with me as backup?"

"Yes, take DS Roycroft. If you both tell me Faulkner's dead, I just might believe it."

⊸o⊷

They had agreed to meet on the Circle line between 9:00 and 9:15 that evening. They would board the tube at different stations and meet up in the rear carriage. The meeting would last no more than five stops; they didn't want to risk being seen together for any longer than was necessary. Once their business had been completed, they would get off at different stations and go their separate ways.

DS Jerry Summers boarded the train at Barbican, pleased to find the rear carriage was almost unoccupied. But then, the hour had been chosen carefully, and couldn't have been described as "rush."

It hadn't taken Summers long to find out why Lamont had opted for early retirement, despite the success of Operation Trojan Horse. The phrase *hand in the till* was one being bandied about in the police canteen, and it had only taken him a little longer to confirm Lamont's gambling habit. A few casual inquiries over an after-work drink had made it possible for him to join up the dots and as Lamont had returned all the money in exchange for the commander turning a blind eye, he realized he shouldn't be difficult to turn.

When the tube train drew into Aldgate, Summers was joined by his former station officer, who had been waiting at the end of the platform. Lamont stepped on board and took the seat next to him, but they didn't acknowledge each other. Out of habit, Lamont scanned the carriage, but the only other passenger to have got on at his stop was a young woman who had taken a seat at the far end of the carriage and immediately began reading a paperback.

Although she was well out of earshot, they still spoke in hushed tones.

"Good to catch up with you again, Jerry," said Lamont. "And congratulations on your well-deserved promotion."

"Thank you, sir."

"Bruce, please. Don't forget I'm no longer a serving officer."

"Thanks to the Choirboy," said Summers.

"You know the bastard?"

"We were at Hendon together. He came out top in everything except booze and birds, so we were never going to be natural friends."

"I'm glad to hear that," said Lamont.

"So, if you felt he needed to be taken down a peg or two, I just might be able to help."

"What do you have in mind?"

"I wondered if you would be available for a little well-paid part-time work?" Summers emphasized the words "well-paid." "But perhaps you've already found another job."

"Truth is, there are too many retired police officers out there, describing themselves as consultants, all chasing after the same jobs. I thought about opening a pub, even found the ideal location in Blackheath, but unfortunately I couldn't stump up the down payment."

"How much were they asking?"

"Twenty grand. I could just about scrape together ten, but with two ex-wives and a mortgage, I couldn't make up the difference."

"I know someone who might be willing to help you with that problem," said Summers.

"What would they expect in return?"

"Nothing too demanding. And I can't think of anyone better placed to carry out the job than you."

"I'm listening."

Summers took his time spelling out exactly what his contact would expect in return for ten grand in cash.

"I'll need to give it some thought," said Lamont, once Summers had passed on his message.

"Of course, Bruce. But you'll be well aware of the deadline."

The train came to a halt, and when the doors opened Summers got out without even checking which station it was. Lamont traveled on to Victoria, where he switched to the District line.

The young woman reading the paperback didn't follow him. But then, DC Pankhurst knew exactly where ex-Superintendent Lamont was heading.

---

"I'd like to see the body," said William.

"Are you a member of the family?" asked the elderly priest politely.

"No, Father, but I have a warrant for Mr. Faulkner's arrest," William replied, well aware that his authority didn't stretch beyond the cliffs of Dover.

The priest studied the warrant but was unmoved. "I fear he can now only be judged by a higher authority, my son."

"I'm sure you're right, Father, but I still need to see the body before I can return to London."

"I'm sorry, inspector, but as I said, only members of the family can—"

"I'm a member of the family," said Christina, stepping forward. She opened her handbag and produced her passport, which was still in the name of Mrs. Christina Faulkner.

The priest studied the document, then bowed his head.

"Allow me to offer my sincere condolences on your loss, Mrs. Faulkner. Please follow me."

"May I accompany Mrs. Faulkner?" asked William.

"No, inspector," said the priest firmly.

William and Jackie had no choice but to remain behind as the priest led Christina toward a side door of the little chapel marked NO ENTRY. He stood aside to allow her to enter.

"I would have preferred to see the body myself," said William.

"Me too," said Jackie. "But if there's one person who'll be even more pleased to see him dead than either of us, it has to be the grieving widow."

William nodded. They didn't have to wait long before the door opened again and Christina reappeared, an inappropriate smile on her face. She walked across to join them, with the priest hovering a pace behind.

"It's Miles, all right. I even recovered his favorite watch," she said, holding up a Cartier Tank with the initials "M.H.F." etched on the back. She dropped it into her bag. "Let's go and watch him burn in hell," she whispered.

"If you'll come with me, Mrs. Faulkner, I'll take you to the pew reserved for the family." He led the three of them to the front of the chapel, and once they were seated, left to prepare for the service.

"Have you noticed who's just walked in?" whispered Jackie. "He's taken a seat near the back."

William turned around to see the unmistakable figure of Mr. Booth Watson QC, head bowed as if he were deep in prayer.

"Now I'm convinced Faulkner's dead," said William, "because Booth Watson's the only person I know who would charge for attending a funeral and then bill the estate. Who's the man sitting behind him, a couple of rows back?"

"No idea," said Jackie. "Looks like a Swiss gnome. Probably one of Faulkner's bankers."

"Do you think Booth Watson knows where my paintings are?" asked Christina.

"Of course he does," said William. "But that doesn't mean he's going to let you in on the secret."

"But if he's the executor of Faulkner's estate," said Jackie, "he doesn't have a lot of choice."

"He's well capable of finding a way around that little problem," said William.

"Choirboy, what's come over you?" said Christina.

"Shall we begin by saying the Lord's Prayer," intoned the priest, looking down on his sparse congregation. "*Our Father, who art in heaven . . .*"

"Somewhere Miles won't be going," said Christina under her breath.

The priest continued to conduct the ceremony, delivering several inappropriate prayers to mourners who weren't on their knees.

"Before the cremation takes place," he said, "I know there is one among us who wishes to say a few words in memory of his dear departed friend."

William couldn't hide his disbelief as Booth Watson made his way slowly to the front of the chapel and turned to face the congregation.

"I had the privilege of knowing Miles for over twenty years," he began, "both as his legal adviser and a close friend."

"As long as he paid your fees," whispered Christina.

"He was a man given to great acts of generosity and kindness, always putting the interests of his fellow men before his own."

"Are we thinking about the same man?" Christina muttered.

"He gave unheralded service to his local community, while sharing his wealth in the national interest. He will be sadly missed by his many friends."

"I don't see too many of them here today," said Christina, looking around.

"Behave yourself," mocked William, as Booth Watson continued to extol the virtues of his dear departed client, while failing to acknowledge the fact that two police officers from Scotland Yard made up half the congregation. He ended his eulogy with the words, "I cannot express how much I will miss him."

"Not to mention his fees and retainers," whispered Christina, as Booth Watson turned to face the coffin, and gave a slight bow before returning to his seat.

William watched closely as the priest pressed a button and the coffin began to move slowly along a platform of electronic rollers. Two small doors opened, and it disappeared from view, drawing a curtain on Miles Faulkner's life.

After a few moments of silence, the priest returned to the chapel steps to deliver the final blessing. This was followed by a piped recording of the "Hallelujah" chorus that Handel wouldn't have approved of.

After the service was over, Christina made her way outside to the garden of remembrance, accompanied by William and Jackie. Booth Watson was standing in the middle of the narrow path, clearly waiting for them.

"I wonder if I might have a private word, Mrs. Faulkner?" said Booth Watson solicitously.

"Anything you have to say to me, Mr. Booth Watson, can be witnessed by my friend, Detective Inspector Warwick," said the widow, standing her ground.

"As you wish, Mrs. Faulkner. You will be aware that under the divorce settlement drawn up by Sir Julian Warwick, you are entitled to half of my late client's considerable art collection."

"You know where it is?"

"It's presently stored in the vaults of a private bank here in Geneva," said Booth Watson. "You are free to claim the works at any time you wish."

"How about today?" said Christina defiantly.

"However," continued Booth Watson, ignoring the question, "what you will not be aware of—"

"Now for the small print," said Christina.

"—is that your late husband died intestate. As your divorce had not yet been declared absolute by a court of law, and Miles had no surviving blood relations, you are therefore his legal next of kin and the sole inheritor of his estate."

"I get everything?" said Christina in disbelief.

"Everything, madam," said Booth Watson, giving her a slight bow.

"Now I really do believe he's dead," said William as the priest approached them, head bowed. "Because the only way you'd get your hands on that man's art collection, would be over his dead body. . . ."

"I'll arrange for the ashes to be sent to you, Mrs. Faulkner," he said. "I'm sure you'll want to scatter them somewhere appropriate."

"In hell?" suggested Christina.

---

Three letters landed on the mat that morning, two of them in brown envelopes. One was his Ladbroke's credit statement, reminding their client of the names of several horses that didn't have the same confidence in themselves that he had shown in them. The second was a tax demand from the Inland Revenue, with a reminder that interest would be added if the full amount wasn't paid by the end of the month.

The third envelope, the white one, was from a solicitor whose signature he couldn't make out, reminding him that his second wife's alimony payment was a month overdue and threatening legal proceedings. . . . That was when he made the decision.

Lamont left his flat in Hammersmith at ten minutes to ten, and instead of turning right and heading for the nearest tube station, as he'd done every weekday morning for the past eight years, he turned left. After about a hundred yards he turned left again, and continued walking until he reached a telephone box at the end of the road. Looking around to check that no one was following him, he pulled the door open and stepped inside.

He paused for a moment, still uncertain if he should make the call, but when he heard a nearby church bell toll ten, he picked up the receiver and dialed a number he knew by heart, as he couldn't afford to leave it lying about for his wife to come across.

He dialed the seven numbers slowly, aware that Summers would be waiting in another phone box on the other side of town. His call was answered after only one ring.

"Hello?" No names, no pack drill.

"I accept your offer. But not your terms. I need an advance."

"That's not what we agreed."

"Then you'll have to find someone else to do your dirty work."

A long silence followed before he heard the words, "How much?"

"Two grand, and the rest when I deliver."

"When and where?"

"This evening, same time, same place." Lamont put down the phone and began to walk home. For a moment he had an uneasy feeling that the young woman waiting at the bus stop near his home looked familiar.

As a No. 211 pulled up, DC Pankhurst climbed on board, wondering if he'd spotted her. If Rebecca had looked back, she would have known the answer.

# 6

"We have a full agenda today," said the commander, taking his place at the head of the table, "so don't let's waste any time. Can we begin by closing the file on the Miles Faulkner case? DI Warwick."

"DS Roycroft and I," began William, "traveled to Geneva last Thursday to attend Faulkner's funeral. And while he may not roast in hell, at least we saw him burn on earth. The merry widow returned to England a few days later with far more than her ex-husband's ashes, which she scattered over her land at Limpton, so we can indeed close the file on the late Miles Faulkner."

"You look disappointed, inspector," said the Hawk, raising an eyebrow.

"I am, sir. I'm reminded of the words of Hilaire Belloc on learning of the death of his Member of Parliament. 'Here richly, with ridiculous display, the politician's corpse was laid away. While all of his acquaintance sneered and slanged, I wept: for I had longed to see him hanged.'"

The team burst out laughing and banged the table with the palms of their hands.

"And what are Mrs. Faulkner's plans for the future?"

"She will remain in England until the paintings have all been sold, and then she'll join her sister in Florida."

"I won't miss either of them," admitted the commander as he closed one file and opened another. "Let's move on to DS Summers. Are we any nearer to proving he's worth investigating? He seems to have a record second to none as a thief catcher."

"And second to none for letting other villains off the hook," said Paul. "Which might explain why he's so successful."

"Speculation and proof are two different things, DS Adaja," the Hawk reminded him.

"I agree, sir," said Paul, "but both DC Pankhurst and PC Bailey have come up with some interesting facts."

William looked across the table at Paul, who over the past couple of months had become a close friend on and off the field of battle. He wasn't a clock watcher when it came to fighting crime and, like the Hawk, considered bent coppers even worse than professional criminals.

"For the past month," continued Paul, "DC Pankhurst has been shadowing Lamont, while PC Bailey has joined the Romford division as a WPC. Her remit over and above her normal duties is to keep a close eye on Summers and find out if he's quite as pure as he would have us all believe."

William turned his attention to the two young constables who had recently joined the unit, and smiled at the thought that they couldn't have been more different.

DC Pankhurst had proudly announced at her interview that she was a descendant of Emmeline Pankhurst, who had been arrested on numerous occasions as the leader of the suffragettes, and had spent a great deal of her time in prison on hunger strike. William had happily signed up this bright, tenacious young woman to his team. He quickly discovered that he and Paul had to stay wide awake just to keep up with her. She didn't hesitate to correct them without ever appearing to be insubordinate.

By contrast, Nicola Bailey had never known her father, who had also spent a great deal of time in prison. She'd left school at fourteen and drifted from job to job, before applying to join the police force. She'd been turned down three times, but Nicky wasn't someone who gave up easily. William had asked her to join the team because, like Rebecca Pankhurst, she had a mind as sharp as any criminal.

"DC Pankhurst," said Paul, "bring us all up to date."

"I've been keeping a round-the-clock eye on the former superintendent," said Rebecca. "There was nothing of interest to report until I followed Lamont onto a tube train at Aldgate, where he joined his former colleague DS Summers."

"There could be a perfectly innocent explanation for that," said the Hawk, playing devil's advocate. "Don't forget that he and Summers served together at Romford, so they might just be friends."

"Then why meet at the far end of the rear carriage of an almost-empty tube train for their innocent get-together," said Pankhurst, "when they could have had a pint at their local?"

"Then what happened?" asked the Hawk, chastized but not chastened.

"They talked for about fifteen minutes, no more, before Summers got off at Westminster, while Lamont traveled two more stops before changing trains at Victoria."

"That's all I need," said the Hawk.

"When Lamont left his home in Hammersmith the following morning—" Rebecca checked her notes—"at nine fifty-one, he walked to a nearby phone box, and made a one-minute call. I wondered why he didn't make the call from his home."

"Perhaps he didn't want his wife to know who he was calling?" suggested the Hawk.

"His wife was at the hairdresser at the time, sir."

"Can it get any worse?" asked the Hawk.

"I'm afraid so, sir," interjected PC Bailey. "After DS Summers came off duty yesterday evening, I followed him to the nearest railway station. He switched to the tube at Liverpool Street, and three stops later was once again joined by Lamont."

"In another empty rear carriage, no doubt," said Paul.

"Yes, sir."

"What are they up to?" said William, almost to himself.

"All I can tell you, sir, is that Summers handed Lamont a thick brown envelope, and then he got off at the next station."

"Did you continue to follow him?"

"No, sir. DS Adaja had instructed me to remain on board and see where Summers got off."

"Enlighten me," said the Hawk.

"Monument. He then returned to Liverpool Street and took the next train back to Romford."

"DC Pankhurst, were you still trailing Lamont?"

"Yes, sir. He returned to his home in Hammersmith, arriving back just before ten."

"Do you think he spotted you?" asked William.

"It's possible, but there was no sign he did."

"If he's worked out what you're up to, you'll never be sure. Don't forget he's an old pro, and quite capable of running circles around you long before you get on the Circle line."

"If one of them was to approach either of you," said William, "do you have cover stories?"

"Yes, sir," said DC Pankhurst. "I'm an assistant librarian at Hammersmith Public Library."

"Credible," said Paul. "But it wouldn't bear too much scrutiny."

"I work there every Saturday morning as a volunteer," said Rebecca, "and the senior librarian knows exactly what to say should a DS Summers or Lamont ever get in touch. We were at university together."

The Hawk touched his forehead. "Chapeau," he said.

"And you, PC Bailey?" asked William.

"I never went to university, sir. Left school at fourteen."

They all burst out laughing, except the Hawk.

"Answer the question, PC Bailey," he said.

"As long as Summers continues to believe I'm just a raw recruit on the beat, I couldn't have a better front."

"Agreed," said the Hawk. "But if either of you ever has the slightest sense you've been sussed, abort the operation and make sure you're never seen in Romford or on the Circle line again, and I'll put a replacement team on the job."

"Understood," said Paul. "Especially as Jackie and I can't risk being seen anywhere near Lamont. But I hope to leave PCs Bailey and Pankhurst on surveillance for as long as possible."

"No risks," said Hawksby firmly.

"It may interest you to know, sir," said William, "that a recent survey conducted on behalf of the Yard found that when women carry out surveillance, they are seventy-two percent less likely than men to be spotted by their mark."

"No risks," repeated the commander. "Now, let's move on," he said, turning to another file. "Are you fully prepared for Rashidi's trial?" he asked, turning his attention back to William. "Because you'll need to be more than a yard ahead of that man if we're going to secure a conviction."

"The Crown's lead prosecutor is confident they have more than enough evidence to put him behind bars for a very long time," said William, without mentioning his father's name.

"Rock solid?"

"He left behind a number of hand-tailored suits in the master bedroom of his Brixton flat, along with a dozen shirts from Pink's on Jermyn Street."

"Rashidi's five foot nine, and of medium build," said the Hawk. "Booth Watson will claim they could have been made for any one of a thousand customers, including two or three members of the jury."

"Not with the initials 'A.R.' sewn on the inside pocket he can't, and according to the labels in the suits, they were all made by Bennett and Reed of Savile Row," said William, checking his notebook. "I've already been in touch with Mr. Bennett."

"Is he willing to give evidence under oath?"

"Reluctantly. We may have to pursue a witness summons if we want him to appear."

"Don't we have anything better than suits and shirts as evidence?" asked the Hawk.

"A photograph of Rashidi's mother, that I found on the bedside table in the Brixton apartment," said William.

"That's more like it," said the Hawk. "And do we have any more reliable witnesses than a reluctant tailor?"

"Yes, sir, a Mr. Gerald Sangster, who's turned Queen's evidence, in exchange for a lesser sentence."

"I hope he's not residing in the same prison as Rashidi," said the Hawk. "Because if he is, you can be sure he won't make it to the witness box."

"He's been living in a safe house for the past five months, and we won't be bringing him in until the opening day of the trial. The former doctor has one piece of evidence that Booth Watson won't find easy to explain away."

"Namely?"

"He was responsible for making up the drugs before they were distributed by his dealers, and Rashidi checked them regularly before they were allowed onto the streets."

The Hawk smiled for the first time before asking, "How is Rashidi being transported from the prison to the Old Bailey? I ask because he'll have worked out that's his only chance of escape."

"He'll be in an armored van accompanied by three police cars and a dozen outriders," said William, "along with a helicopter tracking every inch of the route."

"So was Faulkner," the Hawk reminded him, "and he still managed to fool us."

"But unlike him," said Adaja, "Rashidi won't be stopping off to attend his mother's funeral on the way."

"Just be sure not to lower your guard for one moment, otherwise it will be your funeral he's attending. That man's got enough resources to bribe everyone, including the driver and anyone who can fix a set of traffic lights. Don't forget the trial is set to last for several days. Rashidi won't make a move on the first day, but the moment we begin to relax . . ."

"We're on top of it," said William.

"Are you also fully prepared to be torn apart by Booth Watson from the moment you enter the witness box?"

"Overprepared, sir. I spent last weekend being grilled by my sister, Grace, who didn't show me any mercy."

"I'm glad to hear it," said the Hawk, "because Booth Watson considers policemen fair game, even more so when they're the son of the Crown's leading counsel."

---

First, he had to decide on which day of the week he would carry out the deception, aware that he now had a shadow. He settled on the Sunday before the trial. Next, what time of the day or night he was least likely to be noticed; he chose 3 a.m., as only a skeleton crew would be on duty at that time in the morning. And finally, should he be in uniform or in mufti? He came to the conclusion he'd be less likely to be remembered if he was dressed in civilian clothes.

At three o'clock the following Sunday morning, he was standing on the pavement outside Scotland Yard, a small package under his left arm.

He used his entry pass to open the glass door before he approached the reception desk, which was manned by a young woman reading a fashion magazine. He flicked open his warrant card.

"Good morning, superintendent," she said, slipping the magazine under the counter.

"Just got to pick up something I left on my desk," Lamont explained. "Shouldn't be too long."

"Of course, sir," she said, swiveling the night log around so he could sign in. But he was already on the way to the lift, and she didn't feel she could leave the desk to chase after a superintendent. She'd have to catch him on the way out.

He kept his back to her while he waited for the lift to arrive, and stepped inside immediately the doors opened. He then pressed 7, Administration, the least likely department to have anyone working at three o'clock on a Sunday morning.

When the doors opened, he got out into an unlit corridor and waited for a few moments before walking to the far end, where he opened the fire-escape door and jogged down the stone steps to the basement. He stepped into another unlit corridor, but didn't turn the light on. He knew exactly where he was going.

He walked slowly along the corridor until he reached the end door. Having already checked who'd be on duty, he felt sure the nightwatchman would either be fast asleep or reading the *Racing Post.* Only the idlest volunteered for the early-morning shift, knowing they would still be paid even if they occasionally dozed off.

"Good morning, Sam," he said as he marched in, disturbing the ancient constable's slumbers. "Just need to check on something. Won't be a moment."

"Be my guest, super," said Sam, hoping he wouldn't be put on report.

Lamont walked straight past him, pushed his way through another door, and headed for the evidence room. It only took him a few minutes to find what he was looking for, and to carry out the switch. The small package fitted neatly into his raincoat pocket.

"Good night," he said when he returned to find Sam head down, trying to assess the runners and riders for the 4:30 at Kempton Park the following day.

"'Night, super," he replied, without looking up.

He took the stairs to the ground floor, where the early-morning cleaners were signing in. He walked quickly across the entrance hall toward the door, ignoring the receptionist's cry of "Excuse me, sir!" By the time she'd thought about chasing after him, he was already out of sight.

When he reached Buckingham Gate, he hailed a taxi. A necessary expense. Couldn't risk someone recognizing him on the long walk back to Hammersmith. Police officers look at you more carefully at that time of night. He settled back in the corner of the cab, where the driver wouldn't be able to see him in his rearview mirror, and smiled. The whole exercise had been carried out in less than fifteen minutes. Tomorrow morning, he would collect the other £8,000, and his problems would be sorted. But for how long?

# 7

Beth poured him a second cup of coffee, surprised that he hadn't touched his bacon and eggs. William seemed preoccupied, even anxious, and at times like this she felt shut out.

She tried an old ploy. "What's the problem, Caveman? It's not as if you haven't appeared in a witness box before."

"But this could be my last appearance. If I make a balls-up of it and the jury decide that Rashidi is a decent, upstanding citizen who's been wrongly arrested by an overzealous copper."

"That seems a little far-fetched," Beth said, as she started to feed the twins.

"Far-fetched is Booth Watson's stock in trade. And don't forget what he hinted at when I last faced him in the witness box. . . ."

"And don't you forget, he lost the case," said Beth, "and Faulkner ended up getting eight years."

"Which will only make him more determined to—"

"But you spent the whole of yesterday afternoon being grilled by your sister, and Grace doesn't take prisoners."

"True, but even she can't always second-guess what Booth Watson will come up with, and it's me who has to face the grand inquisitor."

"Why isn't Lamont giving evidence instead of you? After all, he was the senior officer on the case."

"Booth Watson took him apart last time, and he'll know only too well why Lamont retired early."

"Did your father give you any advice?"

"He never left his study the whole afternoon. He was preparing his cross-examination of Rashidi. When I left, all he said was to look out for Booth Watson's googly."

"What's a googly?"

"As you've never shown any interest in cricket, my darling, it would take me a week to explain," said William, picking up his knife and fork and poking at a yolk that had gone hard.

"You'll be fine," said Beth, trying to reassure him. "The jury won't be in any doubt which one of you is telling the truth. A notorious drugs baron, or the Choirboy."

"I wish it was that simple." William gave up and pushed his plate aside. "Booth Watson is a past master when it comes to planting doubt in a juror's mind, whereas my father, as prosecution counsel, has to prove his case beyond reasonable doubt."

"How come Booth Watson is representing Rashidi?"

"Because of a mistake we made, and didn't give a second thought to at the time," said William after taking a sip of his cold coffee. "They put Rashidi in the same prison as Faulkner, so it was only going to be a matter of time before the magnet attracted the filings."

"I wonder if Rashidi's having bacon and eggs this morning."

⊸o⊷

"Another cup of coffee, Mr. Rashidi?" asked one of the officers.

Rashidi nodded, as he broke into his second three-and-a-half-minute boiled egg.

"What do you want me to do while you're at the Old Bailey?" asked Tulip, now a regular at the top table.

"Just keep things ticking over in my absence. You can bring me up to date every morning at breakfast, and at church on Sunday. Meanwhile, have you dealt with the officer who was skimming?"

"He's been transferred to another prison. In Wolverhampton."

"But have you found someone to take his place?"

"There was a queue, boss, and all of them have worked out the consequences of crossing you."

"Brief me fully tomorrow morning."

"You may not be coming back," said Tulip, grinning. "The case might be thrown out of court."

"Don't count any chickens," said Rashidi, checking the marmalade was Frank Cooper's Oxford before he removed the lid. "Although my QC says the biggest problem has been taken care of, as Warwick will discover when he takes the stand."

"I'm surprised he's still alive."

"Booth Watson didn't give me a lot of choice. But once the trial is over . . ."

"What about the good doctor? He might still prove a problem?"

"Not when the jury discovers just how bad a doctor Sangster was. I'm more worried about my tailor," said Rashidi, touching the lapel of his jacket, to check the initials A.R. were sewn on the inside.

"Don't worry, he's been well stitched up," said Tulip, laughing at his own joke.

"Your car has arrived, Mr. Rashidi," said a duty officer, appearing by his side.

"Remember to send my mother some flowers," said Rashidi before he drained his coffee.

"Will she be in court?"

"I hope not," said Rashidi.

Rashidi got up from the table. "What's my escort looking like?" he asked one of the officers who accompanied him out of the canteen.

"Three armored cars, a dozen outriders, and a helicopter. No one's had that sort of treatment since the Kray twins were on trial."

"It doesn't matter who drives me there," said Rashidi. "Only who drives me back."

"Sorry about this," said the warder, clapping a pair of handcuffs on the prisoner. "Regulations."

As Rashidi stepped out into the prison courtyard, two police officers took him firmly by the arms and led him toward the second of three armored cars.

⊸o⊷

Grace skipped breakfast so she could be in chambers before her father arrived. She knew she'd have to be up very early in the morning to achieve that. It didn't help that he had a comfortable flat in Lincoln's Inn that he always stayed in the night before a major trial.

Her partner, Clare, would have chastised her for skipping breakfast—*Go to work on an egg* was the first advertisement Grace remembered as a child—but Clare had already left for Brent, where she was appearing in a child-protection case, so she'd never know. Clare had called to wish her luck just before Grace left for chambers.

It was still dark when Grace closed the front door of her flat and headed for the tube station. The sun was only just making an appearance when she stepped out at Chancery Lane twenty minutes later. She cursed as she hurried across Lincoln's Inn's cobblestone courtyard in her high heels, not because of the slight drizzle but the sight of a glowing lightbulb in the head of chambers' office.

When she reached 1 Essex Court, she dashed up the stairs to the third floor and knocked on senior counsel's door, as she always did, before entering her father's domain.

Like a Roman orator, Sir Julian was proclaiming his opening lines to the rising sun.

"M'lud, members of the jury, I appear before you today on behalf of the Crown, while my learned friend Mr. Booth Watson QC represents the defendant. I would like to open the Crown's submission by declaring that in all my years at the Bar, I have never come across a more dastardly criminal."

"Almost your exact words when you prosecuted Faulkner," said Grace, as she began to unpack her bag in search of her amended copy of the opening address.

"A different judge and a different jury," said Sir Julian, "so no one will be any the wiser."

"Except for Booth Watson. And 'dastardly criminal' sounds Victorian, not Elizabethan. I've suggested 'evil individual' instead," said Grace.

Sir Julian nodded, and made the change. "Assem Rashidi," he continued, "is a well-educated and gifted man who could have succeeded in any profession he chose, but decided instead to use his undoubted talents not to benefit his fellow men, but to—"

"And women?" suggested Grace. "There will be several of them on the jury."

"—fellow men and women, but to harm them. Never forget, members of the jury, his sole and single purpose was to—"

"Sole and single are synonymous. You should ditch one of them."

"His only interest was to make more and more money while showing no interest in the suffering he caused to others."

"You've used 'interest' twice in the same sentence. His overriding desire?" suggested Grace.

Her father nodded, and made a further emendation to his script, before continuing. "Mr. Rashidi was the chairman of a respectable family company that already made more than enough profit for him to enjoy a way of life far beyond most people's wildest dreams." He jotted down, *Look directly at the jury.* "However, that was not enough for this greedy and self-indulgent man, who chose instead to lead a double life. A respectable tea merchant by day, and a merchant of death by night. A modern Janus."

"Will the jury know who Janus is?"

"Possibly not, but His Lordship will," said Sir Julian. "One always needs the occasional line for the judge," he said before continuing. "Every Monday afternoon he would leave his office in the City, and without any of his colleagues or his secretary knowing, would travel to Brixton by tube, where he entered his other world. But such was his vanity and arrogance that he could not forgo life's luxuries, and that will surely prove to be his downfall. On the nights he remained in Brixton, he lived in a millionaire's apartment in the next block to his drugs factory. Members of the jury, once you have seen photographs of that apartment for yourselves, you will be in no doubt about how much he was making from the alternative life he chose to lead. And perhaps more important, who lived there?

"On the top three floors of the adjoining block, a world away from his luxurious apartment, were the squalid headquarters of his illegal drugs business. Not one that specialized in importing selected grades of tea from Malaysia and Sri Lanka for sale in the high street, but one that imported heroin, cocaine, and cannabis resin from Colombia and Afghanistan for sale in the back streets.

"In the City he employed thirty people who returned to their families at five o'clock every evening extolling his virtues. In Brixton, he imprisoned thirty illegal immigrants who toiled for him through the night, fearful of being reported to the police if they did not carry out his bidding."

"Carry out his demands," interrupted Grace. "'Bidding' is too old-fashioned. More F. E. Smith than J. N. Warwick."

"At that moment I will pause," said Sir Julian, "which should give you enough time to put the large floor plan of Rashidi's drugs factory on an easel so I can describe what was taking place there, while you point to each of the rooms in question. That way the jury can't fail to appreciate the sheer size of the operation. Be sure to put the chart at an angle so they and the judge can see it clearly. No one else matters."

Grace nodded.

"The twenty-third floor of that block," continued Sir Julian, turning a page of his script, "was where the sordid deals were carried out. Cash changed hands, and in return drugs were supplied. An average day's takings were around ten thousand pounds. Ten times as much as Mr. Rashidi could expect to earn in a week as chairman of Marcel and Neffe. And don't forget, not a penny would be paid in tax."

"That allusion has always worried me," said Grace. "It hints, if somewhat obliquely, that you might approve of the sale of drugs as long as the profits were taxed. I came up with an alternative last night that I hoped you might consider."

Sir Julian raised an eyebrow.

"In his position as chairman of a respectable tea-importing company in the City of London, Mr. Rashidi's business was conducted in the open and above board, while in his role as a drugs baron in Brixton, it was conducted in the dark and out of sight."

Sir Julian crossed out the passage and replaced it with his junior's words. "Thank you, Grace," he said, giving her a warm smile.

"M'lud, members of the jury, the Crown will demonstrate beyond reasonable doubt that this cynical and corrupt individual, while posing as the respectable chairman of a City company, led a double life as an international drugs baron, taking advantage of the vulnerable and the wretched in our society. He cared nothing for the consequences even when his actions resulted in innocent human beings losing their lives."

"You've already said that in so many words, Father. Why repeat it?"

"Because it's the image I want to leave in the jury's minds, as well as ending up on the front pages of tomorrow morning's papers. So if Booth Watson tries to convince the jury of the virtues of his churchgoing, charity-donating client, universally admired and respected by his fellow men, the seed of doubt will already have been sown, and all the press will have to do is water the plant. So, when BW goes on to suggest that his client was nothing more than an occasional smoker of pot in the privacy of his own home, and was innocently caught up in the crossfire that night, the jury will dismiss the idea out of hand."

"I presume you'll ask why Rashidi even had a flat in a tower block in Brixton, when he could have lived in the West End, or with his mother in The Boltons?"

"He could also have rented a flat nearer the City. I can't wait to find out how Booth Watson tries to wriggle out of that one. However, I fear he won't allow Rashidi anywhere near the witness box, and neither would I. By the way, how did William get on under your cross-examination yesterday?"

"He's well on top of his brief, and I've no doubt the jury won't find it difficult to choose between a corrupt drugs baron and the Choirboy."

"We can't afford to take anything for granted while Booth

Watson is involved," said Sir Julian as he returned to the first page. "One more time.

"M'lud, members of the jury, I appear before you today . . ."

⊸o⊷

Booth Watson was seated at his usual table in the Savoy Grill devouring a full English breakfast while reading *The Times.* Just a few column inches alerted the paper's readers to the upcoming trial of the *Crown v. Rashidi* that would be heard before Mr. Justice Whittaker in court number one of the Old Bailey that morning. Booth Watson was sure that at that very moment Sir Julian Warwick would be rehearsing some pithy rejoinder in the hope that it would not only influence the jury, but guarantee lurid headlines in the more sensational rags the following morning, which he feared most of the jury would probably read, despite the judge instructing them not to do so.

Booth Watson had warned his client that after Sir Julian had delivered his opening statement, the jury would be convinced he was the Devil incarnate. But, he reminded him, it was defense counsel who had the last word.

"More coffee, sir?" inquired an attentive waiter.

Booth Watson nodded, before filling in six more squares of *The Times* crossword. About the only thing he had in common with his esteemed colleague. *Was it possible for one's innermost thoughts to be sarcastic?* he wondered.

Any other customer who noticed Booth Watson tucking into a hearty breakfast that morning might have been surprised to learn that in a couple of hours' time he would be appearing at the Old Bailey, defending a man who on the face of it looked as if he might be spending the next twenty years in prison. However, Booth Watson was well aware that only the first salvo would be delivered that morning, and he was unlikely to be called upon until later in the afternoon, when he would cross-examine Mr. Cyril Bennett, the Crown's first witness—a hapless tailor from Savile Row. If the little ploy he had hatched with his client overnight worked, it would leave the jury puzzled and unsure about who to believe.

Next would come the turncoat who was hoping to save his own skin by turning Queen's evidence in exchange for a lighter sentence. However, his junior had done some in-depth research on Mr. Gerald Sangster and had come up with a couple of gems that even the General Medical Council had missed.

Next to appear in the witness box would be Detective Inspector Warwick, who he suspected would be cross-examined by his sister, not their father. A decision he hoped to make them regret. Sir Julian may have thought he had a smoking gun, but he would discover otherwise when Booth Watson pulled the trigger. If his second bullet hit the mark, there would be no need to call his client to give evidence, because the trial would be over and Assem would be free to leave by the front door, at which point Booth Watson would double his fee.

"Another coffee, sir?"

"No," said Booth Watson. He folded his newspaper, checked his watch, and said, "Just the bill."

# 8

DC Pankhurst sat in the corner of the crowded bus shelter, but when the No. 72 pulled in, she didn't climb on board. She had a perfect sightline of Lamont's front door, and as long as there were enough people hanging around waiting for the next bus, whatever the number, he couldn't possibly see her.

The front door opened just after seven that morning, and Lamont emerged and began walking toward the bus stop. When a No. 211 appeared in the distance, she decided to take a risk.

As the bus approached the stop, Lamont began to jog, a clue that gave her enough confidence to get on. She climbed the stairs to the upper deck and sat at the back, not wanting to risk sitting downstairs now it was possible he might recognize her.

Rebecca looked out of the window to see Lamont glancing around. Once he was confident she was nowhere to be seen, he climbed aboard. Rebecca smiled. Her ploy had worked. But she was still anxious that her cover had been blown, and they'd have to replace her. She could feel the hand of Emmeline Pankhurst slapping her on the wrist.

Lamont took his usual window seat on the lower deck. Whenever the bus came to a stop, Rebecca checked to see if he got off, although she was fairly confident she knew where he was going.

But today he didn't get off at his usual stop and head straight for the betting shop. Instead he remained on board until the bus reached Victoria station. Another slap on the wrist—she should have anticipated that. After all, the betting shop didn't open until nine.

*Could he be going to Scotland Yard?* she wondered. But no, he headed toward the underground. It had to be the Circle line and another clandestine meeting with Jerry Summers. But she was taken by surprise a second time, when he stopped at a newsstand, bought a packet of cigarettes and a copy of the *Daily Mail.* He sat on a nearby bench, lit a cigarette, and pretended to be reading his paper while regularly glancing across at the steps that led down to the tube station.

Rebecca slipped into a coffee shop and ordered a cappuccino. She took a seat near the window, which gave her a clear view of her mark. She doubted whether he would be able to see her sitting in the crowded café, but he never once glanced in her direction. His eyes remained focused on the entrance to the underground. He was obviously waiting for someone. But who?

And then she spotted Lamont's prey. Commander Hawksby strode out of the station and began walking up Victoria Street in the direction of Scotland Yard. DC Pankhurst switched her attention back to Lamont, who was stubbing out his cigarette and folding his newspaper. He got up and followed the Hawk, but made no attempt to catch up with him.

Rebecca left the café and continued to shadow Lamont. What the hell was he up to? A stalker stalking a stalker.

The Hawk continued toward Scotland Yard at a brisk pace, but to Rebecca's surprise, about halfway down Victoria Street he turned right and disappeared from sight. Lamont maintained his distance, knowing that he couldn't risk getting too close.

Rebecca entered the square and tucked in behind a small group of Japanese tourists who were heading toward Westminster Cathedral, umbrellas up even though it wasn't raining. She was just in time to spot the commander disappearing down the side of the vast building. Lamont didn't follow him, but entered the cathedral by the main door, leaving Rebecca even more puzzled.

She stuck closely to the tour group as they went inside, and spotted Lamont making his way down the center aisle. He took a seat near the front, among a few devout worshippers, heads bowed, oblivious to those around them. Shedding the tourists, Rebecca slipped into a pew toward the back, partially obscured by a marble pillar, although she could still just about see Lamont, who was now kneeling, his head bowed and turned slightly to his right. She remained puzzled as to why Lamont had followed his old boss all the way to the cathedral and then let him out of his sight. What did he know that she didn't?

Then came the third surprise, far more of a jolt, when Rebecca saw a man who looked like the commander walking slowly up the south aisle dressed in holy vestments. She did a double-take, only to confirm it was the Hawk. A quick glance at Lamont showed that she wasn't the only person observing him carefully. The only difference, he was clearly expecting him.

The priest made his way to a confessional box and stepped inside as if he was going about his clerical duties. A few moments later a man entered by the side door, sat down, and drew the curtain.

Rebecca now knew why Lamont was on his knees in the cathedral, pretending to pray. He was there simply to identify the commander's UCO so he could warn Summers to be on the lookout for a tall, slim, middle-aged man, slightly balding with a brown mustache. She thought about alerting her boss there and then, but realized that would be the last thing he'd want, as all of their covers would then be blown. So she sat and waited to see what would happen next.

Fifteen minutes later the UCO reappeared. He bowed to the cross like a real pro, before making his way toward the west door. Lamont got up off his knees and followed him cautiously out into the square, with Rebecca not far behind. The UCO was good. He stopped several times to look in shop windows, an old trick to check if he was being tailed. He then disappeared into a jewelry shop, and when he came back out he was holding a small package. This was followed by his most audacious ploy, entering a discreet boutique hotel with the air of someone who was staying there.

Lamont didn't follow him inside, too much of a risk. Instead he retraced his steps back to Victoria station, where he disappeared below ground. After all, he now knew what the Hawk's Marlboro Man informer looked like.

Rebecca didn't continue to follow Lamont, not just because she knew where he was going, but because she needed to report back to the commander as quickly as possible.

⊸o⊷

Ross allowed a little time to pass before he made his next move. Once he was satisfied that all three of them had left the cathedral and wouldn't be returning, he made his way slowly across to the confessional box, and stepped inside.

"Lamont followed you here, sir," were his opening words, after he'd drawn the curtain closed. "And when your innocent penitent finally left, he followed him out of the cathedral and hasn't come back."

"Then he'll have a long journey," said the Hawk. "He was a businessman from Montreal who wanted to confess about a visit to a strip joint in Soho last night, before returning home to his wife and children in Canada. But from now on, we're going to have to change our venue and the way we exchange messages in the future."

"Understood," said Marlboro Man. "And by the way, the new girl's good."

"The new girl?"

"The one that followed Lamont out of the cathedral. I hadn't spotted her until then. It will be interesting to hear where they all ended up."

Hawksby smiled, as he expected DC Pankhurst was already sitting outside his office waiting to tell him what she'd just seen.

"When we next meet," he said, "I'll be on the move." A coded message MM fully understood. "But until then, my son, go in peace, and may the good Lord bless you, because your next mission will be to save a sinner who I fear is beyond redemption."

---

It was a fortnight before PC Nicky Bailey came across DS Summers, although she had been regularly dropping into the police canteen given the slightest opportunity. She had begun to form an opinion of the man she was meant to be keeping a close eye on, even though she had to make do with eavesdropping on her colleagues' conversations whenever his name came up. She never showed the slightest interest in their comments or asked any questions.

The words "lucky," "a chancer," and "a good thief catcher" were common, along with the advice to any new female recruits not to go back to his flat on their own, especially if they'd had one too many. Nicky had formed an opinion of Summers's character long before he strolled into the canteen that morning, but the reality was something she hadn't anticipated.

Detective Sergeant Jerry Summers was six foot two, powerfully built, with an unruly mop of fair hair and piercing blue eyes that reminded her of Paul Newman. She tried not to look a second time, but didn't have much choice when he crossed the room and sat down next to her. Although she was flattered, Nicky knew it was only because she was the new girl on the block. Nevertheless, she was fascinated to find out what his approach would be: subtle, crass, charming? Or perhaps a combination of all three?

DS Roycroft had made it clear she was to find out as much as possible about what Summers was up to without getting too close to him. If she did, Jackie had warned her she would be taken off the assignment, and worse, dropped from William's team altogether. She would probably end up on traffic duty in an outer borough. Not part of her career plan.

"Hi. Jerry Summers."

"Nicky Bailey," she replied, taking care to sound unaware of how important he thought he was.

"You're new around here."

"But not green," she said dismissively.

He laughed. "Then I'll have to watch out, won't I?"

"It might be wise. Especially as I'm already in a relationship," she said, adding another line to her backstory.

"Lucky man. Well, I've got to run. Criminals to catch. Have a good day, constable."

Nicky had her next line ready, but he was already halfway to the door before she could deliver it, and he didn't look back.

# 9

"All rise!" bellowed the clerk of the court.

Mr. Justice Whittaker entered court number one to find it looking more like the opening night at a West End theater than the first morning of an Old Bailey trial. The actors, the critics, and the packed audience were all in place, waiting for the curtain to rise.

The judge knew it was his duty to be neutral and unbiased, and to make sure the jury was given every chance to reach a verdict, based on evidence, that was beyond reasonable doubt. Before his appointment to the bench he'd been a QC for many years, and he believed that in the course of his working life he had witnessed few, if any, serious miscarriages of justice. But after reading the submissions for this case, it was difficult not to have formed an unfavorable opinion of the defendant long before the jury filed into their places.

What made it worse for the judge was that he'd had to wrestle with his conscience, as his youngest son had been sent down from university after being caught smoking cannabis in his rooms. He was well aware that a lot of undergraduates experimented with drugs, but Roddy had had the misfortune of being caught. He had suggested to the Lord Chancellor that, given the circumstances, another judge should perhaps be considered for this case.

However, Lord Havers was adamant. He needed an experienced, well-respected judge to preside over such a high-profile trial.

Mr. Justice Whittaker took his place in the high-backed leather chair at the center of the dais, rearranged his long, red gown, and adjusted his ancient wig that, like a Test cricketer's cap, gave an indication of how many matches he'd played.

He looked down at counsels' bench, all too aware that the next of his prejudices would be more difficult to hide.

He admired Sir Julian Warwick, both as an advocate and a fellow bencher. A man who would do everything in his power to win a case without ever overstepping the mark.

Mr. Booth Watson, on the other hand, didn't know where the mark was. His only interest was to win at any cost, and the judge already feared that, as the trial progressed, defense counsel would test his patience to its limit. However, he was determined not to be provoked. Over the years Booth Watson had somehow managed to escape the full wrath of the Bar Council, which had shown him several yellow cards, but never a red one. But surely even he must accept it would take a miracle to prevent his client from ending up in jail.

The judge turned his attention to the jury, and gave them a beneficent smile. It was important they believed he was being neutral at all times, because he knew if there was one thing a jury couldn't abide, it was the feeling that a judge had made up his mind even before the trial had begun.

He glanced across at the seven men and five women who would decide Assem Rashidi's fate, paying particular attention to the man they had selected as their foreman. He sat bolt upright, giving the impression of being a professional man who might have worked in the Square Mile. He looked as if he was a firm believer in the rule of law and, equally important, that he was well aware this could be among the most important decisions he would make in his life, and of the need to carry the rest of the jury with him.

"Ladies and gentlemen of the jury," said the judge. "Before proceedings begin, I feel I should alert you to an anomaly concerning this particular case. . . ."

All twelve jurors' eyes were fixed on the judge.

"The Crown will be represented on this occasion by Sir Julian Warwick QC while his daughter, Miss Grace Warwick, will act as his junior. That in itself is not unusual. However, Sir Julian's son, Detective Inspector William Warwick, might at some point be called on to appear as a Crown witness. I therefore took it upon myself to ask Mr. Booth Watson if he had any objection to this arrangement, and he assured me he did not. But given the circumstances, I would like him to confirm that in your presence."

Booth Watston rose slowly from his place, and with what passed as a smile said, "I have no objection, m'lud; in fact, I welcome it."

The expression on the Crown prosecuter's face revealed nothing but Sir Julian had to admit Booth Watson had won the opening round before the bell had been struck.

The judge turned his attention back to Sir Julian, who was waiting patiently to begin proceedings. His small wooden lectern had been set up, with his opening statement in place. He glanced across at Booth Watson, who was seated at the other end of counsels' bench, picking his nails, displaying an air of nonchalant indifference to all that was happening around him.

The clerk of the court rose from his place and faced the dock.

"Will the defendant please rise," he said portentously.

Rashidi stood up. Dressed in a bespoke suit, white shirt, and blue silk tie, he looked every bit the chairman of a City company who wouldn't know where Brixton was.

"On the first charge, the production of a controlled drug, how do you plead?"

"Not guilty."

"And on the second charge, possession of a controlled drug with intent to supply, how do you plead?"

"Not guilty," repeated the defendant.

"And on the third charge, possession of a controlled drug, how do you plead?"

"Not guilty."

The judge waited for the court to settle before he said, "Sir Julian, would you begin proceedings by delivering your opening statement?"

"Thank you, m'lud," said the Crown's advocate. He rose slowly from his place, gave the judge a bow, and looked down at the first page of his script, which he knew almost by heart.

"M'lud, members of the jury," he began, "I appear before you today on behalf of the Crown, while my learned friend Mr. Booth Watson QC represents the defendant." He barely gave his adversary a glance, and certainly not a bow.

"I open the Crown's submission by telling you that in all my years at the Bar . . ."

The jury listened attentively to Sir Julian's every word, as jurors always do on the first day of any trial. The judge could tell already that the Crown's senior silk was on particularly good form, and his concluding remarks would have left no one in doubt about what he believed the verdict must surely be.

"You and you alone," Sir Julian proclaimed, staring directly at the jury, "will decide the fate of the man standing in the dock. After you've considered all the evidence in this case, I want you to imagine that it's your own child who has suffered at the hands of this unscrupulous man."

The judge gave an involuntary shudder, which he hoped no one noticed.

"The world would undoubtedly be a better place if Assem Rashidi had not been born. You now have it in your power to ensure he can never again ruin the lives of the young, the vulnerable, and the helpless in our society. Your own child," he repeated, his eyes never leaving the jury.

By the time Sir Julian resumed his seat, the jury looked as if they would have been happy to bring back the death penalty, while the journalists scurried out of the court to give their editors tomorrow's headline, YOUR OWN CHILD, aware that anything said in court could be printed in block capitals without any fear of libel proceedings.

"Thank you, Sir Julian," said the judge. "You may call your first witness."

---

"But does he know that we know he knows?" asked the commander.

"I don't think so, sir," said Rebecca, "because we both followed the wrong man out of the cathedral, and ended up at the Goring Hotel. So neither of us has any idea what Marlboro Man looks like."

"Let's keep it that way," said the Hawk.

"But why does Lamont need to know who MM is?" asked Paul. "That's the real mystery."

"My bet," said Jackie, "is that he suspects he's still under surveillance, after some money went missing following the three-bags-full incident."

"Every penny was returned," said the Hawk abruptly.

"Or perhaps he wants to get in touch with MM for some reason we don't know about?" suggested Rebecca.

"Not much point second-guessing," said the Hawk. "For now, DC Pankhurst, continue to keep Lamont under close surveillance, but if you suspect even for a second that he's sussed you, disappear, because the moment that happens we'll have to replace you."

"Understood," said Rebecca.

"And what about you, PC Bailey?" asked the Hawk. "Have you anything worthwhile to report?"

"Not a lot," admitted Nicky. "I've at last had a face-to-face meeting with Summers, but I can't pretend it went well."

"Bide your time," said Paul, "and he'll eventually show his true colors. Have you been able to check up on any of his more recent investigations?"

"Yes, and they're pretty impressive. He's made a number of arrests over the past year for drug offenses, burglary, and one for GBH when he clearly showed a lot of courage. He's admired by his colleagues even if he's not particularly liked."

"Have you come across anything that looks at all suspicious?" asked Jackie.

"There's a petty criminal he turned into an informant who on several occasions has come up with intel that's resulted in arrests for burglary and another for supplying drugs."

"Does this phantom have a name?" asked Paul.

"John Smith. Hardly original, but then no detective wants to give away the identities of their informants. Once their real name is revealed, both of them are out of business."

"Has he been paid for his services?" asked the Hawk.

"Several times. Very much above board, small amounts, always authorized by his controller, a local inspector who rarely sets foot out of Romford."

"That's not untypical of a lot of the force," said Hawksby. "Well done, PC Bailey. And Paul is right. Bide your time, because if Summers is bent, it will be the little things that give him away."

"Like what?" asked Nicky.

"His lifestyle, clothes, possessions, even his girlfriends. But be careful, because if he's bent he's also likely to be on the lookout for anyone who's on to him. So don't be in any hurry. Right, let's all get back to work," said the commander, "and hope that Booth Watson trips over his own shoelaces."

"He was wearing slip-ons," said Paul.

⤙o⤚

"Call Mr. Cyril Bennett," said the clerk of the court.

A short, immaculately dressed man entered the courtroom and made his way to the witness box. As he took the oath, Grace noticed that his three-piece suit was almost identical to the one Rashidi was wearing.

"Before I begin my examination, m'lud," said Sir Julian, "I should point out that Mr. Bennett had to be summonsed as he was reluctant to give evidence."

The judge nodded, and made a note on his yellow pad before taking a closer look at the witness.

"Would you please state your name and occupation for the record," said Sir Julian.

"My name is Cyril Bennett. I am a bespoke tailor, and the proprietor of Bennett and Reed of Savile Row."

"So it would be safe to say you make suits for some of the most fashionable people in London."

"And well beyond London, sir."

"Let me ask you, Mr. Bennett, how much would it cost to have a suit made by Bennett and Reed of Savile Row?"

"That would depend."

"Top of the range?"

"It could be as much as three hundred pounds."

"So, you cater only for the wealthiest customers?"

"If you say so."

"As three hundred pounds is almost double the average weekly wage for a worker in this country, yes, I would say so."

"I have no idea what the average weekly wage is for a worker in this country."

"I'm sure you don't, Mr. Bennett," said Sir Julian, smiling at the jury. "Now, I'm going to show you a hand-tailored suit that was found at the defendant's flat in Brixton."

Booth Watson was quickly on his feet.

"I must object, m'lud. The Crown has produced no proof that my client ever lived in Brixton, let alone owned a flat there."

"I apologize, m'lud," said Sir Julian. "But be assured, we will. However, I would still like Mr. Bennett to confirm that this particular suit found in an apartment in Brixton was made by Bennett and Reed. Item number nine, m'lud."

The clerk of the court took a suit across to the witness, who studied it for some time, but made no comment.

"If you look at the distinctive red label on the inside of the jacket," said Sir Julian, "you will see that the suit was made by Bennett and Reed."

The witness stared at the label before saying, "It would appear so."

"And do you also see the neatly sewn initials on the inside jacket pocket?"

"Yes, I do."

"Would you tell the court whose initials they are?"

"I have no idea whose initials they are."

"If you say so, Mr. Bennett. Then perhaps you would tell the court what the initials are?"

"A.R."

An outbreak of loudly whispered comments erupted from some of those seated in the court. Sir Julian waited for a moment before looking directly at the jury and repeating, "A.R." He then turned his attention back to the reluctant witness and said, "Who did you make this suit for, Mr. Bennett?"

"I have no idea who it was made for," said the witness. "Those initials could have been added after the suit had been purchased."

"Then let me make it easier for you. Do you see any of your customers in court today?"

Mr. Bennett looked slowly around the court. His eyes settled briefly on the defendant, but moved on until he finally looked up at the judge and said, "I believe we have made suits for you in the past, m'lud."

Mr. Justice Whittaker nodded, looking slightly embarrassed.

"You have never seen the prisoner in the dock before?" said Sir Julian, trying to recover from this unexpected blow.

"No, I have not," said Bennett.

Grace looked across at Rashidi, who was leaning forward and staring at the witness, like a mongoose with a cobra in its sights. She smiled when she spotted a red label on the inside of Rashidi's jacket. She scribbled a note and handed it across to her father.

"But you're not denying this suit was tailored by your company, Mr. Bennett."

"I can confirm it was made in my workshop, but then I employ some twenty tailors and have over a hundred customers on my books, including His Lordship."

"I'm sure you do. However, I wonder how many of them are five feet nine, of average build, and have the initials A.R. I imagine that would reduce the numbers considerably."

"I wouldn't know."

"I suspect you know every one of your customers, Mr. Bennett," said Sir Julian with an exasperated sigh. "No more questions, m'lud," he added before resuming his seat.

"Do you wish to cross-examine this witness, Mr. Booth Watson?" asked the judge.

"Just a couple of questions, m'lud," he said, rising slowly from his place.

"Mr. Bennett, can I confirm that your distinguished company has never made a suit for the defendant?"

"I checked our books before coming to court this morning and couldn't find anything to suggest we have ever made a suit for a Mr. Rashidi."

Sir Julian read Grace's note and realized if Rashidi were to enter the witness box, that sentence would trap him. He turned around and nodded to his daughter.

"My learned friend made great play of the fact that the initials A.R. are sewn on the inside of the jacket," said Booth Watson. "Have you by any chance ever made a suit for a Mr. Arthur Rainsford?"

Sir Julian looked taken aback.

"Not that I'm aware of," said Bennett, bang on cue. "Why do you ask?"

"They just happen to be the initials of the father of my learned friend's daughter-in-law. But let me assure the court," said Booth Watson, throwing his arms up in mock horror, "it's just another coincidence, because like Mr. Rashidi, Mr. Arthur Rainsford doesn't have a flat in Brixton, hasn't had a suit made by Bennett and Reed, and isn't a drug dealer. No more questions," he concluded, offering the jury his most ingratiating smile.

⤚o⤙

"Enter lover boy," she muttered disdainfully.

Nicky looked up from her table by the window as Jerry Summers strolled into the pub and walked across to join a colleague at the bar, where a pint was already waiting for him.

"Still, you should be safe," said the WPC who sat opposite her, sipping a Coke. "Jerry Summers is only interested in blondes with big boobs."

Nicky could hardly conceal her surprise. Liz Morgan, her constable mentor, was usually the sole of discretion when it came to discussing colleagues, but clearly not on this occasion.

"You speak from experience?" she risked.

"I lasted a couple of weeks before he moved on."

"That long?" said Nicky, trying to make light of it. "But let's be fair, everyone says he's a good thief catcher."

"The best," admitted Liz. "More arrests and more convictions than anyone else in the division. But I'm told it doesn't stop him making a few bob on the side."

"You mean he's bent?" said Nicky, feigning shock.

"There's a thin line between bent and straight. It's what you might call malleable. But no one's going to complain about Summers while he has a grass who delivers on such a regular basis."

"So he's able to make a little extra cash on the side?" said Nicky. "Where's the harm in that?"

"Which he flaunts. Doesn't make him the most popular person in the nick. Anyway," Liz continued, looking across at the bar, where the two officers were sharing a joke, "DI Castle seems happy to sign all the necessary forms to keep their little arrangement legal and above board. Mind you, I wouldn't be surprised if he gets more than the occasional pint for his trouble," she added bitterly.

"What are we doing tonight?" asked Nicky, wanting to change the subject, as she'd picked up quite enough intel for one evening.

"Hornchurch Youth Club. Some of the locals have been complaining about the all-night raves. Can't say I blame them. I think we'll have to pay them a visit and give their team leader a slap on the wrist."

"And if that doesn't work?"

"We'll charge in next week, torch the joint, and throw the little blighters in jail."

Nicky laughed, finished her drink, and said, "Time to leave if we're not going to be put on report."

They got up and headed for the door. Nicky glanced back, to catch Summers staring at her. He grinned, and she couldn't believe that she blushed. Nicky quickly closed the door behind her and made her way back to the station.

# 10

"You may call your next witness, Sir Julian."

"Thank you, m'lud. I call Mr. Gerald Sangster."

"Call Gerald Sangster!" roared the clerk of the court, and moments later his words were echoed in the corridor outside.

The door swung open and a slightly stooped, middle-aged man, whose hair and tightly clipped beard were prematurely gray. He entered the court and made his way slowly across to the witness box. He was wearing a navy-blue blazer, his old school tie, and neatly pressed gray flannel trousers, giving the impression of a professional man who'd recently retired. Booth Watson considered him far too young for that.

The clerk held up a card, and the witness delivered the oath with a confidence that belied his self-effacing demeanor. Booth Watson made a note on his yellow pad and passed it to his junior, who quickly scurried out of court.

"Would you please state your name and occupation for the record," said Sir Julian.

"My name is Gerald Sangster, and I'm currently unemployed."

Booth Watson made a second note.

"Can I get on the record, Mr. Sangster, that in the past you have been a drug addict?"

"That's true, sir, but I'm clean now. I've been through rehab, and haven't touched a drug for months."

"And before that, you were a doctor," said Sir Julian, "with a successful practice in Harley Street?"

"That is correct."

"But as a result of your addiction your name was removed from the Medical Register, and not long after that sadly your marriage broke down."

Sangster bowed his head.

"Bring on the violins," said Booth Watson, and not to himself.

"That was when you went to work for Mr. Rashidi."

"Something I will regret for the rest of my life."

"I won't be waiting that long," said Booth Watson.

"Do you see Mr. Rashidi in the courtroom today?"

"Yes, sir," said Sangster, pointing toward the dock.

Rashidi stared blankly back at him as though they had never met.

"May I ask what role you played in Mr. Rashidi's empire?"

"I have a degree in chemistry, and was able to advise Mr. Rashidi on the strength and makeup of the drugs he distributed, particularly cocaine."

"Would you please go into a little more detail, Mr. Sangster, as I expect the jury, like myself, are swimming in unfamiliar waters."

"A wrap of cocaine, probably two grams, would be of a higher quality and would cost more for a wealthy customer in Mayfair, than an inferior wrap sold to a junkie on a street corner in the East End. I was in charge of quality control. I checked each batch, after which the dealers, like any salesmen, decided on the price, according to their knowledge of the customer."

"Could you be more specific as to how you went about that?"

"I would take the finest Colombian cocaine, which is usually around ninety percent pure, and then mix it with baking powder to make it go further, while still looking like the real thing. The more sophisticated customers would taste a sample and reject it if it wasn't of the highest quality. I was also responsible for the quality control of heroin, crack cocaine, methamphetamine, and marijuana. Occasionally we gave some of our stock away for free."

"Why would you do that?" asked Sir Julian, well aware what the answer would be.

"You give a child a week's supply and they'll become hooked. That's when you start charging."

"Who are the dealers in these cases?"

"Usually other kids, who give away the gear in school playgrounds."

"And do these children go on to become fully fledged drug dealers after they leave school?"

"It doesn't take them long to work out they're already earning more than their parents, besides which, it's often the only work they can get. There's never been a better example of a womb-to-tomb job."

"Your own child," repeated Sir Julian, looking directly at the jury, before he moved on. "And where did you carry out this work, Mr. Sangster?"

"In Mr. Rashidi's drug factory."

"Could you be more specific?"

"His factory was on the twenty-third, twenty-fourth, and twenty-fifth floors of a tower block in Brixton."

Grace walked across to a plan of the block resting on an easel, and pointed to each floor as Sangster mentioned it.

"And how often was Mr. Rashidi on the premises?"

"Most of the time. He oversaw the entire operation from his office on the twenty-third floor when he wasn't in his apartment."

"He had an apartment in the same building?"

"No, it was in the adjoining block. But there was a walkway linking the two buildings, which was his escape route should the factory ever be raided."

"Did he attempt to use that exit on the night of the raid?"

"Yes, sir. But it must have been blocked, because a couple of minutes later I saw him rush back into the room accompanied by his two bodyguards. But he didn't have time to get out of the front door before the police turned up."

"When did you next see him?"

"He was on his knees in the middle of the room pretending to be one of the workers."

"Were you there when he was arrested?"

"No, I wasn't."

*Why not?* Booth Watson wrote on his pad before Sir Julian moved on.

"Which floor did you work on?"

"Number twenty-four. The one where the drugs were prepared for distribution."

Grace pointed to the twenty-fourth floor.

"How were you paid?"

"In cash at the end of every working day."

"And how much could you earn in a week?"

"At least a grand. Sometimes more."

"Over fifty thousand pounds a year," said Sir Julian, emphasizing each word. "More than six times the average annual wage for a working man in this country. And who was your paymaster?"

"It was always Assem Rashidi. No one else was allowed to handle payments."

"Could you earn extra for overtime?"

"Of course. The key hours for any drug dealer are between ten at night and four in the morning. If you were willing to work through the night and at weekends, you could double your income."

"So how much could an experienced dealer hope to make in a week?"

"A couple of grand."

"Over a hundred thousand pounds a year," said Sir Julian, feigning disbelief.

"Even a runner still at school can make two or three hundred pounds a week. But if you got hooked on the stuff yourself, you didn't last too long. And if you were caught skimming the goods, or with your hand in the till, they cut it off."

"I presume you don't mean literally," said Sir Julian.

"Quite literally," said Sangster. "On the dealers' floor, with all the other dealers present to witness the punishment."

Sir Julian remained silent for some time to allow the jury to take in what they'd just heard.

"Did any of the victims ever report these barbaric atrocities to the police?"

"Only one that I know of."

"And where is he now?"

"I never seen or heard of him since."

Sir Julian turned to look at the jury to see that several heads were bowed, but not the foreman's; he was staring directly at the defendant in the dock.

"Would it be fair to say that you are risking far more than losing a hand by agreeing to give evidence in this trial?"

"I'm currently under police protection," said Sangster, "so I feel relatively safe while Rashidi's in jail. But if he was released," he added, looking directly at the defendant, "I'd be on the first plane out of the country."

"And who could blame you?" said Sir Julian. "I'm sure we all salute your courageous decision to give evidence in this trial, Mr. Sangster, considering what the consequences might be should the defendant be set free."

"It's the least I could do," said Sangster, turning to face Rashidi. "I only hope that by giving evidence today I'll have played a small part in ensuring that justice is finally done for all those helpless victims, young and old, who have suffered at the hands of this monster."

"A little over-rehearsed," said Booth Watson, just loud enough for the jury to hear.

Sir Julian ignored the comment as Booth Watson's junior rushed back into the court and handed his leader a note. Booth Watson smiled as Sir Julian looked up at the judge and said, "No more questions, m'lud."

---

"What's your poison?' he asked as he climbed on the stool next to her.

"Half a shandy," said Nicky. She would normally have ordered a pint of bitter if she'd been out drinking with the team. But not this evening.

Jackie had warned her to be cautious, because it wouldn't be too long before he made his first move. The Jerry Summers of this world, Jackie had assured her, don't hang about. They consider anything in a skirt is fair game. It was legendary at the Yard that when Jackie was a trainee constable an inspector had once placed a hand on her thigh, and she'd knocked him out with one punch. While it hadn't helped her chances of promotion, that was the first and last time she'd suffered wandering hands.

"Let him do the talking," Jackie had advised. "If he's hoping to get you in the sack, he'll start showing off, exaggerating his exploits. But if you think even for a moment that he suspects you're working undercover, report back to me immediately and I'll have you out of there the same day."

"A pint of bitter and half a shandy," said Summers, giving the barman a wink. "So how are you enjoying life on the beat?" he asked.

"Great fun," said Nicky, not wanting to admit that she hated being back in uniform.

"And Liz?" he asked tentatively.

"I'm lucky to have her as my constable mentor."

"Just be careful. She's not quite as friendly as she appears."

"What do you mean?"

"She's bound to see you as a rival when it comes to promotion."

"But she's got three years' service under her belt."

"True, but unlike you, those three years weren't spent at university. With a degree, you have a far better chance of accelerated promotion."

Nicky had forgotten just how much of her backstory she'd already told him.

"What's it like being a detective?" she asked, changing the subject.

"Never a dull moment. You should think about taking the exam. You'd make a great detective."

"I've only been on the beat for a couple of months, but I must admit I have thought about it," she said as she took a sip of her shandy.

"You know Liz failed the detective's exam, so don't raise the subject with her."

Nicky did know, and hadn't. "So, what have you been up to today?" she asked.

"Arrested a drug dealer outside the Midland Bank. Right little villain. Didn't see me coming."

"On the high street?" said Nicky.

"Yeah. He tried to slip out of sight when he saw you and Liz coming down the road and walked straight into my arms."

"Good work," said Nicky. "We had to be satisfied with a shoplifter who'd stolen a tin of salmon."

"Life imprisonment," said Summers after a long gulp of bitter.

Nicky laughed. "Did your dealer put up a fight?"

"No. Only wish he had, because I've got a black belt, so he would have soon discovered it doesn't pay to mess with me."

Nicky looked suitably impressed, even though she knew black was in fact brown. "It must be exciting never knowing what or who you'll be facing tomorrow."

"Tomorrow," said Summers, "I'm going to arrest a car thief who's stolen one Jag too many."

"How can you be sure?"

"I've had him under surveillance for several days. Even know the garage, the model, and the exact time he intends to strike," Summers said as he downed his pint. "Got time for another?"

"No, thanks. I ought to be getting home. I'm on the early-morning shift tomorrow."

"Where do you live?"

"Peckham. I share a flat with a friend."

"A girlfriend, I hope?"

Nicky nodded as she finished her drink.

"Is she one of us?"

"No, Rebecca's far too sensible for that," she said, immediately regretting her slip of the tongue. "She's a librarian in Hammersmith. We were at school together," she added, delivering another snippet of her backstory. "Perhaps I'll see you in the morning," Nicky said as she got up to leave.

"I know where I'd like to see you in the morning," said Summers, giving her a kiss on the cheek.

Nicky didn't respond. But as she made her way to the station she couldn't help wondering. . . .

# 11

"Do you wish to cross-examine this witness, Mr. Booth Watson?"

"I most certainly do, m'lud," responded defense counsel as he rose from his place. He readjusted his wig and tugged the lapels of his black gown, before looking down at a long list of prepared questions. He took his time before he spoke; an old ruse that guaranteed everyone would be waiting for his first question.

"Mr. Sangster," he began, fixing the witness with a gimlet eye. "I would like to take you back to the first words you uttered after you delivered your solemn oath, because I'm going to ask you the same question as my learned friend. Would you please state your name and occupation?"

The witness looked puzzled. "Gerald Sangster, and I'm currently unemployed."

"If I had asked you that same question eighteen months ago, how would you have responded?"

Sangster hesitated for a moment before he said, "Dr. Gerald Sangster."

"When a doctor returns to being Mr., it's usually because they've been appointed a surgeon, or a consultant. Is that what happened in your case?"

"No."

"Then perhaps you'd like to explain to the court why you are no longer entitled to call yourself a doctor."

"The court has already been told that the General Medical Council removed my name from the register."

"'Struck off,' I believe, is the correct term. And what was your offense, may I ask?"

Sangster hesitated for a moment before he admitted, "I was accused of violating my Hippocratic Oath."

Booth Watson couldn't resist another long pause.

"'Violating,'" he repeated. "What does that actually mean?"

"I overprescribed controlled drugs that proved harmful to some of my patients."

"How many patients were involved?"

"There were three witnesses who gave evidence at the hearing."

"That wasn't the question I asked, Mr. Sangster," said Booth Watson, as his junior passed him a thick file.

"Eleven," said Sangster, more quietly.

"Can you tell the court the fate of one particular patient, a Ms. Amy Watson?"

"Sadly, she died."

"How did she die?"

"From an overdose."

"Of drugs prescribed by you, Mr. Sangster. How old was she?"

"Twenty-seven."

"And another of your patients, a Ms. Esther Lockhart. How did she die?"

"Suicide."

"She hanged herself," said Booth Watson, before turning another page of the GMC's report. "I won't go into the details of the other nine unfortunate patients who were in your care, Mr. Sangster, unless of course you'd like me to."

Sir Julian rose from his place. "M'lud, I hadn't realized that Mr. Sangster was on trial in this case."

"He isn't, m'lud," interjected Booth Watson before the judge could respond, "but the credibility of his evidence is, and I'll leave the jury to decide if they can believe a word this witness says."

"You've made your point, Mr. Booth Watson. Move on."

"As Your Lordship pleases," said defense counsel, before turning back to face the witness. "Mr. Sangster, when were you struck off the Medical Register?"

Sangster hesitated again.

"Come, come. I can't believe that date isn't etched in your memory."

"July ninth last year."

"And how long do you claim that you worked for Mr. Rashidi?"

"I joined him quite recently."

"How recently?"

"A few weeks before the factory was raided."

"I think two weeks would be more accurate, wouldn't it, Mr. Sangster? But then, accuracy is not your strong suit."

"It was more than two weeks."

"Well, let's say three, shall we? How many times during those three weeks did you come across Mr. Rashidi?"

"Several times."

"And was one of those occasions during the police raid?"

"Yes, it was," said Sangster firmly.

"When you yourself were arrested?"

"Mr. Booth Watson, tread carefully," said the judge firmly.

"I'm simply trying to get at the truth, m'lud. And were you charged on that occasion, Mr. Sangster?"

"Yes."

"With what offense?"

"The supply of illegal substances."

"In contravention of the Misuse of Drugs Act 1971. And when your case came to court, how did you plead?"

"Guilty," said Sangster, so quietly he could barely be heard.

"Would you repeat that, Mr. Sangster? I'm not sure the jury heard you."

"Guilty."

"And your sentence?"

"Two years."

"Only two years for an offense that usually carries a tariff of seven? That seems an unusually lenient sentence for such a serious crime. Can I presume you're still in prison?"

"No, I was released last week."

"How convenient. Just in time to give evidence in this trial."

"You've made your point, Mr. Booth Watson," repeated the judge. "Move on."

Booth Watson looked at the jury, and had to agree with the judge. He put down one file, picked up another, and turned a few pages before embarking on his next ploy. "Mr Sangster, I'm interested to find out how well you know Mr. Rashidi. For example, can you tell me the name of the company of which he's been chairman for the past ten years?"

"Marcel and Neffe," said Sangster, almost in triumph.

"And what do they do?"

"Import tea."

"Which I don't think we'll find is listed as an illegal substance under the 1971 Misuse of Drugs Act."

Several people smiled, one or two of them on the jury.

"And where are the offices of Marcel and Neffe?"

"In the City."

"Could you be a little more precise?"

Sangster bit his lip, but didn't reply.

"No, of course you can't, Mr. Sangster, because I would suggest that there's not a lot you do know about Mr. Rashidi, other than what you've read in the press, or picked up when you were in prison."

"I know where his drug factory was, because I worked there."

"I don't doubt you worked there, Mr. Sangster, I just doubt you ever saw Mr. Rashidi there, other than on the night of the raid."

"But I know he had a flat in the same block."

"In the same block?" repeated Booth Watson word for word, to make sure it was on the record.

"I meant in the adjoining block."

"Perhaps it was you who had a flat in the same block," suggested Booth Watson, but was met with a stony silence.

Sir Julian frowned and passed a note to Grace.

"Did you ever visit that flat?"

"No, I wasn't a friend of Rashidi's."

"Then how do you know about this supposed flat?"

"It was common knowledge."

"It is common knowledge, Mr. Sangster, that Queen Elizabeth the First met Mary, Queen of Scots in Fotheringhay Castle, but I can assure you that no such meeting ever took place. I would suggest that you have never met Mr. Rashidi, and that your whole story is nothing more than a few scraps of 'common knowledge' you picked up in prison, embroidered with some elaborate inventions of your own that would guarantee you a shorter sentence."

"That's not true. I worked for Rashidi."

"And was it Mr. Rashidi who offered you the job?"

"No, a dealer recommended me."

"Your personal dealer?"

Another long silence followed before Sangster responded. "Yes.

In the past, as I've admitted, I was an occasional user of cocaine, but that's all behind me now."

Booth Watson picked up the GMC report once again, and took his time finding the relevant page before he said, "'Occasional' wasn't the word the chairman of the GMC used to describe your addiction."

Sangster made no attempt to defend himself.

"You are clearly someone who has only an *occasional* association with the truth." Sir Julian began to rise from his place. "But before my learned friend protests, let me ask if that was the same dealer with whom you shared a cell during your surprisingly brief period in prison?"

This time the hesitation was even longer.

"And was it during that time he told you the story of a drug dealer who lost his hand?"

"It might have been."

"In which case it would be nothing more than hearsay, and the jury can dismiss it for what it's worth. And where is this dealer now?" asked Booth Watson before the witness could recover.

"He's still in jail."

"Another unreliable witness, who I imagine Sir Julian will not be calling on to give evidence in this trial," Booth Watson said as he turned to face the jury. "So, allow me to sum up your evidence, Mr. Sangster. You were a doctor before you were struck off the Medical Register for violating your professional code of conduct. You're a drug addict who's happy to give evidence under oath that turns out to be hearsay picked up from another prisoner while you were in jail. You only worked in the drugs factory for two, possibly three, weeks, yet you claim to have known the defendant for some considerable time. You were struck off for harming your patients by overprescribing dangerous drugs, and later you received a surprisingly lenient two-year sentence, and you somehow ended up serving less than a year. That at least is common knowledge."

"You're twisting my words," shouted Sangster.

"I think they were already twisted, Mr. Sangster. But I'm happy to give you a chance to straighten them out before I ask any further questions."

Booth Watson stared impassively at the Crown's star witness, waiting for a reply, but none was forthcoming.

"The truth is, Mr. Sangster, that you're a super-grass with no grass. I can only hope the Crown will be calling on some more reliable witnesses to support their rather weak case."

The judge didn't look pleased. "Do you have any more questions for this witness, Mr. Booth Watson?" he asked.

"None that I suspect would elicit an honest answer, m'lud," said defense counsel before resuming his place on the bench with an exaggerated sigh.

—o—

"*There's nothing wrong with wanting to be a millionaire,*" said Marty.

Jerry placed an arm around Nicky's shoulder and pulled her gently toward him.

"*That's all very well for you to say, but I'm penniless.*"

"*Then you'll have to learn how to steal from the rich, and be sure not to give anything back to the poor.*"

Her head rested on his shoulder.

"*But that's immoral.*"

He turned to face her and smiled, not that she could see him in the darkness of the cinema.

"*Where do you draw the line when it comes to breaking the law?*"

He leaned over and kissed her gently on the lips.

*"I don't. I leave my lawyer to make those decisions."*

Their tongues touched.

*"So how do I join the greed club?"*

She broke off and turned her attention back to the screen, although she'd lost the plot.

*"First you identify a family company with a strong asset base, that's currently being managed by the third generation."*

He placed a hand on her thigh.

*"What kind of assets?"*

She gently removed his hand.

*"Land, property, paintings, jewelry even. Anything you can dispose of quickly."*

He kissed her again with a practiced confidence that left her in no doubt this wasn't the first time he'd sat in the back row. Possibly even in the same seat.

*"What's my next move?"*

His hand slipped under her jumper.

*"Start buying the company's shares in different names, but not in large amounts or they'll work out what you're up to."*

He unclasped her bra.

*"And if you pull that off?"*

He began to gently massage her breast.

*"You replace the management and sack all the workers."*

*"How will it end?"*

Her nipple hardened.

*"You sell off all the assets and make a killing, before the shareholders find out what you've been up to."*

This time she didn't resist.

*"What's that called?"*

*"Asset stripping."*

⊸o⊷

"It could have gone better," admitted William.

"Enlighten me," said the commander, as he sank back into his favorite chair by the fireplace and listened carefully.

"My father began with the forensics specialist, who produced several items from the drugs factory that clearly revealed Rashidi's fingerprints."

"I don't think Rashidi will be denying he was there," said the Hawk.

"Dr. Webb, the government's drugs supremo, was next up. She was totally convincing and didn't leave the jury in any doubt about the scale of the operation Rashidi was running. Booth Watson didn't even bother to cross-examine her."

"Sounds as if we're well ahead—"

"Until Mr. Bennett, the Savile Row tailor, made an appearance. I'm afraid he wasn't exactly helpful. Said he couldn't recall ever meeting Rashidi, let alone making a suit for him."

"Then he's got a very selective memory," said Hawksby.

"Especially as I think Rashidi was wearing one of his suits in court."

"If that's the case, he'll be trapped the moment he enters the witness box."

"*If* he enters the witness box, which is unlikely, as he won't want to admit whose photograph it was we found on the bedside table in his flat."

"He and Booth Watson will have been thinking about that for weeks, so we can assume that by now they'll have come up with an alternative explanation."

"They won't be able to get away with suggesting I planted the photo. How would I ever have got my hands on it in the first place?"

"When you visited his mother's home in The Boltons to question her?"

"Since his arrest she's refused to have anything to do with him, so he may not even know I visited her."

"She has a chauffeur and a housekeeper, paid for by Rashidi, so he'll know," said the Hawk. "But how about Sangster? Surely the jury found his evidence compelling?"

"After my father had completed his examination, the jury looked as if they weren't in any doubt that Rashidi was Sangster's boss. In fact, I thought we were home and dry until Booth Watson got back on his feet."

"Not again."

"I have to admit his cross-examination was lethal. By the time he sat down, the jury could have been forgiven for wondering if it was Sangster who should have been in the dock."

The Hawk let out a long sigh. "So it will now be up to you, William, to make sure that after you've given your evidence tomorrow, the jury will be back on the side of the angels."

"On a wing and a prayer," said William.

"Take them through how you found out that Rashidi was leading a double life," said the Hawk as if he hadn't heard the comment, fearing he might be regaled with its derivation. "And finish up with what happened on the night of the raid. Then we can leave the jury to decide who they believe—the drug baron or the Choirboy."

"If I can pull that off," said William, "Rashidi might even consider giving evidence in a last desperate attempt to avoid being sent back to prison."

"Booth Watson will advise him against doing anything quite that foolish. However I suspect Rashidi might well ignore his advice.

He's a last-throw-of-the-dice man, who'll believe he can convince the jury of his innocence, whatever the odds."

"He can't be that stupid," said William.

"No, but he might be that arrogant."

"Any advice on how I should handle Booth Watson?"

"If you do your job properly, I suspect he won't even bother to cross-examine you. He'll want the Choirboy's evidence erased from the jurors' memories as quickly as possible. But be sure you get a good night's sleep, just in case," the commander added, before putting down the phone.

"Fat chance of that," said William as Beth entered the room.

"Fat chance of what?" she asked.

⊸o⊷

Nicky woke just after five the following morning. She blinked as she took in the unfamiliar surroundings.

After the film, not much of which she could remember, they'd skipped sharing a Margherita at the local pizza house and gone back to his place. Rule number one broken. After a couple of drinks, that turned out to be a bottle of wine, she told him she ought to be leaving, but who was she kidding.

Their first effort at making love, clothes ripped off long before they reached the bedroom, ended up with them lying in each other's arms exhausted on the floor. Her initial thought afterward was that she could still catch the last train home, but not long after that she fell asleep in his arms.

She lay there painfully aware that sooner or later she would have to admit what had happened to DI Warwick. She'd not only have to resign, but might well have to look for a job stacking shelves at Tesco. Part of her backstory that might soon be her front story.

She didn't laugh. Nicky didn't want to admit even to Rebecca that she hadn't felt this way about anyone for a long time. She hoped it would turn out that Jerry might have taken the occasional risk but couldn't be thought of as a criminal.

She looked around the room, taking in the large television set resting on a stylish chrome console table that wouldn't have looked out of place in a West End duplex. Clearly not all the stolen goods Summers had recovered after his impressive number of arrests for burglary had made it to the police-station property store. At least that would be something worthwhile to report when she saw Jackie later that morning, although she wasn't sure how she would explain ending up in bed with the suspect.

She felt him stir, and a hand moved across and gently pulled her toward him, putting off the decision for a few more minutes.

"Do you have time for breakfast?" he asked when she finally climbed out of bed and headed for the bathroom.

"No, I should go home and change. I can't turn up for work looking like this."

"If you moved in with me that wouldn't be a problem."

Nicky couldn't believe what she'd just heard, and wondered if it was simply a line he used with all his conquests. As she was leaving, he kissed her once again. Not the kiss of a one-night stand. She dreaded the walk of shame from Jerry's house to the station, and was relieved not to bump into any of her colleagues on the way. She had plenty of time to think about the consequences on the long journey back to Peckham. Had Jerry really meant what he'd said?

When the train finally pulled into her local station, she jumped off and jogged all the way home, arriving outside the front door of her flat just after six. She turned the key slowly in the lock, hoping to make it to her room without Rebecca seeing her. She quietly closed the door behind her, slipped off her heels and padded silently upstairs, relieved to see a light shining under Rebecca's door. A few more paces and she'd make it. Once safely inside her bedroom, she threw off last night's clothes and put on her dressing gown. Moments later she was in the bathroom taking a second shower.

They passed each other in the corridor with a breezy "Good morning," before Nicky returned to her bedroom and got dressed. Jerry was constantly in her thoughts.

Over breakfast, they discussed anything but work, a golden rule, before heading off together for the commander's morning briefing. They were all seated around the boss's table by 7:55, waiting for the Hawk to open proceedings.

"Let's begin with you, PC Bailey," said the commander, "as I know you have to be back in Romford in time for the afternoon shift. Bring us up to date on your progress with Summers."

"Not a great deal to report, sir. He invited me out for a drink last night, but didn't show up."

"Typical," said Jackie. "But that will just be part of his long-term plan, so hang in there."

"How long did he keep you waiting?" asked Paul.

"About an hour. Then I called it a day and went home."

Rebecca was surprised by Nicky's reply, but decided to say nothing to William until her flatmate had left for Romford. Even then, she was torn.

# 12

William took the Bible in his right hand and delivered the oath with a confidence he did not feel.

Grace Warwick rose from her place on the advocates' bench, tugged at the lapels of her black gown, and adjusted her wig, unconsciously imitating her father.

"Inspector Warwick," she began, giving her brother a warm smile, "would you tell the court your name and rank for the record."

"My name is William Warwick, and I'm a detective inspector attached to Scotland Yard's drugs squad."

"On the night in question, Inspector Warwick, were you the officer who arrested Mr. Rashidi, following the raid on his drugs factory in Brixton?"

Booth Watson rose slowly from his place, a look of exasperation on his face, and delivered the words, "I must object, m'lud," before William had a chance to answer the question. "It has yet to be established who owned the property, and my learned friend's casual assertion might lead the jury to believe it was the defendant, while in fact nothing could be further from the truth."

"I apologize, m'lud," said Grace, "but had I been allowed to continue my line of questioning, the jury would have been left in no doubt who was in charge of the drugs factory that night, and who occupied the spacious apartment in the adjoining block."

Sir Julian allowed himself a smile, while Booth Watson sank back into his place.

"DI Warwick," continued Grace, looking back at her prepared questions, all of which she was confident she knew the answer to, "following the arrest of Mr. Rashidi, did you later interview him at Brixton police station?"

"I did, ma'am," replied William, addressing his sister that way for the first time, and wondering if he would ever get used to it. "And following that interview, I charged him with three offenses under sections four and five of the 1971 Misuse of Drugs Act."

"Would you tell the court the substance of those charges?"

"Section four of the Act covers the production of a controlled drug. Section five relates to the possession of a controlled drug with intent to supply, and the lesser offense of being in possession of a controlled drug."

"How did the defendant react when you put these allegations to him?"

"On the advice of his legal representative, he chose not to respond."

"No more than his legal right," snorted Booth Watson.

"And did you find any illegal substances on him?"

William hesitated. "A small cache of cannabis."

"Nothing more?"

"Sixteen pounds in cash and a bus ticket."

Booth Watson smiled and made a note on the yellow pad perched on his leg: *Bus ticket.*

"He claimed he was on his way home from work and had dropped by the flat to buy a small quantity of cannabis for his personal use over the weekend, only to find himself caught up in the maelstrom," said William, reading directly from his notebook.

"Did the defendant use the word 'maelstrom'?" asked the judge.

"He did, my lord," said William.

The judge made a note. "Please continue, Miss Warwick."

"And before the raid took place, inspector, had you already been investigating Mr. Rashidi?"

"Yes, ma'am. Over a period of nearly six months, we had been closely monitoring his daily activities."

"We?"

"At that time I was heading up a small unit of highly trained officers who established in the course of their investigations that the defendant was living a double life. During the day, he posed as the chairman of a respectable family tea company based in the City of London, while at night he was running an illegal drugs factory from the top three floors of a tower block in Brixton."

"How were you able to raid that factory without Mr. Rashidi's knowledge, given the fact that it was situated on the top three floors of a tower block, and was presumably well protected?" asked Grace.

"It was indeed, ma'am, but my team mounted an undercover operation, known as Trojan Horse. We were well aware of the tight security surrounding Block A, the building in which the drugs factory was located. It included four lookouts stationed at ground level outside the entrance to the building, making it almost impossible for any of my officers to reach the upper floors before Mr. Rashidi could be warned of our presence, giving him more than enough time to reach the safety of his apartment on the twenty-third floor in the adjoining building, Block B, which is connected to Block A by a walkway on that floor."

Booth Watson wrote the words *Block B* on his yellow pad.

"Taking all this into account, inspector, how could a team of armed police officers hope to reach the twenty-third floor of Block A before the defendant could escape to his apartment in the adjoining block?"

"My learned friend is at it again, m'lud," said Booth Watson, rising more quickly this time. "It has not been established that my client had an apartment in the adjoining block. In fact, the Crown's star witness claimed the defendant lived in the same block—Block A—as I feel sure you recall, m'lud."

The judge wrote down this observation, as did the foreman of the jury.

"And *my* learned friend is at it again," said Grace. "If he would be a little more patient, I promise to supply him with all the proof he requires."

Booth Watson sat back down, while Sir Julian could barely stop himself applauding.

"Having established the existence of an escape route from the drugs factory in Block A to an apartment in Block B, how did you overcome that problem?"

"Moments before the raid began, a carpenter who was already waiting on the landing of the twenty-third floor of Block B boarded up the entrance to the walkway. That gave my men enough time to reach the drugs factory before Rashidi was able to escape."

Grace turned to Booth Watson and gave him a warm smile, which he didn't reciprocate.

"And having arrested Mr. Rashidi on the premises, you took him to Brixton police station where he was held overnight?"

"Yes, ma'am."

"On the following morning, you gained access to an apartment in Block B. What was the purpose of that visit, inspector?"

"Under section eighteen of PACE, I had the authority to search any apartment in that building in order to establish if it had been Mr. Rashidi's place of residence whenever he was in London."

Booth Watson smiled as he penned the word, *If.*

"And were you able to do so, inspector?"

"I found a wardrobe in the bedroom full of tailored suits that had been made by Bennett and Reed of Savile Row, along with a dozen handmade shirts from Pink's on Jermyn Street that just happened to fit the defendant perfectly."

"Fitted up, more like," said Booth Watson as he rose to his feet. "M'lud, has my learned friend conveniently forgotten that the tailor in question confirmed that Mr. Rashidi was not one of his clients?"

"Let us move on to a piece of evidence that even my learned friend won't be able to dismiss quite so easily. Inspector," said Grace, turning back to face her brother, "during your investigation of the luxurious apartment in Block B, did you come across anything that proved beyond reasonable doubt that it was Mr. Rashidi who must have spent his nights there during the week?"

"Yes, ma'am. On a side table in the master bedroom I came across a photograph, the silver frame of which was engraved with the letter *A*."

"And you assumed that the *A* stood for Assem."

"Yes, I did."

Booth Watson was quickly on his feet, but Grace continued before he could intervene.

"However, that turned out *not* to be the case?"

"That's correct, ma'am. I later discovered that the *A* stood for Asprey, the well-known luxury goods company in Bond Street."

"Then what led you to believe there was any connection between that photograph and the defendant?"

"It was a photograph of Mr. Rashidi's mother."

A tumult of chatter broke out in the court, and Grace had to wait for some time before she was able to ask her next question. "The photograph is part of the Crown's evidence, m'lud, and has been accepted by both sides." She gave Booth Watson a warm smile, before adding, "And with your permission, I'll ask the clerk of the court to show it to the witness so he can confirm it was the photo he found on the bedside table of the spacious apartment in Block B."

The judge nodded, and the clerk extracted a silver-framed photograph from the bundle of evidence, walked across to the witness box, and handed it to Detective Inspector Warwick.

"Inspector," said Grace, "can you confirm this is the silver frame you found on a bedside table of the apartment in Block B?"

"Yes, I can."

"Do you recognize the woman in the photograph?"

There was total silence as the court waited for William's reply.

"No, I don't," he said finally, staring down at the image. "Someone must have replaced the original photograph."

By the time order had been restored, Booth Watson was back on his feet.

"M'lud, I wonder if the jury, and indeed you and I, might be allowed to see the photograph in question, as the inspector no longer appears to believe it proves my client's guilt," he paused, "beyond reasonable doubt."

Mr. Justice Whittaker hesitated before nodding.

The clerk handed the photograph up to the judge, but after studying it, he looked none the wiser. He passed it back to the clerk, who in turn handed it to the foreman of the jury. He took his time looking at the photograph of an elderly lady before showing it to his fellow jurors.

Grace and Sir Julian were the next people to consider the evidence, before it finally reached Mr. Booth Watson, who gave the photograph only a cursory glance before giving it back to the clerk of the court. Sir Julian leaned across and whispered a clear instruction to his daughter, who carried out his bidding.

"M'lud," she said, "I wonder if you would grant us a short recess, in order that the Crown might consider its position."

"I will allow you thirty minutes, Ms. Warwick," said the judge. "No more." He checked his watch. "Counsel will be back in their places by eleven fifteen."

"All rise."

⊸o⊷

Rebecca couldn't help thinking about what had happened earlier that morning, when Nicky had crept into the flat just after six, obviously hoping she wouldn't be seen.

When she'd joined her flatmate for breakfast, Nicky didn't mention where she'd spent the night. She was usually open about the men in her life and often had Rebecca in fits of laughter about her would-be Romeos. Nicky's diary was always full, while Rebecca's was full of blank pages.

Whenever her mother raised the subject of boyfriends, which was almost every other weekend, Rebecca told her it was difficult because of her job and the hours she kept. Most men backed off, she explained, once they discovered she was in the police force. Mind you, that didn't seem to prevent Nicky from leading a busy social life. Rebecca hoped this was just another one-night stand, and a long way from Romford. But if that was the case, why hadn't Nicky . . . Rebecca sat down at her desk and began to write a report. . . .

⊸o⊷

"When did you last see the photograph?" asked Sir Julian, as he closed the door of a private consultation room.

"A couple of days ago," said Grace, "in the presence of Booth Watson's junior and the exhibits officer, when we agreed on the prosecution's bundle of evidence. Someone must have switched the photographs over the weekend."

"Obviously," said Sir Julian. "But who?" he demanded, thumping the desk with a clenched fist.

"Someone in the pay of Rashidi, who was able to get in and out of Scotland Yard unchallenged. I have no idea who the lady is," said Grace, looking more closely at the photograph. "But I can tell you one thing. It isn't Mrs. Rashidi."

"That's for sure," said Sir Julian, "but I have a feeling we're about to find out who it is."

⊸o⊷

"That's all I need," said the Hawk once he'd finished reading Rebecca's report.

"Let's hope I'm wrong, sir."

"But if you're right," said Jackie, "we're going to have to play them at their own game."

"What do you have in mind, DS Roycroft?" asked the Hawk.

"In future, we'll have to hold two separate meetings. One at which Nicky is present, and another when she isn't, along with two different agendas."

"But how can we keep an eye on her while she's in Romford," interjected Paul, "without it being obvious?"

"I will have to get Marlboro Man to do that job," said the Hawk. "I'll leave you to get in touch with him, DS Roycroft, and arrange a meeting as soon as possible."

Jackie nodded.

"And DC Pankhurst, I would quite understand if you felt unable to spy on your friend. However, if PC Bailey has switched sides . . ."

"I'm still hoping I've made a terrible mistake, sir, and that Nicky spent the night with some other bloke. But I fear everything points to Summers."

"I agree with you," said the Hawk. "So we should assume the worst for now. And while we're on the subject of switching sides, what's the latest on Lamont?"

Rebecca opened her notebook. "Yesterday morning he left home just after nine, and took the tube to Moorgate, where he spent the day seated in the back row of the public gallery of court number one at the Old Bailey."

"What was he doing there?" asked the Hawk, but no one offered an opinion.

---

Sir Julian and Grace were back in court only moments before the judge reappeared.

Grace was looking resigned as her brother passed her on his way to the witness box. She waited until everyone had settled before she rose from her place and said, "M'lud, the Crown has no further questions for this witness."

William took a deep breath, and like a heavyweight boxer took up his stance in the middle of the ring and waited for Booth Watson to throw the first punch. It was a sucker punch.

"Do you wish to cross-examine this witness, Mr. Booth Watson?" asked the referee.

Booth Watson took his time before responding.

"No, thank you, m'lud," he said, barely rising from his place.

"You may step down, Inspector Warwick."

William left the witness box unsure if he was relieved to have escaped unscathed, or annoyed he hadn't even been allowed to put up a fight.

Grace rose again, but waited for her brother to leave before she addressed the court. "M'lud, we will not be calling any further witnesses, so that completes the case for the prosecution."

"Thank you, Miss Warwick." The judge switched his attention to the other end of the bench. "You may call your first witness, Mr. Booth Watson."

"Thank you, m'lud." Defense counsel took his time studying a list of names before he said, "I call Mr. Tony Roberts."

⊸o⊷

William couldn't hide his anger as he walked out of court number one and headed for the nearest telephone. Someone, somehow, had switched the one piece of evidence that would have left the jury in no doubt of Rashidi's guilt, and put him behind bars with a life sentence.

As he picked up the phone and dialed the commander's number, he was still trying to figure out who could possibly be the latest recruit on Rashidi's payroll. Which of his henchmen had access to Scotland Yard or the Old Bailey?

"Hawksby," announced the familiar voice.

"We've been snookered," said William.

He didn't need to refer to his notebook to repeat verbatim what had taken place in court number one earlier that morning.

"It would seem that Rashidi is every bit as resourceful as Faulkner," said the commander, "and has found his own way of escaping."

"He also has Booth Watson on his side, so switching the photo may turn out to be the least of our problems."

"Then you'd better get back and find out who Tony Roberts is. Call me the moment court is adjourned for the day, because another problem has arisen that could blow up in our faces."

"A clue, sir?"

"No. I want you to find out who Tony Roberts is, before I share that piece of news with you."

The commander put the phone down, opened the file in front of him, and reread DC Pankhurst's report. A frown didn't leave his face.

# 13

"Please state your name and occupation for the record," said Booth Watson.

"My name is Tony Roberts, and I own a chain of newsagents south of the river."

"And your home address?"

"Flat 97, Napier Mansions, Brixton."

"Can I confirm, Mr. Roberts, that your apartment is on the twenty-third floor of Block B?"

"Yes, sir."

"And how long have you lived there?"

"Just over ten years. I was rentin' it for four years, and then I bought the place when the government made that possible, six years ago."

Sir Julian made a note, underlining *Ten years*.

"And yours is a larger apartment than any other in the block."

"That's right, I got plannin' permission to knock two flats into one."

Sir Julian wrote the words *Check whose name is on planning permission,* and passed his query across to Clare, who was sitting on the solicitors' bench behind him.

"So, your newsagents business must be fairly successful?"

"Can't complain. Took over my old man's shop when he retired. And since then, the business has grown like Topsy."

"And how many shops do you own now?"

"Eleven, with a couple more under offer."

"As your business is so successful, Mr. Roberts, have you ever considered opening a newsagents on the other side of the river?"

Sir Julian put a cross through one of the questions he had intended to ask.

"I'm not a toff like you," said Roberts. "Born in Brixton, went to the local secondary modern, married a Brixton girl, and when my time comes, I'll be buried in Brixton."

"But you must cross the river occasionally?" said Booth Watson. "Because I can't believe the suit you are wearing was purchased in Brixton."

Sir Julian crossed out another question on his list.

"Sunday best," said Roberts. "The wife thought it would be appropriate for my appearance in court."

"May I ask who the tailor is?"

Roberts opened his jacket with a flourish to reveal the red label of Bennett and Reed of Savile Row.

Sir Julian made a further note that he added to his list of questions.

"Mr. Roberts, I'm going to show you a photograph that was found on the bedside table of your apartment."

Once again, the clerk retrieved the silver-framed photo from the bundle of evidence and handed it to the witness.

"Do you recognize the lady in the photograph?"

"Course I do. It's my dear departed mother, God rest her soul."

Grace made a note, and passed it to her father.

"Where were you on the night the police raided the adjoining block, Block A?"

"Havin' a few jars at the Rose and Crown, with some mates."

"So you were unaware of the raid?"

"At the time yes, but by the time I got home both buildin's was surrounded by coppers. So many uniforms I thought the third world war must have broken out."

One or two people in the court laughed, including a member of the jury.

"You weren't aware there was a drugs factory operating in the block next door?"

"Heard rumors, of course. If it's true, I hope the bastards get what's comin' to them," he said, staring directly at Rashidi.

"Brilliant," whispered Grace. "A National Theatre player couldn't have delivered that line more convincingly."

"I agree," said Sir Julian. "But let's see what he's like under cross-examination, when he doesn't have a prepared script to rely on, with the occasional prompt from the wings."

"I'd like to move on to the day after the raid took place," said Booth Watson, "when the police obtained a warrant to search your apartment and came away with a number of your suits and shirts, and the photograph of your mother you have just identified."

"Not to mention the money that went missin' from my safe."

"Some money went missing?" said Booth Watson, feigning surprise while looking directly at the jury. "May I ask how much?"

"A few bob short of seven hundred quid, which I'd intended to bank the next mornin'."

This time it was Clare who made a note and handed it to counsel. Sir Julian nodded and added the question to his list.

"I presume you made an official complaint to the police?"

"What's the point, when it was them what took it?"

Uproar broke out in the court, as the journalists began to pen a story they hadn't anticipated. Booth Watson waited patiently for the chatter to cease before he put his next question. "Were you able to find out which officer was responsible for conducting the search of the apartment in your absence?"

"Yep, I've got a mate who works in Brixton nick. He told me it wasn't someone from our local patch, but an outsider from the other side of the river. Scotland Yard, no less."

"Did he give you a name?"

"Sure did. Detective Inspector William Warwick."

Several people turned around and stared in William's direction. Only the journalists remained head down, scribbling away.

Sir Julian was on his feet at once. "I must protest, m'lud."

"Of course you must," said Booth Watson. "After all, he's your son."

Now the journalists had their banner headline, and it was still YOUR OWN CHILD. It was some time before the uproar had died down enough for anyone to be heard. Mr. Justice Whittaker stared down at defense counsel.

"That was uncalled for, Mr. Booth Watson," he said, barely concealing his anger.

"I apologize unreservedly," said defense counsel, giving the judge a slight bow. "However, m'lud, I should point out that I didn't ask the witness who had stolen his money, only who had conducted the search."

The judge was still seething, but managed to control his temper. "Very well. You may continue, Mr. Booth Watson."

"Allow me to ask you once again, Mr. Roberts, how long have you lived in your apartment in Block B?"

"Just over ten years."

"And would you now look carefully at the man standing in the dock." The witness looked across at Rashidi. "Have you ever seen him before?"

"No, never," said Roberts without hesitation.

"Thank you, Mr. Roberts," said Booth Watson, who turned to the judge and said, "I have no more questions for this witness, m'lud," before sinking back down into his place, well satisfied with his afternoon's work.

Grace, who had remained outwardly calm during the bitter exchanges, leaned across and whispered to her father, "Have you noticed that Roberts and Rashidi are wearing identical suits?"

Sir Julian took a closer look at both of them before saying, "You could be right. But I can't do anything about it unless Rashidi gives evidence from the witness box, and I shouldn't imagine BW will allow that."

"Do you intend to cross-examine this witness, Sir Julian?" asked the judge.

"I most certainly do, m'lud," said the Crown's leading advocate, as he rose from his place.

"Mr. Roberts, if that is your real name," he began, looking directly at the witness.

"What are you gettin' at?" said Roberts defiantly.

"I only wondered if Tony Roberts was the name on your birth certificate. Think carefully before you answer the question, because I'm confident the judge will allow me a recess so I can visit the General Record Office to check the original document."

"OK, I was born Tony Burke. What of it?"

"And when did you change your name to Roberts?"

"Can't remember the exact date."

"Could it have been about ten years ago?"

"Might've been."

"Did you do so for any particular reason?"

"Didn't like being called a right berk, simple as that." The witness leaned back, waiting for someone to laugh, but no one did.

"I don't think it can have been quite as simple as that," said Sir Julian, "because the initials sewn on the inside of your jacket . . ."

"A.R., Anthony Roberts. My God-fearing mother never called me Tony. I only wish she was still alive today, then she could tell you 'erself."

"So do I," said Sir Julian, "because I could then have asked her some more questions about her son."

"Like what?" said Roberts, defiantly.

"If he knew the way to Savile Row."

"She'd have said yes."

"So when you leave your home in Brixton to visit your tailor for another fitting, which bridge do you cross?"

"No idea. I always take a cab." He paused. "It's somewhere in the West End, if I remember right."

"Somewhere in the West End," Sir Julian repeated, looking at the jury. "So let me ask you about a venue with which you appear to be more familiar, the Rose and Crown."

"My local."

"You told the court that on the night the police raided the drugs factory in Block A, you were 'having a few jars at the Rose and Crown, with some mates.'"

"Yes, and what's more, I can name every one of them."

"I feel sure you can," said Sir Julian. "However, you went on to say that by the time you got home later that night, both blocks were surrounded by the police. You thought the third world war must have broken out, if I recall your exact words."

"At least you got somethin' right."

"What time did you leave the pub?"

"Just before ten. Don't forget I own several newsagents so I have to be up early."

"And how far is it from the pub to your home in Napier Road?"

"About half a mile."

"So it must have taken you ten, perhaps fifteen minutes to reach home?"

"Sounds 'bout right."

"I must tell you it's a matter of record that the police didn't turn up in Napier Road until after ten thirty that night. So how do you account for the missing fifteen minutes?"

A worried look appeared on the witness's face for the first time, before he blurted out, "Oh yeah, I forgot. I left the pub with one of my mates, and we stopped off at his place for another jar."

"Can you remember the name and address of that mate, Mr. Roberts?"

"Can't say I do, but then it was more than six months ago."

"But only a few moments ago you told the court you could name every one of your mates who were in the pub that night."

The witness pursed his lips, but made no attempt to reply.

"Well, let's move on to something you appear to remember in great detail. You told my learned friend that the police visited your home the morning after the raid and removed a number of Savile Row suits, a dozen shirts, a silver-framed photograph of your mother, as well as 'a few bob short of seven hundred quid,' which you later found was missing from your safe."

"Spot on. And I'd like to know who stole it."

"So would I," said Sir Julian, "because you also told the court that you intended to bank the seven hundred pounds that morning."

"That's right. I deposit the previous day's takings on my way to work every mornin,' without fail."

"But you did fail on this occasion, Mr. Roberts, because you told the court the money was still in your safe when the police searched your home."

"Must have forgotten for once."

"Then let me ask you something you couldn't possibly forget if, as you claim, you've lived in that flat for the past ten years. What's your telephone number?"

"Two seven four—" Roberts began, then stopped and stared blankly at Sir Julian.

"It's not a trick question, Mr. Roberts. I imagine every member of the jury can remember their home telephone number, especially those who've lived at the same address for the past ten years." He was rewarded with some involuntary nods from the jury box.

"I think it might have been changed recently," said Roberts.

"Not according to British Telecom," said Sir Julian, holding up a letter for the court to see. "The accounts manager for the Brixton area assures me," he said, reading the words Grace had underlined, "this number has not been changed since it was installed in 1976."

"If you say so."

"I don't say so, Mr. Roberts, but British Telecom does." Sir Julian didn't move on until he was certain the jury had realized the witness had no intention of responding. "I would like to return to the Asprey's silver frame found in your flat, displaying a photograph of your late lamented mother."

"God rest her soul," said Roberts.

"Yes, indeed," said Sir Julian, "because had she lived, there is another question I would have liked to ask her. How often did she pop into Asprey's to buy presents for her son?"

"What are you suggestin'?"

"Just as we learned earlier that you didn't know where Savile Row is, despite having a wardrobe full of handmade suits from one of its long-established tailors, I have a feeling your mother never visited Bond Street."

"You can't prove that."

"You're right, I can't." Roberts assumed a smug expression, until Sir Julian asked, "Do you believe in coincidence?"

"What are you gettin' at?"

"Allow me to explain exactly what I'm getting at. Ten years ago, you changed your name, rented a brand-new apartment in a recently built block, and acquired a bespoke tailor, even though you're not entirely sure where Savile Row is. At that time you were the proprietor of a single newsagents shop, and you now own eleven, with another two under offer."

"What does that prove?"

"That you're a very resourceful man, Mr. Roberts. But the jury might find it quite a coincidence that all this happened at the same time as Mr. Assem Rashidi moved into the area, opened a drugs factory in the next block, and might have needed someone local who could move into his apartment at a moment's notice, and look as if he'd lived there for the past ten years despite the fact he didn't even know the telephone number of the flat."

"It was always my flat, not Assem's," shouted Roberts, pointing at the defendant.

"Shall we let the jury decide if it was your flat or *Assem's*?" said Sir Julian, allowing himself a smile. "No more questions, m'lud."

# 14

The taxi turned left out of Scotland Yard and headed toward Westminster. The FOR HIRE sign had been switched off, but that didn't stop one or two hopeful customers from trying to flag him down. The driver ignored them because he already had a booking.

He headed down Victoria Street, with Westminster Abbey on his right and, on his left, the QEII center, which had recently been opened by the Queen. As always, the traffic in Parliament Square was almost at a standstill, but that suited his purpose. He looked up at Big Ben as England's timekeeper struck twelve times, the chimes echoing around the square.

He eased across to the inside lane and slowed down. His timing needed to be perfect. The lights turned red as he swung left, coming to a halt at the top of Whitehall, allowing a mass of pedestrians to cross the road. There are no zebra crossings in Whitehall, because if there were, the traffic would be at a perpetual standstill, as would the seat of government.

A woman tapped on his side window, having noticed that although the yellow light was off, no one was sitting in the back.

"Are you free?"

"No, madam. I have a booking."

She looked surprised when an unlikely looking passenger opened the back door of the taxi, and climbed in. The traffic light turned green.

As the driver moved off he glanced in the rearview mirror to see a scruffy, unshaven individual lounging on the backseat, who most cabbies would have refused to pick up. But not the commander.

"Good morning, sir," his fare said as they drove past the Foreign Office.

"Good morning, Ross," replied the Hawk, as he slipped into the bus lane.

"As instructed, I've been keeping a close eye on our former colleague, Superintendent Lamont, and I'm sorry to report that your worst fears have been realized."

The commander let out a deep sigh as they passed the Cenotaph and headed toward Trafalgar Square. "Don't paper over the cracks, Ross," he said.

"After you put pressure on him to return the cash, or at least most of it, that had been temporarily mislaid following the raid on Rashidi's slaughter, he decided, as you know, to resign from the force rather than face an inquiry. As a result of that decision he ended up in considerable debt. He even thought about buying a pub in Blackheath, but his wife put a stop to that. I'm afraid he's in a bad place and Summers found it only too easy to take advantage of the situation."

"How come?"

"A nag problem, sir, caused by a high-maintenance wife and low-maintenance horses."

"Don't spare me the details."

"His wife, Lauren, thinks Harrods is the only store she should be seen frequenting, and the Caprice the only restaurant worthy of her patronage."

"Poor man."

"And poor is the result, because whenever he does have the occasional win at the races he celebrates, and forgets all about the far more frequent losses. That's why until recently he was always broke."

"Until recently?"

"In the past couple of weeks he's paid off all his debts to the bookies, and several other substantial outgoings that aren't easy to explain," said Ross as the taxi swung out of Trafalgar Square and headed down the Mall.

"Like what?" asked the Hawk, as Buckingham Palace loomed into sight.

"He's recently made a down payment on a bigger house in Fulham that comes with an even larger mortgage. His wife is kitting it out with furniture from Harrods, and he's driving a new Audi which he paid for in cash. He's certainly not getting that sort of money from his pension pot."

"We've got a pretty good idea who his paymaster is," said the Hawk. "Lamont's had three separate meetings with DS Summers during the past month. They get on and off at different stations on the Circle line, and never spend more than a few minutes together. On one occasion our undercover officer saw a bulky brown envelope changing hands. What we don't know is what Lamont is offering in return, although we strongly suspect he was responsible for switching the photograph that blew a hole through the Crown's evidence at Rashidi's trial." He threw on his brakes and cursed as a jogger ran in front of the cab. "We already knew about the connection between Lamont and Summers," the Hawk mused, "but what's the connection between Rashidi and Summers?"

"That's easy to explain," said Ross. "The Turner family. They control the drugs racket in Romford, and were among Rashidi's best customers. I wouldn't be surprised if Summers is on their payroll."

"Then let's concentrate on the source of the money as it's always the best motive. Anything new at the Romford end?"

"PC Bailey has spent the past three nights at Summers's home. I'm informed by a reliable source that most of his girlfriends last about a week, two at the most. If it goes into a third week, you might have a more serious problem."

"That's the understatement of the year. An officer on my investigation squad sleeping with the person she's meant to be investigating. How am I going to explain that to the commissioner?"

Marlboro Man didn't offer an opinion.

"Keep an eye on both of them," the Hawk eventually managed, "and let's meet up again in a week. Same time, same place. If you find out what Lamont's up to, get in touch with Jackie and let her know immediately."

The commander came to a halt at the traffic lights opposite the Army and Navy Store. His passenger hopped out of the cab, fare unpaid, and disappeared among the morning shoppers.

"Can you take me to the Guards Club, my good man?" inquired an elderly gentleman, tapping a cane on the side window.

"No, I can't," said the Hawk, and quickly accelerated away.

"I don't know what the country's coming to," growled the old man.

The Hawk turned into Victoria Street, still trying to work out what Summers was expecting from Lamont in return for the latest bulky brown envelope. As he parked in his reserved space at Scotland Yard, he said out loud, "I can't believe he'd sink that low."

---

"Dr. Goddard, would you please tell the court your occupation?" said Booth Watson, smiling warmly at his next witness.

"I am the clinical director of a drugs rehabilitation center in Bromsgrove."

"And how do you know the defendant?"

"He was a patient of mine at one time, but I am happy to say he is now fully recovered."

"Dr. Goddard, for how long was Mr. Rashidi a patient at your clinic?"

"He was in rehab for a couple of months."

"And during that time did you ever see a photograph on his bedside table?"

"Yes, a silver-framed photo of his mother, who regularly visited him at the clinic."

"And was there a large 'A' engraved on the top of the frame?"

"Yes, sir," said Goddard, looking surprised.

"Do you know what the A stood for?"

"Asprey. But I only discovered that when his mother told me she had purchased the frame in Bond Street."

"And when Mr. Rashidi left your care, did he take the photograph with him?"

"Yes, he did."

"How can you be so sure?"

"Because I saw it again when I had tea with him at his mother's home in The Boltons."

"After being discharged, did Mr. Rashidi continue to take an interest in your clinic's invaluable work?"

"More than an interest. I would describe him as one of our most committed supporters. Not only does he visit the clinic on a regular basis, but for the past ten years his family company has made an annual donation of a hundred thousand pounds in support of our work."

"Just the price of another get-out-of-jail-free card," muttered Sir Julian, sotto voce, while Clare wrote down the words *Ten years.* Another coincidence?

"So, over a number of years," continued Booth Watson, "your clinic has benefited to the tune of around a million pounds thanks to Mr. Rashidi's generosity."

"Over a million," said Goddard, "as he recently made a one-off donation when we needed to build a new ward.

"After he was arrested no doubt," said Sir Julian not so sotto voce.

"What was your reaction, Dr. Goddard, when you heard that Mr. Rashidi had been arrested and charged with being a drug trafficker?"

"I assumed the police would quickly realize they'd arrested the wrong man and release him. After all, no one could have done more to assist the unfortunate victims of drugs."

"And no one could have done more to put them there in the first place," murmured Sir Julian.

"You say Mr. Rashidi has fully recovered from his addiction, but when he was arrested, he was found in possession of a small quantity of cannabis."

"Assem has always been quite open about the fact that he enjoys the occasional marijuana cigarette at weekends, but then so do over five million people in this country. Perhaps they should all be locked up? However, I can assure you, Mr. Booth Watson, he hasn't touched anything more serious for over ten years."

"Just sold it to the highest bidder," muttered Sir Julian under his breath.

"I have no further questions, Dr. Goddard, and I'm sure we are all grateful for your contribution. But could you remain in the witness box, as I suspect my learned friend will want to question you further, having made so many observations from a sedentary position."

"I most certainly do, m'lud," said Sir Julian and was about to rise when Grace placed a hand on his arm. "Don't go there, Father," she whispered. "He's just an innocent bystander, and unlike Tony Roberts, nothing will be gained by cross-examining him."

"But what about the silver frame, it must be the same one—"

"Possibly," said Clare, leaning forward from the row behind, "but the manager of Asprey told me that it's one of their most popular items. They sold more than two hundred of them last year."

"But how could Rashidi possibly afford to pay out over a million pounds to Goddard's clinic when his only official source of income is his declared profits from a small tea-importing company."

"Goddard can't possibly know the answer to that question," said Grace.

"But at least I'd get it on the record," insisted Sir Julian.

"Save your firepower for Rashidi, when it will be far more effective."

"That's assuming Booth Watson allows him to set foot in the witness box."

"He's bound to," said Grace, "if he's to have any hope of turning the tables after Roberts's disastrous testimony."

Sir Julian sank back onto the bench. "I can only wonder where you get your wisdom from," he remarked, with the suggestion of a smile.

"Will you be cross-examining this witness, Sir Julian?" asked the judge.

"No, m'lud," said the prosecution counsel, bobbing up briefly from his place.

⊸o⊷

Marlboro Man drove down to Romford soon after he'd left the commander.

He couldn't risk taking the train, even though he knew exactly where Lamont, Summers, and Bailey were at that moment. Lamont was sitting at the back of the public gallery in court number one at the Old Bailey making notes, although Ross still couldn't work out why. Summers was interviewing a petty crook who specialized in stealing Jaguars, while PC Bailey was out on the beat and wouldn't be reporting back to the nick much before six.

For the fourth day in a row he parked just down the road from Romford police station. It wasn't a perfect view, but it had the advantage that he was unlikely to be spotted.

PC Bailey arrived back at the nick just after six o'clock, and reappeared fifteen minutes later, dressed in her civilian clothes. He climbed out of his car and began to follow her, while keeping a safe distance. First surprise, she didn't head for the station, but their favorite pub.

He crossed the road and slipped into a small café, where he bought a black coffee and a cheese-and-tomato baguette. Always grab some grub whenever you can, his old SAS training sergeant used to say. He took a seat near the window that gave him a clear view of the pub. He ate his sandwich a little too quickly, but then, he couldn't be sure when he'd be on the move again.

Summers swaggered into the pub about fifteen minutes later. Ross assumed Jaguar Man must be safely locked up in a cell for the night.

Another twenty minutes passed before they reappeared, holding hands, and headed off in the direction of Summers's flat. Marlboro Man returned to his car and selected another spot from where he had a clear view of the fourth-floor window. Despite it being his job, he still felt like a peeping Tom, especially when it came to spying on a colleague. He didn't switch the ignition back on until just after eleven, when the bedroom light finally went out.

He would normally have gone home and tried to grab a few hours' sleep, but instead he decided to head for Jackie's flat in

Lambeth so he could pass on the latest intel. He hoped she'd be tucked up in bed—alone.

He parked in a side street just after midnight and for a moment considered not waking her, but he knew the commander wouldn't want to wait a week to discover that PC Bailey now appeared to be a permanent fixture in the Summers household. Or at least that was his excuse.

He climbed up the fire escape like a professional burglar: slowly, silently. When he reached the third floor he peered through a tiny gap in the curtain. He could see her, but couldn't make out if she was alone.

He tapped gently on the window, three one three, to let her know it was him. A few moments later a sleepy figure appeared, drew the curtains, and pulled up the window.

"Business or pleasure?" Jackie asked, managing a smile.

"I was hoping we might manage both," her UCO replied.

---

"There's not a lot more we can do tonight," said Sir Julian as the clock on a nearby church tower struck midnight.

"Or even this morning," remarked Grace, looking down at the long list of questions they'd prepared in the hope of trapping Rashidi.

"Booth Watson would be pleased to know we've been up half the night preparing to cross-examine a defendant he probably has no intention of putting on the stand."

"But surely after Tony Roberts's dismal contribution, he'll have no choice but to want to tell the jury his side of the story, however improbable."

Sir Julian shook his head. "Roberts may not have helped their chances, but Dr. Goddard was convincing, and it doesn't help that the one piece of evidence we had that would have left the jury in no doubt of Rashidi's guilt conveniently disappeared into thin air. All I can say is, if Rashidi was my client, I wouldn't allow him anywhere near the witness box."

"But don't forget," Grace reminded him, "BW told the judge after Goddard stood down, that he would be calling his final witness in the morning. So if it's not Rashidi, who could it possibly be?"

"Rashidi's mother?"

"No, she's on the side of the angels, so he won't risk calling her."

"Then I agree, it has to be Rashidi."

"If it is, I can't wait to find out where he's been sleeping during the week for the past ten years if it wasn't in the apartment in Brixton."

"In a suite at the Savoy would be my bet," said Sir Julian. "And you can be sure Booth Watson will produce all the necessary bills and receipts to prove it. Just another get-out clause in his fully paid-up comprehensive insurance policy."

He rose from behind his desk, gathered up his papers, and headed for the door.

"Booth Watson will still have to explain what his client was doing in Brixton that night, because it can hardly be described as on the way back to his country home in Oxfordshire, and it's a long way to go and pick up a couple of joints when there's a dozen pubs in the City that would happily supply them over the counter," Grace remarked as her father helped her on with her coat.

"Don't tell William that," said Julian, "or he'll set the dogs on them."

"Have you decided what to do if Rashidi is wearing the same suit tomorrow as he did on the first day of the trial?" she asked as they began walking down the creaky wooden staircase.

"I may not do anything," said Sir Julian. "Frankly, I don't think it's a risk worth taking."

"But Clare spotted a red label with the initials A.R. on the inside of his jacket."

"Which Booth Watson and Rashidi might well have intended her to see," said Sir Julian. "Never ask a question unless you can be sure of the answer," he reminded her as they strolled across Lincoln's Inn Fields. "Let's meet up and go over the questions one more time later this morning," he suggested. "You can be Rashidi, and I'll cross-examine you."

"But that man is so devious, I can't begin to imagine what he's likely to come up with."

"Try to think like him, although I'm still not convinced Booth Watson will risk putting him in the witness box."

"Then who else can it be?" said Grace as she shivered and buttoned up her coat against the cold night air.

"Remember to bring a flask of black coffee and a bacon butty. And don't even think about telling your mother."

Grace laughed as her father headed off to his flat on the other side of the square, while she went in search of a taxi. Rashidi and Booth Watson accompanied her all the way back to west London. In her thoughts.

# 15

Sir Julian and Grace arrived at the Old Bailey just after nine that morning.

Overnight, Clare had come up with some more incisive questions that she felt would catch Rashidi off guard, and Sir Julian appeared a bit more hopeful that Booth Watson had been left with no choice but to allow his client to enter the witness box.

By the time they arrived in court, Booth Watson was already setting up his stall in preparation for the final witness. Sir Julian would have liked to have sight of the list of questions he had prepared for Rashidi, but accepted that he would have to wait like everyone else, until the clock struck ten.

When their eyes met the two gladiators barely raised their visors.

Next to enter the arena was the defendant, who took his place in the dock. Booth Watson looked around and gave him a warm smile. If Rashidi was nervous about giving evidence in his own defense, there was no sign of it.

"I'm pretty sure he's wearing the same suit as he did on the opening day," ventured Grace after a surreptitious glance in Rashidi's direction.

"You may be right," said Sir Julian, "but I'm still not convinced it's a risk worth taking. After all, BW's second-guessed everything else we've come up with so far."

Bang on cue the referee entered the arena. Mr. Justice Whittaker bowed low before taking his place in the high-backed chair above them, and waited for the seven men and five women to file in and resume their places in the jury box. Grace felt they all looked especially alert that morning, no doubt in anticipation of the main attraction.

William slipped in a few moments later and took a seat at the back of the court, just as proceedings were about to begin.

"Mr. Booth Watson," declared the judge, looking down from on high. "You may call your next witness."

"Thank you, m'lud," said defense counsel, who once again glanced in Rashidi's direction before saying, "I call Mr. Bruce Lamont."

William was momentarily stunned, while everyone around him began talking at once. Even so, he assumed his father wouldn't have been taken by surprise, until he saw him leap to his feet.

"M'lud, the Crown has not been informed about the possibility of this witness giving evidence, and has therefore had no time to prepare for such an eventuality. We had assumed that Mr. Rashidi would be the defense's final witness."

"I can't imagine why," said Booth Watson, with an air of innocence. "After all, I registered my intention to examine this witness with the clerk of the court yesterday afternoon, after some new evidence had come to light, and asked him to inform Your Lordship without fail."

"Which he did," said the judge. "Perhaps it would have been courteous to have also informed the Crown of your intention."

"That was remiss of me," said Booth Watson. "I'll make sure I don't make the same mistake again."

"It wasn't a mistake," said Grace, unable to restrain herself any longer.

"Am I my sister's keeper?" said Booth Watson with a sigh.

"As the witness is waiting to be called," said the judge, "I will allow defense counsel to carry out his examination-in-chief. If you then feel, Sir Julian, you need more time to consider the witness's evidence, I would of course be willing to grant an adjournment before calling on you to conduct your cross-examination."

"As Your Lordship pleases," said Sir Julian, not looking at all pleased. He pushed aside the long list of questions he and Grace had spent the previous night preparing, and the early morning rehearsing, in exchange for a virgin yellow pad and a fountain pen. He was pleased to see that both Grace and Clare already had their pencils poised.

William was still seething at the back of the court when a familiar figure walked in, and made his way to the witness box. Lamont was dressed in a dark blue double-breasted blazer, a freshly pressed pair of gray slacks, cream shirt, and Metropolitan Police tie. William recalled his oft-repeated homily: always dress smartly when you're in the witness box. It helps to get the jury on your side.

The clerk handed Lamont a Bible, which he held in his right hand. He delivered the oath confidently, without looking at the proffered card, adding the words, "So help me God."

---

"What is the one sentence in MM's report that screams out at you, DS Roycroft?" asked the commander.

"They spent another night together in the flat," suggested Jackie.

"No, that didn't surprise me. But something else did."

Jackie quickly skimmed through MM's two-page report once

again, but couldn't spot what the Hawk was getting at. He put her out of her misery.

"When the two of them left the pub, they were holding hands. Summers doesn't strike me as the hand-holding type, so we have to assume this is a more serious relationship than we'd originally thought. Which presents us with a different kind of problem."

"Plan B?" suggested Paul.

"We don't have much choice, DS Adaja," said the commander. "With that in mind, all future team meetings will be held only when PC Bailey is on duty in Romford. We will also have to rely on DC Pankhurst to update us on Nicky's movements, if she's not to become suspicious. Naive she may be, but a fool she is not."

Rebecca nodded, but didn't comment.

"The one exception will be our usual Monday-morning meetings, which must still go ahead, with PC Bailey present. She can continue to give us her weekly progress reports, which should prove illuminating."

"Perhaps she'll come clean," said Rebecca, "and admit what a terrible mistake she's made?"

"I wouldn't put your wages on it, DC Pankhurst," said the Hawk.

"Please state your name and occupation for the record," said Booth Watson after the witness had taken the oath.

"My name is Bruce Lamont, and until recently I was a detective superintendent with the drugs squad based at Scotland Yard."

"And you were the officer in charge of the successful operation known as Trojan Horse, that took out the drugs factory in Brixton."

"I was indeed, sir."

"And was it you who arrested my client, Mr. Assem Rashidi?"

"No, sir, I was on the battle bus at the time, in charge of overall strategy for the operation."

William was glad the Hawk wasn't in court to hear this claim.

"An operation that was hailed by the press and public alike as an overwhelming success."

"We all thought so at the time, but I began to have my doubts a few days later."

"But your team had arrested twenty-eight criminals that night, among them several drug manufacturers, dealers, runners, and most important, Mr. Assem Rashidi, the man you believed to be their controller."

"I thought so at the time, but after further investigation, I began to wonder if we'd arrested the wrong man."

Sir Julian couldn't help noticing that the jury were hanging on Lamont's every word.

"You're no longer convinced that the leader of the drugs ring was among those you arrested and charged that night?"

"No, I am not, sir."

"Do you think he might have escaped?"

"No, sir. I don't think he was there when we turned up."

"How could that be possible when the operation had been planned so meticulously for several months?"

"I have reluctantly come to the conclusion that someone must have tipped him off before we arrived."

"Could that someone possibly have been a member of your inner team?"

"Perhaps, but I still don't want to believe it."

"Do you have any idea who that person might be?"

"I have my suspicions," said Lamont, looking directly at William. "But suspicions alone should never be enough for a good copper."

William could feel his body tense, but accepted he could do nothing except sit and wait to find out what was coming next.

"Nevertheless," continued Booth Watson, "my client was arrested and charged with the despicable crime of manufacturing and distributing illegal drugs. Was it you who arrested him?"

"No, sir. It was Detective Inspector William Warwick who arrested and charged him. He seemed convinced he'd got the right man. But then, Mr. Rashidi conveniently fitted the perceived profile of a drugs baron."

"I'm not sure I understand what you're getting at, superintendent," said Booth Watson, understanding only too well.

"An Algerian immigrant who ran an import company, previously had a drugs problem, and just happened to be on the premises at the wrong time. We thought we'd hit the jackpot, but it all seemed a little too convenient for me. So I began to carry out a more in-depth investigation of my own."

"But surely, superintendent, you must have been tempted to remain silent and bask in your success?"

"Tempted, yes," said Lamont, "but then I thought about how even more disgraceful it would be for an innocent man to be sent to jail for a crime he hadn't committed."

"And in the course of your investigations, did you discover anything that would explain why Mr. Rashidi just happened to be on the premises at the time of the raid?"

"He was on his way home from a small warehouse in Battersea that he visits every Friday evening."

"For what purpose?" asked Booth Watson.

"Mr. Rashidi's family company imports tea, and he always checks next week's orders on a Friday evening before returning to his home in the country."

"That doesn't explain what he was doing at the drugs factory later that night."

"My surveillance team were able to establish that he did occasionally visit the factory, but never for more than a few minutes. I came to the reluctant conclusion he was simply an occasional customer, and not the man we were looking for."

"But he could have got any amount of drugs in the City. Why go all the way to Brixton?"

"Not everyone wants to piss in their own backyard, if you'll excuse the expression, m'lud," said Lamont, looking up at the judge.

"The Crown would have us believe that Mr. Rashidi resided in a luxurious apartment in the adjoining block during the week."

"I also investigated that possibility, and quickly established that the defendant returned to his home in The Boltons every night after carrying out a day's work in the City."

"Did you find anyone who could confirm that?"

"Yes, sir—the housekeeper and his chauffeur, a Falklands veteran, who are both willing to testify."

Clare wrote *What about his mother?* on her yellow pad, before passing the observation to Sir Julian.

"It may also be relevant that the house is in Mr. Rashidi's name," continued Booth Watson.

"Of course it is," murmured Grace. "And guess who pays the wages of both the chauffeur and housekeeper."

"None of this explains DI Warwick's claim that he found a photograph of Mr. Rashidi's mother on a bedside table in an apartment in Block B."

"If he did," said Lamont, "I never saw it. The only photograph I came across in the flat was the one of Mr. Roberts's mother that was presented to this court as evidence. However, I did look into the possibility that the silver frame might be rare, or even unique."

"And was that the case?"

"No, sir. Asprey informed me that they sell around two hundred such frames every year. It's one of their most popular items."

Clare nodded, Sir Julian frowned, and William could barely restrain himself. He assumed his father couldn't wait to tear Lamont apart.

"And the empty safe that Mr. Roberts testified had seven hundred pounds in it," pressed Booth Watson. "What do you have to say about that?"

"At the time I took DI Warwick's word and assumed it was empty."

William became aware that almost everyone in the court was now staring at him.

"Did you mention to any of your superiors the possibility that Mr. Rashidi might be innocent?"

"I was reluctant to do so because everyone, including the commissioner of the Met, was convinced Trojan Horse had been an overwhelming success. Indeed, soon after Rashidi's arrest, DS Warwick was promoted to inspector. So it would be understandable if he had turned a blind eye. I confess I made the same mistake when I was a young detective sergeant, and I've regretted it ever since."

"Brilliant," whispered Sir Julian. "He's not only got it on the record but turned it to his advantage."

"But you also turned a blind eye, superintendent."

"To begin with, yes, sir, but once I realized that no one was willing to consider the possibility this could be a gross miscarriage of justice, I took what I believed to be the only honorable course of action given the circumstances, and resigned from the Metropolitan Police."

Sir Julian placed his head in his hands, while William could only stare in disbelief at Rashidi, who clearly was getting his money's worth.

"Is it also true, Mr. Lamont, that had you remained in the force for another eighteen months, you would have been eligible for a full pension, and no one would have been any the wiser?"

"That is correct, sir. But by then, I was convinced that an innocent man had been stitched up for a crime he hadn't committed, and I didn't want that on my conscience for the rest of my days."

"Understandably, Mr. Lamont," said Booth Watson. "I commend you for the fortitude and courage you have shown in wanting to set the record straight, rather than taking the easy way out. I have no further questions. But please remain in the witness box, as I'm sure my learned friend will want to cross-examine you."

Sir Julian rose from his place and was about to ask for an adjournment when Booth Watson got back onto his feet. "I do apologize, m'lud, but there is one more question I should have asked this witness."

The judge nodded his consent, and Sir Julian reluctantly resumed his seat.

"Earlier in this trial, Mr. Lamont, the Crown made great play of the fact that my client had his suits made in Savile Row by Bennett and Reed, and we know that Inspector Warwick removed several suits from the apartment in Block B as evidence that Mr. Rashidi lived there. Did your personal investigations include looking into that claim?"

"Indeed they did, sir. And despite trooping up and down Savile Row for hours on end, I was unable to find anyone who'd ever heard of Mr. Rashidi, let alone made a suit for him."

"Were you able to discover where Mr. Rashidi had his suits made?"

"Yes, sir. During the course of my investigations, while questioning Mr. Rashidi's mother to confirm that he resided with her in The Boltons during the week, I asked if she knew where he had his suits made. She told me—" Lamont paused, and looking up at the judge, said, "May I be allowed to refer to the note I made at the time, m'lud?" Mr. Justice Whittaker nodded, and the court waited while Lamont flicked through several pages of his notebook until he found the one he was looking for. "Mrs. Rashidi's exact words were, 'I think Assem gets all his suits off the peg from Harrods. He's a regular size, and doesn't like to waste money unnecessarily.'"

Sir Julian began to write a note.

"And did you then—"

"Forgive me for interrupting you, Mr. Booth Watson," said the judge, "but could this matter not be resolved quite simply by asking the defendant to show us the label on the inside of the jacket he is wearing?"

"Do you not consider, m'lud," said Booth Watson, "that would be more appropriate when my client is being examined in the witness box?"

"I would agree with you, Mr. Booth Watson, if you hadn't already informed my clerk that Mr. Lamont will be your final witness. Besides which, if the defendant were to give evidence, he would have more than enough time to change into another suit."

"Couldn't have put it better myself," whispered Grace. Sir Julian didn't look convinced.

"You are of course under no obligation to reveal the label of the suit you are wearing, Mr. Rashidi," said the judge, looking across at the defendant. "However, it might assist the jury in their deliberations if you felt able to do so."

Suddenly, all eyes were looking in one direction. It was clear from the expression on Rashidi's face that he was reluctant to go along with the judge's suggestion.

"Got you," murmured William, as their eyes met for a second time, pleased to see the self-satisfied smile had been wiped off Rashidi's face.

Rashidi rose slowly from his seat in the dock, unbuttoned his jacket, and pulled it open to reveal a familiar green-and-gold label that read HARRODS. There was no sign of the initials A.R.

Sir Julian requested an adjournment, which the judge agreed to.

⸻

"How much do you think Lamont was paid to perjure himself?" asked William.

"A damn sight more than thirty pieces of silver," replied Grace, with considerable feeling.

"Don't forget this is the same man who stole a holdall full of money," said William, "and probably switched the photographs."

"We don't have proof of that," said Sir Julian, "despite the receptionist reporting that it was a superintendent she'd seen that morning, but the duty exhibits officer wasn't able to confirm it was Lamont."

"Wasn't able to," said Grace, "or wasn't willing to?"

"Be that as it may," reflected Sir Julian, "I couldn't help noticing that several members of the jury looked convinced by Lamont's sincere and heartfelt testimony. To make matters worse, although it was a complete set-up, the Harrods label didn't do us any favors."

"Mea culpa," said Grace. "I fell for that little ruse on the opening day, when Rashidi was wearing a suit with a Bennett and Reed label inside."

"The jury may also have been under the illusion that it was a first-night performance they were attending," said Sir Julian, "but it had all the hallmarks of a well-rehearsed production, with Booth Watson as the director, Lamont as the lead actor, and neither of them being paid equity rates."

"But that's against the law," said William. "Barristers aren't allowed to coach witnesses."

"Choirboy," said Sir Julian and Grace in unison.

"If we could get Mrs. Rashidi to give evidence," said Grace, "we could still blow Lamont's testimony out of the water."

"Possibly, but when William interviewed her following the raid, she was adamant she would never bear witness against her son," said Sir Julian, "however much she disapproved of his criminal activities. If I were to subpoena her, it could well backfire, because the jury's sympathy would be with a dignified old lady being asked to condemn her only child, by a prejudiced old man trying to defend his."

"But we know she never told Lamont that Rashidi stayed at her house every night during the week," said Clare.

"No doubt. But her housekeeper will say he did, and his driver will confirm he drove him from The Boltons to the City every morning and back again at night. What's more, you can count on Booth Watson keeping them both in the witness box for so long the jury will have forgotten Mrs. Rashidi's testimony. No, we'll have to spend the weekend going over Lamont's evidence with a fine-tooth comb and try to identify any inconsistencies, because you can be sure Booth Watson will be doing the same thing as they attempt to anticipate every question I might throw at him. I might even have to consider taking the occasional risk."

Grace wasn't sure she'd heard her father correctly.

# 16

"Mr. Lamont, I would like to begin by asking you why you resigned from the police force only months before you would have been eligible for a full pension."

"As I stated under oath, Sir Julian, it was a matter of conscience. I couldn't stand by and watch an innocent man being convicted for a crime he hadn't committed."

Clare, who, as the consulting solicitor, was sitting a row behind the QCs, placed an X against question number one. 0–1.

"You told the court that Mr. Rashidi returned to his home in The Boltons every evening during the week, and that he then stayed there overnight before being driven back to work in the City the following day."

"That's what his mother told me, and I had no reason not to believe her."

"When exactly did you see Mrs. Rashidi?"

Lamont looked up at the judge. "M'lud," he said, "may I refer to the notes I made at the time?" The judge nodded. Lamont opened his notebook and flicked through several pages. "May twelfth, fourteenth, and nineteenth," he pronounced. "I also interviewed Mrs. Rashidi's housekeeper and Mr. Rashidi's driver."

Clare placed an X against that question. 0–2.

"You also told the court that you were the officer in charge of Operation Trojan Horse. Was that entirely accurate?"

"I was in charge of the day-to-day planning, but I reported to Commander Hawksby, who as head of the unit joined us on the night of the raid. He in turn reported to the assistant commissioner of the Metropolitan Police."

"Got himself off the hook with that reply," conceded Clare. 0–3. She had to admit that so far, Sir Julian hadn't laid a glove on him.

"You also informed the court that your private investigations revealed that on the night of the raid, Mr. Rashidi had visited a warehouse in Battersea, as he did every Friday evening. Having done so, he then went on to the drugs factory to purchase a small amount of cannabis for his personal use, which you suggest explains why he was there when the premises were raided."

"That is correct."

"How far is it from the warehouse to the drugs factory?"

Lamont hesitated for the first time. "About a mile," he said, "which would account for the bus ticket we found in his pocket at the time of his arrest."

"Why would Mr. Rashidi need to take a bus to the drugs factory, when he had a car and driver?"

For the second time Lamont looked as if that was a question he hadn't been prepared for. He glanced desperately at Booth Watson, who sat there, head bowed. 1–3.

"Since you appear to have no answer to that question, I will move on. What time did the warehouse close that night?"

"I have no idea," admitted Lamont.

"But didn't you tell the court you had carried out a thorough investigation after you were convinced Rashidi had been wrongly arrested?"

Another question that clearly hadn't been on Booth Watson's crib sheet. 2–3.

"Then allow me to tell you," said Sir Julian. "A notice on the warehouse gate states that they close at six o'clock. Are you suggesting Mr. Rashidi stood at a bus stop for three hours waiting for the 127, when he could have walked there and back several times?"

Lamont didn't offer an opinion, so Clare put an X next to the question. 3–3.

"Once again, the jury won't have missed the fact that you failed to answer the question," said Sir Julian. "So I'll move on. Mr. Lamont, you told the court that when you went to what the police presumed to be Mr. Rashidi's apartment in Block B on the day after the raid, the only photograph you saw there was of Mr. Roberts's mother."

"That is correct," said Lamont, back on track.

"I'm now going to ask the clerk of the court to show you another photograph, Mr. Lamont, and I'd like you to tell me if you've ever seen it before."

Sir Julian handed a silver-framed photograph to the clerk who in turn passed it to Lamont. He studied the image for a few moments before admitting, "Yes, I have seen this photograph before. It was in Mr. Rashidi's drawing room at The Boltons when I interviewed his mother."

"He saw that one coming," whispered Clare, and added another X to her list. 3–4.

"Then I'm bound to ask," said Sir Julian, "how the police got hold of a copy of the same photograph, that just happened to be in an identical frame?"

"I have no idea. But I have a feeling your son might be able to answer that question."

One or two members of the jury smiled, and Clare put another

X against that question. 3–5. She glanced at the next one and felt more hopeful.

"How many times did you interview Mr. Rashidi while you were carrying out your private investigations?"

"On three separate occasions."

"I notice that you didn't need to check the dates in your notebook this time." 4–5.

"You didn't ask me for the dates," said Lamont. "Only how many times." 4–6.

"Then I'm bound to ask how many times you have seen Mr. Rashidi since you resigned from the Metropolitan Police."

"Not once," said Lamont confidently.

"And Mr. Booth Watson?"

Booth Watson was quickly on his feet. "I can answer that question, m'lud."

"I'm sure you can," said Mr. Justice Whittaker. "But it's Mr. Lamont's response the jury will want to hear, not yours."

Booth Watson reluctantly sat back down. 5–6.

"Twice," said Lamont, not sounding quite as confident. "When I provided him with written evidence under oath, with a witness present."

"Were you compensated for your trouble?"

"That is a disgraceful suggestion," said Booth Watson, even before he'd had time to rise.

"Possibly," said the judge, "but once again, I would like to hear the witness's response."

"No, sir," said Lamont, turning toward the judge. "I received nothing for telling the truth." 4–7.

"Then how much did you receive for telling lies?" asked Sir Julian. 5–7.

As the court erupted, Sir Julian turned around to Clare, who handed him a large brown envelope. He opened it slowly and extracted three photographs, which he took his time considering.

"Was last night one of the occasions on which you visited my learned friend?"

Booth Watson leaped to his feet.

"Sit down, Mr. Booth Watson," said the judge, "or I'll hold you in contempt."

Booth Watson hovered like a cat waiting to pounce, but finally slunk back down.

"Let me ask you once again," said Sir Julian. "Did you have a meeting with Mr. Booth Watson last night, which as you must know is against the law, while you're still giving evidence?" 6–7.

Lamont stared at Booth Watson, who kept his eyes down.

Sir Julian waited for some time before saying, "As Mr. Lamont seems unwilling to answer the question, m'lud, I would be happy for my learned friend to confirm or deny whether such a meeting took place." 7–7. Extra time.

Booth Watson didn't stir. Sir Julian placed the three photographs of the young William as a choirboy back into the envelope, before handing it to Clare. 8–7.

"I have no more questions for this witness, m'lud."

Lamont stepped out of the witness box and quickly left the court, without looking at Rashidi or Booth Watson. Final whistle.

---

Lamont had anticipated almost every one of Sir Julian's questions, until he'd produced those photographs. But he hadn't shown them to the court. Was he bluffing? Lamont had been about to call *his* bluff, and say that he hadn't seen Booth Watson the previous night, but at the last moment he wondered if Marlboro Man had tailed him and witnessed him turning up for the clandestine meeting. If he had, it wouldn't just have been Rashidi who ended up in jail, because Booth Watson would have been hauled up in front of the Bar Council for the last time. So Lamont had decided to follow another of Booth Watson's pieces of sage advice: if in doubt, remain silent.

The oleaginous QC couldn't have made his position clearer when they'd met the night before. If Rashidi got off the main charges, Lamont would be well rewarded. But if he didn't . . .

Lamont realized that he still had one last chance to influence the jury and redeem himself with Booth Watson. Fortunately, the judge had halted proceedings until Monday morning when he would begin his summing-up.

He'd already carried out in-depth research on all twelve of the jurors, just in case things started to go wrong. And things had gone badly wrong. However, all was not lost when Lamont discovered he could stitch up two of them for the price of one.

As the proceedings had been wrapped up earlier in the week, he'd followed juror number three as she left the court, and was surprised when she dropped into a local hotel. Moments later juror number seven appeared and entered the same hotel. Lamont hung around on the far side of the road, in the freezing cold, for just over an hour, before juror number seven reappeared. He headed quickly off toward the nearest tube station.

A few minutes later juror number three came out of the hotel, and began walking in the opposite direction.

It didn't take Lamont that long to find out they were both "happily" married, with five children between them, one of whom had recently announced her engagement in the *Farnham Gazette*. The other was hoping to be elected chairman of his local golf club at the AGM next month.

He already knew where they both lived, and the journeys they took home from court each day. He would be on the same train as juror number seven this evening.

# 17

"It is your duty," began Mr. Justice Whittaker, looking down at the jury, "when considering your verdict, to take into account only the evidence you have heard in this court. Anything you've read in the press, or opinions expressed by your family or friends, should be ignored. They have not heard all the evidence.

"You are under no time pressure. A man's future is in your hands. Once you retire, the only verdict I can accept is a unanimous one. Let me remind you the burden of proof is on the prosecution to show that the defendant is guilty, beyond reasonable doubt.

"You will now retire to the jury room to consider your verdict." He nodded at the clerk of the court, who stood in front of the jury and declared, "I swear by Almighty God that I will keep this jury in some private and convenient place. I will not suffer anyone to talk to them nor will I talk to them unless it is to ask whether they have reached a verdict."

He then led his twelve charges out of the court to the jury room.

The seven men and five women had already spent ten days together, and had got to know each other fairly well. Friendships had developed and rivalries surfaced, not least when it had come to selecting who should be appointed foreman. Mr. Anscombe had triumphed over Mrs. Parish, but Mrs. Parish was turning out to be a sore loser.

Anscombe wasn't in any doubt that Rashidi was guilty on all three counts. However, he felt as foreman it was his duty not to impose his views on the other members of the jury, but to listen attentively to all their opinions.

He had been a schoolmaster all his working life, ending his career as the headmaster of a local grammar school in Kent. But this wasn't a staff meeting to decide if a boy should be put in detention, or even expelled. They were about to determine whether a man should be set free or sentenced to a long term of imprisonment.

Once they had all taken their places, he looked around the table, trying to remember everyone's name, as he'd always done with his boys. Although he'd thought he'd got to know them quite well over the course of the trial, he was about to discover that in fact he didn't know them at all.

"It might be helpful," he began once they were settled, "if we were to take a vote and find out if we are all of one mind, and therefore able to reach a verdict fairly quickly."

"Couldn't agree more, foreman," said a voice from the other end of the table. Several other members of the jury nodded, and there was even one "Hear, hear!"

"Then I'll begin by asking how many of you consider the defendant is guilty," said Anscombe. "So as not to exert any undue influence as your foreman, I will not vote at this juncture." He counted the raised hands and, attempting to conceal his surprise, wrote the number 8 on the pad in front of him. "And those who think he is not guilty?"

Two hands immediately shot up. Mrs. Parish's followed a few moments later.

As he wrote the number 3 on his pad he recalled the judge's words: "The only verdict I can accept is a unanimous one."

"Shall we begin," said Anscombe, "by listening to the views of the three of us who consider Mr. Rashidi is innocent on all three charges?"

Beth was waiting impatiently by the door when William arrived back from the Old Bailey.

"Guilty or not guilty?" she demanded.

"Do you mean me or Rashidi?"

"Rashidi, of course."

"The jury's still out."

"And you?"

The expression on William's face left her in no doubt this was not something that could be discussed on the doorstep. He led his wife through to the front room and waited for her to sit down before telling her what had happened in court, and the commander's decision.

"But why?" she protested angrily.

"He had no choice but to suspend me after Lamont, who was the senior officer in charge of Trojan Horse, all but accused me of stealing seven hundred pounds from a safe in the apartment."

"So what happens next?" asked Beth.

"My suspension is only temporary, pending an inquiry."

"But how long will that take?"

"Three or four months at the most. And before you ask, I'll remain on full pay, and the Hawk thinks the whole episode will be laughed out of court long before then."

"Perhaps you should take a leaf out of Lamont's book."

"What, become a crook?" said William wearily.

"No, resign. Then there wouldn't be an inquiry, and you could get a job that offers a more realistic wage for the hours you put in, as well as working with colleagues you can trust."

"But that would be tantamount to admitting I'm guilty, which wouldn't make finding another job quite so easy. And what's more, I'd be crucified in the press."

"Are the press going to come after you?" asked Beth, sounding anxious.

"It's unlikely at the moment. The Hawk has issued an internal statement giving me his full support, and has made personal calls to all the leading crime correspondents in Fleet Street leaving them in no doubt which stone they should be looking under, while gently reminding them of the libel laws. If it turns out that I do have to issue a writ, the Met will pick up the bill. For once, my reputation as a choirboy has worked in my favor."

"But surely what Lamont has accused you of is a crime?"

"The Hawk's already made it clear that no criminal proceedings are being considered. That's his way of letting everyone including the press know that I'm innocent, and the finger's being pointed at the wrong man."

"What are you going to do for the next three or four months?" asked Beth, holding back the tears that had replaced her anger.

"Finally master the art of changing a nappy, while feeding two human dustbins at the same time."

"Fat chance of that," said Beth, regaining her composure. "You wouldn't survive three days, let alone three months. But please promise me one thing."

"Anything, darling."

"You may have forgotten we're going to the Fitzmolean tomorrow evening for the unveiling of the Vermeer. Please don't mention your suspension to my parents or yours, otherwise what's meant to be a joyful occasion could turn into a wake."

"I won't say a word until we have lunch with my parents at the weekend. Although my father and Grace have already worked out

I'm likely to be suspended, so it won't come as much of a surprise to them. In fact, they've offered to act as my defense team, with Clare as my solicitor."

"Let's hope it doesn't come to that," said Beth, sounding even more anxious.

William took her in his arms. How he wished he could tell her the truth.

Commander Hawksby took his place at the top of the table to chair the team's Monday-morning meeting. Because William was unable to attend he didn't open with his usual warm greeting.

"As you all know," he said, "following ex-Superintendent Lamont's evidence given under oath, Inspector Warwick has been suspended, pending a full inquiry."

"It's a bloody disgrace," said Paul. "That's like sacking Churchill after he'd won the Second World War."

"Which is exactly what the British people did," the Hawk reminded him. "But don't forget, he returned in triumph in 1951, and served for four more years. However, the commissioner has made it clear we are not to continue with our investigation of Lamont and Summers while the Warwick inquiry is ongoing. With that in mind, DC Pankhurst will be transferred to other duties, which I will come to in a moment. PC Bailey will remain in Romford for the time being, until I find an appropriate moment to transfer her back to the Yard."

"Perhaps it's for the best," said Nicky, "because I'm yet to be convinced Summers is bent. Only last week he made two arrests, including a villain who's been stealing Jaguars, who our boys have been after for years."

The rest of the team listened in silence.

"Rumor is," continued Nicky, "that Summers is about to be put up for another commendation. I'm beginning to wonder if our informant is just another Lamont, looking for revenge."

"Quite possibly," said the Hawk. "So, I'll try and get you back to the Yard without it being too obvious what you were up to."

"Thank you, sir," said Nicky. "I can't wait to rejoin the team."

Not everyone smiled.

"Any more news from court number one?" asked Jackie, changing the subject.

"After Lamont's car crash, I can't believe it will take the jury that long to reach a verdict. But we still have to plan for the unexpected, so should Rashidi somehow manage to get off, one of you will have to watch him twenty-four/seven because once he's out I'm sure he'll lead us straight to the new slaughter. And the same goes for Tony Roberts, or whatever his name is, who I have a feeling has been running Rashidi's operation in his absence."

"He's not bright enough for that," said Paul. "At best he could keep it ticking over until Rashidi returns."

"If that's the case," said the Hawk, "we could end up nabbing them both. If Roberts is even thinking about opening a new slaughter, I'm going to shut it down before it supplies its first customer. We'll then lock him up in a cell far smaller than the apartment he claims he's been living in for the past ten years and this time he won't have a phone number to remember. But now, let's not waste any more time trying to second-guess the verdict," he said as he passed them each a file.

"Excuse me, sir," said Nicky. "I ought to get going. I'm expected back in Romford in a couple of hours."

"Not for much longer," said the Hawk, as she gathered up her files. Once Nicky had closed the door behind her, the Hawk waited for a moment before saying, "Now she's out of the way, let's get back to our original agenda. To start with, DI Warwick has not been suspended. However, I do need Lamont, Summers, and not least PC Bailey to believe he has. With that in mind . . ."

⊸o⊷

The foreman checked a chart that showed the name of every juror. He ticked off number seven. "Mr. Pugh, perhaps I could begin by asking you why you consider Mr. Rashidi innocent?"

The foreman was puzzled as to why Pugh had changed his mind, when earlier in the week he'd told him that life imprisonment was far too good for the likes of Rashidi, and the damn man should be hanged. But he sat back and listened, hoping he would explain his Pauline conversion.

"I'd like to begin," said Pugh, "by reminding everyone that all we know for certain about Assem Rashidi is that he's chairman of a respectable City company, and has never had a conviction of any sort in his life. Not even a parking ticket, as Mr. Booth Watson pointed out."

"Unlikely when you've got a chauffeur," suggested another juror.

"There's no need to be frivolous," snapped Pugh. "And I'm bound to add that I found Sangster's testimony unconvincing, to say the least. Should we allow this case to rest on the word of a convicted drug addict who was struck off the medical register for supplying illegal substances to his patients?"

"That may well be the case," said another juror, "but I'm in no doubt he worked for Rashidi."

"Whereas," continued Pugh, ignoring the interruption, "I found Dr. Goddard's heartfelt evidence compelling. A dedicated professional man who told us that Mr. Rashidi had donated over a million pounds to his clinic. Hardly the action of a drug lord. And you'll have noticed that Sir Julian didn't even bother to cross-examine him."

"But what about Roberts? He was obviously lying from the moment he entered the witness box. Didn't you find it strange that he referred to Rashidi as Assem, when he'd said he didn't even know him?"

"Would you condemn a man to spend the rest of his life in jail on such flimsy evidence?" asked Mrs. Parish, weighing in for the first time. "My children refer to everyone by their first names, even celebrities they've never met."

"He didn't know the telephone number of the flat he claimed he'd lived in for the past ten years!" chipped in juror number eight.

This silenced Mrs. Parish, but only for a moment.

"Don't forget," she came back, "they tried to trap Rashidi on where he bought his suits and that backfired spectacularly."

"If Rashidi was innocent," asked another woman, "why wouldn't he face Sir Julian in the witness box?"

"The judge told us to ignore that," Pugh reminded her. "It's his legal right not to have to give evidence."

"But if he wasn't in charge of the drugs factory," asked juror number two, "what was he doing there at midnight?"

Several jurors nodded.

"I just think he's a wrong 'un," piped up juror number nine, who the foreman had thought was asleep.

"As the superintendent pointed out," said Pugh, "he conveniently fitted the profile for a drugs baron."

"I'm bound to say," said juror number two, "I wasn't convinced that Lamont was telling us the whole truth."

"Try not to forget," came in Mrs. Longstaff, the third dissenter, "that he was prepared to sacrifice his career rather than see an innocent man go to jail."

"That's his story, but I've got a feeling there's more to it than that."

"Like what?" demanded Mrs. Longstaff.

"I don't know," admitted juror number two.

"The judge told us to make our decision on the evidence presented in court, not speculation," the foreman reminded them.

This silenced everyone for a few moments, until another juror piped up.

"If Rashidi was no more than a casual weekend customer, then why pose as an immigrant worker?"

"I was once caught in a brothel," admitted Pugh. "I can tell you I would have posed as anything to make sure my wife didn't find out."

"He doesn't have a wife," snapped back the same juror.

"But he does have a mother," Mrs. Longstaff countered.

"Who wasn't willing to appear in court to even confirm her son lived with her at The Boltons," the foreman reminded them.

"Besides, Rashidi doesn't look like a drug lord to me," Mrs. Longstaff added.

Several members of the jury groaned, and the foreman realized that reaching a unanimous verdict might not prove quite as straightforward as he'd originally thought. He didn't feel any differently after they'd taken a break for lunch. The same arguments were voiced again and again during the afternoon, after the foreman had made it clear that everyone must be allowed to express their personal opinion. However, he hadn't meant the same opinion several times.

The foreman glanced at his watch and when, an hour later, none of the three dissenters had shown any sign of changing their minds, he suggested they call it a day and resume the following morning. At last he'd found something on which they could all agree.

⤙o⤚

"Is it my imagination," said Sir Julian, "or has William not bothered to shave today?"

"I think you'll find it's called designer stubble, my dear," replied his wife. "All the rage."

"Not in Nettleford, it isn't. Let's just be thankful that Commander Hawksby isn't here."

"But he is," said Marjorie. "He and his wife are on the other side of the gallery admiring the Rembrandt."

"Remind me of her name," whispered Sir Julian.

"Josephine. And their children are Ben and Alice."

"I don't know what I'd do—" Sir Julian began as Beth's parents joined them.

"Good evening, Arthur, Joanna," said Sir Julian, giving Beth's mother a kiss on the cheek. "Have you noticed that William seems to have forgotten to shave today?"

"Is that a capital offense?" asked Arthur, grinning.

"It is in our family," said Marjorie. "But more important, how's Beth? She seems to be anxious about something."

"And why wouldn't she be?" said Sir Julian. "It's not every day the museum unveils a Vermeer, and it was Beth who made it possible."

"True," said Arthur. "But like you, Marjorie, I get the impression there's something she's not telling us."

"Could she be pregnant again?" asked Joanna. "I do hope so, because I so enjoy being a grandmother."

"Me too," said Marjorie. "The twins are growing up so fast. Only yesterday—"

"What are you lot plotting behind my back?" asked Beth as she walked across to join them.

"Perhaps you can explain why—" began Sir Julian.

"Shh," said Marjorie, as a waiter handed him a glass of champagne.

"We were talking about the twins," said her mother, "and how quickly they're growing up."

"Artemisia is almost crawling, while her brother looks on . . ."

The sharp tap of a gavel on a lectern caused them all to turn around, to see the museum's director standing on a raised platform smiling down at them.

"Good evening, ladies and gentlemen," he began. "Thank you for joining us on this auspicious occasion. In a few moments we will unveil the gallery's latest acquisition, Vermeer's *The White Lace Collar,* a bequest made possible by our most generous benefactor, Christina Faulkner."

A warm round of applause followed, and William glanced across the room to see Christina standing next to a distinguished-looking gentleman who must have been a shade over six foot, and considerably older than her usual consorts. His trim white beard, graying hair, and tanned face suggested he'd spent more time at sea than on land.

"But before we unveil this masterpiece, I have an announcement to make. Sam Waterstone, the Keeper of Pictures, will be retiring at the end of the month, having served the Fitzmolean for over thirty years, so I considered it appropriate that he should perform the unveiling ceremony."

Beth smiled as her head of department ambled up to the microphone, looking like a disheveled schoolmaster. He turned an academic gaze on the guests as if they were a bunch of unruly students.

"Thank you, Tim," he began. "Johannes Vermeer of Delft was unquestionably one of the foremost Dutch masters of the seventeenth century. Sadly, he only lived to the age of forty-three, and just thirty-four of his pictures survive, so we are indeed privileged to own one of them."

Without another word he stepped back and pulled a cord. A pair of velvet curtains parted to reveal *The White Lace Collar.*

Gasps were followed by loud applause.

"Thank you, Sam," said the director, and turning to the audience he added, "Before I allow you all to continue enjoying this special occasion, I have another announcement to make, and one that I suspect won't come as a complete surprise to some of you. It gives me great pleasure to tell you that Sam's successor as Keeper of Pictures will be our very own, and very special, Beth Warwick."

This time the applause was even louder, and several people turned around to smile at the new Keeper.

"Beth," continued the director, "has played a leading role in securing three of the museum's most treasured masterpieces: the long-lost Rubens, the fabled Rembrandt, and now this magnificent Vermeer. When Sam recommended Beth should take his place, it took me a nanosecond to agree, and the board confirmed her appointment this morning."

William squeezed Beth's hand. "I'm so proud of you, Keeper," he said, as the rest of the family gathered around to congratulate her.

"I couldn't have done it without you and Christina," she whispered.

"Not to mention Miles Faulkner," said William, "who died so conveniently."

"I also played a small part," Commander Hawksby reminded them, as he shook Beth's hand and added his congratulations.

"Or at least that's what I told the commissioner of the Met," said William, in a clipped voice. He immediately regretted his words, until everyone, including the Hawk, burst out laughing.

"Arsenal versus Chelsea, same time, usual place," whispered Hawksby to William, before walking away to take a closer look at the Vermeer.

"Many congratulations, my darling," said a voice coming from behind her. Beth turned to see Christina and the distinguished-looking gentleman sailing toward her.

"Thank you, Christina. And the gallery will be eternally in debt to its most generous benefactor."

"It was all made possible by William," she replied. "If he hadn't been able to show that Miles's paintings weren't destroyed after he'd burned down Limpton Hall, I'd be a penniless waif."

"And stray, which certainly wouldn't suit you," said William, leaning over and kissing her on both cheeks.

"I'd like to introduce you to Captain Ralph Neville," said Christina. Her companion stepped forward and shook hands with William and Beth rather formally.

"May I add my congratulations on your appointment, Mrs. Warwick," he said. "But frankly it didn't come as a great surprise after all Christina has told me about you."

"Christina!" said the director as he bustled over. "How do I begin to thank you?"

"My pleasure, Tim. May I introduce my guest, Captain Ralph Neville."

"Good evening, sir," said Neville, as William and Beth slipped off to take a closer look at the Vermeer.

"And I thought it was only me who could keep a secret," said William. "You didn't even hint you might be appointed Keeper of Pictures, or that Christina had a new escort."

"I wasn't confident enough to tell you about the promotion, and only found out quite recently about Captain Neville. In fact it's the first time I've met him."

"I like the cut of his jib," mocked William, stealing one of his father's expressions.

"How appropriate. Apparently, Ralph was a captain in the Royal Navy, recently retired."

"And he certainly looks as if he'd like to lower his anchor, if he hasn't already," William added.

"Behave yourself, Caveman," said Beth, looking around to see Christina and the captain chatting to the director.

"A bit of a contrast to her late, unlamented husband," said William.

"Not to mention the string of toy boys who've been sponging off her recently."

"I think she always knew what she was getting in return."

"This one looks a little more promising," said Beth. "So let's be happy for her."

"Dare I ask, as you seem to be keeping me in the dark on so many things, if all the other pictures have also been returned to Christina?"

"The entire collection, she tells me. I think Christina plans to sell them all and continue to live in a manner few of us can dream of."

"Then let's hope Captain Neville doesn't turn out to be another gold digger," said William, taking a closer look at the new man in Christina's life.

"We're off to Monte Carlo for a few days," Christina was telling the director. "Ralph is looking forward to seeing my little hide-away."

"That isn't how William described your Monte Carlo home," said Tim. "More like a palace filled with masterpieces."

"Well, I have my dear departed husband to thank for that. As the paintings won't be around for much longer, you must come and see them while you still have a chance."

"Nothing would give me greater pleasure," said Tim, who had already been warned by Beth that Christina intended to sell the entire collection.

"I'm afraid we'll have to leave fairly soon," said Christina. "We're catching an early flight to Nice in the morning and won't be returning until after Christmas. But early in the New Year I'm planning to give a dinner party for a few friends, and do hope you'll be able to join us."

"I'll look forward to it," said Tim, giving her a slight bow before he left them to mingle with his other guests.

"Let's slip away," said Christina. "We've been here quite long enough."

She and the captain held hands as they walked slowly across the room, left the gallery, and made their way down the wide, carpeted staircase and out onto the street.

Christina's chauffeur opened the back door of the Rolls to allow them to climb in, before returning to the driver's seat. He eased out and joined the early-evening traffic, but it wasn't until he'd turned the corner that Christina looked at her companion and said, "Do you think we got away with it?"

# 18

"Good morning, Mrs. Faulkner. How nice to see you."

Christina had to admire the way Booth Watson could lie so unashamedly, while keeping a straight face. She sat down in the seat opposite him, but did not return his salutation.

"Miles felt we should meet in order to avoid any possible misunderstandings in the future."

"How thoughtful of him," said Christina.

"As you know, he is content to make your life as comfortable as possible," said Booth Watson, ignoring the barbed remark, "but in return, he will expect you to abide by certain rules."

"Like what?"

"He'll buy you a house in the country, continue to pay the rent on the flat in Chelsea, and supply you with an income of one thousand pounds a week. And of course you'll be able to keep your car and chauffeur."

"What about the half million we agreed on in the divorce settlement?"

"An agreement that was unfortunately never formalized. In any case, you've recently sold the land on the site of Limpton Hall for—" he checked the figure—"seven hundred and seventy thousand pounds, so you're not exactly broke," he added.

"I'll need at least two thousand pounds a week to cover my living expenses. That was also agreed in our divorce settlement, in case you've forgotten."

"Miles anticipated you might say that, and being a generous man, he will agree to fifteen hundred a week."

"What about the paintings? Half of them belong to me."

"Possession is nine-tenths of the law. And they are now well beyond your reach."

"Two thousand a week."

"Very well. As long as you make no attempt to reclaim the Vermeer from the Fitzmolean should you for any reason fall upon hard times."

"Only if Miles agrees not to steal the painting from the gallery a second time."

"He's unlikely to do that," said Booth Watson, "as it wouldn't take the police long to work out that he's still alive."

"If I do agree to his terms, what will he expect in return?"

"You will keep up the myth that he is dead, especially with your friend Beth Warwick and her husband. As long as they continue to believe he is Captain Ralph Neville, a recently retired naval officer, he'll be able to go about his business without fear of being exposed."

"It wouldn't take William long to discover that no such Royal Navy officer ever existed."

"Ah, but he does," said Booth Watson, "and he's recently retired on a far larger pension than he would have thought possible before he met Miles, on the one condition that he never sets foot in England again."

"And if I refuse to go along with your plan and decide to expose him?" said Christina, defiantly.

"The country house will never be yours, the flat in London will undergo a rent review that you won't be able to afford, and your weekly allowance will dry up overnight."

"You've forgotten the car and chauffeur," said Christina sarcastically.

"Your chauffeur would be made redundant, and the Rolls-Royce might just be involved in an unfortunate accident, reminding your friends that after years of having a driver, you were no longer safe on the road."

Christina gave an involuntary shudder. "Even Miles wouldn't go that far," she eventually managed.

"You may well be right, but you'd certainly have to think about it every time you got into the car."

Christina tried *not* to think about it.

"And there's something else I should mention, while we're on the subject of your future. The paintings are no longer in Monte Carlo, and all of Miles's assets have been deposited in several numbered accounts in Zurich, Geneva, and Bern, so if you don't want to end up living on social security, I suggest you keep to your end of the bargain."

"Does that mean I can no longer see Beth Warwick, because she's about the only friend I've got?"

"On the contrary, we want you to go on seeing Mrs. Warwick. Just make sure she remains convinced you're a widow, because the day she isn't, you may as well be."

"Am I also expected to live with Miles?"

"No, that's the last thing he wants. He has no objection to you continuing your former lifestyle, as long as you're discreet. However, there will be occasions when you'll have to be seen in public together in order to keep up the pretense."

"Does Miles actually believe he'll get away with it?"

"I hope so, for your sake. He tells me he passed the Vermeer unveiling test with flying colors, so clearly the Swiss plastic surgeon did an excellent job. And don't forget, no one gave him a second look when he sat in the row behind me at his own funeral. Any more questions?" he asked abruptly.

"How will I know when I'm required to play my role?"

"I'll be in touch. I'll try to give you at least twenty-four hours' notice."

"How considerate of you."

"I hope you'll quickly accept, Mrs. Faulkner, this is an amicable arrangement that will suit both parties. However, should you ever need any legal advice, do feel free to call on me."

"How kind of you, Mr. Booth Watson, but fortunately Sir Julian Warwick fulfills that role quite admirably."

"Not in the future, he won't," said Booth Watson firmly.

"You're frightened of him," said Christina, feeling that at last she'd scored a point.

Booth Watson hesitated for a moment. "Not frightened," he eventually managed, "but I do have a certain respect for his professional skills. So, you are never to call on his services again."

Christina was about to protest when Booth Watson added, "It's a deal breaker." She remained silent.

Booth Watson swiveled the agreement around, offered her a pen, and said, "You sign here, here, and here. By the way," he added, "I thought your performance at the funeral was quite brilliant. But then, it was always in your best interests to convince Inspector Warwick that Miles was dead."

⊸o⊷

The morning session the following day had gone better once Mrs. Parish finally accepted that the only reason Rashidi could have been visiting a drugs factory after midnight was to buy some drugs. However, she wouldn't budge when it came to the main offense, of being a dealer and the mastermind behind the entire operation.

The foreman once again called for a vote on all three counts, and on the lesser charge of possession, he finally secured a guilty verdict of ten to two. But on the two more serious charges, the vote remained nine to three.

The foreman looked around the table, before he suggested to his exhausted cohorts, that "Perhaps the time has come for us to send a note to the judge and ask His Lordship if he would consider a majority verdict."

No one raised an objection.

Mr. Justice Whittaker listened carefully to the foreman of the jury and the intractable problem he was facing.

"I'm going to ask you to retire again, and strive once more to reach a unanimous verdict. If you are unable to do so, I will accept a verdict upon which at least ten of you are agreed."

The foreman bowed, and the bailiff once again led his charges back to the jury room.

The judge returned to his chambers and scanned a long line of leather-bound volumes on the shelves behind his desk. He extracted one before sitting down and consulting the index. He turned to page 213 and checked the maximum sentence he could impose for the possession of cannabis, and if there were any aggravating circumstances that would allow him to increase the sentence. He frowned. He was rereading the relevant paragraph, when he was interrupted by a tap on the door, and his clerk entered the room.

"The jury are returning, m'lud," he said, as he held open the door.

⊸o⊷

PC Bailey was out pounding the streets on the ten-to-six shift when William drove into Romford. She was late returning to the station because she'd had to deal with a traffic accident. It was only a minor prang, but one of the drivers didn't have a license, so when she finally got back to the nick, there were several forms to fill in.

She didn't emerge again until 6:32 p.m. She was dressed in her civilian clothes, and headed in the direction of Summers's flat, stopping on the way to pick up one of his suits from the dry cleaner's. At 6:58 she let herself into the house.

⊸o⊷

William put down his biro after completing the latest entry in his log-book. He turned on the radio and listened to the seven o'clock news.

The Rashidi drugs trial was still the lead item, and the only new piece of information was that the judge would pass sentence in the morning.

Two years is the maximum period the judge can impose for possession, his father had reminded him when they had spoken on the phone that afternoon.

"Which means he's quite literally got away with murder," said William. "And remembering he's already served over six months, he'll be released in a few weeks' time, and we still don't know where his new factory is."

"I'm sure he'll lead you to it on the day he's released," was the Hawk's opinion.

William's thoughts turned to Lamont, who was every bit as guilty as Rashidi, having worked hand in glove with Booth Watson to get him off. But one of the ex-superintendent's favorite bon mots had been, *Crime pays, laddie,* and William didn't doubt that Lamont was now earning far more as one of Booth Watson's lackeys than he ever had in the Met.

He could hear Beth asking once again if the time had come for him to consider resigning, and he still hadn't come up with a convincing response.

When a light appeared on the third floor, William tried to concentrate. After five nights of surveillance, he had roughly worked out the layout of Summers's flat. Nicky must now be in the kitchen, probably preparing supper.

The news was followed by *The Archers*; much more of this and he'd become an addict. He was listening to *File on 4,* who were debating the removal of hereditary peers from the House of Lords, when he spotted Summers entering the building. A few moments later he watched as the two of them embraced before Nicky drew the curtains. William only wished he could have overheard their conversation.

The Hawk had applied for an order to have the flat bugged, but the application had been rejected by the assistant commissioner of Specialist Operations as a fishing trip. ACSO suggested they supply some more convincing corroborating evidence before approaching him again. He referred the commander to the Interception of Communications Act 1985.

A second application just to bug Summers's phone was also turned down. Britain wasn't a police state, the Hawk had been reminded by the commissioner. William couldn't disagree with him, even though it made his job that much more difficult.

⊸o⊷

"Supper will be ready in a few minutes," said Nicky, as she sat down on the sofa next to Jerry, who was watching an FA Cup match: Aston Villa versus Chelsea. Although Jerry had been born in Birmingham, he'd always wanted to join the Met, so headed down to the smoke the day after he left school. But he still supported Villa.

"From about the age of five," he'd explained to Nicky, "you decide which team you support. And you stick with them through thick and thin for the rest of your life."

She was thinking about the rest of her life as she snuggled up next to him.

"This is a fantastic TV," she said, not interested in the match.

"Part of a job lot," said Summers, putting an arm around her. "I arrested this guy a couple of months back who had half a dozen of them in his front room. Only five ended up back in the nick's property store."

"I only saw four."

"I wouldn't be surprised if another one went missing before the desk sergeant filled out the charge sheet."

"Don't you ever worry that one day a thief will shop you?" said Nicky, once again wrestling with her conscience, as she had been doing a lot recently.

"Unlikely," he said, his eyes not leaving the screen. "Any sensible villain would rather be charged with stealing four TVs than six, and in any case, it would be his word against mine. Goal!"

---

William listened to a debate on the future of Trident between Tony Blair and Michael Heseltine—both regarded as potential future leaders of their respective parties—when the lights went out in Summers's living room at 10:41. He turned the radio off and made another entry in his notebook. A few moments later a light went on in the bedroom. Once again, the curtains were drawn, and once again, he would have liked to be able to hear what they were talking about. Pillow talk might be even more revealing than television banter, and despite the fact William had heard on the news that Chelsea had won 2–1, which pleased him, he thought Summers might become more expansive.

⊸o⊷

"Who do we have to thank for the new hi-fi?" Nicky asked as she began to get undressed, still uncertain whose side she was on.

"John Smith," said Summers, hanging up his suit.

"The politician?" asked Nicky, grinning.

"No, my number one informer, who makes it possible for me to have a few extra luxuries on the side."

"He's a legend in the canteen."

"And so he should be. He was responsible for me finally nailing Ted Payne when that shipment of cocaine came in from Brixton."

"Now that half of the Payne family are safely locked up, will you be turning your attention to the Turners?"

"Not while they keep supplying me with information about every other criminal on the patch."

"But they're crooks," Nicky said as she climbed into bed.

"Sometimes you have to turn a blind eye if you want to keep your arrest sheet ticking over."

"So is John Smith a member of the Turner family?"

"Let's say he's a close relation," Summers replied, as he took her in his arms.

⊸o⊷

He had chosen the venue. Somewhere she'd never been before. As she pushed her way through the swing doors, she spotted her former boss seated in a dimly lit alcove at the far end of the pub, his back to her. Two pints were on the table in front of him. He didn't stand up when she joined him.

"Am I off the hook?" were Lamont's first words.

"Yes," she said, after taking a sip of beer. "The Hawk told me there's no point going after you. Thought you'd suffered enough, remembering you returned all of the money that was in the third bag. I like to think I played my part. It was touch and go, because Warwick still thinks you should be arrested and hung out to dry."

"Keep trying to convince the little prick otherwise, and I'll make it worth your while. There's more than enough money swilling around in that trough for both of us. Unless of course you're in Warwick's camp."

"Haven't seen a lot of him lately," said Jackie. "He's been suspended while the corruption unit investigate the seven hundred quid that went missing from Roberts's safe."

"Will you be giving evidence?"

"Probably. But don't worry, I won't be helping his cause."

"'I wasn't in the room at the time' will get you off that hook," said Lamont.

"Don't forget, it was Warwick who stopped me getting my sergeant's stripes back."

"I would have promoted you ahead of him," said Lamont.

"I know you would, Bruce, which is another reason I wish you were still a member of the team."

Lamont finished his beer. "Let's continue to meet from time to time so we can keep each other up to date."

"Sure. But what's in it for me?"

He took an envelope out of an inside pocket and pushed it across the table. "There's more where that came from," he said.

She slipped the package into her bag and smiled. "Better get going," she said. "I'll be in touch again when I've got anything worthwhile to report."

⊸o⊷

The light in the bedroom went out just after 11:30, and William made another entry in his logbook. William didn't enjoy undercover work, and certainly didn't like snooping on a colleague. However, the Hawk had pointed out that if he was going to arrest PC Bailey as well as Summers, he would need MM's reports to be confirmed. William leaned back, thought about Beth and the twins, and fell asleep almost immediately.

⊸o⊷

The sound of a horn in the distance snapped him out of his slumber. He rubbed his eyes and checked his watch. Just after four. He looked up at the third floor, relieved to see the flat was still in darkness. It was another couple of hours before a bedside light was switched on.

⊸o⊷

"So what are you up to today?" asked Nicky, stifling a yawn.

"I'm due to give evidence in court at ten. Jaguar man is coming up in front of the local magistrate."

"How long will he go down for?"

"It's his first offense, so he'll probably get a suspended sentence, while I'll end up owning a second-hand Jag, with only seven hundred miles on the clock."

"Won't someone want to know how a DS can possibly afford a Jag?"

"I'll just remind them it's second-hand, not unlike the inspector's Volvo."

"You two are quite a double act," said Nicky, as she joined him in the shower.

"If you ever want to join our team, just let me know."

"What use would a humble PC on the beat possibly be?"

"You're out on the street, picking up information that could lead to an arrest, and that just might turn out to be profitable, especially if Mr. Smith gets to hear it before you make your report."

Once again, Nicky thought about coming clean, and making a full report on everything she now knew about DS Summers, but realized that if she did, she would lose him, and her job.

"How about you?" he asked, as he stepped out of the shower and grabbed a towel.

"Day off. I'm going to visit my mother in Tooting, and take her out to lunch. I should be back around six."

"When I'll take you for a spin in my new Jaguar."

William turned on the seven o'clock news. Not a lot had changed overnight. He made another entry in his logbook when Summers emerged from the building at 7:34, and set off in the direction of the local nick as his radio sprang to life. He listened carefully to what Paul had to report, and said he'd deal with it as soon as he was back in the office.

PC Bailey appeared a few minutes later, and to William's surprise, she headed in the direction of the railway station. He waited until she'd taken the first train into central London before getting out of the car and walking across to a phone box on the other side of the road.

Rebecca picked up the phone after a couple of rings.

"She's on her way back into London," William said. "She should be with you long before I can make it."

"Not a problem," said Rebecca. "Nicky thinks I'm off today, so she won't be surprised to find me at home."

"Meanwhile, you're going to have to keep an even closer eye on Lamont. Jackie's just phoned in to tell Paul that following her meeting with him last night, he now believes he's in the clear. She got a thick brown envelope for her trouble, which she's left on my desk."

"Jackie's the best," said Rebecca. "I only wish I could say the same about Nicky."

"Don't give up on her. She may yet come to her senses," said William before ringing off.

He returned to the car and made a final entry in his logbook. Surely another five nights in a row would be enough to convince the commander that Nicky had switched sides. But he accepted that the Hawk must have his reasons for not wanting to break cover yet. William closed his notebook, turned the key in the ignition, and headed back into London. He was passing the Tower Hotel when Nicky put her key in the front door, and Beth was woken by the twins.

⤙o⤚

Rebecca was doing the washing-up when she heard the front door open.

"Do you want some breakfast?" she asked as Nicky joined her in the kitchen.

"No, thanks, I'll just grab a bowl of cornflakes before I go off to see Mum."

"Dare I ask?" said Rebecca, giving her a grin.

"I think this one could be a bit special. I've never felt this way before."

"Details, details," pleaded Rebecca, not turning around to face her.

"He's an estate agent, looking after mainly rented property, shops, and offices in the Croydon area, and he's just been made a junior partner."

*Too much detail, too carefully thought out, and too smoothly delivered,* thought Rebecca. "Does Mr. Perfect have a name?"

"Alan Mitchell. He's from Nottingham originally, but he's now living in Romford."

"When do I get to meet him?" ventured Rebecca.

"Not just yet," said Nicky. "I want to be absolutely sure. While we're on the subject, how's your love life?"

"What can I tell you? I'm the original wallflower. I'm surprised you don't water me once a week."

"How about work? Has the Hawk given you something interesting to do, now you're no longer shadowing Lamont?"

"I'm investigating a sergeant from West End Central. We think he may be taking backhanders from the owner of a local strip joint, who's hoping to get a liquor license in return."

"That sounds interesting," said Nicky, as she poured some milk on her cornflakes.

"Actually, it's rather sad and a bit sordid, if the truth be known." Rebecca couldn't help feeling that her cover story was more credible than Alan, an estate agent who worked in Croydon, who had just been made a junior partner, and happened to live in Romford.

⤚o⤙

"Will the defendant please rise?"

Assem Rashidi rose from his place in the dock, and faced the judge, a look of studied indifference on his face.

Mr. Justice Whittaker opened his red leather folder, and looked down at the words he'd written earlier that morning. "Mr Rashidi, you have been found guilty of possession of five ounces of marijuana, and I sentence you to two years in prison, the maximum the law permits for this offense," he added, unable to hide his contempt for a man he would happily have sent down for life.

The judge closed his folder and was about to leave the court when Rashidi said, "Thank you, m'lud. Do pass on my best wishes to your son."

"Send the prisoner down," growled the judge.

# 19

"It's the pride of the Fitzmolean's collection," said Beth as they both stood there admiring the Vermeer.

"And it couldn't have found a better home," said Christina. "But I have to tell you that since Miles's death, art dealers and auction houses have been beating a path to my door wanting to know what I intend to do with the rest of the collection."

"If you ever decide to sell any of your paintings, we'd be happy to advise you. It's the least we could do in return for your generosity."

"That's kind of you," said Christina, "but that's not why I invited you to lunch."

"Monte Carlo?" asked Beth, raising an eyebrow.

"Couldn't have been more perfect," purred Christina. "Ralph was so kind and considerate, and such good company. Between us girls, the sex isn't bad either."

"Well, I'm pleased for you. William was a little worried that—"

"Ralph might only be interested in my money?"

Beth looked embarrassed.

"Why don't you both come over for dinner one evening, then you can get to know him a little better."

"I didn't mean to imply . . ." began Beth. "It's just that William always—"

"Thinks like a policeman. How is he, by the way?"

"He's up to something," Beth replied, trying to get off the hook. "But I'm not sure what."

"Another woman?" suggested Christina, laughing.

"Not the way he's looking at the moment, unless she's sleeping rough. Are you still thinking of moving to Florida?" asked Beth, keen to change the subject.

"I no longer need to. I've ended up with the apartment in Mayfair, the villa, and a yacht, not to mention a captain who can't wait to sail her."

"You sound quite serious about Ralph."

"Yes, I am. He's changed my whole life. Sinatra was right, love's much lovelier the second time around. But I'll tell you everything over lunch," Christina said as she linked arms with Beth and they left the gallery together.

---

He checked his watch: 2:20 p.m. Kickoff at 3:00. Forty thousand fans were all heading in the same direction. The majority were wearing red-and-white scarves, although a large contingent wore blue-and-white. The two rival tribes had only one thing in common: each were convinced they were supporting the winning team.

A lone figure, in a red-and-white scarf, strolled past Arsenal tube station, as even more supporters poured out onto Gillespie Road. Moments later he was joined by another red-and-white scarf.

"I'm listening," said the commander, to a scruffy-looking young man who might have just been released from prison, rather than being a recently promoted inspector with the anti-corruption unit.

"If you only consider his record," said William. "Summers is doing an impressive job. Just a shame he's as crooked as a corkscrew."

"Are he and PC Bailey still an item?"

"Rebecca certainly thinks so, but who knows how much longer it will last? On Summers's previous form, she's well past her sell-by date."

"I imagine that like most gamblers, he has a system he considers infallible."

"Until he has to double up."

"Enlighten me."

"There are two major criminal gangs who work out of Romford: the Turners and the Paynes. I'm convinced Summers is in the pay of the Turners, not least because half the Payne family are currently locked up in Wormwood Scrubs, while the Turners only make an occasional appearance at the local magistrates' court, and rarely come away with more than a fine or a suspended sentence," William said as Highbury loomed up in front of them and the prejudices of the vast crowd became even more vocal with each stride they took.

"Is there any chance we could infiltrate the Payne hierarchy, and play Summers at his own game?" asked the Hawk.

"They're a very tight-knit family, and you can be sure there aren't any coppers on their Christmas card list."

The Hawk nodded as they passed the main entrance to the stadium, ignoring the turnstiles.

"However," continued William, "I have come across one member of the family who has a proper job. Adam Payne works in the Barking and Dagenham Council housing department. He's married, two children, and considered the black sheep of the family. Which must make things a bit awkward for him, as his father, Reg, heads up the drug racket in Romford, and his brother is a dealer."

"Does he keep in touch with any other members of the family?"

"Only his mother. He visits her every other weekend, when the rest of the tribe can be found at White Hart Lane, supporting Tottenham."

"Try and make contact with him, and find out if he'd be willing to pass on a message to his mother requesting a meeting with Reg Payne. It's a long shot, but worth a try."

William nodded, but didn't look convinced.

They'd walked a few more yards before William asked, "What are the rest of the team up to in my absence?"

"Rebecca's still shadowing Lamont, who seems to be in debt with the bookmakers again, while Jackie's trying to find out why he's still in contact with Summers. Everyone outside of the inner team still thinks you've been suspended and are preparing for your tribunal."

"Should your phantom board find me guilty," said William, "I'm thinking of joining the Turner gang. Far better pay and shorter hours."

"Don't even joke about it," said Hawksby. "Because I fear that's exactly what Lamont has done. I suspect he's now working directly for Summers, who's in the pay of the Turners, who are among Rashidi's many outlets. That man has a chain of command any general would be proud of."

"When's Rashidi due to be released?"

"In just over a month's time, when I'll want you to drop everything and dog his every step, from the moment he leaves prison until we've got him safely back inside. That should still give you more than enough time to contact Adam Payne. But never forget, if his father thought for one moment you were double-crossing him, he'd slice you up like a piece of salami."

"Thank you, sir, that's most encouraging," said William as they arrived back at the main entrance to the stadium.

"I'll see you again in two weeks' time, when we play Leicester," said the Hawk. "But don't hesitate to call me at home if you come up with anything worthwhile."

He headed for the nearest turnstile, while William made his way to the Gunners' tube station, where he boarded an empty train back to Fulham.

⊸○⊷

"If the Law Society Bar Council were to find out you're alive, and I'm still acting for you," said Booth Watson, "I would undoubtedly be disbarred, and probably end up in prison."

"That's why I never complain about your exorbitant fees, BW."

"Nevertheless, Miles, anything we do in the future will have to be in the name of Captain Ralph Neville, because as far as I'm concerned, Miles Faulkner is dead. I know because I attended his funeral."

"So did I," said Miles, "and nobody gave me a second look other than you. In fact, that was what gave me the confidence to move on to stage two of my long-term plan. Now it's time for stage three. But first, how did your meeting with Christina go?"

"She put up a fight, but not much of one. Settled for two thousand a week after I explained what the alternatives were."

"Sackcloth and ashes didn't appeal to her?"

"I think it was the ashes part that finally convinced her."

"Good, then that's settled. Let's move on, as another problem has arisen."

Booth Watson unscrewed the top of his fountain pen and prepared to make notes.

"I'm still in possession of all my paintings that are worth several million, but if I were to sell even one of them on the open market, some inquisitive busybody might start to wonder if I was still alive, not least Detective Inspector Warwick, even though he also attended my funeral."

"Why not let Christina put them up for auction? That way no one need become suspicious."

"I've already thought about that, but it's too much of a risk. My deal with Christina ensures she keeps her end of the bargain as long as she believes that if she doesn't, her only source of income will dry up. If she was able to get her hands on one of my pictures, let alone the entire collection, she'd pocket the proceeds and disappear off the face of the earth, but not before she'd shopped Captain Ralph Neville and made sure he walked the plank."

"If the open market is out of the question, what about the closed market?" suggested Booth Watson. "I represent several clients who are cash rich, and following the government's recent guidelines on money laundering, are stuck with large sums of money they can't easily dispose of."

"I can't think of a better example of supply and demand," said Miles. "One of your clients could buy a painting from me with some of their surplus cash, put it up for auction, then collect a legitimate check, which they could then deposit in any bank they choose, while I make at least fifty percent on the deal."

"What about the problem of provenance?"

"They could say they bought it from Mrs. Christina Faulkner, and it was part of her late husband's estate."

"She'd expect a cut."

"Give her ten percent of the sale price, and promise her there'll be more where that came from, as long as she keeps her side of the bargain. She has absolutely no interest in my collection, but does like money. Now all you have to do is decide who my first client will be."

"Your friend Assem Rashidi is getting out of prison in about a month's time. I happen to know he's sitting on millions in cash that's locked in a bank vault that he can't transfer to his regular account, not least because the moment he's out, the authorities will be watching him like a hawk."

"An unfortunate simile," said Miles. "But why don't you set up a meeting?"

"That would only create another problem."

"Namely?"

"If I invited you both to my chambers, we might as well ask William Warwick to join us and take notes."

"But Christina told me he's been suspended, and is facing a disciplinary hearing."

"That doesn't mean he's sitting around twiddling his thumbs. No, we need to select somewhere he'd never think of, and I believe I've found the ideal location. But even so, a meeting with Mr. Rashidi would create yet another problem."

"Like what?"

"He would be added to the list of those who know you're still alive."

"Assem's a friend, and in any case, it's in his interests to keep his mouth shut."

"Until he stops being a friend," said Booth Watson, "and it's in his interests to open his mouth, then he'd have us by the balls."

"Not as long as he's hoping to open another slaughter when he comes out," said Miles, "in which case we'll be holding each other's balls."

"Then I'll arrange a meeting as soon as he's released, and let you know when and where, as it certainly won't be in my chambers. By the way, how did you get on with Rashidi when you were inside?"

"Liked him, but wouldn't trust him an inch."

"Funny. He said the same thing about you."

# 20

"Number twenty-two!"

William stood at the back of the room waiting patiently for the right moment. There were three housing officers available that morning, all seated behind thick glass screens, like bank tellers.

He'd arrived at the Town Hall when the doors opened at nine o'clock, but still had to join a long queue. He'd explained to the woman on the inquiry desk why he was there.

"Stick to the truth whenever possible," the Hawk had advised. "That way you're less likely to be caught out by some silly mistake."

"I'm married with two children [true], and currently live in Fulham [true]. I've just been offered a job with the Ford Motor Company in Dagenham [untrue], and am looking for accommodation in the area [untrue]."

The woman handed him a long form, a short pencil, and a small wooden disc with the number 26 etched on it.

"Fill in the form," she said, "and when your number's called hand the disc to the next available officer."

He took a seat in the second row, opposite Adam Payne. After he'd filled in the form, he watched all three officers carefully. He knew he only had a one-in-three chance of ending up at the right window, so tried to work out how he could lower the odds.

"Number twenty-three."

William noticed that Payne took his time dealing with clients. He had a kind, reassuring manner that clearly put them at ease as he listened to their problems. He made copious notes, often showed them photographs, and each person left looking satisfied. Would he be able to achieve the same result with William?

"Number twenty-four."

A heavily pregnant woman shuffled forward and sat down opposite Payne. She slid her form under the window and began to explain her situation. William had already calculated that on average Payne spent eleven minutes dealing with each application, while the world-weary-looking older woman to his left took around seven, and the younger man on his right took about eight.

"Number twenty-five."

A young couple with a baby stood up and walked toward the left-hand cubicle. William checked his watch. He was pretty sure the young man would finish with his client before Payne had dealt with the pregnant woman.

"Number twenty-six."

Although it was his turn, he leaned across to an elderly gentleman on his left and said, "I'm in no hurry, sir, why don't you take my place?"

"Thank you," he said. They swapped discs, and the old man walked slowly across to the younger officer's window.

"Number twenty-seven."

"Damn," said William under his breath. The older woman had finished far too quickly, and he couldn't see who had number 28.

"Number twenty-eight."

William flew out of the blocks and made his way quickly across to Payne's window, leaving number 28 with no choice but to join the woman in the end cubicle.

"Good morning," said Payne. "How can I help you?"

William handed him his form. Payne read the details slowly before he offered an opinion.

"Well," he said, "I'm afraid you can't be considered a priority, but I can still put you on the council's waiting list. However, I fear we might not be able to offer you suitable accommodation for at least a year." He extracted another form from a drawer below his desk, and began to fill it out.

"Is there any way I can jump the queue?" asked William.

"No, sir," said Payne firmly. "Each case is assessed on its merit, so like everyone else, you'll have to wait until the appropriate accommodation becomes available."

"Even if I was a friend of your father's?"

Payne stopped writing, unable to hide his embarrassment. "You know my father?"

"No, but I'm keen to meet him."

"Then it's time for you to leave, Mr.—" he looked down and checked the form—"Warwick. You've picked the wrong man."

"It could be mutually beneficial."

"If you don't leave immediately, Mr. Warwick, I shall have no choice but to call the police." He placed a hand on the phone by his side.

"I am the police," said William, producing his warrant card, which caused the blood to drain from Payne's face.

"How can I help, inspector?" he asked, their roles suddenly reversed.

"I need to speak to your father on a private matter."

"I'm not in contact with him, and haven't been for years."

"I'm aware of that. But you do see your mother every other weekend, so perhaps she could arrange a meeting."

"Never," said Payne firmly. "I don't want anything to do with my father's world."

"I quite understand, but if you felt able to help, I can assure you it could make a difference."

"Two wrongs don't make a right, detective inspector. I'll have to ask you once again to leave."

William took a card from an inside pocket and slid it under the screen. "If you change your mind, don't hesitate to call me at any time."

"You won't be hearing from me."

William reluctantly rose from his place, as the housing officer tore up his application form and dropped it in the wastepaper basket.

"Number thirty."

William made his way out of the crowded town hall, and paused at the top of the steps to consider what had just happened. He wasn't looking forward to telling the Hawk that his approach to the only law-abiding member of the Payne family had ended in failure. Then he saw her. He slipped behind a pillar until she'd passed by. The Hawk would be disappointed to hear he'd failed to convince Adam Payne to assist him, but to have to admit he'd been spotted by PC Bailey . . .

---

"How are the twins?" asked Josephine Hawksby after the waitress had served them with afternoon tea.

"They never stop eating!" said Beth. "William and I live off their leftovers."

Josephine smiled as she poured her guest a cup of tea.

"And then there are the clothes. When I was a child, I wore a gray school uniform until I was seventeen, when I got my first pair of jeans, which my father didn't approve of, and I can't tell you what he said when I discovered miniskirts."

"My first dress almost reached my ankles," said Josephine, after she'd selected a cucumber sandwich.

"Do you remember daps?" They both laughed. "So forgive me if I finish off the sandwiches before I go home to feed the children."

"Who takes care of the twins while you're at work?" asked Josephine.

"Both our mothers are wonderful," said Beth. "We also have a nanny who does so much overtime she earns almost as much as I do."

"You're a thoroughly modern couple," commented Josephine as she selected another sandwich. "Jack wouldn't allow me to go back to work."

"Do you think there's anywhere else left on earth where cucumber sandwiches are still on the menu?"

"Along with scones and clotted cream," said Josephine. "Probably only Wimbledon, and that's just for a fortnight. But I have a feeling the menu isn't why you wanted to see me."

"No," admitted Beth. "I just thought you might be able to fill in one or two missing pieces in the latest jigsaw, and I rather hoped Commander Hawksby might be a little more forthcoming than William."

"Not a chance. When Jack's at home, he leaves Scotland Yard behind him. You wouldn't even know he was a police officer. But tell me which pieces of the jigsaw you think are missing, and I'll see if I can help."

"I know William's been temporarily suspended, and can't return to work until the tribunal clears his name."

"Whenever the subject arises, 'temporarily' is the word Jack repeats."

"That's a relief," said Beth. "But can you explain why he's out most nights, only shaves at the weekends, and dresses like a gardener, when we don't have a garden?"

Josephine spread some raspberry jam on a scone before she replied. "The only time 'double-breasted' Jack ever dressed like that was when he was working undercover. Do you have any other clues?"

"Only that when I was ironing a pair of his trousers last week, I came across a receipt for a meal in Romford."

"Can't help you on that one."

"And last Saturday, when he left the house after lunch, he was wearing a red-and-white scarf, which came as a bit of a surprise as he supports Chelsea."

"Ah, their first mistake," said Josephine, "because Jack supports the Gunners, and has done since he was a child."

"I'm none the wiser," said Beth.

"He told me all about Bob Wilson and Frank McLintock on our first date."

"Now I'm completely lost."

"Last Saturday Arsenal were playing Chelsea at home, so now we know where they both spent the afternoon."

"But I thought they weren't allowed to be in contact with each other while William is under investigation?"

"What proof do you have that he's even under investigation?"

Beth thought for some time before she replied, "None, other than what he's told me."

"Men will always tell you what they think you want to hear, and policemen are even worse. I suspect you've just been working on the wrong jigsaw. But if he ever admits he was never under investigation, don't let him know you already knew. Meanwhile, for an underfed mother, I can recommend the chocolate gâteau."

---

"Right," said the commander. "As PC Bailey has left for Romford, perhaps someone can bring me up to date on her activities. Let's start with you, DI Warwick."

William opened his notebook. "PC Bailey spent every night of last week at DS Summers's flat in Romford. She not only does the shopping and laundry for him, but also has her own latch key. On Thursday, she booked two tickets for a holiday in Malaga next month, so I think we can safely assume they're an item."

"DC Pankhurst, do you have anything to add?" asked the Hawk, switching his attention to the other side of the table.

Rebecca didn't need her notebook. "Nicky hasn't slept at our flat for the past fortnight. She made a brief appearance on Saturday morning, when she told me more about her latest boyfriend, who bore no resemblance to DS Summers."

"Did you press her for details?" asked Paul.

"Yes. She said his name was Alan Mitchell, and that he worked for an estate agent in Croydon, but she didn't say which one."

"Don't press her any further," said Paul. "Now we know the truth, we don't need her to become suspicious."

"Understood, sir," said Rebecca, looking relieved.

"Pity Nicky doesn't know the difference between getting laid and being screwed," said Jackie.

"Right, William," said the Hawk without comment, "you can come off night duty and turn your attention to DS Summers's day-time activities. I'm keen to find out more about his informer, John Smith, and if he actually exists."

"Surely he exists," said Rebecca. "Otherwise where's the money going?"

"Straight into his back pocket," said Jackie, "because he's nothing more than a figment of Summers's imagination?"

"How does that work?" asked Rebecca.

"It's not unknown," said the Hawk, "for a bent copper to invent an informer who regularly comes up with information he already knows about, so when it comes to paying off his snitch, there's only one pig's snout in the trough."

"I've recently come across a variation on that particular scam," said Paul. "After a major crime has been committed, the bent copper backdates an earlier intelligence report crediting his informer with supplying the original information. It's a system known as double and quits."

"I must be getting old," said the Hawk, "because I've never come across that one before."

"As the crooks become more sophisticated," said Jackie, "so do the bent coppers."

"So must we," said the Hawk, "if we're to stay ahead of them."

"Well, that could explain Summers's new Jaguar, the flashy suits, and a holiday in Malaga," said William. "But it would certainly help us prove Summers is bent if we were able to show that John Smith doesn't even exist."

"I think I may have come up with how we can do just that," said the Hawk. He handed out a single sheet of paper to each member of the team. "I'll allow the three of you a week to take my plan apart, or better still, improve on it, so when we meet again next Monday I can give DI Warwick the authority to set the whole operation in motion. Which reminds me—as far as anyone outside this office is concerned, and that includes PC Bailey, DI Warwick is still suspended, and his tribunal won't be sitting for at least another six weeks. So you all know exactly how much time you've got to nail Rashidi, Lamont, Summers, and Roberts. Any questions?"

"Yes, sir," said Jackie. "If Lamont gives me another brown envelope, can I book a holiday to Malaga?"

# 21

Rebecca followed Lamont down the crowded escalator with Marlboro Man a few steps behind. Lamont didn't spot her, and neither of them noticed Ross.

When Lamont reached the platform, he made his way to the far end, and didn't have to wait long before the next train came whooshing in. He climbed into the rear carriage, and although it was almost empty, he sat down next to a man who was reading *The Evening Standard.* They didn't acknowledge each other.

Rebecca found a seat at the other end of the carriage, and opened her paperback, but didn't start reading.

"You wanted to see me, sir," said Summers. He still couldn't get out of the habit of calling his old gaffer *sir.*

"You wouldn't have anything I could help you with, by any chance?" asked Lamont. "I'm a bit skint at the moment."

"Not right now," said Summers. "But in a couple of weeks' time we could both be back in business."

"Can't be too soon," said Lamont, trying not to sound desperate. "I've got one or two bills that I can't put off for much longer."

"I'm sorry to hear that," said Summers, who was delighted to hear it, as it gave him the whip hand. "Anything in particular?" he asked, like any good detective.

"I've had a bit of a bad run on the horses lately, and the bookies are beginning to breathe down my neck."

"And they have such bad breath."

"Also, the new house is turning out to be more expensive than I'd budgeted for, and my wife will kill me if we have to put it back on the market." He paused before saying, "You're not married, are you?"

"No. Never found the right girl."

"I've found three of them," said Lamont, "and none of them turned out to be right. Should have taken Jimmy Goldsmith's advice. If it flies, floats, or fucks, rent it."

Summers burst out laughing, which caused Rebecca to look around, but not MM.

"Don't have that problem myself," said Summers. "There's more than enough skirt at the nick to satisfy my needs, not to mention out there on the street."

"I thought you had a girlfriend," said Lamont, glancing toward the other end of the carriage.

"Not for much longer. She's just about reached her sell-by date."

"I've seen that woman somewhere before," whispered Lamont.

Summers looked in Rebecca's direction. "Not my type."

"Do you think she could be following us?"

Summers took a closer look.

Rebecca became uncomfortably aware the two men were taking an interest in her. She'd have to get off at the next stop and inform William her cover had been blown. He'd already told her he was surprised she'd lasted that long. She turned another page of her book, painfully aware that it was the same novel she'd been reading every time she'd traveled on the Circle line.

When the train pulled into Green Park, Rebecca got off and never once looked back. MM didn't move.

"Perhaps I was just imagining it," said Lamont as she disappeared out of sight.

"I'm getting off at the next stop," said Summers. "I'll be in touch as soon as the shipment arrives," he added when the train came to a halt. "Do you still have your old uniform, sir?" he asked as the doors opened.

⊸o⊷

"I'm off to the match," said William.

*Why bother to lie?* Beth wanted to ask him. Did he assume she hadn't worked it out when a schoolboy would have realized he wasn't going to the match? Chelsea were playing away at Newcastle, so he couldn't hope to make the three o'clock kickoff unless he had a helicopter standing by. And then there was the red-and-white scarf he'd started wearing every other Saturday. Josephine Hawksby had told her they were the colors of the team her husband supported, and William despised. So he must be going to see the commander. Or was that just another deception?

She thought about following him, but decided against it for two reasons. He would have spotted her before he'd turned the first corner, and more important, she trusted him. Beth assumed it had to be undercover work that he couldn't tell her about. But he was suspended, and not allowed to be involved in any police duties until his name had been cleared by the tribunal. Or was that just another lie, and Josephine had been right all along?

William opened the front door as the phone in the hall began to ring.

"If it's for me," he said as Beth came out of the kitchen, "tell them to call back after the match. Don't want to miss kickoff."

Beth picked up the phone. "Hello?"

"I want to speak to your husband," said a gruff voice.

"I'm afraid he's just left, but if you could call back later—"

"I won't be calling back."

"Please hold on," said Beth, sensing the call might be part of William's elaborate deception. "I'll see if I can catch him." She put the phone down and ran out of the front door, to see William striding away.

"William!" she cried at the top of her voice, but he didn't stop walking. She began to chase after him, shouting his name until he finally stopped and turned round.

"There's someone on the phone for you," she said, catching her breath. "Said he wouldn't be calling back."

William began to sprint toward the house, wondering if it could possibly be Adam Payne and he'd spoken to his mother. He charged through the open door, grabbed the phone, and said, "William Warwick."

"Why do you want to see me?" demanded an unfriendly voice William didn't recognize, though he knew exactly who it was.

"Mr. Payne. I'm currently carrying out an undercover investigation that doesn't involve you or any member of your family, but the Turner mob and one of their close associates."

"Detective Sergeant Summers, no doubt," said the voice, "along with his cooperative desk sergeant."

William was left speechless. Reg Payne already had him on the back foot.

Beth quietly closed the front door and made her way back into the kitchen, leaving the door ajar.

"I understand you're currently suspended, inspector. So what are you really up to?"

William, still reeling from the first blow, decided that only the truth would get this man on his side. "We have reason to believe that Summers and his desk sergeant are working hand in glove with the Turners."

"Who've recently recruited PC Bailey into their gang, although I'm still not sure which side she's actually on," said Payne.

William could only wonder how much more the man knew.

"The other thing I can't work out is where ex-Superintendent Lamont fits into the scheme of things. Of course, I know he was an inspector stationed in Romford when Summers was still on the beat, but that was before he was transferred to the Yard and joined the drugs squad. But then he suddenly resigns without explanation, despite the success of the Trojan Horse operation. I assume that after all the porkies he told during the Rashidi trial he's been well rewarded. But I can tell you the cash didn't last for long, because he's broke again. Not surprising, remembering how he manages to lose so consistently at almost every race meeting he attends."

"Is there anything you don't know, Mr. Payne?" asked William, butting in.

"Yes. Why you want to see me."

"I want to set a trap to catch Summers and the Turners, that would put them all out of business for a very long time."

"So you're looking for a thief to catch a thief."

"Something like that," admitted William, who went on to spell out his plan in detail. Payne didn't interrupt, other than to ask the occasional shrewd question.

"Impressive," he said after William had come to the end. "But then, I'd expect nothing less of the Hawk. I'll have to speak to my family before I let you know my decision."

The line went dead. William put the phone down and checked his watch. He wasn't going to make the match on time and would have to call the Hawk at home after the game. At least this time he would have something worthwhile to tell the commander.

He joined Beth and the twins in the kitchen.

"I won't be going to the match after all," he said, without explanation.

"Why not? Didn't your helicopter arrive on time?"

William was left speechless for the second time that day.

"Isn't it time you told me what you're really up to?" said Beth. "Because it's obvious you haven't been suspended."

William accepted that it was going to be one of those days when he was always on the back foot.

---

"We'd adopt a child if we could," said Grace. "But that's just not possible at the moment."

"More's the pity," said Marjorie. "Any child would be fortunate to have you and Clare as parents."

"It's kind of you to say so, but sadly not too many people agree with you. In fact, a judge told me quite recently he thought it just wasn't the natural way of things."

"One enlightened Liberal member of parliament has a private member's bill in front of the House that would make adoption by two members of the same sex legal," said Clare.

"But I'm told it won't make a second reading," said Grace. "In fact, it's likely to be years before it becomes law, and by that time it will be too late for us."

"Would you prefer a boy or a girl?" asked Sir Julian, taking the rest of the family by surprise.

"It wouldn't matter to us," said Grace, looking at Clare. "Like Liquorice Allsorts, we'd take whatever we could get and love them to death."

Everyone burst out laughing.

"You can have the twins until they're six," said William.

"Why six?" asked Marjorie.

"That's when they'll start playing football," explained Beth.

"Peter would walk into the present Chelsea team," said William, "who somehow managed to lose three–nil to Southampton last week."

"While we're on the subject of winning teams," said Sir Julian, "has a date been set for your tribunal?"

"Not yet," said William, delivering a well-prepared response.

Beth watched with interest to see how the rest of the family would react.

"The sooner you get back to work the better," said Sir Julian. "If you send me the relevant papers, I'll look over them and give you an opinion. Mind you, the case against you is so weak, even Grace would get you off."

"Thank you, Father, for that vote of confidence," said Grace. "However, Clare and I have already been asked to represent the defendant, and we don't require a junior."

"Touché," said Sir Julian, reaching for the port.

"More important," said Marjorie, who was sitting on the floor with the twins, "is that Julian and I have decided to set up a trust fund to pay for Peter's education."

"What about Artemisia?" demanded Grace.

"Beth's parents have already taken on that responsibility. In fact, it was Arthur and Joanna's idea in the first place."

"Lucky children," said William, ruffling Peter's hair.

"I thought Eton and Cheltenham Ladies' College," said Sir Julian, well aware that he was tossing a hand grenade into the middle of the room.

"And I thought Fulham comprehensive would suit them both perfectly well," said Beth.

"What fun," said Marjorie. "Something for us all to endlessly fight over before we finally murder each other."

"It's already been decided," said Beth, joining her children on the floor.

"That wasn't how it worked when I was a boy," said Sir Julian, removing the pin from the hand grenade.

"You were never a boy," said Marjorie. "You were born middle-aged."

Sir Julian was lost for words, something the rest of the family didn't experience often, so William took advantage of it.

"We should be off," he said. "It's been a long day for the children."

Once Peter and Artemisia had been strapped into their car seats, good-byes were exchanged followed by waves, as William made his way slowly down the drive to the sound of Harry Chapin's "A Better Place to Be."

"I think your father knows perfectly well there isn't going to be an inquiry, and you haven't really been suspended," said Beth as they turned onto the main road.

"What makes you say that?"

"There would have been an endless stream of questions if he'd thought for one moment you were in any trouble, and while he can still draw breath, he certainly wouldn't allow Grace to represent you at the tribunal."

# 22

"Assem Rashidi will be released from Pentonville at ten o'clock tomorrow morning," said the Hawk, "and I expect a welcoming party to be waiting for him. Three of you will watch him twenty-four/seven. If Rashidi even thinks about going anywhere other than his office in the City, or his mother's home in The Boltons, I want to be informed immediately. I've already briefed Superintendent Watts, the new head of the drugs squad, about our immediate plans. He'll have sixty officers on standby who can move at a moment's notice. This time we'll shut down Rashidi's operation even before he's given the chance to poison his first customer."

"While at the same time, we must arrest those associates who've been keeping the business ticking over in his absence," said Paul.

"We won't need to mount a Trojan Horse operation to achieve that as we'll be charging in the front door. Try not to sprain your ankle this time, DS Adaja."

Paul looked embarrassed.

"How did you sprain your ankle, sarge?" asked Rebecca innocently, although she'd been told the tale of the Trojan Horse many times.

Jackie suppressed a grin.

"Before your time, DC Pankhurst," was all Paul had to say on the subject.

"Superintendent Watts thinks it's no coincidence that a large shipment of drugs from Colombia arrived at Felixstowe just a few days ago," said the Hawk, "so he's issued an all-ports alert."

"Any further intel?" asked Paul, coming in on cue.

"Only that he thinks Rashidi's mules will be distributing large amounts of cocaine and heroin across London during the next few days. I have a full list of likely recipients," said the Hawk, opening a thick file. "One of them is on the Romford patch. A family called Payne. I presume you've come across them, PC Bailey."

"Yes," said Nicky. "A right bunch of villains, but thanks to DS Summers, there are more of them in jail than there are on the outside enjoying the comforts of home cooking."

"That's good to hear. Right, let's make sure we're all ready for Rashidi when he's released tomorrow morning, and keep me informed of any developments."

The team gathered up their files, left the commander's office, and returned to their desks, except for PC Bailey, who signed off before leaving for Romford. DC Pankhurst had earlier left the building and taken up a position across the road from where she could see the entrance to St. James's Park underground station.

She didn't have to wait long before Nicky appeared, and jogged down the steps into the station. Rebecca returned to the Yard and reported to DS Adaja. Fifteen minutes later, the team reconvened in the commander's office where William was waiting for them.

"The hare has been let out of the trap," said the Hawk, "but the hounds must allow her to run a couple more circuits around the track before we move in."

"What do you have in mind, sir?" asked Jackie.

"Marlboro Man will deliver the gear to Reg Payne's home at one o'clock on Friday morning," said the Hawk. "No sooner than that, because we don't want Summers or Bailey to become suspicious."

"Do we move in once they've gone inside?" asked Paul.

"No," said the Hawk firmly. "If we did, Summers would claim he was just about to arrest Payne when we turned up, and he's got enough gall to try and take the credit for the ambush. No, we'll have to let him place the noose around his own neck before we open the trapdoor. Once MM has delivered a kilo of cocaine and ten grand in cash, we'll wait to see if Summers arrests Payne and takes the merchandise back to the nick. If he hands in less than ten thousand and not a full haul of the drugs we supplied, our suspicions will be confirmed."

"Is that when we move in, sir?" asked Jackie.

"No," said William. "We'll still need to keep our powder dry. I want to find out how many people are involved, and how they distribute the cocaine and dispose of such large amounts of cash. And don't forget, we have the serial numbers of those banknotes."

"What if Summers arrests MM when he comes out of Payne's house?" asked Jackie.

"Then we'll know he's straight. But if he's bent, he won't be interested in the delivery boy, only what's being delivered."

"He might arrange for someone to follow MM," suggested DC Pankhurst, "and then he'll find out he's one of ours."

"Don't worry about that, Rebecca. MM would lose them before they reached the first corner. But that doesn't mean there won't be some surprises along the way, because Summers is a shrewd operator, and he's certain to have a backup plan that turns him from being a villain into a hero. Be prepared to move at a moment's notice, even if it's the middle of the night."

"And PC Bailey?" asked Rebecca.

"She may get caught up in the crossfire," said the Hawk. "If so, she'll have to face the consequences."

"There's something else you should know, sir," said Rebecca.

They all turned their attention to DC Pankhurst.

"Nicky's pregnant."

---

Summers was delighted when Nicky told him her news.

"The delivery will be early Friday morning, you say?"

"Yes," said Nicky as she turned a steak over in the pan.

"Where did you pick up such valuable intel?"

"From a runner on the street, in exchange for turning a blind eye."

"You're learning fast," said Summers, sitting down at the kitchen table.

"Is this one for your snitch?" Nicky asked as she placed a steak in front of him.

"God, no," said Summers. "This one's for us. That way it'll be far more profitable."

Nicky took the seat opposite him and thought about his response. He'd given her another chance to escape, and she might have done, if he hadn't taken her by surprise.

---

William sat in the back of a taxi that wasn't for hire. His eyes never left the front gate of the jail, although he knew the prisoner wouldn't be released for at least another thirty minutes. He checked his watch every few seconds, but the door at the side of the main gate remained resolutely closed.

A dark blue Mercedes swept past them and came to a halt outside the prison as if it were a country club.

"Same car?" asked William.

"No, sir," said Danny. "Same number plate, AR1, but that's the latest model, straight off the production line."

"Is it the same driver?" asked William, trying to get a closer look.

"I'm a driver," replied Danny. "If you dress like that, I think you'll find you're a chauffeur. But yes, it's the same man."

William laughed, although it wasn't a morning for laughing.

Ten chimes rang out from a nearby church tower, but still the door didn't open.

"Perhaps he likes the place so much he doesn't want to leave." Danny's idea of humor.

Finally the door swung open, and a short, muscle-bound man covered in tattoos and carrying a black leather bag stepped out.

"Burglary," said Danny, without giving him a second look. The newly released prisoner took one look at the Mercedes and gave the driver a V sign, before heading for the nearest bus stop.

Two more prisoners slipped out through the door. William couldn't help wondering how long their freedom would last. Some of them treated prison like a second home, especially if they were sleeping rough, and a minor crime meant they could spend the winter in a warm cell, with three meals a day and a television.

At last the unmistakable figure of Assem Rashidi appeared. William didn't need to say, *That's him,* as unlike his fellow inmates, he'd lost weight, not put it on. He wore a similar well-tailored suit, white shirt, and silk tie as he'd been wearing on the final day of his trial. William wondered if there was a Harrods label on the inside of the jacket. He could have been the prison governor, except that the governor drove himself home each evening in a Morris Minor.

The chauffeur leaped out and opened the back door of the Mercedes for his boss, as if it was a normal Monday morning, and he was being picked up from his country home to be driven to work. He touched the peak of his cap as Rashidi slipped into the backseat. William ducked out of sight as the car moved serenely past the waiting taxi and turned left.

Danny swung the taxi around, and took care to keep his distance. He slipped in behind other black cabs whenever possible so the chauffeur wouldn't realize he was being tailed.

"He could be heading for Brixton or The Boltons," said William, staring out of the front window as they drove along Upper Street.

The Mercedes never crossed the river, but continued to head east, and thirty minutes later they passed two mounted silver dragons bearing cast-iron shields, indicating they had entered the City of London.

"It has to be his office," said William.

The Mercedes eventually came to a halt outside the headquarters of Marcel and Neffe. Once again the chauffeur jumped out and opened the back door for his boss.

As Rashidi entered the Tea House he received a second salute from another man in a peaked cap, as if he'd never been away.

William didn't follow him inside, but then he knew he would be going up to his office on the eleventh floor. He was more interested in when and by which exit Rashidi would be leaving the building. The Mercedes drove off.

"Stay put, Danny," said William, "and don't take your eyes off the entrance. If Rashidi reappears, get me on the radio and I'll nip back out. If you should miss him," he added as he opened the cab door and stepped out onto the pavement, "start looking for a fare, because it's the only money you'll earn this week."

Danny didn't laugh as William jogged off in the direction of Moorgate tube station.

It had been some time since he'd discovered how Rashidi had

discreetly left his office without anyone noticing. He took up his preferred vantage point next to a small newsstand, from where he could observe anyone who left the Tea House by the unobtrusive door that few were aware of unless they worked in the building.

He resigned himself to the fact he could be hanging about for some time, if Rashidi was being brought up to date on the company's affairs during his absence. He might even have become a reformed character, as he'd promised the judge he would, though William thought that was unlikely.

Perhaps Danny would call him at around six o'clock and they'd follow Rashidi to The Boltons, where he would have supper with his mother and spend his first night of liberty, at her home, especially if he thought, even for a moment, he was being watched.

An hour passed, during which time several City workers slipped in or out of the discreet door, but Rashidi was not among them. William was becoming bored, and considered spending a few minutes with Danny in the back of the warm cab, but that would surely be the moment Rashidi would choose to leave his day job in search of alternative employment.

During the third hour, he purchased a copy of *The Evening Standard* for 20p, but never got far beyond the headline on the front page before once again checking that door.

"Are you going to be here much longer?" asked a traffic warden.

"As long as it takes," said Danny, producing his warrant card.

The warden touched the corner of his cap, surprised that the cab driver was Met, not City police.

William remained rooted to the spot for hour upon hour, getting colder and older, until a man appeared through the side door, wearing a baggy gray tracksuit, his head covered in a hood. An outfit William could never forget. He joined the early-evening commuters as they made their way toward the escalators. William might not have been able to see his face, but it was definitely the same tracksuit, and the same walk. But more important, the same black leather gloves.

Rashidi stepped onto the escalator, as William slipped in behind a broad-shouldered man who shielded him from his prey. By the time William reached the bottom step, Rashidi was already out of sight. Not that there was much doubt where he was going. William headed for the Northern line's southbound platform, and arrived just as a train pulled in. He spotted Rashidi climbing aboard at the other end of the platform, and slipped into the nearest carriage.

Although William was sure he knew where Rashidi would be getting off, he still double-checked at every station. But he was right, because Rashidi didn't leave the train until it pulled into Stockwell, where he made his way across to the Victoria line for the one-stop journey to Brixton.

William allowed his mark to disappear from sight once again, as he was confident he knew where he was going. When he strolled onto the platform he hung back among the waiting passengers at the far end. He didn't intend to travel any farther. Now the old pattern had been reestablished, Paul would take over and be waiting for Rashidi outside the station tomorrow afternoon hoping that he would lead him to the new slaughter.

William glanced to his right to see Rashidi shaking hands with a man he immediately recognized along with two muscle-bound bodyguards, who stood one on either side of him. Rashidi had already returned to his other world.

A rush of wind from inside the dark tunnel announced the arrival of the next train. William was about to return to the Yard, when Rashidi took a step forward, and before he had a chance to react, the two bodyguards grabbed an arm each and with one violent movement hurled Rashidi onto the track.

The train screeched to a halt, but it was too late. The horrifying sound of metal and body colliding caused several passengers to scream, while others turned away.

William sprinted toward the three men, but they had chosen their spot next to an exit carefully, and by the time he reached the escalator they were already approaching the top step, barging their way past several startled passengers. He charged on, taking two steps at a time, but by the time he reached the top, they were almost at the exit.

The older man was gasping for breath in an attempt to keep up with the younger, fitter bodyguards. William had nearly caught up with him, and was about to pounce when he felt two arms encircle him and he was tackled before reaching the try line. His arms were thrust behind his back by one man while another handcuffed him.

"You're under arrest," said a voice.

---

When William arrived back at the Yard, he immediately briefed the commander on the violent and premeditated murder of Assem Rashidi, and how he'd ended up being arrested by mistake.

"At least that solves one of our problems," said the Hawk, taking William by surprise. "Rashidi can no longer harm you. But what I want to know, detective inspector, is did you recognize the man he shook hands with?"

"Yes, sir. It was Tony Roberts, the owner of eleven newsagents, who claimed at the trial he'd been living in Rashidi's apartment for the past ten years. He must have been running Rashidi's empire in his absence, and clearly decided he wanted to take over the business with a sleeping partner."

"Foolish mistake," said the Hawk. "Roberts is only at best a number two, and by killing his paymaster, he's made it far easier for us to bring down the entire empire."

"What do you want me to do next, sir?"

"Go home, inspector, and leave me to get a Murder Team mobilized."

William was disappointed not to be the officer who would arrest Roberts. He hoped it would be Paul, so the sprained ankle would be relegated to folklore.

⊸o⊷

As William sat on the tube back to Fulham Broadway, he knew the Hawk would already have dispatched a Murder Team to Brixton, with the drugs unit not far behind. By the time he'd written up his report and handed it over to the Hawk's secretary, it would not only be out of date, but ancient history. He would have to wait for the team meeting in the morning to find out what had happened next.

When he arrived home, he found Beth and the twins in the bathroom, almost as much water on the floor as in the bath. "Have you heard about Rashidi?" were Beth's first words. His silence told her everything she needed to know.

"I'll fill in the details later," he said. "Not least how I ended up being arrested for the murder," he whispered as the phone began to ring. William left Beth with the children splashing around in the bath, and picked up the phone on the landing.

No greeting, no name, no small talk. But he knew who was on the other end of the line.

"I've spoken to the family, and we're willing to go ahead with your plan. But there's a condition."

William didn't need to be told what that condition was. He could only wonder how the Hawk would react. He returned to the bathroom to find Beth drying the children before putting on their pajamas.

"Who was it?" she asked.

"I'm going to have to make a phone call," William said, not answering her question. He picked up the twins, one under each arm, and carried them giggling to their bedroom, where he tucked them up and turned out the light. He returned to the landing, picked up the phone, and dialed an unlisted number.

"Commander Hawksby speaking."

# 23

DRUG LORD THROWN UNDER TRAIN

The Hawk glanced at the front page of the *Daily Mail* before tossing it aside.

"Yesterday's news," he declared. "Tony Roberts and his two sidekicks were arrested last night, and all three will be charged with Rashidi's murder later today. As a bonus, the drugs squad moved in and were able to shut down another slaughter in a different part of Brixton that looked as if it had recently been set up in preparation for Rashidi's return."

"Can't wait to read the headlines in tomorrow's papers," said Jackie.

"I've already briefed the commissioner on what to expect, and taken all the credit. None of you got a mention."

Laughter broke out among the team, as they banged the palms of their hands on the table in approval.

"As you were responsible for arresting Roberts, DS Adaja, perhaps you could bring us all up to date."

"A Murder Team moved in immediately after the senior investigating officer's call," began Paul. "The eleven newsagents purportedly owned by Roberts were, as you always suspected, sir, nothing more than an elaborate front to launder Rashidi's drugs money.

Although most of Roberts's employees kept shtum, one of them broke down when it was suggested she might be charged with assisting an offender. Her information led us to a local brothel, where we found Roberts on the job. He made no attempt to resist arrest. The young woman who was with him, well, on top of him, was a fount of information once we'd promised to keep her name out of the papers. It seems her mother is chairman of the local Conservative Association."

"Everyone has their price," said the Hawk. "What about Roberts's two accomplices?"

"Not the sharpest tools in the box, sir. They were found celebrating in a local pub. They put up a fight, but not much of one. They'll be appearing in front of the magistrate this morning along with Roberts, all three of them will be charged with murder."

"I hear you had an equally worthwhile evening, DS Roycroft," said the Hawk, switching his attention to Jackie.

"As Paul pointed out, sir, Roberts is no Rashidi. Once he'd been charged with murder he broke down, blamed it on the two thugs, and even told us where Rashidi's latest drug factory was. Claimed he was nothing more than a fall guy who'd been paid to say he lived in Rashidi's flat. When I mentioned the words life imprisonment, he offered to turn Queen's evidence in return for the possibility of a shorter sentence."

"I'm sure we can get a couple of years knocked off," said the Hawk, "so that he's released in time to go straight into an old people's home."

More banging of palms on the table.

"Following Roberts's revelations," said the Hawk, "I can report that Superintendent Watts and sixty of his men swept through Brixton last night and netted a shoal of minnows, a dozen runners, and more important, a couple of leading dealers who we've been after for years. Second only to Trojan Horse, is how I described it to the commissioner."

"Did they find enough evidence to back up their charges?" asked Paul.

"Seven kilos of coke, three of heroin, and countless bags of marijuana," said the Hawk. "I'll be issuing photographs of the haul to the press later today."

"However," said Jackie, "Superintendent Watts is convinced this was only a small part of a larger consignment that was recently shipped in from Colombia, and the rest of the haul has already been distributed across London."

"Has any of it turned up in Romford?" asked the Hawk, looking across the table at PC Bailey.

"Not that I'm aware of, sir," said Nicky. "There's nothing in Book 66 to suggest it has, no significant drugs arrests have been made during the past week and nothing's been handed in."

"Remind me," said the Hawk. "Isn't it the Turner family who would be the most likely recipients of any drugs being distributed in Romford?"

"No, sir, the Paynes. The Turners haven't been causing any trouble lately."

Either she's lying, thought Rebecca, or Summers doesn't trust her enough to tell her what he's up to. The detective suspected the first, while the friend wanted to believe the second.

"I expect all of you to have your reports on my desk by midday," said the Hawk. "What do you have to say for yourself, DC Pankhurst?" he asked the one person who had remained resolutely silent.

"The extended liquor license application for the strip club in Soho has been turned down, sir, and the officer concerned has had to unpick his three stripes and is back on the beat."

A coded message that her latest intel would have to wait until they reconvened in an hour's time, after Nicky had left for Romford.

The Hawk nodded. He couldn't bring himself to look at PC Bailey, and wondered how much longer it would be before she had to admit who was the father of her unborn child, because he certainly didn't move from Croydon.

---

Funerals, they say, are how the departed discover how popular they were. Just a pity they're not present to find out.

The attendance at Assem Rashidi's funeral might have been described as meager at best. His mother was the only one who shed a tear when the body of her only child, or what was left of it, was lowered into the ground. The Catholic priest who presided over the service had never met him, and wouldn't have agreed to perform the ceremony had Rashidi's mother not been a regular attendee at the Brompton Oratory and, more important, one of the parish's more generous benefactors.

Booth Watson stood a pace back from the small group of mourners, dressed in suitably somber attire, head bowed, representing his client for the last time. Although he had hopes that Rashidi's only known living relative might soon find herself in need of his services.

Two heavily built men, squeezed into tight-fitting suits, observed the burial from afar, looking as if their only purpose was to make sure the body didn't miraculously rise from the dead. The little gathering was immediately doubled by the presence of four gravediggers.

Even farther back stood William, shielded from view by a vast memorial statue of three angels, while behind him was a photographer who would have pictures of everyone present on the commander's desk by noon.

The priest delivered the final blessing, followed by the sign of the cross. Not that he believed this particular sinner had much chance of entering the Kingdom of Heaven.

A few spots of rain began to fall. Booth Watson raised his umbrella and accompanied Mrs. Rashidi back to her waiting car.

"It was kind of you to attend Assem's funeral, Mr. Booth Watson," she said almost in a whisper.

"A much-misunderstood man," he said gravely. "If there is anything I can do to assist you in the future, madam, please don't hesitate to call upon my services." He handed her one of his embossed cards.

"As it happens, Mr. Booth Watson," she replied, "I do need advice on a private matter. My son died intestate, and I want someone to advise me on how to handle his—" she hesitated—"somewhat complicated estate."

Booth Watson opened the back door of a black Mercedes, lowered his umbrella, and stood aside to allow his new client to climb in.

"I shall wait for a suitable time to pass, Mrs. Rashidi, to allow you to mourn, before I get back in touch."

"Don't leave it too long," she said as he closed the door.

"Always follow the money," said the commander when the team reconvened after PC Bailey had left for Romford. "But first, let's recap on our most recent intel. At one o'clock last Friday morning, Marlboro Man visited the Paynes' residence. He observed two men watching him from a parked car about a hundred yards away.

"Once MM was inside the house, he handed Payne's father, Reg, one kilo of cocaine, half a kilo of heroin, and ten thousand pounds in marked notes, all delivered in a Sainsbury's bag. I have receipts for all of them, and they were authorized by the assistant commissioner.

"After leaving the house, MM drove off, but when it was clear no one was following him, he doubled back, and returned to a spot he'd identified earlier from which he could remain out of sight, but still have a clear view of Payne's front door.

"A few minutes later, two men got out of the parked car and entered Reg Payne's house." The Hawk handed around several photographs. "You will note that MM is no David Bailey, but to be fair, he couldn't use a flash, and he was some way off."

The officers studied the pictures for some time before the Hawk asked, "Any observations?"

"The tall one is Summers," said Jackie. "Could the other one, in the raincoat, be his partner in crime, DI Castle?"

"I don't think so," said William. "Castle is a lot older than that. But what's he holding in his right hand?"

"It's Lamont," said Paul, who was examining one of the photographs through a magnifying glass.

"What makes you think that, DS Adaja?" asked the Hawk.

"It's a police cap. And if I'm not mistaken, that looks like silver braid on the peak."

"Impersonating a police officer may turn out to be the least of Lamont's problems. However, it's still a mistake he might live to regret," said the Hawk as he handed around another set of photographs of the two men coming out of the house twenty minutes later.

"Can you spot the difference?"

"Summers is now carrying the Sainsbury's bag MM took in earlier," said Jackie.

"And what does that tell us, DS Roycroft?"

"They are now in possession of the drugs and the money."

"And more important?"

"No one's been arrested," said Rebecca. "So they must have made a deal."

"Don't forget that PC Bailey told us nothing was recorded in Book 66, and Summers turned up at the nick the following morning empty-handed," said the Hawk.

"So now we have three bent coppers—if you include Lamont," said William. "But the fourth is nowhere to be seen."

"Perhaps Nicky was unaware of what was going on?" suggested Rebecca.

"Seems unlikely, as MM has confirmed she spent Friday night at Summers's home. But let's give her the benefit of the doubt for the time being," said the Hawk, sounding unconvinced. "Who's got the next question?"

"Where did Summers and Lamont go after they left Payne's house, if it wasn't back to the nick?" asked Rebecca.

"Good thinking," said the commander, handing out another set of photographs.

"MM followed them to the home of Jimmy Turner, the head of the family who lives on the other side of the patch. They were clearly expected, because the ground-floor light was on, and the front door was opened even before Summers knocked."

"Then what happened?" asked Paul.

"The two of them emerged about half an hour later, without the Sainsbury's bag. So what can we assume from that, even though it wouldn't stand up as evidence in court?"

"They handed over the drugs to the Turner family, but held on to the cash?"

"Which is why I emphasized at the beginning of this meeting that you must always follow the money," said the Hawk. "We now know they're in possession of our original ten thousand, and in time can also expect their cut on the drugs money. But what they don't know is that we have the serial numbers of every one of those banknotes, so the minute they try to spend any of the money, we'll be on to them."

"They're unlikely to go on a spending spree immediately," said William. "Lamont's far too canny to allow them to do anything that crass. Don't forget, the only reason you were able to get the holdall full of cash back after the drugs raid was because he hadn't started spending it."

"Summers might not be quite as patient, so he could still be our best bet."

"I think Summers has already done something even more stupid," said Rebecca, who couldn't resist pausing for a moment to ensure she had everyone's attention.

"Spit it out, DC Pankhurst," said the Hawk.

"When Nicky came down to breakfast on Sunday morning, she was wearing a diamond ring."

"Sunday morning?" repeated the Hawk. "But that was five days before they got their hands on the money."

"So it's still possible she wasn't involved in the raid," said Rebecca. "However, there's something else I think you ought to know, sir. The ring Nicky was wearing was a diamond solitaire. If it's real, it would have cost far more than a detective sergeant earns in a year."

"I suspect the ring went missing after a recent burglary when Summers was the arresting officer," said William. "In which case it shouldn't be difficult to trace, and we'll have them both bang to rights."

"How can you be sure it was a diamond solitaire?" asked the Hawk, switching his attention back to DC Pankhurst.

"It's not dissimilar to my mother's engagement ring," she said, looking embarrassed.

"We'll make a detective of you yet, DC Pankhurst," said the commander. "But on which finger is PC Bailey wearing the ring?"

Rebecca held up the third finger of her left hand.

"Poor girl," said the Hawk, sounding unusually sympathetic. "But we still can't afford to make a move yet. Any other developments on that front?"

"Yes," said Jackie. "Lamont has asked to see me again. We're having a drink on Saturday night."

"What does he want?" said Paul.

"After my lapse on the tube," said Rebecca, "I expect he wants to find out if he's being followed."

"So what do I tell him?" asked Jackie.

"What he wants to hear—no, he isn't," said William.

"Mind you," said the Hawk, "there will come a time when I want him to know he's under surveillance, but not quite yet."

William smiled, while Jackie looked puzzled, but neither of them asked the obvious question, because they knew they wouldn't get an answer.

"If Lamont gives you another brown envelope," said the Hawk, "we'll know he still thinks you're as bent as he is."

"Dare I ask how much was in the first one?" asked Jackie.

"No idea," said William. "I handed it straight in to the property store. But I'm looking forward to getting another one."

Jackie had the grace to smile.

⊸o⊷

"You have to understand, Mr. Booth Watson, I had no idea my son was a drug dealer. I thought he was the chairman of a small, reputable tea company. When he was arrested, it was as much of a shock to me as it was to my friends that he had been leading a double life."

Booth Watson steepled his hands as if in prayer but said nothing.

"I appreciate, Mr. Booth Watson, that you succeeded in having him cleared of the most serious charges, but I should tell you that I prayed he would be found guilty, and punished for his sins."

Booth Watson looked suitably contrite, but still made no attempt to interrupt his client while she was in a confessional mood.

"I'm sure you will recall my telling you at the time that I was loath to give evidence at the trial, as I would have had to admit I only saw Assem once a week on a Friday afternoon, and then just for a couple of hours." She paused for a moment before adding, "I confess that his death came as a blessed relief."

Booth Watson bowed his head.

"Most of my friends have deserted me," she continued, "so there's no longer any reason for me to remain in this country. I intend to move back to France as soon as possible. I pray that our Lord will not extend my life on this earth for much longer."

Booth Watson smiled at his client like a benign spider that had caught a large fly in its web, and had no intention of letting it escape. The last thing he wanted was for Mrs. Rashidi to die.

"With that in mind, I'm asking you to put my affairs in order, so I can return to my native Lyons."

"Be assured, madam," said Booth Watson, "I have been working night and day on your behalf, with that single purpose in mind. But your affairs, I fear, are somewhat complex. However, as time is of the essence, I may have come up with a solution to your problem."

"Which is, Mr. Booth Watson?"

The benign smile returned, the spider having spun some more threads in its web. "You could leave for Lyons whenever you wished, if—"

"If what?"

"If you felt able to grant me power of attorney over your affairs in your absence. I would be honored to represent you to the best of my ability. Of course, I would be only too happy to visit you in Lyons from time to time to keep you up to date."

"What would I have to do to make that happen?"

"If you sign this document, Mrs. Rashidi," he said, placing two sheets of paper in front of her, "your problems will become mine, and you can rest easy in the knowledge that I will always have your best interests at heart."

He handed his client a pen, and guided her to two penciled crosses. Mrs. Rashidi didn't spend a great deal of time reading the document before she signed it.

BW waited for the ink to dry before saying, "I remain your humble servant, madam," while giving her a slight bow.

"No, no, Mr. Booth Watson. It is I who should thank you."

---

Nicky came off duty just after four. She had decided the time had come to tell people she was pregnant, as it wouldn't be much longer before her condition was blindingly obvious. She glanced at her ring and smiled. She intended to take advantage of the three months' fully paid maternity leave offered to WPCs, after which she would decide whether to return to work or resign. One copper in the family was quite enough, in her opinion.

She let herself into the flat, and wasn't surprised to find it was in a mess. After all, she'd been away for the weekend. A stack of washing-up had been left in the sink, food still stuck to the plates. Rinsing was clearly not an activity Jerry considered a priority. She opened the kitchen window and set about washing up, hoping she would have completed the job before he came off duty.

Once she'd finished in the kitchen, she turned her attention to the bedroom. The bed was unmade, and Jerry's silk dressing gown had been left strewn on the floor. Just like James Bond, he'd once told her. She hung it on the back of the door before plumping up the pillows and pulling back the top sheet. She just stood there and thought she was going to be sick when she saw a pair of red lacy knickers in the middle of the bed. They certainly weren't hers. She collapsed on the floor and burst into tears. Had someone left them there deliberately, knowing she would be certain to find them?

How many times had Jerry sworn blind that he'd turned over a new leaf since he'd met her? *I've found the woman I want to spend the rest of my life with,* he'd told her often enough. Didn't the ring mean anything at all? Or was it in part exchange, just like her?

It didn't take long for Nicky's tears to turn to anger, as she thought about how many risks she'd taken for him, only to be discarded like an empty wrapper. She wanted him to walk in right now, so she could tell him exactly what she thought of him.

After an hour had passed, and he hadn't come home, she decided it was time to turn her thoughts into actions.

She got up off the floor, walked slowly back into the kitchen, and selected a large pair of scissors from a drawer. She returned to the bedroom and opened the wardrobe to find half a dozen suits, a couple of blazers, three pairs of gray flannel trousers, and a dozen silk ties.

She took out the first suit and cut off both sleeves of the jacket. The trousers followed, and by the time she'd finished, they could only have been worn by a schoolboy. The other suits were next in line, then the blazers, followed by the gray trousers, and finally the ties. Even a black bow tie, rarely worn, didn't escape execution.

She surveyed the carnage strewn across the floor, before returning the scissors to the kitchen drawer. She next took a hammer out of the tool kit under the sink before setting about destroying the TV in the lounge. Finally, she turned her attention to the vases, plates, cups and saucers, saving until last the dinner set that was only brought out for special occasions. Jerry had claimed it was a present from his mother. More likely John Smith. When Nicky was finished, she stood back and surveyed the damage. A bull in a china shop would have been proud of her.

Nicky sank to the floor, exhausted but exhilarated. Once she was fully recovered, she decided on her encore.

She sat down at Jerry's desk in the front room, took a large envelope from the top drawer, and dropped the lacy knickers and the diamond ring inside, before sealing it. She was about to close the drawer when she spotted his diary.

She turned the pages slowly until she was up to date. Seeing the words *Playboy Club, Park Lane,* underlined, she realized he wouldn't be back before midnight. She tried not to think about the bunnies.

She took a sheet of paper from the solid silver letter rack in front of her and wrote a short note that she would deliver on her way home that evening in the hope that DI Warwick would be left in no doubt whose side she was on.

# 24

They both arrived at the bank a few minutes before their appointment with the area manager. The young woman behind the reception desk checked their names on her clipboard and ticked them off.

"If you take the lift to the fifth floor," she said, "Miss Davis, Mr. Simpson's PA, will meet you and accompany you to the manager's office."

The two men carried out her instructions, and didn't speak in the crowded lift until the doors opened on the fifth floor where they were greeted by a young woman.

"Good morning," she said. "I'm Mr. Simpson's PA. He's looking forward to meeting you."

She led them down a long corridor to a door that announced in gilded letters, R. C. SIMPSON, AREA MANAGER. She knocked once, and didn't wait for a reply before opening the door and standing to one side.

"How nice to meet you," said Simpson, rising from behind his desk to shake hands with his potential new customers.

"You too," said Booth Watson politely. Faulkner didn't offer an opinion.

"Please take a seat," the manager said. Miss Davis sat behind him, notebook open, pen poised.

"Although all your papers were in order," said Simpson once his guests had settled, "I took the precaution of calling Mrs. Rashidi in Lyons to check that the bank had her authority to fully cooperate with you."

"I would have expected no less," said Booth Watson, offering his most benign smile.

"Mrs. Rashidi confirmed not only that you had full power of attorney, but I was to answer any questions you might have concerning her late son's estate. I am at your service, gentlemen."

"Thank you," said Booth Watson. "Perhaps I could start by seeing the details of any private accounts held in Mr. Rashidi's name, and the latest annual report from Marcel and Neffe."

Mr. Simpson handed over two thick files, having clearly anticipated both requests.

Faulkner turned to the back page and started with the bottom line, while Booth Watson continued with his list of prepared questions.

"Are there any other assets lodged with the bank for safekeeping that are not shown on Mrs. Rashidi's current account?"

"Her fifty-one percent holding in Marcel and Neffe. I can tell you in the strictest confidence that the other four shareholders would be willing to dispose of their stake in the company if they were to receive a realistic offer."

"As the share price has collapsed," said Faulkner, speaking for the first time, but not looking up, "I'm bound to ask what they would consider realistic."

"I think they would be willing to let their forty-nine percent go for two million pounds."

"Offer them one million, and make it clear it's a final offer, and there's no room for negotiation."

"But the company made a profit of three hundred thousand last year."

"That was last year. Frankly, I'd be surprised if they broke even this year. So I repeat, it's a final offer."

"I'll pass on your message," said Simpson, not sounding hopeful.

"Are there any other assets we should be aware of?" inquired Booth Watson, continuing to play the good cop.

"There most certainly are," replied Simpson. "Mr. Rashidi rented seven safety-deposit boxes that are kept in our vaults, but of course I have no idea of their contents. You may check them whenever it's convenient."

"It's convenient right now," said Faulkner, standing up and placing the files back on the manager's desk.

Simpson was taken by surprise, but quickly recovered. "That won't be possible, I'm afraid, unless of course you're in possession of Mrs. Rashidi's key."

Booth Watson produced the key from an inside pocket.

"Miss Davis," said Simpson, "please accompany Mr. Booth Watson and his colleague to the basement. I'll phone the head of security to warn him that they're on their way."

Miss Davis closed her notebook, rose from her place, and said, "Follow me, gentlemen."

Booth Watson shook hands with Simpson once again, before following Faulkner and Miss Davis out of the room and back to the lift.

"Nice weather we're having for this time of year," Miss Davis ventured as the lift made its way slowly down to the basement.

"Yes, indeed," said Booth Watson, who made no further observation on the weather or any other subject before the lift doors opened once again.

This time they were greeted by a tall, smartly dressed man, holding a large bunch of keys.

"Good morning, gentlemen. Please follow me," he said before leading them down a dimly lit corridor, until they reached a vast steel door. It took three of his keys and a six-digit code entered on a keypad on the wall before he was able to pull the heavy door open, revealing a room lined from floor to ceiling with hundreds of safety-deposit boxes. The security man checked several numbers in a small notebook before pulling out seven boxes and placing them on the table in the center of the room.

"We'll leave you now, gentlemen," said Miss Davis. "When you've completed your business, please press the green button on the wall. The door will open automatically, and I'll accompany you back to the manager's office."

"Thank you," said Booth Watson. Miss Davis and the head of security made a discreet exit, closing the door behind them.

Booth Watson took his time opening each of the seven boxes before they both checked their contents: cash, diamonds, bonds, and share certificates filled the first six boxes, but not the seventh. Booth Watson felt that Aladdin's Cave would have resembled a charity shop compared with the treasures that now surrounded them. It took him over an hour to make a complete inventory of the contents.

"I estimate," he said, "that there's over two million in dollars, and almost another million pounds in sterling. However, although they're used notes and therefore untraceable, the latest money-laundering laws will make it difficult for you to dispose of them in large amounts."

"That shouldn't prove a problem," said Faulkner. "There are plenty of members of the aristocracy who are only too happy to part with the odd family heirloom for cash, as long as I can produce a convincing copy to hang in its place, ensuring that there's no need for them to trouble the taxman. And you can also be assured there's no shortage of wealthy foreigners who are only too eager to acquire masterpieces in case they become suddenly persona non grata in their own countries and find themselves in need of disposable assets."

"That doesn't solve the problem of how you buy the remaining shares in Marcel and Neffe. Simpson would never accept a cash payment for that amount. Any transaction will have to be transparent and above board."

"And so it will be," said Miles. "Rashidi had three legitimate bank accounts, one of which is just over a million pounds in credit. So we can buy the other forty-nine percent of the company with his own money."

"How do you expect me to explain that to Mrs. Rashidi? She might not be quite as green as the banknotes."

"You can tell her it's tainted money, acquired by her son from illegal drug deals. Then she won't want anything to do with it."

"But what about her fifty-one percent holding in Marcel and Neffe?"

"I'm confident she'll part with those shares in exchange for Raphael's *Madonna di Cesare*."

"But that must be worth millions."

"It would be, if it was the original."

"What if she were to put it up for sale?"

"Not a chance. That God-fearing woman would rather die than sell the Virgin."

"Unless she comes across the original."

"That's highly unlikely, since I own it, and have no intention of putting it on the market."

"And how will I benefit from your master plan, bearing in mind that none of this," said Booth Watson with a grand sweep of his arm, "would have been possible without me?"

"You will handle the successful takeover of Marcel and Neffe, after which you will become the company's legal adviser, on a monthly retainer high enough to ensure that you never need to represent another client."

"With bonuses," suggested Booth Watson, looking at the piles of cash on the table in front of them.

"Of course," said Faulkner, taking several sealed packets of twenty-pound notes from one of the boxes and handing them to Booth Watson. "This should take care of life's little necessities for the time being. And should you run out, there's plenty more where that came from."

Booth Watson's smile remained in place as he dropped several wads of cash into his Gladstone bag, which was joined by the contents of the seventh box. "I'll take all the personal items to Lyons," he said, "and hand them over to Mrs. Rashidi. The photos, letters, and a few family mementos that I know she'll appreciate."

"Along with the copy of the Raphael, which I'm confident she won't be able to resist," said Faulkner.

"All in all, a good morning's work," declared Booth Watson, as he picked up his heavy bag while Faulkner pressed the green button. The door swung open to reveal Miss Davis and the head of security waiting for them. "We've finished for now," said Booth Watson. "But I will be returning from time to time."

⊸o⊷

Beth was feeding the twins when she heard the gate click. She looked out of the window to see a young woman pushing an envelope through their letterbox. *Probably a parish circular or an invitation to a local Conservative Party drinks evening,* she thought, both of which would be disappointed. She looked at the woman more closely as she walked back down the path. There was something familiar about her, but Beth couldn't place where or when she'd seen her before.

She was carrying the children upstairs when she heard the gate click a second time, and smiled at the thought that William was home early for a change. Once the twins were tucked up in their cots, she returned downstairs to find him reading a one-page note.

"Did you see who delivered this?" he asked, not looking up.

"Yes. And how lovely to see you too."

"Sorry," he said, taking her in his arms.

"I only got a brief glimpse of her. She was young, mid-twenties maybe, dark hair. I think she might have been pregnant."

William nodded and read the note a second time.

*Be at the Playboy Club in Park Lane at 7:30 this evening. Ignore the bunnies, keep an eye out for the poachers.*

"I've made your favorite dinner, Caveman," said Beth, "so I do hope you're hungry."

William handed her the note. After she'd read it, she said, "Hmm, that's somewhere you'll be able to mix with a lot of other cavemen, but I'd be willing to bet they don't serve shepherd's pie at the Playboy Club."

# 25

William arrived at the Playboy Club in Park Lane just after seven, confident that he'd have more than enough time to familiarize himself with the premises, as he knew Summers didn't come off duty until eight.

After signing in, he climbed the stairs to the first floor and entered the casino. He walked slowly around the gaming room, checking out the different ways of losing money. A dozen blackjack tables and several roulette tables manned by croupiers who spun the wheels while their customers followed the progress of a little white ball, fervently hoping that it would select their chosen number. Ninety-three percent of the time it didn't. At the back of the room William noticed a door marked PRIVÉ, through which he assumed only the high rollers were invited. An invitation that would never be extended to him.

After a second perambulation of the gaming hall, he took a seat at the end of the bar and waited for Summers to make an entrance.

"What can I get you, sir?" asked an attentive barman.

"An orange juice, please," said William, taking out his wallet.

"On the house, sir," said the barman to the first-time customer.

An hour passed, and still there was no sign of Summers. After a second hour, William was beginning to wonder if PC Bailey had set him up in the hope of getting her boyfriend off the hook, while leaving him to wish he stayed at home.

William almost fell off his barstool when the door opened and Bruce Lamont strolled in. William quickly headed for the nearest stairs, not even knowing where they led. When he reached the top step, he was greeted by the maître d.'

"Will you be joining us for dinner, sir?" inquired a man who was used to customers dining alone.

"No, thank you," said William. "I've already eaten." He glanced over the balcony to see Lamont standing at the bar just a few places away from where he had been sitting only a moment before. "But I would like a coffee," he said, eyeing a table at the far end of the balcony.

"Of course, sir. If you'd like to take a seat, a waitress will be with you shortly."

William's new vantage point gave him a panoramic view of the casino floor, while he remained half hidden behind a fake-marble pillar. Lamont was sipping champagne and chatting to the barman when Summers strolled into the casino and walked across to join him at the bar.

"What can I get you to drink, sir?" asked a young woman dressed in an outfit that left little to the imagination.

"Just a coffee," said William, trying not to stare at her trademark large rabbit ears and fluffy bobtail. "Black."

He turned his attention back to the bar, where Lamont and Summers were deep in conversation. William was beginning to wonder if they had chosen the club as their meeting place simply because they were unlikely to bump into anyone who would recognize them, but then the talking stopped. Summers stood up and headed for the nearest roulette table.

He handed the croupier a cellophane packet containing five

hundred pounds in five-pound notes that William had last seen in the Hawk's office. The croupier spread the cash out on the green baize and counted it before dropping the money into a plastic box for all to see. He then pushed a small stack of chips across the table to his new customer.

William didn't know a great deal about gaming, but he did know that roulette was one of the easiest ways to lose money. Nags and fillies came a close second, his father had warned him at an early age. If that weren't the case, he explained, it would be the casinos and the bookies, not the punters, who ended up broke.

A few minutes later Lamont joined him, taking the seat opposite, without acknowledging him. He handed over another five hundred, and also received a pile of chips. William sipped his coffee as he tried to work out what they were up to.

"*Faites vos jeux,*" said the croupier as he spun the wheel.

Lamont put five chips on black, while Summers placed the same amount on red, ensuring that one of them was certain to win, while the other was just as sure to lose.

"*Rien ne va plus,*" declared the croupier. The ball continued to spin around the outer rim before dropping toward the numbers where it bounced around for some time, finally settling in red 27.

The croupier raked in all the losing bets, including Lamont's, before pushing another five chips in Summers's direction.

"*Faites vos jeux,*" he announced again.

Some punters stuck with their favorite numbers without rhyme or reason, while others pursued supposedly infallible systems, ignoring the fact that a thousand books had been written on the subject, most of them out of print.

Lamont placed five more of his chips on black, while Summers stuck with red. Red 11. Summers won again, while Lamont lost. After two spins, between them they'd lost nothing and gained nothing, just broken even. It didn't take William long to work out exactly what they were up to.

They were simply and methodically disposing of the Hawk's numbered notes in exchange for chips that they would eventually cash in for a casino check. Their winnings could then be deposited at any bank, *the result of a run of luck at the tables,* should anyone ask. On two occasions zero came up, and they both lost their five-pound stake. A small blip in their overall plan, as they didn't have to pay for their free champagne and smoked salmon sandwiches.

After an hour had passed, Summers and Lamont gathered up their chips and headed for a different table, where once again they each handed over a cellophane packet containing five hundred pounds before continuing with their joint enterprise. William knew there was nothing he could do about it. He could imagine the Hawk's response if he called the local Crime Squad and asked them to raid the joint.

Another hour passed before they moved on to the next table, their pockets now bulging with chips. This strategy continued until the last packet of cash had been disposed of, when they finally left the table to join a small queue at the cashier's window. A teller made out two checks for three thousand nine hundred pounds each in exchange for their chips.

Summers and Lamont left the club with two hundred pounds less than they'd come in with, but with one essential difference. They'd disposed of the original banknotes.

William had to acknowledge that they'd found a way of laundering money right under the noses of the casino bosses and the police. He could only wonder how long it would be before a law would be passed to prevent others playing the same game.

Despite the late hour, William knew the commander would be sitting by his phone at home, waiting for a call. He came on the line before the second ring could disturb his wife.

"Enlighten me," said the Hawk, aware that only one person would be calling him at that time of night.

William took him through his evening at the Playboy Club, and when he came to the last spin of the wheel, all the Hawk had to say was, "Clever."

"But they made one mistake, sir," said William, "which might still catch them out."

"Enlighten me," he repeated.

"As far as I could tell they didn't launder all of the money. It looks to me as if they got rid of around eight thousand pounds in cash, so there's still two thousand out there somewhere."

"Don't forget that DI Castle will have been paid his share."

"I hadn't, sir. In fact, I was going to suggest we obtain search warrants for all three premises, and if we come across any of our numbered notes, we'll have them bang to rights."

"Castle and Lamont will be far too shrewd to make that kind of mistake," said the Hawk. "However, we might get lucky with an overconfident detective sergeant."

"At the same time," said William, "I think we should raid Jimmy Turner's place. I suspect the Turners have got lazy, and think that as a local copper is on their payroll they have nothing to fear. We may find a lot more than just the drugs Summers took from the Paynes and delivered to the Turners."

"Good thinking, William. Have everyone except PC Bailey in my office by seven o'clock tomorrow morning. If we're going to mount a full operation, we'll need to move quickly."

“Summers is off to Malaga for the weekend, sir, so while he’s out of the country it might be the ideal time to strike.”

“Agreed, but not until he’s boarded the plane and is on his way back.”

# 26

Every member of the team except PC Bailey was seated around the table in the commander's office long before seven the following morning.

William had told Beth over breakfast that he still couldn't make up his mind if Nicky was in bed with Summers, as well as sleeping with him.

"You can't have one without the other," suggested Beth, for whom things tended to be either black or white.

William didn't pass on his wife's opinion when the Hawk asked him to bring the team up to date. His description of how he ended up at the Playboy Club the previous night had them all on the edge of their seats.

"Well done, William," said the Hawk. "On balance, I think you were wise not to call in the local Crime Squad. However, we now have a genuine chance of mounting a successful operation without their help. Let me build you a skeleton before we all put some flesh on it."

As he began to share his initial ideas with the team, it became clear to William that the Hawk couldn't have gone back to bed after his phone call. When he had finished, all he said was, "Observations?"

Rebecca was the first to speak.

"Lamont may well be paying off his debts once again," she said, "but it's a rare day when he doesn't visit the bookies, or his wife can't be found loitering with intent in Harrods."

"And Summers?" said the Hawk, turning his attention to Jackie.

"He's traded in his old Jag for the latest model, paying on the never-never, so no one can query where the money's coming from. On Saturday he flies to Malaga with a Miss Karen Turner, also the latest model, although I have a feeling she won't be on the never-never."

The Hawk frowned. "What about DI Castle?"

"Lying low at the moment. No obvious extravagances that can't be explained."

"We could always visit the Playboy Club and check all the banknotes?" suggested Paul.

"No point. We'd never be able to prove who'd handed them over, and it would simply alert Summers and Lamont that we were on to them. We have to accept we've lost that one. Let's hope that while Summers is away we find some of the banknotes in one of their homes. What about PC Bailey?" said the Hawk, switching his attention back to Rebecca. "I thought she was meant to be going to Malaga with Summers?"

"Apparently not, sir. She came home last night in a foul temper, and perhaps more important, she was no longer wearing her engagement ring."

"Whose side do you think she's on now?" asked Jackie.

"Certainly not Summers's," said William, "otherwise she wouldn't have delivered that note to my home."

"We'll soon find out," said the commander, "because there's one more job I need her to do. So let's hope hell hath no fury like a woman scorned."

"Do you know where that saying comes from?" asked William, leaning back in his chair.

"*The Mourning Bride,*" said the Hawk, without missing a beat.

"Written by William Congreve in 1697," added Paul.

"A Restoration writer and dramatist who was educated at Trinity College Dublin," offered Rebecca.

"Born in 1670 and died in 1729," said Jackie, stifling a yawn.

William threw his arms in the air and accepted he'd been set up.

"Nevertheless," said Rebecca, "scorned or not, I think she's still in love with Summers." After telling the team everything Nicky had told her over breakfast that morning, she produced a small leather box and placed it in the middle of the table. "She left this on the hall stand this morning before she went back to Romford."

"I presume it's empty," said Paul, flicking open the lid.

"Yes, but as I said, Nicky was no longer wearing the ring, so she clearly wanted me to find the box."

William studied the gold lettering inside: *House of Garrard, founded 1735. 24 Albemarle Street, London W1.*

"It's often something small and unexpected that finally catches them out," said the commander. "Well done, Rebecca. However, I don't consider it would be appropriate for you to follow up this particular lead. Leave that to DI Warwick. Now let's all get back to work. We've only got a few days before Summers returns from Malaga, so remember, there's no sleep—"

"For the wicked," they all chorused.

William was standing outside the entrance of Garrard's in Albemarle Street forty minutes later, only to be greeted with a CLOSED sign. He checked the opening hours printed in neat black letters on the glass door: MON–SAT 10–5. He had to agree with F. Scott Fitzgerald: the rich are different.

He decided to take a walk around the block to kill some time before the jewelers opened. As he passed the Royal Institution, he spotted a poster in the window: *Visit Michael Faraday's laboratory.* It opened at nine o'clock.

He went inside, and joined a trickle of visitors as they descended the stairs that led to the laboratory of the great nineteenth-century scientist. William marveled at the genius of the man who'd first turned electrical power into mechanical motion, and vice versa. It amused him to read what Sir Robert Peel had said at the time, "But tell me, Faraday, what's the point of it?" To which Faraday had replied, "What's the point of a newborn baby, prime minister?"

It was only after the clock struck ten that William reluctantly stepped back into the twentieth century. He made his way upstairs and headed back to Garrard's. Running through his mind were the questions he'd prepared on the tube to Green Park earlier that morning. He remembered that Beth had once told him she would happily strangle anyone who even thought about stealing her engagement ring.

A uniformed guard opened the door for him as if he were a customer about to spend thousands of pounds on a bauble. He walked across to one of the counters and presented his warrant card to a young woman.

"Would it be possible to speak to the manager?"

The woman picked up a phone, pressed a button, and passed on the message. After a brief pause she put down the phone and said, "Please follow me, inspector."

She led him up an elegant spiral staircase to the first floor, where the manager was waiting for him.

"Good morning, inspector. My name is Paul Gumbley."

They shook hands, and Gumbley opened a door that led into an inner sanctum where kings, maharajahs, presidents, and the occasional dictator were invited to view treasures mere mortals would never see.

"How may I be of assistance, inspector?"

"I'm investigating the theft of an engagement ring that was purchased here," said William, as he handed over the little leather box bearing the Garrard's insignia.

"I'm afraid there's not a lot I can tell you from this," said the manager. "I don't suppose you have the receipt?" William shook his head. "Have you any idea how long ago it would have been purchased?"

"I'm not sure," said William.

"Oddly enough, one of your colleagues visited me some time ago, and asked about the theft of some jewelry." He opened a drawer in his desk, took out a diary, and began to turn back the pages.

*Tell me his name was Summers*, prayed William.

"Ah, yes, here it is," said Gumbley, after turning several pages of his diary. "An Inspector Prescott from West End Central. He came in to inquire about some jewelry that had been stolen from a house in Mayfair. Although I'm unable to reveal the name of the customer concerned, I can confirm that an engagement ring was among the items stolen."

"I'm grateful," said William. "Just out of interest, how much did the ring cost?"

"A little over three thousand pounds," said Gumbley casually.

"Then you're never going to meet my wife," said William, with a smile.

Gumbley accompanied him back downstairs. "I hope you find the man who stole the ring," he said, as he opened the shop door.

"He's not the one I'm after," said William, leaving a puzzled look on the manager's face.

Once he was back on Albemarle Street, he immediately headed for West End Central police station in Savile Row. He passed several art galleries on the way that he would have liked to drop into and browse for an hour or two, but not today.

When he reached the nick he went inside and presented his warrant card to the station officer, who checked it before taking a second look at him and asking, "How can I help, inspector?"

William wondered how old he'd have to be before other officers didn't look surprised by his rank. "Is Inspector Prescott on duty?" he asked.

"I saw him go up to his office earlier this morning. I'll give him a bell." He picked up the phone and said, "I have an Inspector Warwick at the desk, sir. He wondered if you could see him."

"Send him up!" barked a voice.

"Top of the stairs, first door on the right, sir," said the desk sergeant.

William thanked him, climbed the stairs, and knocked on the first door, waiting until he heard the command, "Come!" before entering.

William was greeted by a colleague who was clearly nearing the end of his career. A lined and crumpled face that had experienced a life of crime. He shook William warmly by the hand and said, "How can I help?"

"I'm following up a burglary in your manor. The theft of an engagement ring, among several other expensive pieces of jewelry. The manager of Garrard's told me that you visited him about it."

"Mr. and Mrs. van Haeften," said Prescott. He got up from behind his desk, walked across to a filing cabinet, and flicked through several files, before extracting one.

"Mr. van Haeften reported the theft last year," he said as he returned to his desk. "They'd only been married a few months, and Mrs. van Haeften left me in no doubt that she wanted her engagement ring back, and I should drop every other case I was working on until I found it."

William began to turn the pages, occasionally pausing to make a note and to sip from a mug of foul coffee. "Thank you, inspector," he said finally, handing back the file.

"Do you know who was responsible for the burglary?" asked Prescott.

"No. But I'm pretty sure I know the thief catcher who stole the ring from the thief."

Inspector Prescott knew when not to press for more information. "Please give my regards to the Hawk," he said.

"You know my boss?"

"We were at Hendon training college together. That's where he got his nickname. Are you by any chance Choirboy?"

⟜⟞

"Good work, inspector," said the Hawk, after he'd read William's report.

"Where do we go from here, sir?"

"You'll recall I said at this morning's meeting there was one more thing I needed PC Bailey to do."

"I think I've already worked out what that might be, sir."

"Enlighten me."

"You want her to check all of Summers's crime sheets to find out if he arrested a burglar soon after the theft of the jewelry from the van Haeftens' home, because that would explain how he got hold of a ring he clearly couldn't have afforded. Depending on her answer, we'll know whose side she's on."

"And if she's on the other side?"

"I'll arrest her the same day Summers comes back from his holiday."

"And just in case you thought this was going to be an easy week, inspector, you might be interested to know that Mr. Justice Ramsden has begun his summing-up in the Tony Roberts case."

"My father tells me it can only go one way. In fact, he was surprised Roberts didn't plead guilty after I'd told the court I saw him on the platform talking to the two men who threw Rashidi onto the track."

"That might not be enough to convince the jury. They may conclude he was no more than an innocent bystander who was as shocked as everyone else on the platform by what happened."

"Then why did he start running the moment he saw me?"

"Good question."

"And what about the dozen witnesses who also gave evidence?"

"Unfortunately, there are also a dozen people on the jury who may have been persuaded by Booth Watson's silver tongue."

"If we lose this case," said William, "I'd abolish the jury system."

"No, you wouldn't," said the Hawk. "That way lies tyranny."

---

"Can you remember when my birthday is, Caveman?"

"Today," replied William, as he took Beth in his arms. "I would have wished you a happy birthday this morning if you hadn't been sound asleep when I left."

"So where's my present?" she demanded, holding out both hands.

"Waiting for you on our table at your favorite restaurant."

"The Ritz?"

"Not yet. I'll have to make commissioner before we can spend an evening at the Ritz. Until then, you'll have to settle for Elena's."

"Where we went on our first date, how romantic."

"And before that, we're going to the Palace theater," said William.

"To see what?"

"*Les Misérables,*" said William, just as there was a knock on the door.

"Who can that be?"

"The babysitter. It's Suzy's night off. Why don't you go and get changed while I introduce her to the twins."

When Beth came back down thirty minutes later, William couldn't stop staring longingly at her.

"Not a chance, Caveman. After dinner if you're good."

William grinned as he took her hand. "The children are tucked up in their cots, and your carriage awaits, my lady."

"I don't think you can describe a second-hand Austin Allegro as a carriage? More like a pumpkin, I would have thought."

They both enjoyed the show from the moment the curtain rose, but Beth still rang home in the interval to check if the children were asleep. After they'd left the theater she sang "I Dreamed a Dream" all the way to the restaurant.

Gino guided them to their table in the corner, as he had done that first evening five years before. A green leather box awaited her. Gino uncorked a bottle of champagne while she opened it, to discover a necklace of cultured pearls. She gasped.

"Did you steal these when you visited Garrard's, Caveman?"

"No, my grandmother left them to me in her will, to be given to the woman I married."

"What took you so long?"

"I had to be sure you'd last," he teased, leaning across the table and placing the pearls around her neck.

Beth opened her compact and looked at her present. "Wow," she said. "Your grandmother had good taste."

"As did my grandfather, who brought them back from Tokyo to celebrate their thirtieth wedding anniversary."

"Do you think we'll make it to our thirtieth?" asked Beth, taking his hand.

"If we don't," said William, grinning, "I'll want the necklace back."

"Not a hope," said Beth as Gino reappeared at their table, notepad open, biro poised. "What's it to be?" he asked.

"We'd like the same meal we had on our first date," said William.

"Of course, but I will replace the bottle of Frascati with a vintage champagne," said Gino as he refilled their glasses.

"I have another surprise for you," said William after Gino had left them. "It shouldn't be too long before I rejoin the unit and officially go back to work at the Yard."

"What's changed?"

"PC Bailey. I think she's back playing for the home team, which will make all our lives easier."

"Will she have to face an inquiry?"

"With a bit of luck that won't be necessary," said William as a waiter placed a bowl of stracciatella in front of him.

"Did I really order soup on our first date?"

"Followed by spaghetti bolognese. While I had the smoked salmon and the veal piccata with lemon sauce and creamed spinach."

"How did I ever get a second date?"

"I could see the raw potential," said Beth. "Even if you're taking your time about it."

"Are you the director of the Fitzmolean yet?" asked William, fighting back.

"No, but there's a rumor that Tim will be awarded a knighthood in the New Year's honors list, and he may soon be moving on to greater things."

"As may you?" asked William.

A waiter was whisking away their first course when Beth suddenly grabbed William's hand. "Don't look now, but Christina's just walked in."

"Is she with the captain?" whispered William, as their main course was placed in front of them.

"No, a rather dishy younger man I've never seen before."

"I wouldn't have thought Elena's was her style," said William, twirling a forkful of spaghetti.

"Unless she doesn't want to be seen by any of her friends."

"Didn't you tell me she was getting quite serious about Captain Neville?"

"That was certainly the impression she gave me when I last saw her, which was only a few days ago. She told me they were going on holiday to New York—on the *Alden,* no less. Frankly, I'm surprised she's gone back to her old ways."

"I'm not," said William.

"Do you think we should go over and say hello?"

"She wouldn't thank you for that," said William, "so I'd stay put."

"I feel sorry for Ralph. I rather liked him. But then, you always thought he was a gold digger."

"It's not quite that simple," said William. "There's something about Captain Ralph Neville that doesn't ring true," he added, as their plates were cleared away.

Gino rejoined them a few moments later carrying a birthday cake. He took a deep breath and was just about to deliver a raucous version of "Happy Birthday" when William whispered firmly, "Not tonight, Gino."

"Why not, *signore*? I'm known as the Pavarotti of Potters Bar."

"No doubt, but we're trying not to attract the attention of a certain lady who's sitting on the other side of the restaurant."

"Ah, *Signora* Christina," whispered Gino, joining in the game.

"Is she a regular?" asked William.

"Certainly. It's the gentlemen who aren't."

Beth laughed. "Is there any way we can get out of here without her noticing?"

"Not a problem," said Gino. "I'll take you through to the kitchen and out of the staff entrance."

"Not before I've paid," said William, reaching for his wallet.

"This one's on the house," said Gino as he began to wrap up the birthday cake in a napkin. "By the way, I love the necklace."

⊸o⊷

"Harrison. Craig Harrison," said Nicky when she joined Rebecca for breakfast the following morning. "A petty thief with a record as long as your arm."

"Did Summers arrest him for burglary earlier in the year?"

"Yes, on May the twenty-third, for a separate offense," confirmed Nicky, taking a seat at the kitchen table, although Rebecca noticed that she didn't touch her breakfast.

"Was he charged?"

"The following day, and when he came up in front of the magistrate, he pleaded guilty and asked for eight other offenses to be taken into consideration. But I suspect there's only one the Hawk will be interested in."

"Will you be briefing him?"

"I've already left my report on his desk."

"That's good news," said Rebecca, taking her hand.

"I've also decided I won't be returning to the force after the baby is born."

"I wouldn't tell anyone else that," said Rebecca. "After all, you may feel differently in a few months' time."

"That seems unlikely," said Nicky, "since the child's father will be serving a long prison sentence, and I'll be the one who turned him in."

"Summers is the father?"

"Oh, come on. There's no need to pretend you didn't know."

Rebecca sat down next to her friend and put an arm gently around her shoulder.

"Do the rest of the team know?" asked Nicky.

"Yes. They have done for some time, and I'm afraid I'm to blame."

Nicky turned to face her flatmate, tears streaming down her face.

"As soon as I saw the ring, I knew Summers couldn't afford a diamond that size on a copper's salary."

"It could have been given to me by someone else."

"Like an estate agent from Croydon, for example? I don't think so."

"But I gave it back," said Nicky defensively, "and left the Garrard's box where you couldn't miss it."

"I handed it to DI Warwick that same morning."

"I assumed you would."

"And it's thanks to you," said Rebecca, "that we now know Summers arrested Harrison after he'd stolen the ring, so—"

"Will I be arrested?"

"Let's hope it doesn't come to that," said Rebecca gently. "I know the commander doesn't think you were involved in any of DS Summers's criminal activities, and he's well aware you alerted DI Warwick about his visit to the Playboy Club, which must count in your favor."

"But not in Jerry's."

"He doesn't deserve your sympathy."

"You've been such a good friend," said Nicky, taking her hand.

"Not as good as I'd like to have been."

---

"Do you find the prisoner at the bar, Anthony Roberts, guilty or not guilty of murder?"

The foreman of the jury rose slowly from her place. She looked up at the judge and said, "Guilty, m'lud." William leaped up and dashed out of court, forgetting to bow as he pushed his way through the doors and headed for the nearest phone. "Guilty," he said when he heard the Hawk's voice on the other end of the line.

"So you won't be abolishing the jury system after all?"

"No, sir. But I may change my mind if Summers is acquitted."

"You may not have a job if Summers is acquitted," responded the Hawk.

# 27

"We've got a problem."

"Don't spare me," said Miles.

"Not over the phone."

"That bad?"

"I'm afraid so," said Booth Watson. "Where will you be later this morning?"

"I've got a board meeting in the City at ten."

"Cancel it. Join me in chambers as quickly as possible."

"But I'm chairing the meeting—"

"You may not be chairman by this evening."

"That bad?"

⊸o⊷

Danny ignored the double yellow lines, restricted areas, and short-term parking signs as he drove the commander into Gatwick Airport and headed toward a gate the general public were unaware of.

A guard checked Commander Hawksby's warrant card before pointing to the far end of the runway, where he was met by Chief Superintendent Bob Fenton, the head of airport security, and three uniformed officers.

"Good morning, Bob," said the Hawk as he stepped out of the car and the two men shook hands. "Can you bring me up to date?"

"Flight zero one six took off from Malaga at nine thirty-five this morning," said Fenton. "About fifteen minutes behind schedule. It's due to land in about thirty minutes."

"Perfect timing," said the Hawk, who returned to his car and asked Danny to get DS Adaja on the radio. A few minutes later a familiar voice came crackling down the line.

"Morning, sir."

"Morning, Paul. Summers is safely on board, and his flight is about half an hour away from Gatwick, so no one can get in touch with him. I want you to move in and arrest Castle, and at the same time DS Roycroft's team should carry out a meticulous search of his home. I'm looking for any items that look expensive and out of place. Drugs and numbered notes would be a bonus."

"What about Summers's house?"

"Tell Jackie to take the place apart. If you come across a diamond ring, call me immediately, because that's all the evidence we need."

"DC Pankhurst and her team are already stationed outside Summers's home waiting for you to give the order," said Paul. "On your command, the search party will immediately move into action, while I go to the local nick and introduce myself to DI Castle."

"Get on with it," said the commander as he handed the radio back to Danny.

"Zero one six has requested permission to land," said Fenton. "They'll taxi to gate forty-three where your colleague and two of my men are already waiting. Perhaps we should join them."

"Superintendent Watts on the line," said Danny, handing the radio back to the Hawk.

"Good morning, Chris," said the Hawk to the new head of the drugs squad. "Was Jimmy Turner expecting you and a few friends to drop in for breakfast this morning?"

"No, sir. He was still in bed when I raided his home and arrested him along with three other members of his family."

"What did you charge them with?"

"Possession of eight kilos of cocaine, among several other illegal substances. Some of which just happened to be in a Sainsbury's bag."

The Hawk smiled. "I look forward to telling DS Summers the good news when I arrest him in a few minutes' time."

"I'll see you back at the station, sir," said Watts. "Let's hope they've got enough cells to accommodate them."

"Well done, Chris. I'll try to remember to let the commissioner know the role you played."

"I'm sure you will, sir," said Watts, laughing.

"Let's get going," said the Hawk as he passed the radio phone back to Danny. "Mustn't keep DS Summers waiting."

---

Miles handed the cab driver a pound note and told him to keep the change. He made his way slowly across Middle Temple, still trying to fathom why Booth Watson wanted to see him so urgently. Two young women walked past him, one pulling a small case, the other wearing a barrister's gown. He recognized both of them, but they didn't recognize him.

When he reached No. 1 Fetter Court, he didn't have to scan the list of names painted on the white brick wall to discover on which floor the head of chambers resided. He climbed the creaky wooden staircase to the second floor and knocked on the door. Not for the first time, he felt like a naughty schoolboy about to face the headmaster's wrath for failing to hand in his weekly essay.

The door was opened by Miss Plumstead, the head of chambers' secretary, who showed him through to Booth Watson's inner sanctum.

"Good morning, Captain Neville," said Booth Watson, as he waited for his secretary to leave the room.

"What can possibly be so important that I'm expected to cancel a board meeting and come running?" said Miles once the door had closed.

"Mrs. Rashidi's dead." Booth Watson paused to allow his client to take in the news. "She died peacefully in her sleep yesterday afternoon," he said as his client collapsed into the nearest chair.

Miles was silent for some time before he asked, "Who did she leave the Raphael to?"

"She's left everything, including the Raphael, to the Brompton Oratory, her church in Kensington," said Booth Watson, reading directly from the will.

"That's all right then," said Miles. "The Oratory will hang the painting in the church for all its parishioners to worship, and no one will be any the wiser."

"That might well have been the case if the Oratory didn't need a new roof, which will cost over a million pounds. I understand the church council considered it nothing less than a miracle when Raphael's Madonna appeared at the moment they most needed her."

"Then we have to get it back before anyone finds out it's a fake," said Miles. "Offer them a million."

"That may not be enough. Unfortunately, one of the church wardens is a director of Christie's, so you can be sure the council will seek his opinion. But I think I may have a solution to the problem." At that moment the door opened, and Miss Plumstead appeared with a tray of coffee and biscuits.

"I would be honored to be the guest speaker at your Falklands reunion dinner in October, Captain Neville," said Booth Watson without missing a beat, as she poured them both coffee.

"I'll inform the committee at our next meeting. And we'd hoped you'd propose the health of the club, which I, as secretary, will be replying to," said Miles, as Miss Plumstead left the room.

"So what's your solution?" pressed Miles, the moment she had closed the door behind her.

"As we both know, Raphael's *Madonna di Cesare* is a fake and not the original. . . . What makes it worse," continued Booth Watson, "is when I handed over the picture to Mrs. Rashidi, in exchange for her shares in Marcel and Neffe, the contract included the original paperwork and proof of provenance, so neither the Oratory nor Christie's will have any reason to doubt its authenticity."

"So what are you advising me to do?"

"You have no choice but to buy it back when it comes up for sale at Christie's. If the Oratory were to discover it's a fake, it wouldn't take them long to find out who sold the painting to Mrs. Rashidi in the first place, and then work out where the original is."

"But I'm dead," said Miles. "Just in case you've forgotten."

"And Christina is still very much alive, and this would give her another stick to beat you with because she knows the original is hanging in Monte Carlo."

"I still don't fancy coughing up over a million for a fake when I already own the original."

"I sympathize with you, Miles, but it's a better alternative to spending the next ten years in solitary."

"I could kill Christina."

"Then you'd end up spending twenty years in solitary. No,

I think I've come up with a better solution for how to deal with Christina."

"Namely?"

"Marry her."

⊸o⊷

Danny drove slowly around the perimeter of the airport before coming to a halt at gate 43. The commander got out and introduced Fenton to his colleague.

"Good morning, inspector," said Fenton. "I hope we haven't kept you waiting too long."

"About six months, sir," said William, as he shook hands with the chief superintendent.

"Well, you won't have to wait much longer," said the Hawk as they watched flight 016 touch down at the far end of the runway and begin to taxi toward them. It took several minutes for the plane to come to a halt at the gate and as it approached, the commander had to hold on to his hat to prevent it being blown off by the thrust of the engines.

Two ground staff pushed a flight of steps toward the aircraft door.

"Summers and his companion are in row nine, seats A and B," said Fenton, checking his booking sheet, "so they should be among the first off the plane."

The plane's door swung open, and the Hawk walked across to the bottom of the steps and began scanning the passengers as they made their way down onto the tarmac. It wasn't long before William said, "That's him. Six foot two, navy blazer, jeans, and an open-neck shirt."

"And I assume that's Karen Turner behind him," said the Hawk.

"What makes you say that, sir?" said William.

"Look at the third finger of her left hand."

William switched his attention to an attractive blonde who looked as if she had just spent a fortnight in the sun.

"This is going to be a holiday she'll never forget," said William. "Do we arrest both of them?"

"No, just Summers. I'll take Miss Turner to one side and relieve her of the engagement ring," said the Hawk. "Let's hope they haven't set a date for the wedding before 2010."

As Summers and Miss Turner stepped onto the tarmac, five officers headed toward them. William and two young constables blocked Summers's path, while the commander and a WPC took his companion to one side.

"DS Jerry Summers," said William, who produced his warrant card. "I'm Detective Inspector Warwick, and I am arresting you on suspicion of handling stolen goods and misconduct in a public office. You do not have to say anything, but it may harm your defense if you do not mention, when questioned, something which you later rely on in court. Anything you do say may be given in evidence."

Summers looked shocked, and quickly glanced back at Karen, only to see her being led away by an older man and a WPC. Two uniformed officers thrust his arms behind his back and handcuffed him before he was taken to the waiting police car. He said nothing.

⊸o⊷

"Let me begin this meeting," said the commander, "by officially welcoming back Detective Inspector Warwick. He's been on what the civil service call gardening leave, even though he doesn't have a garden. Whereas in fact, as you all know, for the past five months he's been operating as my UCO, and kept me well informed, which is why I've been able to stay a yard ahead of the rest of you. Even his wife has been kept in the dark, such was the secrecy of this operation."

*Well, not quite,* William wanted to say, but decided against it.

"PC Bailey must have worked it out," said Paul, "because she tipped William off about Summers's and Lamont's visit to the Playboy Club, which proved they were working in tandem."

"Nicky certainly played her part by briefing me on why I should go to the Playboy Club that night," said William.

"Agreed," said Jackie. "But we shouldn't ignore the fact that PC Bailey withheld vital information for some time, which could have speeded up our investigation."

"Perhaps we should also remember," said DC Pankhurst, "that she doesn't intend to return to the force after her baby is born."

"Which would solve one problem," said the commander. "Because I'm still to be convinced she played any part in Summers's illegal activities."

"Though she was happy to flaunt an expensive diamond ring given to her by Summers," said Jackie, "which she must have known he couldn't afford, and therefore had to be stolen."

"But she gave it back to him," Rebecca reminded her, "and left the Garrard's box where I was certain to find it. If she's guilty of anything, it's poor judgment, something all of us have been at some time."

"If she did apply to rejoin the Met in the future," said Jackie, "would you be willing to turn a blind eye?"

"She must know that would be unwise, given the circumstances," said the commander, looking directly at DC Pankhurst. "Now, let's move on to Summers and the Payne family, and what we have planned for them. Inspector Warwick?"

"I arrested Detective Sergeant Summers at Gatwick Airport

yesterday morning, and charged him with handling stolen goods and misconduct in a public office. To my surprise he was granted bail—until I found out that Booth Watson was his defense counsel."

"Summers couldn't begin to afford his fees," said DS Adaja.

"But Karen Turner's father certainly can," said William. "And he doesn't want his daughter's fiancé ending up in jail. So we can expect Summers to appear at the Old Bailey in about six months' time, which should give us more than enough time to prepare our case."

"And him to prepare his," said the Hawk. "What about Castle?"

"We didn't find enough evidence to charge him," said Jackie, not bothering to open her file.

"You didn't find anything incriminating in his home?" pressed the Hawk.

"A brand-new TV and a gold cigarette lighter he claims is a family heirloom. Not nearly enough to be confident of securing a conviction."

"He'll still have to resign," said the commander, "once everyone works out why his home was searched."

"And Lamont?" asked William.

"I couldn't lay a glove on him," admitted Rebecca. "My team didn't find any money with the serial numbers we're looking for at his home, or anything else that would implicate him, so like Jackie, I couldn't charge him. Impersonating a police officer and spending an evening at the Playboy Club with his friend Summers is a long way from being beyond reasonable doubt."

"So he's going to get away with it again?" said William.

"Unless DS Roycroft has something worthwhile to tell us following their latest get-together," said the Hawk.

"He was on a fishing expedition, sir," said Jackie. "Told me he'd read about Summers's arrest in the press and wondered if we'd picked up the connection between the two of them."

"What did you tell him?" asked William.

"I looked suitably surprised when he told me he'd been an inspector at Romford when Summers was a recruit, but claimed he couldn't remember him."

"Then he's got a very short memory," said the Hawk. "Did you let slip the one piece of information we wanted him to know about?"

"Yes, I did, sir."

"And were you appropriately rewarded?"

Jackie opened her handbag, took out a brown envelope, and handed it over to the commander, who tore it open and extracted a thick wad of five-pound notes. He distributed them among the team, who immediately set about checking the serial numbers, but without producing any cries of "Gotcha!"

"I suppose that would have been too much to hope for," said the Hawk as he put the money back in the envelope and handed it to William. "See that it's logged into the property store, along with DS Roycroft's report."

William nodded.

"So for now, let's concentrate on Summers. Did you find anything incriminating in his flat, DS Roycroft?"

"No, sir," said Jackie. "It's somewhat ironic that PC Bailey trashed the place, because that could be what saves him."

"How's that possible?" asked the Hawk.

"She destroyed all the relevant evidence. We found what was left of it on a local council tip."

"That wasn't the reason she did it," said Rebecca.

"Possibly not," said Jackie, "but it might get her boyfriend off the hook."

"He wasn't her boyfriend by then."

"Cut it out, you two," said William sharply, "and try to remember that we'll be needing PC Bailey to act as a defense witness at Summers's trial." He turned his attention back to Jackie. "So what it comes down to, DS Roycroft, is that you didn't find anything that could be used as evidence?"

"Just a silver letter rack, a couple of designer watches, and a few pounds in cash, but none of the serial numbers matched up with our original batch."

"However, thanks to Summers's arrogance, greed, overconfidence, call it what you will," said the Hawk, "we've got the diamond ring, which should be more than enough to send him down and set a trap for Lamont. Congratulations to you all on a job well done. But remember, by the time the case comes to court, you can be sure that Summers will be able to explain away the ring, the designer watches, the silver letter rack, and anything else we come up with. So none of us can afford to relax until we see him being driven away from the Old Bailey in a Black Maria, and not driving himself off in his latest Jag."

"Would you like to hold him?" said Nicky, as she handed the baby to Rebecca.

"You're so lucky," said Rebecca, cradling the little bundle in her arms.

"I don't always feel that way," admitted Nicky, "considering that Jake may not be seeing his father until he's a teenager."

"You can always visit him in jail."

"Not while he's engaged to another woman. In any case, I'll never allow my son to see the inside of a prison. That's how they get used to the idea."

"Does that mean you've agreed to give evidence against Summers?"

"The Hawk didn't give me a lot of choice, unless I wanted to join him in the dock."

"Your evidence could prove crucial," said Rebecca as she handed the little boy back to his mother.

"I'm aware of that," said Nicky quietly. "I won't let you down this time."

"You still love him, don't you?"

It was some time before PC Bailey responded. "Yes, but that won't stop me giving vital evidence that will put Jerry away, even though it means I'll also end up serving a life sentence."

---

There was a gentle tap on the door of Beth's office. Before she could respond, it opened and Christina swept in. She was wearing an Armani suit and a silk Hermès scarf and carrying a Gucci handbag that wouldn't have left anyone in doubt why she suffered from the illusion of entitlement, not unlike a minor member of the Royal Family.

It amused Beth that Christina never made an appointment to visit her at the gallery. Not only did she assume her friend would be there whenever she called, but she would always be available. Her accomplices, Rembrandt, Rubens, and Vermeer, didn't harm her cause.

"Lovely to see you," said Beth, as if she had nothing better to do. She kissed Christina on both cheeks. "To what do I owe this unexpected pleasure?" she added.

"I was just passing and thought I'd drop by."

Beth knew only too well Christina was never just passing. She always had a motive for her unannounced visits. She sat down in the most comfortable chair in the room, to indicate this wasn't going to be a short meeting.

"I have a couple of pieces of news I wanted to share with you."

Beth took the seat opposite the Fitzmolean's most generous benefactor, interested to discover what had caused her to rise so early that morning.

"But first, how is my favorite inspector?"

"He's spending most of the time preparing for a major corruption trial at the Old Bailey, when he'll have to be at his best, because he's up against Booth Watson again."

"Not a man I've ever cared for," said Christina. "I much prefer your father-in-law."

"Sir Julian will be representing the Crown on this occasion, which doesn't make life any easier for William. But do tell, why did you want to see me?"

"Ralph has asked me to marry him."

"And you said?"

"Yes! I do so love the man."

"Congratulations," said Beth, attempting to look suitably delighted, although she couldn't help recalling that the last time she'd seen Christina was at Elena's, and it wasn't Ralph's leg she had a hand on.

"It's beautiful," said Beth when Christina thrust out her left hand to reveal a simple diamond solitaire, looking a little lost among its more sparkling rivals.

"Have you fixed a date?"

"August the twenty-second."

"Weren't you meant to be sailing to New York on the *Alden* around that time?"

"I was, but that's the only Saturday before the end of September when Limpton parish church isn't already booked for a wedding.

So rather than wait until then, we decided to ditch the trip in favor of the more important event. Which was the other reason I wanted to see you. We wondered if you'd like to take our place?"

"You must be joking," said Beth. "We couldn't afford steerage on the *Alden*!"

Christina burst out laughing. "No, you'd simply take over our state room, as we weren't able to cancel the booking at such short notice. If the truth be known, you'd be doing us a favor." She paused to allow Beth to recover. "Unless, of course, you think William might object?"

"If he does," said Beth, "I'll go without him."

"Good. Then that's settled. But there's something even more important I need to discuss with you."

Beth wondered what could possibly be more important than getting married.

"To celebrate our betrothal, Ralph and I would like to present the Fitzmolean with an appropriate gift to mark the occasion."

"How generous of you," said Beth, although she couldn't help wondering what the word "appropriate" meant.

"As I'm sure you know, my darling, a Raphael is coming up for auction in the autumn sales, and we both felt the Fitzmolean is where that particular lady should spend the rest of her days."

"You're not referring to the *Madonna di Cesare,* by any chance?" asked Beth, not attempting to hide her excitement.

"The very same."

"But wasn't that painting originally part of Miles's collection?"

"Yes, but he gave it to a friend just before he died. However, I know he'd originally intended to leave it to the Fitzmolean in his will."

"What an incredibly generous gesture," said Beth, almost lost for words.

"There is one small condition attached to the gift."

*Of course there is*, thought Beth, but remained silent.

"I'll be in Monte Carlo with Ralph when the auction takes place, and will need someone to bid for the painting on my behalf. I couldn't think of anyone better than you to do my bidding."

"I'm flattered. But wouldn't it be more appropriate for Tim Knox to represent you? He is, after all, the gallery's director," said Beth as she began to rummage around in the bottom drawer of her desk in search of the latest sales catalogues so she could check the picture's high and low estimates.

"Eight hundred thousand to one million," said Christina, before Beth had turned to Lot 25, Raphael's *Madonna di Cesare,* the property of a lady.

"And how high would you allow me to bid?"

"A million should see off any rivals."

"That's way beyond the gallery's limit, so I'd need some form of security."

"I thought you might say that," said Christina. She opened her handbag, took out a check, and handed it to Beth.

Beth's hand started trembling when she saw the figure of £1,000,000.

"Of course, if someone outbids you, you won't need to cash the check, but that seems unlikely."

"What I don't know," said Beth, "is how to begin to thank you."

"Wait until the Madonna is hanging on the wall of the Fitzmolean before you do that," said Christina, "and don't forget, it has to remain our little secret."

"Yes, of course," said Beth, although she knew there was one person she would have to tell. So did Christina.

"Don't forget the Summers trial opens on Monday," the Hawk reminded them. "However, there are still a couple of jobs that need to be covered before the jury is selected."

William and Jackie opened their notebooks.

"DS Roycroft, I want you to arrange another meeting with Lamont. Tell him something has arisen that he needs to know about immediately."

"What has arisen?" asked Jackie.

"I want you to warn him that while the trial is taking place a team of surveillance officers will be tailing him twenty-four/seven."

"What will I say if he asks why they're tailing him?"

"He'll know why," said the Hawk.

Jackie closed her notebook.

"I haven't got enough officers available for a full surveillance operation," admitted William.

"You won't need them. It will be enough for Lamont to believe he's being watched to ensure he doesn't take any risks. Which brings me on to someone who doesn't give a damn about taking risks. 'Bones' Turner."

William frowned at the mention of Jimmy Turner's youngest son, whose sole purpose in life seemed to be ensuring that members of his family were found not guilty whenever the odds were stacked against them. He didn't bother with bribes or blackmail. He'd discovered the threat of broken bones or a car crash was so much more persuasive.

"He's currently out on probation having served two years of a four-year sentence for GBH," said Paul.

"Then find any excuse to put him back inside for a couple of months until the trial is over."

"He's notorious for turning up late for his weekly meetings with the probation officer. I'll have two officers waiting for him next time, who can ship him straight back to Pentonville, and leave him there until the trial's over."

"Good. While we're on the subject of the trial, William, I hope you're well prepared to be cross-examined by Booth Watson this time?"

"I can't wait," admitted William, "and intend to mention the superb, magnificent, expensive diamond ring again and again, given the slightest opportunity."

# 28

"Will the prisoner please stand up?"

Summers rose from his place in the dock. He was wearing a brand-new suit, a white shirt, and a blue silk tie.

"Jeremy Richard Summers, you have been charged with handling stolen goods, and by so doing, misconduct in public office. How do you plead?"

"Not guilty," said Summers, looking directly at the clerk of the court.

"You may be seated."

Mr. Justice Ramsden looked down from the bench to see Sir Julian quivering, like a greyhound in the slips, waiting to deliver his opening statement. Unlike Mr. Booth Watson, who was slouched at the other end of counsels' bench giving the appearance of a dormouse, half asleep. But then, Booth Watson knew it would be some time before he would need to open his eyes.

"Sir Julian," said the judge, turning his attention to the eminent QC. "If you would care to open proceedings."

Sir Julian rose from his place, tugged at his long black gown, and adjusted his graying wig as he always did before turning to face a jury. He greeted the eight men and four women with a benevolent smile, aware that they were the most important twelve people in the court.

He glanced down at his prepared script, even though he'd considered the possibility that Summers would plead guilty, and all the hours of work would be made redundant with a single word. Years of experience had taught him that wasn't a risk a barrister can take.

"M'lud," he began, looking up at the bench, "I represent the Crown in this case, along with my junior, Ms. Grace Warwick, while my learned friend Mr. Booth Watson appears for the defense." He gave Booth Watson a reluctant bow that was not reciprocated.

"I must open my submission with a warning," said Sir Julian, turning his attention to the jury. "The offense on which you are about to make a judgment is among the most disreputable any public servant can commit. The proof of this is the sentence determined by Parliament should you decide the prisoner is guilty—" he paused, and looked directly at them—"is life imprisonment.

"All citizens when dealing with a servant of the Crown, whether it be a distinguished judge or a bobby on the beat, have the right to assume the integrity of that person is beyond question. When that trust is broken, and in this case it was broken beyond repair, a draconian sentence is surely justified.

"Detective Sergeant Summers appeared to be an outstanding police officer, with a record of arrests and commendations that heralded a brilliant career. But he chose to use those talents to break the law, not uphold it.

"Temptation is part of every police officer's daily experience, and the vast majority of them would never consider even for a moment crossing that line. But unfortunately there are some, though thankfully only a small number, who have no such scruples. Detective

Sergeant Jerry Summers is such a man, as you will discover as this trial unfolds.

"This, ladies and gentlemen of the jury, is not a matter of a single lapse of judgment that might be overlooked when weighed against an otherwise commendable record of service to the community. Detective Sergeant Summers set up a clandestine network as well organized and effective as that of any professional gang in the criminal underworld.

"Members of the jury, you will learn during the course of these proceedings how Summers, on numerous occasions after he'd made an arrest for theft or burglary, then made sure that some of the most valuable stolen goods were not handed in to the police station and detailed on his custody record, but would end up in Summers's home or distributed among his friends and associates.

"Unlike you or me," said Sir Julian, once again looking directly at the jury, "Detective Sergeant Summers didn't need to visit the high street if he wanted a new television set, the latest hi-fi, or even a Jaguar. Instead, he simply removed them from among the stolen goods he had access to during the course of his duty. You may ask why the thieves themselves didn't bring this to the attention of the authorities. But why would they, when a reduction in the number of items they were charged with having stolen meant they might receive a more lenient sentence?

"However, that was still not enough to satisfy Detective Sergeant Summers's wanton greed. For years his local district of Romford had been prey to two rival criminal families, the Paynes and the Turners. He decided to actively assist one of those ruthless gangs, in order to tip the balance in their favor, and perhaps more important, in his.

"He set about arresting members of the Payne family, while allowing his paymasters in the Turner gang to escape scot-free. And while he was lining his pockets with their ill-gotten gains, he was at the same time receiving praise, and official commendations, for his exemplary police work. A modern-day Jekyll and Hyde.

"But like so many criminals, he went one step too far when Scotland Yard set a trap to tempt him that he was unable to resist."

Booth Watson wrote down the words *Set a trap.* A trap he later intended to spring.

"The Crown will produce witnesses who will testify under oath that Summers stole drugs from one gang, sold them to the rival family he was working for, and then pocketed the proceeds. By doing so he was able to make more money in a month than he could hope to earn in a year as a detective sergeant. But then he made one fatal error. He attempted to involve an honest police officer in his crimes, who didn't hesitate to report him to her superiors."

Booth Watson wrote the words *Didn't hesitate* on his yellow pad.

"When that officer gives evidence, you will be left in no doubt of the extent of Detective Sergeant Summers's criminal activities. Your verdict will be a resounding blow in the battle to protect ordinary, decent citizens from a corrupt individual who has betrayed the reputation of the most respected police force in the world."

Sir Julian sat down not to tumultuous applause, but to something far more important, a jury that had hung on his every word. Even Booth Watson had to admit, if only to himself, that he had never witnessed his warring rival on better form. But only the first shot had been fired across his bows.

"You may call your first witness, Sir Julian," said the judge.

"Thank you, m'lud. I call Detective Inspector William Warwick."

⊸o⊷

Lamont looked down at the eight men and four women from his seat at the back of the visitors' gallery, aware that he couldn't risk approaching any one of them after being warned by Jackie that he was being watched night and day.

He suspected that Bones Turner would be given the job of nobbling at least three of them, so the jury wouldn't be able to reach a verdict. However, while the trial was taking place, he would have to avoid contact with any member of the Turner family, or Booth Watson for that matter.

He couldn't complain. He'd been well rewarded for removing the one piece of evidence that Booth Watson was worried about.

William took the Bible in his right hand and sounded confident as he delivered the oath.

"Will you please state your name and rank for the record," said Sir Julian, peering over the top of his half-moon spectacles.

"Detective Inspector William Warwick."

"Inspector Warwick, would you describe to the jury what your current work with the Metropolitan Police involves?"

"I'm attached to a special unit at Scotland Yard investigating corrupt police officers, and one in particular."

"What is the name and rank of that officer?"

"Detective Sergeant Jerry Summers."

"Do you see him in court today?"

"Yes, sir. He is the accused, standing in the dock."

"What caused your unit to open an investigation into DS Summers?"

"The chief constable of Essex informed the Yard that he suspected a serving officer in his constabulary was involved in the handling of stolen goods, and was working with one of the leading drug gangs on his patch."

"Where did you take it from there?"

"We already knew there were two major drugs families operating in the Romford division, and the district commander became suspicious when members of one family kept being arrested, while their rivals appeared to be going about their business undisturbed."

"Armed with this information, detective inspector, what did you do next?"

"I placed one of my inner team, PC Bailey, in the ranks of the Romford constabulary while I continued to work undercover."

Booth Watson wrote *PC Bailey?*

"Were you able to catch DS Summers, to use a colloquial expression, red-handed?"

"Yes, sir," said William, opening his notebook. "In the early hours of Friday, May the twenty-ninth, an undercover officer observed Summers entering the home of Mr. Reg Payne, the head of one of the leading drugs gangs. Summers was accompanied by another man, so our UCO assumed he was about to make an arrest."

Booth Watson scribbled *Will the UCO be giving evidence?* on his yellow pad.

"The two men came back out of the house some twenty minutes later, when the UCO took a photograph of Summers carrying a bulky Sainsbury's shopping bag."

"Did the UCO then pursue the suspect, inspector?"

"Yes, he did, when he drove to Jimmy Turner's home in Westfield Drive, Romford."

"Jimmy Turner?"

"The head of the other family of drug dealers, who we suspected Summers was in league with."

"And how long was he in Turner's home?"

"About thirty minutes."

"At one thirty in the morning?"

"Yes, sir."

"And when he came back out, was Summers still carrying the bulky shopping bag?"

"No, sir."

"What happened next?"

"The officer followed Summers to his flat, then drove back to Scotland Yard where he left a written report of everything he'd witnessed that morning, along with photographs, on my commanding officer's desk."

*Commander Jack Hawksby?* was Booth Watson's next note.

"Once you'd read that report, inspector, what did you do next?"

"I obtained a warrant to search Summers's flat, which was later carried out in his absence by a team under DS Roycroft."

Booth Watson wrote *Was Summers informed of the search?*

"What did they find?" asked Sir Julian.

"A silver letter rack, two designer watches, and some cash. A brand-new Jaguar was parked in the driveway."

"Is that the best you can come up with?" said Booth Watson, loud enough for his rival to hear.

"Patience," snapped Sir Julian, without looking at him.

"I beg your pardon, Sir Julian?" said the judge, looking down from on high.

"I apologize, m'lud, I was just having a quiet word with my learned friend," said Sir Julian before turning his attention back to the witness.

"When DS Roycroft and her team searched DS Summers's flat, inspector, were they looking for anything in particular?"

"Yes, sir, a valuable diamond ring that my colleague PC Bailey had previously seen there."

*When had she first seen it?* was added to Booth Watson's growing list of questions.

"And did they find the ring?"

"No, sir. However, when DS Summers returned from a holiday in Malaga that same day, his companion, a Miss Karen Turner, was seen wearing the ring on the third finger of her left hand."

This time Booth Watson wrote down every word, underlined *Turner*, and added *Revenge?*

"Were you able to establish how DS Summers came into possession of the ring?"

Booth Watson heaved himself up. "M'lud, there's absolutely no proof my client even knew of the existence of this ring, let alone that he was ever in possession of it."

"I hope my learned friend isn't suggesting that it was Miss Turner who stole the ring?" said Sir Julian with a sigh. "Or that DS Summers had gone on holiday with a young woman who was already engaged to someone else?"

Booth Watson sank back into his place.

"After you had arrested DS Summers, did you question him about the theft of the ring?"

"I did, sir, but he refused to answer any of my questions, which didn't surprise me."

Booth Watson was on his feet once again. "M'lud, I must protest. A suspect is perfectly entitled to refuse to answer any questions put to him by the police until his legal representative is present."

"You make a fair point, Mr. Booth Watson," said the judge, and turning to the witness, added, "Stick to the facts, inspector. We are not interested in your opinions."

William looked suitably admonished, but then he knew what his father's next question would be.

"Indeed, let's stick to the facts, shall we, inspector. When Summers's legal representative finally turned up, was he any more forthcoming?"

"No, sir," said William, who wanted to add, *which also didn't surprise me,* but restrained himself.

"Allow me to return to the question my learned friend objected to. Were you able to discover how Summers came into possession of the ring?"

"Yes, sir," said William. "We established that Garrard's, the Mayfair jewelers, had originally sold the ring to a Mr. van Haeften, for three thousand three hundred pounds."

Sir Julian quickly switched tack.

"How much does a police detective sergeant earn in a week?"

"After tax and National Insurance, around a hundred and twenty-five pounds."

"You're not suggesting that DS Summers stole the ring from Mr. van Haeften?" said Sir Julian, back on track.

"No, sir. It was stolen by a burglar called Craig Harrison, who DS Summers arrested a few weeks later for a separate offense. When he was convicted, Harrison asked for eight other offenses to be taken into consideration, among them the theft of some jewelry and other valuable objects from an apartment in Mayfair, which included Mrs. van Haeften's engagement ring."

Sir Julian paused for a moment to allow the jury to absorb this information.

"So you arrested Summers and charged him with handling a stolen ring worth three thousand three hundred pounds when he and Miss Turner arrived back from their holiday in Malaga."

"Yes, sir."

"M'lud, the Crown will now produce the ring in question so the witness can identify it."

The judge nodded in the direction of the clerk of the court, who rose from his place and walked across to the bundle of evidence that had been agreed on by both sides. He checked his clipboard. Item No. 11, one diamond ring in a Garrard's leather box.

He removed the item, walked over to the witness box, and handed the small leather box to the inspector.

"Is that the Garrard's box you mentioned earlier?"

"Yes, it is, sir."

"And more important, Inspector Warwick, does it contain the ring that was taken from Miss Karen Turner when she arrived back in England from her holiday in Malaga with DS Summers?" asked Sir Julian.

Booth Watson allowed the suggestion of a smile to creep across his face.

William flicked open the box and stared down at a diamond ring for some time before saying, "It does."

Booth Watson stared up at Lamont in the visitors' gallery, who, from the expression on his face, wasn't in any doubt he'd been set up by Warwick. Sir Julian leaned across and whispered to Booth Watson, "Once bitten . . ."

"Sir Julian, perhaps the jury should be allowed to see this piece of evidence," suggested the judge.

"I couldn't agree with you more," said the Crown's counsel. "Unless of course my learned friend objects?"

Booth Watson managed a curt nod. William handed the ring back to the clerk of the court, who after the judge had looked at it, walked across to the jury box and passed it to the foreman.

The foreman took her time studying the ring before it was examined by each of her colleagues in turn. The last person to be shown the damning piece of evidence was Mr. Booth Watson, who dismissed it with a wave of the hand.

"Thank you, Inspector Warwick, for your valuable contribution," said Sir Julian. "But could I ask you to remain in the witness box, as I expect Mr. Booth Watson will want to cross-examine you."

An expectant buzz swept around the court as everyone waited for the bull to face the matador.

"Do you wish to question this witness, Mr. Booth Watson?" asked Mr. Justice Ramsden.

Defense counsel rose slowly from his place, but didn't even glance in Warwick's direction before he looked up at the judge and said, "No, m'lud."

The expectant buzz dissolved into a dozen unanswered questions as defense counsel resumed his place. William felt robbed for a second time, having spent so many hours preparing for the encounter. Sir Julian didn't seem at all surprised, though Grace looked puzzled.

"What's he up to?" she whispered in her father's ear.

"We've pulled the rug out from under his feet, so he now can't afford to cross-examine William. Booth Watson was convinced the Garrard's box would be empty. But the Hawk wasn't going to let that happen a second time."

"So should we expect a change of plea?"

"Not a hope. Booth Watson won't throw in the towel while there's the slightest chance of him getting his client off. However, he now knows PC Bailey is his only hope of climbing back into the ring. So don't under any circumstances lower your guard, because she's the one witness Booth Watson will be waiting for."

"Sir Julian, are you ready to call your next witness?" interjected the judge.

"Yes, m'lud. However, with Your Lordship's indulgence, I shall ask my junior to conduct the Crown's cross-examination of this particular witness."

"As you wish, Sir Julian."

The daughter rose to replace the father. From the corner of her eye Grace noticed that Booth Watson was almost licking his lips in anticipation. He may have avoided the Choirboy, but he couldn't wait for the Choirgirl.

Grace looked confidently up at the judge and then across at the jury before she said, "I call Police Constable Nicola Bailey."

# 29

"Are you confident she took the bait?" asked Miles.

"Hook, line, and sinker," said Christina. "Her eyes lit up at the thought of the Fitzmolean getting its hands on a Raphael."

"Which sadly they won't. She's nothing more than a pawn in a far larger game, and she's about to be taken off the board."

Christina felt guilty about the way her friend was being used, but Miles hadn't left her in any doubt what the alternative was.

"You gave her the authority to bid up to a million pounds on your behalf, and made it clear that she couldn't go any higher? And equally important, she mustn't tell anyone she will be bidding on your behalf."

"Not even Tim Knox. She has no idea that check will never be cashed because you're going to outbid her."

"How did she react when you offered her the chance to take our place on the *Alden*?" Miles asked.

"Overwhelmed. She was only disappointed that it meant she wouldn't be able to attend our wedding."

"Let's hope she never finds out the real reason we couldn't risk being seen together on the *Alden*."

"Call Police Constable Nicola Bailey," repeated the clerk, his voice echoing around the court.

A young woman dressed in a simple white blouse and a navy pleated skirt that fell below the knees entered the room. She wore no jewelry and only a hint of lipstick. She and Rebecca had given a great deal of thought to how she should look, with only the jury in mind.

Nicky made her way slowly across to the witness box, not once glancing in the direction of her former lover in the dock, although his eyes never left her. The clerk handed her a Bible and she delivered the oath without looking at the proffered card.

Grace checked the long list of questions she and Clare had spent several days preparing, to make sure that Summers wasn't left with any wiggle room, while at the same time hoping to avoid any traps Booth Watson might later spring.

Clare had instructed Nicky to tell the truth, and admit to the mistakes she'd made, and she mustn't under any circumstances lose her temper, because if she did, Booth Watson would take advantage of it.

Grace smiled at the witness, aware of how nervous she must be.

"Please state your name and rank for the record," said Grace.

"Police Constable Nicola Bailey."

"When you were a serving officer with the Metropolitan Police, which branch did you work for?"

"I was attached to a special unit investigating corrupt police officers, based at Scotland Yard. My final assignment was a posting as a constable in Romford."

Booth Watson wrote the word *Final?* on his yellow pad.

"Why Romford?"

"The unit was investigating a Detective Sergeant Jerry Summers, an officer from the Romford division, who we had reason to believe was involved in serious criminal activities. My job was to try to pick up any information on the ground, while my immediate boss, Detective Inspector Warwick, remained undercover."

*So far so good*, thought William, who was now seated in the back row of the court.

"How did you go about that task?"

"To begin with I was extremely cautious, because if DS Summers had thought I might be working for the Yard, I would have been responsible for blowing the whole operation."

"What information were you able to gather about Summers's activities?"

"I began by checking his daily reports, which I must confess were impressive. But although his arrest record was second to none, there were also some unexplainable anomalies."

"Such as?"

"Two well-known families were between them running the local drugs racket, and while members of one of them, the Paynes, were regularly being arrested by DS Summers, their equally notorious rivals, the Turners, would often get away with a warning, or at most the occasional police caution."

"Did you come up with any explanation for this apparent inconsistency?"

"I did. Summers openly boasted he had a well-placed informer in the Turner gang, who was supplying him with information that resulted in some large drug seizures and a number of arrests."

"Did you pass this information back to Scotland Yard?"

"Yes. I share a flat with another member of the inner team, so that wasn't a problem."

Booth Watson wrote down on his yellow pad *Name and rank of her flatmate?*

"Did you try to establish contact with the subject during this operation?"

"Yes, but it wasn't easy to begin with without making it too obvious," said Nicky. "After all, Summers was a detective sergeant, and as far as he was concerned I was just another trainee bobby on the beat. However, he did speak to me on one occasion in the station canteen, and when I found out which pub he frequented after work, I began to hang out there with another WPC in the hope of seeing him again."

"And did this ploy prove worthwhile?"

"Not at first. But one evening after my friend had left to report for the night shift, DS Summers offered to buy me a drink. I accepted, although I remained cautious, and at the time, kept my distance."

Booth Watson wrote down *At the time* and *Kept my distance.*

"Later that week he invited me to the cinema. Afterward I joined him for a drink at his flat, before going home."

"Why did you agree to go back to his flat? Wasn't that an unnecessary risk that might have jeopardized the whole operation?"

"I wanted to find out if there was anything in his home that looked out of place, and beyond the salary of a detective sergeant."

"And was there?"

"Way beyond. The building he lived in was a bit shabby and certainly in need of a lick of paint, while the garden had more weeds than flowers, but once you were inside DS Summers's home it was a different story. He had all the latest electronic gadgets and top-of-the-range furniture that looked as if it had come from an expensive West End store. There was one notable exception—the curtains were old and worn."

"Why was that?" asked Grace innocently.

"So they'd be in keeping with the other flats in the building, and wouldn't attract the attention of a passerby. I was particularly struck by how well equipped the flat was, because I knew Summers was proud of the fact that, like me, he came from a working-class background, so it couldn't have been family money that allowed him to live in such style."

"Did you report your misgivings to the officer in charge of the operation?"

"I immediately briefed my flatmate, DC Pankhurst, who was a member of the team, the following morning."

Booth Watson wrote *Immediately? DATE?* down on his pad.

"Did Summers ever explain how he came to possess so many expensive and luxurious items on a detective sergeant's salary?"

"Not to me, but in the pub one evening when he was celebrating another arrest, I overheard him telling a young constable that whenever he nabbed a burglar, one or two of the stolen goods might just go missing. 'Call it a perk,' he'd said, without seeming to care who heard him."

Booth Watson began speaking even as he rose from his place at the far end of the bench. "Overheard, m'lud? I can't recall a more blatant example of hearsay."

"I agree, Mr. Booth Watson," said the judge, and turning to the jury instructed them, "You will disregard the witness's last statement."

"Having gained sufficient evidence to have DS Summers arrested," said Grace, "why didn't you return to Scotland Yard and obtain a search warrant?"

"I know I should have," said Nicky, "but I'm ashamed to admit that, like so many others before me, I'd fallen for him by then, and wanted to give him the benefit of the doubt."

"So you didn't pass on your findings to DC Pankhurst?"

"No, not immediately. But at a later date . . ."

*How much later?* Booth Watson wrote on his pad. But no sooner had he put his pen down, than he picked it up again.

"Did you sleep with DS Summers?" asked Grace. The blunt question caused gasps and looks of surprise from all those in court, but she knew she had to get it on the record before Booth Watson cross-examined Nicky.

"I did, even though I'd come across a piece of evidence that I knew would wrap up the case."

"And what was that evidence?" asked Grace, moving quickly on.

"I found a small leather box by the side of Summers's bed that contained a diamond ring. It looked so expensive I knew there was only one way he could have got hold of it."

"Did you retrieve that ring as evidence?"

"No. Summers slipped it onto my engagement finger, and when I got home the next morning, I told Rebecca—"

"Rebecca?"

"DC Pankhurst—that I was engaged."

"To Detective Sergeant Summers."

"No, to an estate agent from Croydon."

"How did she react to the news?"

"When she saw the ring, I knew she didn't believe me."

"So why didn't you tell her the truth?"

"At the time I really believed Jerry wanted to marry me. I hoped I could get him to reform his ways, and have the investigation stopped."

"So you turned a blind eye?"

"Yes," admitted Nicky. "But I soon had them opened."

"What caused that?"

"When I told Jerry I was pregnant, he didn't attempt to hide his feelings, and immediately suggested I should have an abortion."

"How did you respond to that suggestion?"

"I told him never. I wanted to have our child. However, it quickly became clear that the engagement ring was nothing more than another deception, and I even wondered just how many other women had worn the ring before me."

"But not wanting a child isn't in itself proof that he no longer cared for you?"

"I got all the proof I needed a week later when I returned to the flat following my afternoon shift. I let myself in and found he'd left everything in a mess, as usual, so I began to tidy up. I started in the kitchen with the washing-up, and then moved on to the bedroom. While I was making the bed I found another woman's underwear between the sheets. I realized it was his way of letting me know that he'd moved on."

"What did you do then?"

"I was so angry I took all his clothes out of the wardrobe, cut the sleeves off his jackets and shirts, and snipped the trousers off at the crotch."

One of the women on the jury smiled.

"Did you then leave?"

"No, I went back into the kitchen, found a hammer, and destroyed all the things he was most proud of. I now realize that was the most stupid thing I could possibly have done."

"Why?" asked Grace.

"I was destroying the very evidence that could get him convicted."

"But you kept the diamond ring?"

"No, I took it off and put it back on his bedside table, knowing it would be found when the police searched his home."

Booth Watson didn't stop writing.

"And the leather box you'd first seen the ring in?"

"I took it with me when I left the flat that night."

"Why did you do that?"

"It had the name and address of the jewelers on the inside, so I assumed one of my colleagues at the Yard would follow it up."

"Did you take anything else from the flat?"

"Only a few personal belongings. However I did come across Summers's diary, and as I was tearing up the pages I saw that he had an appointment later that night at the Playboy Club in Mayfair."

"Who with?"

"I have no idea, as there wasn't a name in the diary. However, I wrote a note for DI Warwick to let him know what Jerry was up to and dropped it through his letterbox on my way home."

"And your discovery of that vital piece of evidence led to the arrest of DS Summers and another police officer who has recently resigned from the force."

"That's correct, but don't forget I was just one member of a highly professional and dedicated team."

"Looking back over that period," said Grace, "do you have any regrets?"

"If you don't now, you will have by the time I've finished with you," muttered Booth Watson loud enough for Grace to hear.

"Yes, I do," said Nicky, looking at Summers for the first time, but no longer frightened of his piercing glare. "I should never have become so closely involved with the suspect, and once I'd found out the extent of his criminal activities, I should have reported my findings to DI Warwick immediately, and let him take over. But I allowed my personal feelings to cloud my judgment."

"A human enough mistake," said Grace, looking directly at the jury, "which any one of us might have made given the circumstances."

William smiled. Nicky may have come across as naive and foolish, but when he looked at the jury, they appeared to be sympathetic and understanding about what she'd been put through.

"Thank you, Police Constable Bailey, for your frank and honest testimony, which I'm sure the jury will bear in mind when they come to consider their verdict." Grace smiled. "Please remain in the witness box, as my learned friend may want to question you."

"Is that the case, Mr. Booth Watson?" asked the judge, peering down at defense counsel.

"Just one or two questions, m'lud," declared Booth Watson as he rose slowly from a sedentary position. He offered Nicky a warm smile before saying, "I shall not be keeping you long, Miss Bailey, but I'm bound to ask if you have ever heard the expression, 'Hell hath no fury, like a woman scorn'd'?"

"Yes," said Nicky cautiously.

"I would suggest that 'a woman scorned' is a more accurate description of you, than 'frank and honest.'" The two words were laced with sarcasm.

"That's your opinion," said Nicky.

Grace allowed herself a smile.

"It is indeed, Miss Bailey. So I want you to think carefully before you answer my next question, because I'm sure I don't have to remind you that perjury is a serious crime, even more so when it's committed by a police officer." He turned his gaze on the jury before asking, "How long had you been conducting a sexual relationship with DS Summers before you—"

Grace was quickly on her feet. "Is this line of questioning relevant, m'lud? PC Bailey has already admitted her indiscretion. Isn't that enough?"

"Nowhere near enough, m'lud," said Booth Watson before Mr. Justice Ramsden had a chance to respond. "Miss Bailey's behavior goes to the very heart of this case if we are to discover who is telling the truth and who is a blatant liar."

"Cut to the chase, Mr. Booth Watson," said the judge sternly.

"As you wish, m'lud. It's simply that I find it difficult to believe

Miss Bailey's relationship with DS Summers was as fleeting and casual as she claims, when she gave birth to their son only a month ago. The dates just don't fit," he said, emphasizing each word. "So I must ask you again, Miss Bailey. How long did the affair last?"

"A few weeks."

"Months, I would suggest, Miss Bailey."

"Weeks," snapped Nicky.

"Now that we have established there was a long-term sexual relationship between you and the defendant, perhaps we should move on to your account of how you came across the diamond ring you claim to have found in his flat the morning after you'd slept with Detective Sergeant Summers for the first time. Because once again, the dates don't fit." Booth Watson held out a hand, into which his junior placed a single sheet of paper.

"Perhaps you can explain this memo given to DS Paul Adaja by your flatmate, DC Rebecca Pankhurst, both members of the squad of which you told the court you were so proud to be a member." He looked down at the memo, and began reading it out. "'On the morning of May the thirtieth, when PC Bailey joined me for breakfast, she was wearing a diamond ring I'd never seen before, and which looked extremely expensive.'"

Nicky gripped the sides of the witness box as she began shaking uncontrollably.

"Perhaps you've forgotten, Miss Bailey, that both parties in a criminal trial are obliged by law to disclose any evidence they are in possession of that might prove relevant to the case. This little bombshell was found smoldering among the two hundred and twenty-three submissions handed over to the court."

"That doesn't alter the fact that the Garrard's box proves the ring had been stolen by a burglar who was later arrested by DS Summers," said Nicky, trying to fight back.

"Or perhaps it reveals how you yourself got hold of the ring, Miss Bailey? And having discovered it was a little too hot to handle, you then planted it in your lover's flat."

"That's a ridiculous suggestion," said Nicky, almost shouting.

"Then perhaps you could tell us when DC Pankhurst first saw you wearing the ring in your flat in Pimlico?"

"The day after Jerry proposed to me."

"Did he propose to you, Miss Bailey?"

"Not in so many words, but he put the ring on my finger."

"We only have your word for that," said Booth Watson.

"But I returned the ring and gave the Garrard's box to DC Pankhurst, assuming she would hand it in to DS Adaja, which indeed she did."

"I don't doubt that, Miss Bailey. However, I'm more interested in how much time passed between your flatmate first seeing the ring on your finger, and you giving her the Garrard's box. Because unfortunately once again the dates don't quite fit." Booth Watson held up another of the memos. "It would seem you held on to the ring for some considerable time before you put it in a place where, to quote your own testimony, 'it would be found when the police searched his home.' The jury could be forgiven for wondering just who the guilty party is in this case, and who was engaged in stitching an innocent man up."

"Summers is the guilty party, and my only interest was to secure enough evidence to bring him to justice."

"It took you long enough," boomed Booth Watson. He didn't wait for Nicky to recover before he added, "I'm beginning to think, Miss Bailey, that in fact it was you who stole the ring, and that

DS Summers kept quiet about it, because he didn't want you to be arrested and have to face a prison sentence."

"How can that be possible when the ring was stolen before we'd even met?"

Sir Julian allowed himself a smile.

"We only have your word for when you first met."

"You're making this up as you go along!" shouted Nicky.

"As you've been doing from the moment you entered the witness box."

"Next, you'll be saying I planted the ring by his bed as an act of revenge."

Grace grimaced, while Sir Julian bowed his head.

"I congratulate you, Miss Bailey, on anticipating my next question. As you've now admitted, it was the defendant who ended your relationship." He paused and looked at the jury for some time, before saying, "Perhaps because he discovered you were a bent copper and his only crime was to turn a blind eye."

Prosecuting counsel was quickly on his feet.

"I shouldn't have to remind you, Sir Julian," said the judge courteously, "that it is not you who is examining this witness on behalf of the Crown."

Sir Julian sat slowly back down as Grace tentatively rose to her feet, although she wasn't sure what her father had intended to say. "M'lud," she began hesitantly, "Police Constable Bailey is not on trial—"

"That's what you think," muttered Booth Watson, who had remained standing.

"I've already admitted that Jerry and I had a relationship, which I'll regret for the rest of my life," Nicky blurted out.

"Indeed you have, Miss Bailey," said Booth Watson. "But what you apparently don't seem to regret is cutting up his clothes, breaking up his furniture, destroying his electronic equipment, and smashing his mother's dinner service, before planting a diamond ring by the side of his bed to use your words 'as an act of revenge.'"

The journalists on the press benches didn't stop scribbling.

"No, I didn't!" shouted Nicky.

"You didn't ransack his flat after he dropped you?"

"No, I didn't plant the ring."

"But you did wreck your ex-lover's home."

"It was no more than he deserved."

"Or was it because you wanted to destroy the evidence?"

"I only wanted to destroy him!"

William bowed his head.

"Thank you for that frank and honest response, Miss Bailey, because I believe it proves my case," said Booth Watson, "and allows me to remind the jury once again of Congreve's words, 'Hell hath no fury, like a woman scorn'd.' I wonder, Miss Bailey, if you recall the playwright's next line?"

Nicky stared blankly at him.

"Then allow me to remind you: 'For love is oft to foulest vengeance turned.'"

Sir Julian half rose, and then recalled he wasn't examining this witness, otherwise he would have corrected his adversary's deliberate misquotation of Congreve. Booth Watson gave his floored opponent a withering glance, before he turned to the judge and said, "No more questions, m'lud."

---

"You did as well as could be expected in the circumstances," said Sir Julian to Grace as they walked back to Lincoln's Inn after the judge had called a halt to the day's proceedings.

"Nicky should have known better than to lose her temper with Booth Watson and allow it to become personal," said Clare.

"I'm afraid for her it *was* personal," said Sir Julian.

"But God knows, I told her often enough to remain calm, whatever Booth Watson threw at her," said Grace.

"What makes matters worse," said Sir Julian, "is thanks to PC Bailey's faltering performance, Booth Watson can now advise his client there's no longer any need for him to give evidence from the witness box."

"I agree," said Grace. "But surely the jury will realize which of them is the guilty party?"

"I know he's guilty, you know he's guilty, and BW certainly knows he's guilty," said Sir Julian. "But in the end, it's the jury who will decide which one of them they believe."

"I still think we have a fifty-fifty chance," said Clare. "After all, the jury's choice is between a susceptible young woman and the man she was taken in by, who won't even appear in the witness box to defend himself."

"Which is his right in law, as the judge will point out," Sir Julian reminded them. "No, we'll have to hope the jury remember William's evidence, and the fact that BW chose not to cross-examine him after he'd testified that Summers supplied drugs to known criminals in return for cash."

"But we don't have any of those numbered notes to prove it," said Grace, "otherwise Lamont would have had to join Summers in the dock."

"But we do have the stolen diamond ring that he passed on to his next girlfriend, who just happened to be the drug dealer's daughter," said Clare.

"We can only hope the jury has worked that one out," said Sir Julian.

"Yet another reason Booth Watson won't allow Summers to appear in the witness box," suggested Grace.

"Booth Watson even managed to misquote Congreve in support of his case," said Sir Julian.

"Is that why you rose to interrupt BW?" asked Grace.

"Look the quote up," said her father.

"Well, at least you'll be able to put the record straight when you deliver your closing remarks," said Clare, as they reached Essex Court.

"Misquoting Congreve won't cut much ice with the jury, while BW keeps repeating the words, 'arrest record,' 'commendations,' and 'beyond reasonable doubt' during his closing remarks, while forgetting to mention the ring or any other stolen goods Nicky managed to destroy."

"Then you'll have to mention them again and again during your summing-up," said Clare.

"I will. It's just a pity BW will have the final word."

"No, the judge will have the final word," Grace reminded her father, as they climbed the steps to the senior partner's chambers.

"But he will have to present both sides of the case dispassionately, while reminding the jury that their verdict must be unanimous, and more important, beyond reasonable doubt."

"I still think we've got a fifty-fifty chance," said Clare.

# 30

Sir Julian rose early the following morning, and not just because he couldn't sleep. He needed to rehearse his closing summation to the waking birds and seek their approval.

He switched on the bedside light, put on his dressing gown, and padded across to his writing desk. He picked up his notes, looked in the mirror, and began, "M'lud, members of the jury, what an extraordinary case this has turned out to be, and I would suggest that in the end, it simply comes down to who you believe. On the one hand . . ."

Forty minutes later, he ended with the words, "I am confident the jury will use its common sense when reaching a verdict, well aware who is the guilty party."

*But would they?* he wondered as he put the script to one side. He still couldn't be sure which way the jury would fall, and it didn't help that Booth Watson would speak after him and have the final word before the judge's summing-up. He decided to make himself a cup of tea before getting dressed and going across to chambers to find out if Grace or Clare had any last-minute suggestions.

On his way to the kitchen, he stopped to pick up the morning paper from the doormat. He looked at the *Telegraph*'s headline and swore out loud. After reading the front-page article he swore again, even louder.

⤙○⤚

"Do you think they'll find him guilty?" Beth asked as she scooped a second fried egg out of the pan and dropped it on William's plate.

"It's going to be a close-run thing," William replied. "They may feel there's not enough evidence to convict him, after Booth Watson invented a line about revenge that Congreve never wrote."

"Why didn't your father correct him?"

"He couldn't while Grace was representing the Crown."

"But you told me only a week ago you considered it an open-and-shut case."

"And it might have been if our undercover agent had been able to arrest Summers when he came out of Payne's house, and relieve him of the Sainsbury's bag he was carrying."

"Then why didn't he?"

"It's not that easy to arrest two people when you have no backup, unless of course you're James Bond."

"What about at the Playboy Club, when you were given a second chance?"

"Same problem, although thanks to Nicky at least I found out what Summers and Lamont were up to."

"But you were still able to produce the ring as evidence," said Beth, as she began to feed the twins.

"Yes, but it didn't help that Nicky took her time admitting when she first saw it," said William, glancing across at Beth's copy of the *Daily Mail*.

"That's all I need," he said, after he'd read the banner headline on the front page.

⊸o⊷

Grace didn't bother with breakfast that morning as she went over her leader's closing remarks one more time before leaving for chambers.

"It's your father at his most persuasive," said Clare after she'd read the peroration.

"I agree," said Grace as the morning paper landed on the doormat with a thud. "But will the jury end up giving Summers the benefit of the doubt?"

"We'll find out soon enough. Why don't you grab the paper while I make us coffee?"

Clare switched on the kettle as Grace left the kitchen. A few moments later she heard a string of expletives coming from the hall, which only increased in volume as her partner returned to join her. Not the sort of language one would expect from someone who was hoping to be appointed a QC.

Grace burst back into the room and threw *The Guardian* on the kitchen table, saying, "That won't help our cause."

⊸o⊷

Booth Watson still felt the verdict was in the balance as he went slowly over his final submission to the jury. He was enjoying a full English breakfast at his favored table in the Savoy Grill. He was pleased he'd been able to convince Summers he shouldn't give evidence. A risk not worth taking, he'd repeated, several times. Sir Julian would probably mention Banquo's ghost during his summing-up, but at least he had the advantage of following his old rival and responding in kind before the judge addressed the jury.

He made one or two small emendations to his script before pushing it to one side and picking up his copy of *The Times.* His coffee went cold as he read the front-page article a second time.

"Would you care for more coffee, sir?" asked an attentive waiter.

"No," said Booth Watson abruptly. "Get me a copy of every morning paper and put them on my bill. Immediately."

"Yes, sir," said the waiter, who scurried off.

Booth Watson read the article for a third time and smiled. The odds were no longer fifty-fifty. He began to rewrite the last paragraph of his closing speech.

The court was full long before the judge was due to make his entrance, the audience waiting expectantly for the curtain to rise on the final act.

Sir Julian had already set up his little stand, and Grace was double-checking the pages of his manuscript were all in order. Clare sat on the bench behind them, ready to hand over an urgent scribbled note should anything unanticipated arise.

Booth Watson lounged at the other end of the bench, the only person in the crowded courtroom to acknowledge the defendant as he took his place in the dock, accompanied by two officers who looked as if they hoped he'd try to escape.

When the judge appeared, everyone in the court rose and bowed. He returned the compliment as he sat down in the high-backed chair in the center of the raised platform. Once he'd settled, he peered down at the jury over his spectacles and smiled. He finally turned his attention to the prosecution's leading advocate.

"Sir Julian, are you ready to sum up on behalf of the Crown?"

"I am indeed, m'lud," said the Crown's leader as he rose from his place, tugged at his gown, and adjusted his wig, showing that some things never change.

"M'lud, members of the jury, what an extraordinary case this has turned out to be. In the end, I would suggest it simply comes down to who you believe. You could be forgiven for wondering who was on trial, as the defendant refused to answer any questions after he was arrested, and again failed to do so in the presence of my learned friend and finally we were deprived of any explanation he might have to offer when he was given the chance to tell you his side of the story from the witness box. Not unlike Banquo's ghost; you can see him standing there, but he doesn't answer any of Macbeth's questions."

"As is his legal right," grumbled Booth Watson from a sedentary position at the far end of the bench.

Sir Julian turned, smiled at his rival, and said, "At last we've found something we can agree on." One or two members of the jury also smiled.

"Had he done so, m'lud, I would have been able to ask the defendant why he had entered the home of a leading drug dealer at one o'clock in the morning, and what was in the Sainsbury's bag he was carrying when he came back out twenty minutes later. Perhaps there's a simple explanation. If so, we haven't been given the opportunity to hear it.

"And why, you may ask," he continued, turning to face the jury, "did the accused then drive to the home of an equally notorious drug dealer, who was clearly expecting him, because as Inspector Warwick pointed out, the front door was immediately thrown open to welcome him even before he had a chance to knock? When Summers emerged half an hour later he was no longer carrying the Sainsbury's bag. What can have been in it? you may ask. Perhaps he was delivering the groceries?"

This caused more than one member of the jury to smile.

"And then there's the mysterious trip to the Playboy Club, when he was seen apparently parting with a large sum of money. But was he actually losing it, or was he simply exchanging it? Because three hours later he left the club with a check for almost exactly the same amount he'd started out with. I'm sure there's another simple explanation he just didn't feel he could share with us.

"Even more inexplicable is how he came to be in possession of a diamond ring worth over three thousand pounds, which was found in his flat by PC Bailey. My learned friend deftly tried to place the blame onto Constable Bailey herself, by claiming that the dates didn't fit. I'll tell you one date that does fit, and which my learned friend avoided mentioning. The burglar who stole that ring from a house in Mayfair was arrested, charged, and remanded in May, long before PC Bailey had even met the defendant, so it can't have been her who stole the ring, which rather narrows down the field.

"Had the accused chosen to appear in the witness box, and taken an oath to tell the truth, the whole truth, and nothing but the truth, I might have been tempted to ask him how he came to be in possession of the latest model Sony television set, a brand-new VHS recorder, two designer watches, not to mention the latest Jaguar, and furnishings that could have graced a mansion in Mayfair rather than a small flat in Romford.

"However, there is one thing my learned friend and I can agree on." Sir Julian glanced across to see Booth Watson, head bowed, giving the impression he was fast asleep. "Namely, that only one person could have stolen all those items, including the ring." He turned once again to face the jury. "And it certainly wasn't a naive, impressionable young woman who—perhaps unwisely—fell in love with the accused and ended up bearing his child. A child he has made no attempt to acknowledge. In fact, he went on holiday with another woman while PC Bailey was pregnant, and when they returned from that holiday, the other woman was wearing the engagement ring. Members of the jury, you may ask how any man could stoop so low as to try to place the blame for the theft of that ring on an innocent young woman, the mother of his child, in order to save his own skin.

"Before you retire to consider your verdict, I would ask you to think about one more important aspect of this case. If DS Summers is allowed to flout the law and get away with his egregious crimes, what message does that send to all the thousands of decent and dedicated police officers across the land who selflessly and courageously carry out their duties day in and day out in the service of the public?

"I am confident that after you have weighed up all the evidence, you can come to only one conclusion. That DS Jerry Summers is a corrupt, unscrupulous individual, who must now face the consequences of his actions, if only because it will reassure the public that no one is above the law." Sir Julian turned for the final time to face the jury before he said almost in a whisper, "In order to achieve that, you must surely deliver a verdict of guilty."

Sir Julian sat down to an outburst of murmuring that suggested that most of those in the court agreed with him. The journalists continued to scribble away, seemingly convinced that the verdict had already been decided, and there could only be one headline on their front pages the following morning: GUILTY.

The judge waited for everyone to settle before turning to the other end of counsels' bench, where the defense silk was not only wide awake, but clearly impatient to do battle.

"Mr. Booth Watson, are you ready to deliver your closing speech on behalf of your client?" asked the judge.

"More than ready, m'lud." Booth Watson rose from his place, not bothering to tug his gown or adjust his wig. He looked down at the seven bullet points written in capital letters on the back of an envelope. He, too, had been up all night.

## THE MAN

"Members of the jury," he began, looking at them for the first time. "Don't you sometimes think you'd like to hear the other side of the story? The man on trial today has served as a police officer for seven years, attaining the rank of detective sergeant without a blemish on his record." His eyes never left the jury. "On three separate occasions he has been awarded commendations for the outstanding work he has carried out on behalf of his local community. Can this be the same man the Crown has just described? I don't think so."

## THE GOODS FOUND IN HIS HOUSE

"You have been told by the Crown that the defendant's home was full of expensive electronic equipment and luxury goods. Don't you find it strange that not one of these items was offered up as evidence? The reason, we have been told, is that they were all destroyed by one of Scotland Yard's own officers, Police Constable Bailey, before the police could conduct a search of his premises. And what, you may also ask, did they find when they took my client's flat apart?" He paused. "A silver-plated letter rack, a couple of watches, and a Jaguar being paid for on the never-never. Hardly the Great Train Robbery."

One member of the jury suppressed a smile.

## TWO DRUG DEALS

"The Crown went into great detail about how the defendant visited the head of a gang of drug dealers in the early hours of the morning. But isn't it part of a police officer's job to raid suspected drug dealers when they least expect it, in the hope of finding evidence that will enable them to be brought to justice? Not a job many of us would want to carry out in the middle of the night, when we'd rather be safely tucked up in bed. Let's be thankful DS Summers was willing to take on that demanding and dangerous responsibility on your behalf.

"If the undercover officer who'd been watching him night and day was so keen to discover what was in that Sainsbury's bag on the night in question, why didn't he arrest DS Summers and take a look inside? Perhaps he wasn't there in the first place?"

Grace leaned across and whispered to her father, "Surely he realizes undercover agents remain undercover, that's the point of them."

"Of course he does," said Sir Julian. "However, his words aren't aimed at us, but at the jury."

## THE PLAYBOY CLUB

"It would appear, members of the jury, that it's now a crime to visit the Playboy Club and enjoy a night out after a hard day's work. And an even worse crime to leave the club with almost as much money as you came in with."

Booth Watson managed to raise a second smile from another member of the jury.

"Inspector Warwick wants you to believe that the defendant was doing something illegal by playing a game of roulette. If that's the case, why did he once again fail to arrest him? Because once again he knew DS Summers had nothing to hide."

Booth Watson glanced down at his list.

## THE RING

"Let us now turn to the solitary piece of evidence on which this whole charade rests. A diamond ring that was discovered on DS Summers's bedside table. But how did it get there? you may ask. Miss Bailey tells us she left it on his bedside table before returning home. If that is to be believed, why didn't she hand it over to her superiors at Scotland Yard the following morning, when the case could have been solved there and then, and Police Constable Bailey might surely have received a commendation for her outstanding detective work, rather than the suspicion that she hasn't been entirely honest about how she came into possession of the ring. To quote my learned friend, you may well ask why. Is it just possible that Miss Bailey isn't quite as naive and innocent as my learned friend would have you believe?

"After all, we know she held on to the ring for at least a month, possibly longer, and then when things started to unravel, she returned to the defendant's flat when he wasn't there, and left the ring on his bedside table, in the expectation it would be discovered by a search party from Scotland Yard who would arrive the following day all guns blazing. But unfortunately, they didn't find the ring. So, one is bound to wonder who stole it in the first place."

## PERSONAL RELATIONSHIPS

"The Crown made great play of the fact that when Miss Bailey gave birth to her child, DS Summers callously made no effort to visit her or his son. Once again, Miss Bailey only told you her side of the story. What she failed to let you know, members of the jury, and the judge will confirm, is that he issued a ruling that the defendant must not in any circumstances attempt to contact Miss Bailey before the trial began, otherwise his bail would be rescinded. My client sticks to the letter of the law, and she condemns him for it," protested Booth Watson, his eyes never leaving the jury.

## SUMMING-UP

"Members of the jury, the Crown went on to suggest that if my client isn't found guilty and sentenced to a long period of imprisonment, it will send a message to his fellow police officers that they can flout the law with impunity. In fact, the opposite is true. If you find DS Summers not guilty, it will send a message to his colleagues that an innocent man need not fear false and baseless allegations from a vengeful woman, as long as he comes before a jury who believe in justice." He paused for some time before continuing.

"You heard at the beginning of this trial, from none other than my learned friend, that DS Summers is a highly decorated officer, with an extremely promising career ahead of him. Miss Bailey went even further when she testified that his arrest record was, in her own words, "second to none." However, such has been the adverse publicity DS Summers received as a result of this trial that even if you were to find him not guilty, he will be left with no choice but to resign from the police force, as he will no longer be able to carry out to the best of his abilities the job he's always wanted to do since he was a child. You may feel that's punishment enough for such minor indiscretions.

"And finally, ladies and gentlemen of the jury, I wondered if you have had the chance to read any of this morning's newspapers. If you haven't, allow me to show you just a sample of their front pages."

Booth Watson waited for a moment before he held up first *The Times,* followed by the *Telegraph,* then the *Daily Mail,* and finally *The Guardian.* Every one of them displayed the same banner headline: NOT GUILTY.

"Yesterday," continued Booth Watson, lowering his voice, "a prisoner was released from Wormwood Scrubs having served a sentence of fourteen years for a crime he did not commit. I want you just for a moment," he said, his eyes running along the front bench of the jury, "to remember what you were doing fourteen years ago, and all the things that have happened in those intervening years." His gaze moved on to the second row. "And now imagine, ladies and gentlemen of the jury, what it would be like if you were unable to return to your family tonight, because you were about to be locked up for fourteen years, for a crime you had not committed. I feel sure you'll agree it doesn't bear thinking about. But thankfully you now have the opportunity to ensure that an innocent man does not have to serve a similar harsh sentence for a crime he did not commit.

"I would suggest to you that if there's an ounce of doubt in your mind as to DS Summers's guilt, weigh it carefully in the balance. Because if you do, it will surely come down on the side of justice, and you will be left with no choice but to reach a verdict of not guilty."

Once again, he held up his copy of *The Times,* so that the last image the members of the jury saw before they retired to consider their verdicts was NOT GUILTY.

Booth Watson collapsed onto the bench, clearly exhausted. Not for the first time, Sir Julian had to acknowledge that he had no more formidable rival at the Bar.

Low chattering once again broke out around the court. Booth Watson surreptitiously opened one eye and peeked at the jury. He was confident he had sown the seed of doubt, because they all looked as Dickens had once described a jury: in two minds.

"Brilliant," whispered Sir Julian to Grace. "I know he's guilty, you know he's guilty, and certainly BW knows he's guilty. But after that, the jury may no longer feel confident enough to deliver a verdict that could be described as beyond reasonable doubt."

"Perhaps this would be an appropriate time for us to take a break for lunch," said the judge. "If you would return at two o'clock, I shall begin my summing-up."

Mr. Justice Ramsden pushed back his chair, rose, and bowed to the assembled gathering before leaving his court. No sooner had the door closed behind him, than the chattering began once again. Everyone seemed to have an opinion as to whether the defendant would be found guilty or not guilty.

Well, everyone except Sir Julian Warwick and Mr. Booth Watson.

---

"Steak-and-kidney pie and chips," said William.

Grace frowned. "I'm not sure Beth would approve."

"I won't tell her if you don't," said William with a grin.

"I'll have the same," said Sir Julian, handing back the menu. Grace didn't comment.

"I know it's a silly question, Sir Julian," said Clare, "but if you had to put a small wager on the verdict, what—"

"You're quite right, Clare, it's a silly question. We'll just have to leave that decision to the jury. None of us can second-guess."

No further opinion was offered until a waitress reappeared carrying a tray full of food.

"Mine's the green salad," said Grace.

"Don't look now," said William, "but your esteemed colleague—"

Sir Julian, Grace, and Clare glanced across the room to see Booth Watson having lunch with his client.

"BW isn't a colleague, and he certainly isn't esteemed," said Sir Julian. "We just happen to be in the same profession."

"That may well be true," said William, "but even so, I wish I was a fly on the wall."

⊸o⊷

"What do you think?" said Summers as he cut into his steak.

"Once there's nothing more I can do to influence the jury," replied Booth Watson, "I stop thinking. It's a fool's game. But I'll be interested to hear what the judge has to say, because it could in the end all rest on his judgment."

"Two of the women on the jury were looking at me when you sat down after your closing speech, and you said that's a good sign."

"Probably the same two women who were looking at Warwick after he'd given his evidence."

"You couldn't have done any more," said Summers, popping a chip into his mouth.

*But will it be enough?* Booth Watson couldn't help wondering, as a waitress whisked away their plates.

⊸o⊷

"How long do you think the judge's summing-up will take?" said William, checking his watch. "I was hoping to get back to the Yard and catch up on some files in my in-tray that have been gathering dust."

"As long as it takes," said Sir Julian helpfully.

"Could I have a word with you, Father, about Nicky Bailey?" said Grace, changing the subject.

"What about her?"

"Whichever way the verdict goes, I was wondering if we could find her a job in chambers. It won't be easy for her to make ends meet as a single mother."

"Essex Court is not a crèche," said Sir Julian, putting down his coffee. "We're a professional legal chambers."

"I'd be happy to take her on as an investigator," said Clare. "She's bright and capable, and the fact that she fell in love with the wrong man doesn't mean she's not entitled to a second chance."

"Why not employ Summers while you're at it?" said Sir Julian. "After all, he might be also looking for a job."

"Is your father always this chippy?" whispered Clare to her partner.

"Only after he's sat down for the last time and thinks of questions he should have asked."

---

The waitress returned to their table. "Will there be anything else, sir?"

Booth Watson looked at his watch. "No, just the bill," he said, while making no attempt to pay.

Summers smiled at the waitress as she gave him the bill. He glanced at the figure, £7.80, and handed over ten pounds.

"Keep the change."

"Thank you, sir."

"I look forward to seeing you again tomorrow," Summers added with a grin.

Booth Watson didn't offer an opinion other than to say, "Time to make a move. We'd better get back before the judge, otherwise we could both end up in the dock."

They left the restaurant and made their way back to court number one, where Summers returned to the dock, while Booth Watson took his place on the front bench; both of them sat back and waited for Mr. Justice Ramsden to return and begin his summing-up.

As two o'clock struck, the judge entered, a large red folder tucked under his right arm. Like the two leading counsels, he'd also spent most of the night polishing his summation, which was among the most difficult he'd had to write in a long career.

He sat down in his high-backed chair, rearranged his long black gown, and smiled down at the assembled gathering, but the smile disappeared when he observed that the Crown's leader was not in his place. Nor was his junior. He checked his half-hunter to see it was three minutes past the hour. By the fourth minute, he was tapping his fingers impatiently on his open folder, and by the fifth he was becoming increasingly irritated. He had never known Sir Julian Warwick to be late for the start of a session.

Booth Watson made no attempt to repress a smirk as the clock reached six minutes past the hour, and the court doors swung open. Sir Julian, Grace, and Clare came rushing in.

"I do apologize, m'lud," said the Crown's leader, while still on the move.

Mr. Justice Ramsden nodded curtly. "When you are quite ready, Sir Julian," he said. "Perhaps I might be permitted to begin my summing-up."

"Before you call the jury back, m'lud," said Sir Julian, slightly out of breath, "I hope you will allow me to make a legal submission."

"As you wish," said the judge, reluctantly closing his folder and sitting back in his chair.

"With your permission, m'lud, I would like to recall a witness, as some important new evidence has emerged."

"That, as you well know, Sir Julian, would be highly irregular at this stage in proceedings."

"I accept that, m'lud. Nevertheless, if this new evidence were not brought to the attention of the jury, it might undermine the whole purpose of these proceedings. The jury, I am sure you will agree, must be given all the relevant and admissible evidence if they are to come to a considered judgment in this case."

"Do you have any objection to Sir Julian recalling a witness?" asked Mr. Justice Ramsden, turning his attention to the other end of the bench.

"I most certainly do, m'lud," said Booth Watson, rising from his place. "This would, as you've suggested, be highly irregular, considering that the trial has almost concluded, and all that remains before the jury retires is your summing-up."

"I hear you, Mr. Booth Watson, and will need a few moments to consider Sir Julian's request."

Loud chattering broke out the moment the judge had closed the door behind him. Booth Watson was conducting an urgent whispered discussion with his junior about who the witness could possibly be, and more important, what new evidence the Crown had come up with.

The clock had reached the thirty-sixth minute past the hour before the door opened once again and Mr. Justice Ramsden reappeared. The court fell silent as everyone waited for his pronouncement.

"I have given your request some considerable thought, Sir Julian," he said, "and decided that the court will hear this witness's new evidence before I deliver my summing-up."

"He must have sought the Lord Chancellor's advice," growled Booth Watson to his junior, "so there's not much point in objecting."

The judge waited for the jury to return and take their places before saying, "Who is it you wish to recall, Sir Julian?"

"Detective Inspector William Warwick, m'lud," replied prosecuting counsel.

The judge nodded, and the clerk of the court bellowed, "Call Detective Inspector William Warwick."

William entered the court moments later. On his way to the witness box he handed an envelope to Clare.

"I'm sure I don't have to remind you, detective inspector," said the judge, "that you are still under oath."

William bowed, as Clare handed her leader the contents of the envelope, which he double-checked before asking his first question.

"Inspector, would you tell the court exactly what you witnessed a few minutes ago, while we were having lunch in the Silks' restaurant?"

"I saw the defendant, who was lunching with his legal representative, hand two five-pound notes to a waitress after she'd presented him with the bill."

"What did you do then?"

"Once they'd left the dining room, I retrieved the two banknotes from the waitress."

Booth Watson was quickly on his feet. "I'm bound to ask, m'lud, how Inspector Warwick can be certain they were the same two notes."

"She hadn't yet put the money in the till and I asked the waitress if she would be able to identify the customer who'd handed her the notes," said William. He opened his notebook. "Her exact words were, 'Oh, yes, I couldn't forget him, because he was so handsome and he gave me such a large tip.'"

"M'lud," said Sir Julian, "may I ask the clerk to hand the two banknotes in question to Inspector Warwick."

The judge nodded, and the clerk took the notes and passed them to the witness.

"What precisely is the significance of these banknotes?" asked Mr. Justice Ramsden.

"They were part of a batch of ten thousand pounds in cash that was handed to Mr. Reg Payne by the undercover police officer shortly before DS Summers entered his house in the early hours of May the twenty-ninth, as I reported earlier under oath. You will recall, m'lud, that when Summers came out of the house twenty minutes later, he was carrying a Sainsbury's bag that was not, as Mr. Booth Watson suggested, full of groceries, but the ten thousand pounds in cash the undercover officer had handed over to Mr. Payne, and received a receipt for."

"What makes you so sure these two five-pound notes came from the same batch?"

"The serial numbers of the notes given to Payne were recorded at Scotland Yard by Commander Hawksby and witnessed by me. They were," said William, once again referring to his notebook, "AJ142001 to AJ152000."

"And what are the numbers of the two notes you recovered from the waitress, Inspector Warwick?" asked Sir Julian.

"AJ143018 and AJ143019."

"No more questions, m'lud," said Sir Julian.

"Do you wish to cross-examine this witness, Mr. Booth Watson?"

Booth Watson remained slumped in his place and muttered, "If only I'd paid the bill."

# 31

"Ten years," said the commander, "thanks to two five-pound notes, and Inspector Warwick being half awake." The Hawk's idea of a compliment. "And thanks to the rest of the team, DI Castle has taken early retirement. And perhaps equally important, forty-three other Metropolitan Police officers have handed in their notice. Congratulations on a job well done."

"But Lamont got clean away," said Paul.

"Just give me time," said William, almost spitting out the words.

"I'm afraid not, William. You're going to have to leave that to your successor, because the commissioner in his wisdom has decreed that any unit investigating corrupt officers cannot be staffed by the same team for more than one major investigation, for fear that its members become cut off from the rest of their colleagues, and have difficulty returning to normal duties. And I agree with him."

"Perhaps we should all take early retirement?" suggested William.

"Not a hope, detective chief inspector," said the Hawk, sitting back and waiting to see who would be the first to react.

Paul began banging the table with the palm of his hand, and Jackie and Rebecca quickly followed.

"Congratulations, chief inspector," said the Hawk, after the acclamation had died down. As William didn't respond, he added, "And I know you'll be glad to hear that the rest of the team will be joining you in your new assignment."

"Dare I ask what you have in mind for us, sir?" asked Detective Chief Inspector Warwick.

"Murder," said the commander, and then let the idea sink in for a few moments to see how they'd react.

"I think I preferred Art and Antiques," said Jackie.

"Of blessed memory," said the Hawk.

"Or even drugs," said Paul.

"That's as may be," said the commander. "But if you're the best you end up being assigned the worst, because your first task will be to investigate five people who have quite literally got away with murder. However, I'll allow you to indulge yourselves for a few days, before you report back for your new assignment on Monday morning. Eight o'clock sharp."

"Does that mean we get the rest of the week off?" asked Paul.

"I'm amazed you need a razor in the mornings, DS Adaja, you're so sharp. Yes, take some time off, you've earned it. If you decide to go out and celebrate, the first round's on me."

"Did I hear you correctly, sir?" said Paul.

"You did. And don't forget, I have the authority to demote as well as promote. So for you, DS Adaja, it's either back on the beat or murder. Take your pick. But for now, I don't want to see any of you in the office until next Monday. With the exception of DC Pankhurst, the rest of you can bugger off."

William gathered up his files and joined the others as they left the room. He didn't mention that he, for one, wouldn't be taking the rest of the week off, as he still had another private matter to deal with.

The Hawk waited until the rest of the team had left before he spoke to Rebecca. "Despite the team's triumph, DC Pankhurst, in which you played a crucial role, I think there will be one person who's unlikely to be celebrating. Though I don't pretend to understand it, I suspect PC Bailey is still besotted with Summers. However, I need you to tell her that as far as I'm concerned, the case is closed, and there are no plans to take any further action against her."

"She'll be so relieved," said Rebecca. "Thank you, sir."

"Let's hope she'll be able to find another job."

"She's already been offered a position as an investigator in Clare's office."

"Which she's well qualified for," said Hawksby. "But for now, I'd like you to take her out for a drink and try to convince her she has every reason to celebrate. You've proved a loyal friend, DC Pankhurst, and she was lucky to have you on her side."

Rebecca returned to the office to find her colleagues already in a party mood.

"Will you be joining us at the pub, Rebecca?" asked Jackie.

"Thanks, but I have to go home," she said, without explanation.

William gave her a warm smile, aware of the task she faced.

Rebecca decided to walk back to Pimlico, as she wanted a little time to compose her thoughts. She needed to convince Nicky she had done the right thing by giving evidence against her former lover, and it was now time for her to move on.

By the time she reached the front door, Rebecca was well prepared to deal with the tears, the recriminations, and hopefully the relief. She put her key in the lock, and smiled when she opened the door and heard the baby crying. She was so proud that Nicky had invited her to be one of Jake's godparents.

As she climbed the stairs to the first floor, the crying became even louder. She knocked on Nicky's door. Not waiting for a reply, she walked in to find her friend curled up on the floor, two empty bottles of barbiturates by her side. Jake was still crying.

⊸o⊷

"Ten years for stealing a ring worth three grand?" said Miles. "I don't believe it."

"What's more," said Booth Watson, "a ring that had already been stolen by a burglar who only got two years."

"How's that possible?"

"Summers was a serving police officer at the time. If only I'd paid for lunch . . ."

"That would be a first," said Miles. "Whenever I have a meal with you, not only do I end up paying the bill, but you then send me an invoice for a 'consultation.' Breakfast one hour, lunch two hours, and three for dinner. BW, you've brought a new meaning to the word 'refreshers.'"

"It's not my fault you can't be bothered to attend chambers," countered Booth Watson. "In any case, you always have a reason for wanting to see me. So what is it this time?" he asked, before dropping another lump of sugar in his coffee.

"I wanted to make sure you'd sorted out Christina?"

"On several levels," replied Booth Watson. "Where would you like me to start?"

"Was she able to convince her friend Beth Warwick to bid for Raphael's *Madonna di Cesare* on behalf of the museum?"

"Christina even handed her a check for a million pounds, which will never be cashed as I will be putting in the final bid for the painting on your behalf. We wouldn't want the punters to think it might be a fake."

"But why bother to involve Christina in the first place, when she could still switch sides and tell her friend Beth Warwick what we are up to?"

"'Involve' is the relevant word," said Booth Watson. "In the 1967 Criminal Justice Act it comes under the heading 'aiding and abetting a known criminal,' as I'll explain to Christina when we next meet. The maximum sentence a judge can award for this offense is six years, which should be more than enough incentive to ensure she keeps her mouth shut."

"Point taken," said Miles. "I have to admit, you've earned every penny of your refresher for a change. But I still don't see why I have to marry the damn woman?"

"Think of it as an insurance policy," said Booth Watson. "When Christina realizes she could also face a second charge, 'sheltering a known fugitive from the law,' I'll warn her that for that offense the maximum sentence is at the judge's discretion."

"But that still won't stop me having to cough up over a million pounds for a fake."

"It's that or spend the next ten years in jail. Your choice."

"You've convinced me, BW. As I accept that I can't afford to be seen on the *Alden*. However, I still need to rescue the rest of my collection from the apartment in New York."

"Then you'll have to fly."

"I realize that but I'm still not sure why I had to get Christina to hand over our tickets on the *Alden* to Beth Warwick."

"I want the Warwicks as far away as possible when the wedding takes place, and you plan to move into your new home."

"Christina doesn't know about Barcelona . . . ?"

"No one knows other than you and me."

"Thank God for that. But you'll still need to draw up a pre-nup," said Miles, "that leaves Christina in no doubt of the consequences of switching sides."

"I've already completed the first draft," said Booth Watson, "so as long as you don't expect me to act as your best man, my job is done."

"Funny you should mention that, BW . . ."

⊸o⊷

"Death is always a great sadness," said the priest in a somber tone. "All the more so when it comes to someone so young, with so much unfulfilled potential.

"Police Constable Nicola Bailey, Nicky, was such a person. She was tipped for a brilliant career in her chosen profession, but sadly that will now never be realized. We can, however, all share in the memory of her undoubted talent, her unquenchable spirit, and her infectious enthusiasm. Those she has left behind will remember her with affection and respect for the rest of their lives."

The small gathering of mourners who surrounded the grave stood silently in grief as the coffin of Nicola Anne Bailey was lowered into the ground. Rebecca unashamedly wept when the priest offered the final blessing and gave the sign of the cross before the mourners departed. William joined her as they left the graveyard, but didn't interrupt her thoughts. Grace and Clare accompanied Nicky's mother back to her little cottage, where they all assembled for tea.

Mrs. Bailey was touched that Commander Hawksby joined them, and even more so when he told her what an important role Nicky had played in his team. She couldn't hide her pride, despite her grief.

Grace and Clare were the last to leave, and after everyone else had departed, Mrs. Bailey asked if they could spare a few moments, as she wished to have a private word with them.

"Of course," said Clare.

Mrs. Bailey didn't speak for some time, but when she did, it was clear that she'd given considerable thought to what she was going to say.

"Nicky admired you both so much," she eventually managed, "and I'm grateful for all you did for her, especially offering her a job, after all her recent problems."

"We never doubted she was a bit special," said Clare. "That's why I wanted her to join the firm."

"As you know, Nicky hoped the two of you would agree to be Jake's godparents," said Mrs. Bailey, "along with Paul Adaja and Rebecca Pankhurst."

"We were both flattered and delighted when she asked us," said Clare.

"But I wondered, my dears, if I might burden you with an even greater responsibility."

"Anything," said Grace.

"How unlike a lawyer to commit themselves before they've heard the details, and had at least a month to consider the implications."

Grace and Clare laughed for the first time that day.

Mrs. Bailey fell silent for a moment, before she said, "I would like to remove the word 'God' from your new title, and for you to become Jake's foster parents. At my age I'm not capable of raising a young child on my own, and I have no doubt you would make wonderful parents."

Grace was speechless, but not Clare, who immediately said, "Nothing would give us greater pleasure."

⊸o⊷

"Have you been listening to a single thing I've been saying?" said Beth.

"Every word," said William, as he climbed into bed.

"Then what did I just tell you?"

"Tomorrow evening, Christie's will be auctioning Raphael's *Madonna di Cesare*. It's lot number twenty-five."

"One out of ten. Try harder."

"Christina has authorized you to bid up to a million pounds on her behalf, and if you succeed, the painting will be donated to the Fitzmolean."

"Not bad, Caveman. But you're still not off the hook."

"She's given you a check for the full amount, but if someone outbids you, you're to tear it up, and never mention to anyone who you were representing."

"Impressive," said Beth. William placed a hand on the inside of her thigh, but she removed it as if they were on a first date.

"And how will I be bidding?"

"By phone from your office at the Fitzmolean."

"I owe you an apology, Caveman," she said, taking him in her arms. "So now all you have to do is wish me luck."

"Before I do," said William, ignoring her advances, "I need you to stop thinking about what's in it for the gallery, and start thinking about what's in it for Christina."

"Why should I do that?"

"My darling, I'm well aware that you would happily trample over a thousand dead bodies to get your hands on a minor picture by an obscure Dutch artist for the Fitzmolean, so heaven knows what you'd be willing to do to acquire a Raphael."

"Have you forgotten, that's part of my job description? I've already secured a Rembrandt and a Rubens for the museum from the same source, in case you hadn't noticed."

"I did notice, but on both occasions there was something in it for Christina. So what I want to know is, what would she trample over a thousand dead bodies for?"

"You've never liked Christina, have you?"

"Actually, I do rather like her. I just don't trust her."

"I know she's not a saint," said Beth, "but she's been very generous over the years. Why can't you give her the benefit of the doubt for once?"

"Not while she owns several other major works, and her only interest in them in the past has been to find out how much they're worth. So I have to ask myself, why doesn't she just offer the Fitzmolean a picture from her late husband's collection, rather than part with a million pounds of her own money?"

"She told me she wanted to give the Madonna to the Fitzmolean in memory of Miles."

"The only thing she would have been happy to give to the museum in memory of Miles would have been his ashes. So I'm bound to ask, what's the real reason she wants to buy the painting back?"

"I don't know, Chief Inspector Warwick. But why are you always so suspicious of other people's motives, particularly Christina's?"

"That's part of my job description, I'm afraid. But let me ask you another question. Why does Christina need you to bid on her behalf, when she could so easily do it herself?"

"That's easy to answer. She'll be in Monte Carlo on the evening of the sale."

"They don't have phones in Monte Carlo?"

"She doesn't want anyone else to know she's bidding."

"Like who?"

"Tim Knox, for example."

"That doesn't make any sense. He's the director of the gallery and you should certainly let him know what she's asked you to do. If anything goes wrong, he'll never trust you again, and you might even lose your job."

"But Christina would never forgive me if I broke my word."

"Then perhaps you should ask yourself why she chose you, and even more important, who's the seller?"

"The Brompton Oratory," said Beth. "They need the money for a new roof."

"Now that's something I do believe. But who gave the painting to them in the first place? Because it certainly wasn't Miles Faulkner, who worshipped Mammon, not God."

"In the catalog it's described as *The Property of a Lady*, which usually means the owner doesn't want their name revealed."

"If you can find out who the mystery lady is, I suspect you'll also discover why Christina wants you to be seen buying the painting."

"What makes you so convinced of that?" asked Beth.

"The Brompton Oratory just happens to be the church where the late Mrs. Rashidi worshipped, when she lived in The Boltons."

"That could just be a coincidence," said Beth, trying to distract him.

It was William's turn to remove a hand.

"Is it also a coincidence that the late Assem Rashidi was in Pentonville at the same time as Miles Faulkner, the previous owner of the Raphael?"

"What does that prove?"

"I don't know, but it might explain why Christina doesn't want anyone else except you to know that she's the buyer."

"But if I do get the painting for a million or less, your theory bites the dust, and you with it!"

"Agreed."

"In which case Christina is a saint, and you're just a boring old cynic."

"Christina's no saint, and there's only one way we're going to find out if I'm a boring old cynic."

"Enlighten me," said Beth, imitating the Hawk.

"While you're at the gallery bidding over the phone on Christina's behalf, I'll be at Christie's, and I can assure you, I won't be looking at the auctioneer." William turned out the light and began to move a hand up the inside of Beth's thigh.

"Interesting what turns you on, Caveman."

# 32

"What am I bid?" said William, as he climbed out of bed the following morning and headed for the bathroom.

"As long as I get the Raphael for less than a million," said Beth, "I don't really care, because an old cynic will be taking me to Elena's tonight to celebrate my triumph."

"And if it's sold to someone else for more than a million, what then?"

"Humble pie will be served in the kitchen, chief inspector."

"I prefer Elena's," said William as he closed the bathroom door. Not for the first time, he reflected that, for Beth, every glass was half full, which was one of the many reasons he adored her. He hoped he would be proved wrong, but he feared this particular glass was half empty.

He turned on the hot water and looked at himself in the mirror. He occasionally missed that time when he'd been working undercover and didn't have to shave every day. And then he remembered, today he would be undercover.

⟜o⊸

"How much do you think BW will have to bid?" asked Christina, as they waited in the queue at the departure gate.

"A million one, a million two, at most."

"That's a lot of money to pay for a fake," said Christina.

"I don't have much choice," responded Miles. "If another bidder got hold of the painting and then discovered it was a fake, you'd not only have to hand over the original, but clever Inspector Warwick might just put two and two together, and then we'd both end up in the slammer."

Miles handed his boarding card and passport to the officer at the desk, who turned to the last page of his passport, checked the photograph and passed it back to him.

"Have a good flight, Captain Neville," she said.

⊸o⊷

The director listened with great interest to what Beth had to say before he offered an opinion. "You say Mrs. Faulkner gave you a check for a million pounds so you could bid for the Raphael on our behalf?"

Beth handed over the check.

Tim read the figure and smiled. He then began tapping his fingers on the desk, always a sign that he was deep in thought. "We currently have a million pounds in our acquisition fund," he eventually said, "so I'm going to give you the authority to bid up to two million, which should be more than enough to acquire the painting."

"Do I let Christina know your decision?"

"Of course, but don't say anything until I've run it past our chairman of trustees and got his approval."

"What are you grinning about?"

"The thought of the gallery owning a Raphael."

⊸o⊷

Christina picked up the phone, and when she heard the voice on the other end of the line, she was relieved that Miles was out on his morning run.

She listened carefully to what her friend had to say, but didn't respond immediately. Beth was beginning to wonder if Christina had put the phone down on her because she'd broken her word by telling Tim about their arrangement, but then the silence was finally broken. "I can't see any reason why you shouldn't bid up to two million," said Christina. "Good luck."

She smiled at the thought of Miles having to pay double the amount he'd planned to buy back his own fake. She heard the front door slam, and put down the phone without saying good-bye.

William found it hard to concentrate when he briefed Inspector Cole on his responsibilities as the new head of the anti-corruption unit.

"I'm not exactly excited by the idea of spying on my colleagues," admitted Cole, over a pint of Bass and a pork pie.

"I've found it helps if you think of them as corrupt, rather than as colleagues," said William, "and every bit as bad as any other criminal."

Cole went across to the bar and bought a second round of drinks, but when he returned to their table he still didn't look convinced. "So, are you looking forward to leading a Murder Team, as a Senior Investigating Officer?"

"Depends how much it goes for," said William. Inspector Cole looked puzzled. "Sorry," said William, snapping back into the present. "My mind was somewhere else."

Booth Watson ordered a glass of Courvoisier VSOP.

He checked his watch: 6:37. The first lot was due to come under the hammer at seven o'clock. He knew exactly how long it would take to walk from the Ritz to Christie's, and as the Raphael was lot 25, he wasn't in any hurry.

"Your cognac, sir."

⊸o⊷

Beth began to pace around her office like a caged tiger. At seven o'clock she locked the door to make sure she wouldn't be disturbed.

Tim Knox had dropped by earlier in the afternoon to confirm that the trustees had agreed she could bid up to two million pounds for the Raphael. However, they hoped she'd get it for less, and their million wouldn't be required. She checked her watch and poured herself yet another black coffee as she waited for the phone to ring.

The man from Christie's had rung just before midday to brief her. "I'll call you on this number when the auctioneer reaches lot twenty," he'd said. "That will give you more than enough time to prepare. Mr. Pylkkänen has told me he'll open the bidding at five hundred thousand pounds. I'll keep you informed about the progress of the sale, and you can tell me when you want to join in the bidding. But more important, be sure to let me know when you've reached your limit. If yours is the closing bid, you'll have fourteen days to complete the purchase, and after you've done so we'll deliver the painting to the museum."

"When should I expect your call?" asked Beth.

"A little after seven thirty. It might be wise to put me on speaker phone. I've known customers to drop their handset during the bidding, and one accidentally cut himself off and didn't get back in time to make the closing bid. Good luck," he said. "I can't think of a better home than the Fitzmolean for the *Madonna di Cesare*."

Beth recalled the last person who had said that.

⊸o⊷

Booth Watson drained his balloon of vintage brandy, considered ordering a second but thought better of it, and called for the bill. He wrote out a check and added a handsome tip on behalf of his client.

He had walked the short distance from the Ritz to Christie's a few days before—nine minutes—to attend a rare stamp auction, conducted by the same auctioneer who would be on the podium this evening.

He entered the saleroom at 7:42, and took his reserved seat, which he'd selected after some considerable thought. Three rows from the back on the left-hand side. He'd even practiced raising his paddle just high enough for the auctioneer to spot him without anyone in front of him having any idea who was bidding.

⊸o⊷

When the phone on her desk rang, Beth grabbed it as if it were a lifeline.

"We've reached lot twenty, Mrs. Warwick," said the Christie's rep. "Can you hear me clearly?"

"Yes," said Beth, before pressing the hands-free button and replacing the receiver. She could hear a voice in the background saying, "Sold for forty-two thousand pounds," followed by the thud of a hammer coming down.

She turned to the next page of her catalog and was checking lot twenty-one, just as William entered the saleroom.

*Not unlike the opening night of a West End show,* was William's first thought. Every seat had been taken long before the curtain went up. He tucked himself in behind a group of chattering dealers, from where he had a clear view of the auctioneer, while remaining inconspicuous. He scanned the room, but failed to spot anyone he recognized. It didn't help that he was looking at the backs of most of their heads, while he couldn't see some of those seated on the far side of the room.

"Lot number twenty-one."

Booth Watson studied his catalog. A still life by Pieter Claesz failed to reach its reserve price, and the auctioneer brought his hammer down with a thud and murmured, "Pass," to confirm there hadn't been a successful bidder. That was unlikely to be the fate of the Raphael, which the press had dubbed the star attraction of the autumn sales.

"Lot twenty-two," declared the auctioneer, sounding more hopeful. "A drawing of Antwerp Cathedral by Peter Paul Rubens. I have an opening bid at the table of twenty thousand pounds. Do I see twenty-two?" He did, and the drawing eventually sold for £33,000, just below its high estimate.

Beth didn't need to check her pulse to be aware that every time the hammer came down, it rose another few beats.

"Lot twenty-three. A self-portrait by Frans Hals, oil on panel. I'll open the bidding at fifty thousand pounds."

William continued to concentrate on the bidders. A woman in the third row raised her paddle. Her bid was followed by an anonymous phone bidder whose representative stood behind a long table on a raised platform on the right-hand side of the room. His hand was cupped over the receiver so that only his client could hear what he was saying.

William looked closely at the dozen or so gallery assistants who were waiting on the phones for the lot they had been entrusted with by their anonymous clients. He wondered which of them was on the line to Beth.

"One hundred and twenty-five thousand," said the auctioneer, as another bidder raised his paddle.

"Sold!"

⊸o⊷

"It can't be too much longer," said Christina, as the cat leaped onto her lap and settled down.

"Booth Watson will phone the moment the painting's been sold," said Miles.

"You don't seem at all nervous," she said, looking across at a husband she couldn't afford to divorce.

"Why should I be? BW will get hold of it whatever the hammer price."

"Even if it goes for more than a million?"

"No reason it should sell for more than the high estimate," said Miles, matter-of-factly.

Christina continued to stroke the cat, which began to purr contentedly.

⊸o⊷

"The auctioneer has just opened the bidding for lot twenty-four," said the voice over the phone. "It shouldn't be long now. Are you ready, madam?"

More than ready, Beth wanted to tell him, but satisfied herself with, "Yes, thank you."

"Sold for ninety thousand pounds," she heard in the background. There followed what felt like an interminable pause, before she finally heard the words, "Lot number twenty-five, Raphael's *Madonna di Cesare*."

There was an outbreak of excited chattering in the saleroom as the masterpiece was placed on an easel in front of the podium, for all to see. The auctioneer waited until he had complete silence, which made Beth even more nervous.

"I have an opening bid of five hundred thousand pounds. Do I see six hundred thousand?"

"Do you wish to bid, madam?" asked the voice over the phone.

"Yes," replied Beth firmly.

"I have six hundred thousand on the phone," said the auctioneer, turning to his left.

Booth Watson looked across at the line of assistants standing patiently on the right-hand side of the room. Only one of them had a hand cupped over the receiver of his phone, whispering to his client. He knew exactly who was on the other end of the line.

"I'm looking for seven hundred thousand," said the auctioneer. He didn't have to wait long for Booth Watson to raise his paddle.

"Seven hundred thousand has been bid by a gentleman seated near the back of the room," said the voice over the phone. "Will you go to eight hundred thousand, madam?"

"Yes," said Beth without hesitation.

William also knew who was on the other end of the line, but he wasn't able to see who was bidding against her. He couldn't risk taking a step forward for fear of being spotted.

£800,000, £900,000, £1 million followed in quick succession.

"Do I see one million one hundred thousand?" asked the auctioneer.

Booth Watson raised his paddle.

That's when William spotted him.

---

Miles began to pace around the drawing room as he waited impatiently for the phone to ring, while Christina remained on the sofa stroking the cat.

"Surely they've reached lot twenty-five by now," said Miles, checking his watch.

"You would have thought so," said Christina. "But I feel sure Mr. Booth Watson will call the moment the hammer comes down. He's so reliable," she added as she continued to stroke the cat.

They both purred.

⊰o⊱

"One million, eight hundred thousand," said the auctioneer as he continued to switch his attention back and forth between the phone bidder and the gentleman seated near the back who appeared to be the only other person left in the chase. Booth Watson was becoming puzzled by who it could possibly be on the other end of the phone, because it couldn't be Mrs. Warwick. Unless . . .

He raised his paddle once again.

"The gentleman at the back of the room has bid one million, nine hundred thousand, madam," whispered the go-between. "Will you go to two million?"

"Yes," said Beth for the last time. She closed her eyes and prayed that whoever was bidding against her had also reached their limit, and their paddle would fail to rise again.

"I have a bid of two million on the phone," said the auctioneer. "Will you offer me two million two hundred thousand, sir?" he asked hopefully, his gaze fixed on the only other remaining bidder.

After what seemed to Beth to be a lifetime, but was in fact only a few seconds, a paddle was raised.

The auctioneer turned his attention back to the phone bidder. "I have two million two hundred thousand," he said, smiling benevolently.

"Will you bid two million four, madam?" asked a voice that now sounded far away.

"No," said Beth. "I've reached my limit."

"Thank you, madam," said the Christie's representative before putting the phone down. He looked at the auctioneer and shook his head. He didn't tell his client how grateful he was, because it's always the underbidder who decides the hammer price.

"Are there any more bids?" The auctioneer's eyes swept the room, but to no avail. He finally brought the hammer down with a loud thud before declaring, "Sold to the gentleman at the back of the room for two million, two hundred thousand pounds."

A round of applause spontaneously broke out in the room after a new record price had been set for a Raphael. Booth Watson didn't join in.

William still couldn't be certain who had made the closing bid, as he'd only seen the back of his head, but he wasn't going to risk hanging around for fear of being recognized. That moment when the stalker becomes the prey.

He quickly left the saleroom, walked down the wide carpeted staircase, and out of the front door. He didn't look back until he'd crossed the street and reached a narrow alley he'd identified the night before, from where he had a clear view of the entrance to the auction house. William stood shivering in the cold as he waited to confirm his worst fear.

---

The phone in the drawing room began to ring. Miles grabbed it, and listened in silence for a few moments. The blood drained from his face as he repeated: "Two million, two hundred thousand?"

"That's right," said Booth Watson. "I'm about to put down the ten percent deposit. The balance has to be paid within fourteen days."

"Who was the underbidder?" demanded Miles.

"That's the strange thing. There was only one other serious bidder and they were on the phone. I can only assume it had to be Mrs. Warwick bidding on behalf of the Fitzmolean."

"How can that be possible when Christina only gave her a check for one million?"

"I have no idea," admitted Booth Watson. "Perhaps you should ask your wife?"

"I will," said Miles as he slammed down the phone, which caused the cat to leap off Christina's lap and scurry out of the room.

"Did you get it?" Christina asked innocently.

"I did," said Miles, "but ended up having to pay two point two million." He turned to see the flicker of a smile cross Christina's face. *Could it be possible?*

⊸o⊷

After Beth had phoned Tim Knox to tell him the disappointing news, she put on her coat and unlocked the office door. She'd decided to go straight home and share her grief with the twins. At least they wouldn't gloat. She would then prepare a dish of humble pie that she'd have to share with her know-all husband. She only wondered what else he knew.

At least they had the trip to New York on the *Alden* to look forward to, and once they were on board, she would forbid him ever to raise the subject again.

⊸o⊷

The large gathering that had attended the auction were now flooding out of the building and onto the street. Some were looking for taxis, while others headed for their clubs or fashionable restaurants.

William checked every face, but none caused him to take a

second look. He didn't recognize anyone else. He was even beginning to wonder if the £2.2 million might have come from a genuine bidder, and he'd let his imagination run away with him. But he had no intention of going home until the last light in the building had gone out. He accepted it could be a long wait.

⊸o⊷

Booth Watson put down the phone in the lobby and turned to find a young assistant waiting for him.

"Congratulations, sir," he said.

The successful bidder didn't feel congratulations were in order, but he didn't offer an opinion.

"As you know, sir, we will require a two-hundred-and-twenty-thousand-pound deposit to secure the Raphael, with the balance to be paid within fourteen days."

Booth Watson took a check from an inside pocket that had already been signed and dated, but with the amount left blank. He wrote out £220,000, first in words and then in numbers, before he handed it across to the young man.

"Thank you, sir. As soon as we've received the full amount, you can either collect the painting or we'll be happy to arrange delivery for you."

Once again, Booth Watson didn't comment. He left the gallery assistant standing there, and headed for the main exit.

William was about to accept that he must have been mistaken when a familiar portly figure emerged from the auction house, not looking at all pleased. He hailed a taxi that disappeared in the direction of St. James's.

William began to walk slowly toward the nearest tube station, but paused when he spotted a red telephone box on the corner of Piccadilly. William stepped inside, picked up the receiver, and dialed a number that wasn't listed in any telephone directory. When the call was answered by a familiar voice, he pushed a tenpence piece into the slot.

"Good evening, sir. I thought you ought to know that Booth Watson was at the auction, and despite my wife bidding two million for the Raphael, hers wasn't the closing bid."

"Well, one thing's for certain," said the Hawk. "Booth Watson won't have been bidding on behalf of Mrs. Christina Faulkner, as she's a seller, not a buyer."

"Which rather narrows down the field," said William. "In fact I'm beginning to wonder, if it's just possible that Miles Faulkner is still alive."

"I never thought he was dead," said the commander.